THE BROTHERHOOD

Other books by Patrick J. O'Brian

The Fallen

Reaper

For other projects by the author, a detailed biography, and upcoming events, visit **PJObooks.com** online.

THE BROTHERHOOD

Patrick J. O'Brian

Writer's Showcase
New York Lincoln Shanghai

The Brotherhood

All Rights Reserved © 2002 by Patrick J. O'Brian

No part of this book may be reproduced or transmitted in any form or by any means, graphic, electronic, or mechanical, including photocopying, recording, taping, or by any information storage retrieval system, without the written permission of the publisher.

Writer's Showcase
an imprint of iUniverse, Inc.

For information address:
iUniverse, Inc.
2021 Pine Lake Road, Suite 100
Lincoln, NE 68512
www.iuniverse.com

ISBN: 0-595-25445-4 (pbk)
ISBN: 0-595-65174-7 (cloth)

Printed in the United States of America

This book is dedicated to all of the men and women who perished during the 9-11 attacks in New York City, Pennsylvania, and Washington, D.C. May their souls rest in peace, and may their loved ones find the strength and courage to carry on with their lives.

I owe many thanks in the production of this manuscript. Among the contributors who helped make this accurate and meaningful are: John Walston, Mike Dean, Dennis Tyler, Gary Bowden, Eddie Bell, Jeff and Bucky Granger, Don Pence, David Rhum, Scott Gillespie, Steve Haverly, Carol Pyle, Nannette Bell, Renee Johnson, James and Lesa Fullhart, and Tim Hale, who inspired me to write the most memorable quote in this text. Thank you all a hundred times over.

Prologue

For the first time in three years the entire Sheridan family had spent a Christmas morning together, singing carols, opening presents, and drinking ale like they suspected their ancestors in Ireland had at one time.

John and Marie Sheridan had all seven of their children around them for a change. With three of their sons on the local fire department and another working as a police officer, it made for some difficult scheduling anytime the family wanted to get together.

Snow fell outside their rural Illinois home as colored holiday lights glowed outside, wrapped around various trees, and the eaves along the house. A real pine tree put off its alluring aroma after nearly two dozen family members had left for other family gatherings, or the comfort of their own homes.

Of the couple's seven children, only the fraternal twins, Michael and Gregory, stayed behind to visit with their parents into the nighttime hours as the snow continued to fall.

John had retired from the nearby Carvers Grove Fire Department some years before at the rank of captain, only to turn around and become chief of a local volunteer department, a few miles outside of the city.

Mike followed in the footsteps of his father, and two of his older brothers, becoming a firefighter, while Greg chose a different route, becoming a police officer in Carvers Grove.

Night and day in personality, the twins shared their few similar traits passionately, including their devotion to their parents. They also shared a knack for helping people, no matter what the situation.

Greg often felt like the black sheep of the family for choosing such a drastically different career, while Mike was the glue that held the family together, because he got along with all of his siblings.

Though both were thirty-two, Greg had already lost most of his hair, leaving only a brown fringe, which set him apart from his four brothers, who all still had full heads of hair. Occasionally he took teasing about saving money on shampoo and haircuts from his brothers, but Greg took it as best he could.

Wearing a pair of thin-framed glasses, he had a studious look, but Greg had no intentions of ever attaining a college degree. His career choice served him perfectly, so all of his studies went to bettering himself for a promotion down the road.

He had always felt somewhat alienated, but most of his anxiety stemmed from his mistrusting personality.

Almost seventy, John Sheridan relished the holiday because his entire family was around him once more. He had worked too many years and missed too many holidays with his own family not to see all of his kids at one time.

Perhaps for the last time.

"So how's that girlfriend of yours?" John asked Mike, who had taken to picking at the remains of the turkey breast off a plate at the kitchen table.

"She's fine," Mike replied.

Another opposite trait he and his twin possessed was eye color. While Greg had shrewd brown eyes, Mike's baby blues took in the world with an optimism unparalleled amongst everyone who knew him. He often wore a smirk below his rustic red mustache, which matched his hair.

His bangs hung over his forehead, just to make his full head of hair look thicker, as though left that way to irritate his twin brother.

Mike fingered a bit of stuffing from a bowl, receiving a disapproving look from his mother. He grinned, then looked to his father.

"Are you wanting to hear wedding bells soon?" he inquired.

"Well, it's been years since any of you tied the knot," Marie Sheridan stated. "I was beginning to think some of the grandchildren might beat you to it."

"Not likely," Mike said with a tone that indicated he might be popping the question sooner than later.

Greg had engrossed himself in a movie on television. He was dressed for work, since he was due to go in for the midnight shift.

Though more reserved, and in a totally different career than his brothers, Greg was the intellectual pick of the lot. He had ambitions to join the investigative division full-time, and eventually wanted to be part of the front office. Sometimes he felt promotions within his own department were the only way to compete with his brothers.

He and Mike competed more than any of the other brothers. Most of their siblings were considerably older, and by nature, fraternal twins usually want to outdo one another, to set themselves apart.

Unlike Mike, he had already been married.

And divorced.

He had no children to show from his previous marriage, and most days Greg felt better about being on his own. Some days, though, his emotions got the better of him, and the pain was unbearable being alone, feeling like the world was against him.

Greg had tried firefighting once as a volunteer, but the commitment kept him from pursuing his career as a police officer. He volunteered one year before realizing the job would never be for him. On several occasions he had screwed up on the fire scene, and once, a woman died, which could have been prevented by any number of different actions that night.

One of those preventable actions was his own.

Memories of that woman's scream still haunted him, and furthered his separation from the band of firefighters he grew up around. They were his brothers, and they loved him in every way possible, but Greg never truly felt like he was one of them.

If their father ever loved him less, or felt disappointment over Greg never joining the city fire department, John Sheridan never showed it. He was retired, but he was never out of the loop, which kept John far too busy to worry about what all of his kids were doing with their careers at all times.

In some ways John Sheridan seemed a gruff man, loving at times, but indifferent at others. Having seven kids would harden any man, but he never faltered when it came to provision, or making certain his children turned out right.

Greg stood to get some turkey breast before his brother hogged it all, when the dispatch tones came over his father's scanner, nestled neatly on the kitchen counter, like several others strategically placed throughout the house.

All four of the remaining Sheridan clan expected it to be a malfunctioning alarm at some business vacated for the Christmas holiday. John would always speed to the station, go to the business, discover it was a faulty alarm, and be right home.

Not this time.

When the dispatcher came over the air and said they had several reports of a working residential structure fire, the Sheridan family knew someone's Christmas holiday was ruined. John grabbed his keys from the counter, heading for the front door, Mike close behind.

As his father opened the door, Mike turned to look at his twin, who showed no desire to follow the two firemen into battle.

"You coming?" Mike asked, sensing Greg's hesitation, but knowing even Greg's limited experience might be useful on a day where the volunteer department might be shorthanded.

"Okay," the uniformed patrolman said, following his brother and father out the door, turning to see the distressed look on his mother's face before he left.

"Take care of your father," she almost pleaded, knowing her husband was getting far too old to perform heroic acts on a regular basis.

Greg nodded, figuring this would be a routine run, and his father could simply sit back and run the show as he always did.

Five minutes later he realized his guess was incorrect, as they arrived at the volunteer fire station, waited a few minutes, and realized one extra man was all they would be getting. A driver by the name of Al Teal showed up to drive the pumper truck to the scene while the twins grabbed spare gear from inside the station, throwing it on the truck.

God, I hope this is something small, Greg kept thinking, knowing he wanted nothing to do with a full-scale house fire. Sometimes a residential fire would be nothing more than a cooking fire in the kitchen, or a blown furnace.

His uniform was mostly a synthetic material that would burn up quicker than paper confetti if it touched flames. That, and he still had several issues weighing on his mind from previous fires to worry him.

He could hear the screams echoing inside his head, even as his father instructed them on what to expect, and what to do when they got there. Even when he closed his eyes, Greg could not shake the sight of the deadly flames. They taunted him ritually in his sleep, and in the middle of the day when he least expected it.

I don't want to do this, Greg thought amongst the screams in his head.

"Boys, I can see flames over the hill," their father reported from the front seat as both finished donning their self-contained breathing apparatus, pulling the air tanks away from their housings mounted in the truck's jump seats.

Fuck, Greg thought, his stomach tightening. He hadn't done any firefighting in years, and his brain was suddenly mush. He could work any police scenario with the greatest of ease, but this was different. Greg believed the same results could be accomplished from fighting fire outside of the building, but his brothers believed in running inside to fight the beast.

Perhaps they had a hero syndrome, or maybe their desire to save property was far greater than his own, but most cops had no envy toward firefighters concerning the duties they carried out.

As the pumper truck pulled in front of the house, both brothers jumped from their perspective sides as John Sheridan questioned the family standing in front of their house, while sizing up the scene.

An old two-story farmhouse was the scene of the blaze.

The barn behind it had long since fallen in, overshadowed by the house and its flames. Now flames were shooting out the first story windows, and smoke billowed out of the downstairs, and from several ventilation ducts on the second story, indicating the fire was spreading upward.

"My daughter was upstairs sleeping," the woman reported from beside her husband. "We woke up and got out, and when my husband went back to get her, it was just too-"

"I know," John said, reassuring her. "We'll get upstairs and get your daughter."

Their son stood beside the father, clinging to the man's leg as he sobbed uncontrollably. Everything important in their lives was being destroyed right before them on what was supposed to be the happiest night of the year.

Greg watched as Mike pulled his air mask over his head and tightened the straps with a pull, slowly following suit, after tossing his glasses up into the truck. They both pulled their protective hoods over the seals of their masks, then donned their helmets before turning on their air tanks.

Teal had begun pulling off the inch-and-three-quarter hose line from the truck, since he could not begin pumping operations until the hose was clear of its bed. If he tried to charge the rolled hose, he would have a pile of oversized, crumpled spaghetti on his hands, and the hose would be useless to the team.

"Got it," Mike said with an air of confidence his brother could never dream of mustering, pulling the limp hose toward the front door.

Greg followed his brother, his training suddenly coming back to him. It wasn't like remembering how to ride a bike, but firefighting was not rocket science, as his father always liked to say.

"You two knock down that fire," John ordered, putting on a pack of his own. "I'll get upstairs and look for the girl."

"You sure, Dad?" Mike asked, wondering how quickly his father could get his gear on, then get upstairs.

"Yes, Michael. I'll get her and find a window to hand her out of. Let's hope we get some backup real quick."

Mike nodded, then prepared to enter through the front.

Since the front door was unlocked, it was easy to access the inside once the hose hissed with the water coursing through its lined insides. He threw open the door, and both brothers found themselves greeted by flames dancing over their heads.

Mike opened up the nozzle, letting the water begin to knock down the flames as their father darted past them with the department's new thermal imaging camera, ready to find the stairs and a little girl.

"No," Mike said to himself, defying the fire that meant to chase his father up the stairs.

In all of the dense smoke he could barely see the orange glow of the flame, but his father would need the camera more than he would. After all, a life depended on John Sheridan's ability to navigate the house.

Mike could tell the living room, which took up the front of the house, was entirely a loss. He quickly knocked down the flames around him by using a "Z" pattern with the nozzle, but the fire had already spread upward, and toward the back of the house.

The brothers could hear burning wood in the back rooms crackle as the fire made its way along the walls and ceiling. Mike aggressively chased it, using the nozzle to douse the resistant flames, ensuring his father would have to deal with nothing more than the smoke.

"I've got this," Mike yelled through his face mask so his brother could hear. "Go upstairs and help Dad."

"Where the hell are the stairs?" Greg questioned, unsure of which way his father had gone.

"Back there," Mike said, lightly pushing his twin in the right direction. "Get Dad out of here, no matter what."

Greg nodded, barely able to see his brother's form at all through the black smoke. Originally, he worried he wouldn't be able to see without his glasses, but the walls of smoke made certain his eyesight was no factor.

Greg crawled away, forced to stay near the ground from the rising heat, cussing under his breath the entire way.

Upstairs, John had located the little girl, thanks to the thermal camera, but she was not breathing on her own. Though less intense than the smoke downstairs, there was enough on the second story to overcome her small lungs. Hearing himself breathe the air through the air mask like Darth Vader, the retired captain searched for a window facing his pumper truck.

If he couldn't find the right direction, his search would prove useless, and the chances of reviving the girl would dwindle.

His sons had it so much easier on the city department. There would always be plenty of help available on a working fire scene, and they would never have to guess how many people might show up, or if things would get done correctly outside.

On Christmas he knew most of his firefighters would be out of town, or visiting relatives outside the county limits. Some probably wouldn't even have their pagers on.

John had to assume he was alone in his quest to save this girl.

He reached a window, then tried to peer out, finding it covered with a dark film. John had just found a dilemma, because he didn't want to poke out every window and feed the fire the oxygen it craved, yet the girl needed fresh air if there was any chance of saving her.

"Shit," he said, using his elbow to bash the weakened glass outward, finding he was on the side of the house, but able to see his pumper truck.

Teal seemed to perk up at the sound of the broken glass, and John waved to him.

"I've got the girl," he tried to yell through the air mask, but his driver couldn't understand a word of it.

"What?" John saw the driver mouth as he stepped closer.

Tearing off his helmet and air mask, the volunteer chief leaned outside the window.

"Get a ladder!" he ordered. "I've got the girl!"

Teal had no help as of yet, though a few blue lights were flashing in the distance, indicating a few firefighters had finally answered the call. He took a ladder off the side of the pumper truck, carried it over, and struggled to set it up by himself.

John began coughing involuntarily as smoke filtered out the window behind him. As hard as his sons worked to extinguish the fire, there was no ejection fan set up to force the smoke outside. The hazy smoke lingered around the volunteer chief, forcing him to breathe the toxic air as it slowly moved toward the window.

Again, the lack of manpower hurt their efforts, and John was personally feeling the effects as Greg struggled to the top of the stairs, unsure of where his father was.

More than ever, Greg realized his career decision was the right one. He knew he had no business being in this house while it was on fire, but he trudged forward, trying to find his father.

A few seconds later, he reached the floor, noticing the smoke traveled in one direction, probably toward open air.

If his father had popped open a window, he would already be safe, so Greg decided to head the other way, back into one of the bedrooms. He suddenly had the heroic urges to find the girl that his brothers must have sometimes experienced.

As he made his way into the room, the door shut behind him, creating a problem a moment later when he tried to get out. Greg reached for an opening that would let him out, but in the shroud of darkness, only found wall after wall.

He panicked, unsure of where he was anymore, or how to get out, and everything around him was pitch black. No dimly lit window, no light beneath a doorway.

Reaching frantically along the wall for a doorknob, or window, he found nothing except cumbersome furniture, and began yelling for help.

"Dad! I'm lost in here!" Greg screamed through his air mask, the volume of his voice cut considerably by the apparatus.

His brother had the portable radio, so yelling through the dense smoke was the only hope Greg had if he wanted to get found.

As his father handed the girl off to Teal, who had temporarily neglected his pumping duties to set up the ladder, he heard Greg from the other room.

"You got her?" he asked the driver.

"Yeah," Teal answered quickly, ready to head down so he could make sure Mike was getting an adequate water supply inside, and begin trying to revive the girl until other firefighters arrived.

If the water supply was cut off for any reason, Teal would need to fix it, or Mike would be left inside a potential inferno, ready to burst into flashover at any second.

The last thing Mike needed was a wall of flames rolling uncontrollably throughout the room, with no way of defending himself.

Teal quickly found things in working order, and wondered if John would be able to find both boys as he turned his attention to reviving the girl, the family quickly rushing over.

After working at the Red Cross as a volunteer, the mother knew something about CPR, and began helping Teal by administering breaths between his chest compressions, now that they had determined the girl had no breathing or heartbeat.

Upstairs, John had spent a few seconds trying to replace his own air mask, but he could not fasten it and the helmet effectively in the darkness, and Greg's pleas for help were growing more urgent. John had seen inexperienced firefighters panic any number of times in his four decades of public service.

He wondered why Greg had left his brother's side, but he didn't have time to contemplate it thoroughly. John needed to get Greg out of danger, then worry about Mike. Though he stayed close to the ground in a crawl, the chief still took the thick smoke into his lungs, fighting to keep his own wits as he listened for his son.

"Greg!" he called, unsure of where his son was.

"In here!" he heard in reply, finding a doorknob through the slightly thinning smoke.

Perhaps one of the fans had been set up downstairs, because the smoke seemed to have dwindled.

John opened the door, calling for Greg once more, who quickly found him, virtually snorting through the mask because he was breathing so hard. John began leading him toward the window, where he could be relieved by one of the incoming volunteers the chief had heard on his portable radio.

Greg kept a careful hold of his father's left foot as John led the way toward the ladder. The chief reached the ladder first, sticking his head out the window for fresh air, then falling back as he made a strange groaning sound, as though an elephant was standing on his chest, not allowing him to breathe.

"Dad!" Greg cried as his father fell straight back, into his arms, the smoke still filtering past them out the window.

Knowing instantly the stress and physical exertion had overwhelmed his father, possibly into a heart attack, Greg pulled his own helmet and mask off, placing the air mask over his father's face.

Everything after that turned into a slow-motion dream, as other firemen climbed the ladder, helping carry their chief down. Greg looked out the window after the crew, seeing his father appear limp, even helpless, to which he'd never seen the likes of before.

It scared him to see his father like that.

On the ground, everyone began tending to John, trying to ascertain whether or not he was still breathing. Greg felt his brother brush up beside him as both leaned out the window, seeing their father unconscious. Mike gave him a strange look as though he held Greg responsible in some way, then climbed down the ladder to see what he could do.

Greg knew from the moment he'd heard the dispatch over his father's scanner this was going to be a terrible day.

Even his wildest nightmares would never have brought him to the scene laid before him.

CHAPTER 1

John Sheridan survived a moderate heart attack that fateful Christmas night, but his condition deteriorated until he passed away in late February. He died in the hospital, where he had remained since the holidays.

All seven children attended a chilly funeral on the first day of March, and each mourned outwardly, knowing just who and what they had lost.

A procession of over five-hundred firefighters, professional and volunteer, followed the pumper truck carrying John's body through town to the cemetery. Most everyone in the business of firefighting knew who the retired captain was, and just what the Sheridan name meant in their corner of Illinois.

For the family, little changed after the incident on Christmas.

Greg felt like more of an outcast than ever, because he believed in some way he was responsible for his father's untimely death, even though doctors and family assured him it would have been just a matter of time before a heart attack took his father anyhow.

Still, the only cop in the family kept to himself, avoiding any family gatherings, church, and public events he could. He felt positive his brothers and sisters blamed him, in part, for their father's death.

For the rest of the family, things settled down by late April when Wade Sheridan joined the city's fire department just after his twenty-first birthday.

Though his father, the oldest of the Sheridan children, wanted nothing to do with fire department life, his son decided from the time he was in elementary school it was the thing for him.

Today was Wade's first day on his permanent shift, going on actual runs with the department after the tedious two-week mandatory training program. He was excited and nervous, all at the same time, despite working with three of John Sheridan's sons on his shift.

Wade had to admit the training was useful, but most of it seemed to be little more than watching videos, tying simple knots, and working a hydrant correctly. He thirsted for action, but felt nervous as hell about seeing his first fire.

Unlike his uncles, he had no experience whatsoever, even as a volunteer, so he wondered how ready he would be for the real thing when the time came.

Biding his time would be almost painful, waiting for that first chance to prove himself. Everything about this job revolved around respect and trust. He knew that coming in, and earning both would be his top priority.

"You sure you still want to do this?" his uncle, Patrick Sheridan, asked.

Patrick was the battalion chief of the shift his two brothers worked on, and now his nephew would join them. It took the experience of any three other firefighters on the truck room floor to equal the years he had put in with the fire department.

"Yeah, I'm sure," Wade answered. "I guess it's in the blood."

Wade's youth showed in his demeanor.

He was thin as a rail, grinned from youthful optimism, and had a light in his eyes that would eventually fade when he saw what some of his colleagues had already experienced in their years of public safety.

Wade was already accustomed to some of the rookie hazing from other firefighters. He'd been doused with water buckets several times, found his lunch laced with hot sauce one day, and had to fetch a dead fish from the toilet on orders from an officer because the guys said it was the chief's favorite pet, and needed to be properly buried.

Such things were expected, so he would grin, bear it, and moved on.

For the time being, Wade would be stationed at the main headquarters fire station, which housed the battalion chief, a platform aerial truck, and the pumper truck he would be riding on.

After morning cleanup was finished, Wade stood at one of the open bay doors of the fire station, watching the reddish morning sunlight stretch across the blacktop of the city street laid before him. It felt both comforting and lonely all at the same time, but he was happy to finally be where he was.

"I can't believe Dad never wanted to do this," Wade commented to the battalion chief.

"He's happy, and that's what matters," Patrick replied. "He always wanted to do his own thing."

Wade's father constructed and installed commercial antenna fixtures atop all kinds of skyscrapers from New York to Seattle. He reached heights on a daily basis most firefighters on the Carvers Grove Fire Department would never see in their careers.

On his days off, he rode his Harley-Davidson motorcycle with whatever new woman was in his life. Wade resented him for awhile after his parents divorced, but that was years ago, and he was growing accustomed to his father's carefree lifestyle.

After all, he wasn't that much different.

"There's not much I can tell you," Patrick said as they stood at the bay door. "Just listen to your officers, and if you ever have a problem with someone, take it up with that person before you talk to the officers. It'll save you a lot of headaches down the road."

"I don't know what to expect yet," Wade admitted. "Sitting in that class for two weeks didn't make me feel any smarter."

Patrick gave a chuckle.

"Oh, you'll learn quick enough out here. We're just getting into the perfect season for your education, too."

"What season is that?"

"Summertime. You'll get all the fun stuff like attic fires, cookouts gone wrong, and an arson or two."

Wade grinned, clasping his hands a bit nervously. He would pace all morning long, sitting only long enough to eat lunch with the guys.

He found himself unsure of how to act around the other firefighters. He'd known most of them for years, but never worked with them. Wade always respected and liked the guys who worked with his uncles, but this was different.

Now his life was in their hands, and more importantly, he was responsible for them in one way or another.

Strangely, he felt unsure of how to take the hazing. He knew everyone went through it, but it seemed somewhat childish to stick a filled water bottle down someone's pants pocket while they were washing dishes, from behind no less.

Perhaps he felt that way because he was the brunt of the joke.

Soon after lunch, dark clouds moved overhead, and the city of Carvers Grove braced itself for the set of thunderstorms meteorologists had warned about for days. Only when the rains cut loose did the city begin to realize how quickly their roads would flood, and how dangerous being caught in the middle of the storms would prove.

Wade soon found himself on a wild string of runs that began with a false alarm to a department store on the north end of town.

Dispatchers then sent the pumper truck to a reported office fire on the other end of town, because all of the south-end trucks were now involved elsewhere.

By the time they arrived, two other trucks had beaten them to the scene, reporting there was no fire, and that an alarm had malfunctioned. One of the employees had overreacted, calling 911 before truly investigating the situation.

Though all of this was routine to the three other men on his truck, Wade felt his stomach tense, along with a sense of urgency to proficiently don his air pack and mask in case it was necessary. He wondered if his officer wanted him in full gear or not, but Wade didn't dare ask.

After all, he figured the captain had better things to do than answer his silly questions.

They had barely pulled up to the building when the officer in command of the scene released them, letting the dispatcher assign them to another location. In the meantime, the rain had let up from its thunderous downpour, almost completely subsiding.

In its wake, Wade could see cars stranded in water that would reach his waist, along several roads they traveled. He felt compelled to stop and help two older ladies trapped in their car, but the call was not his to make, and the women were in no danger of drowning.

Getting a little wet would be their worst-case-scenario.

Now the clouds let loose a barrage of rain heavier than before, giving no indication it would quit anytime soon.

"One Pump, we have a report of a trash fire behind a restaurant," the dispatcher said over the radio, which Wade overheard from the console beside his captain.

A trash fire? he wondered. How on earth could any fire stay lit in this stuff?

He soon found out, as the truck pulled into a parking lot where a new barbeque business had started just the previous week.

He stepped from the truck, unsure of where to go, or what exactly to wear so far as his equipment went. Wade understood each situation was different, and he remembered being told it was better to be overly prepared than unprepared. It was easier to take extra clothes off after an abated emergency than try and put them on in a hurry.

His captain soon told Wade and the other back-end firefighter to grab the hose line reeled on one side of the truck, since the reported fire was little more than smoldering ashes inside a dumpster. It seemed the owner, or one of his employees, had dumped ashes from the barbeque pit into the trash bin before they were cooled off.

Wade sighed to himself as they went to work putting the small fire out, wondering when he would finally see some real action.

It would be years before he could reach the experience level of his uncles, and he wondered if they had endured the same anxiety he was experiencing on their first days.

He figured they were currently on the same kinds of mediocre runs he was, but then again, they had probably earned the right to have an easy day now and then.

CHAPTER 2

By no means had Mike Sheridan's day begun the way he expected it to.

He started by helping his station's driver complete the inventory report at the station, checked each mechanical piece of equipment to ensure it worked, filled the water jug with ice, and cleaned the restrooms.

Nothing out of the ordinary.

Like his nephew, Mike eventually found himself on a few runs that amounted to nothing, but as they sat outside a restaurant on the south end of town reporting light smoke from their kitchen, he thought about the flooding all around him.

Cars everywhere were stuck in the sudden flood, and he was helpless to make a difference. Their route was based entirely on 911 calls and alarm responses through dispatch. They could not deviate from whatever course they were assigned, until the calls quit coming.

Though highly unusual, the quick flooding was something the city could overcome, and it wouldn't even last more than a few hours.

"You okay?" his lieutenant asked from the front seat, noticing Mike was getting a bit antsy just sitting in the truck.

By nature, Mike was an aggressive firefighter who preferred action-packed calls, not answering faulty security alarms.

"I'm fine," Mike replied. "I was just thinking about those people stuck in their cars back there," he said, nodding toward the floods behind them.

His lieutenant looked quite a bit like him, which was explained by the fact that Kevin Sheridan was his older brother.

Except for a few more lines in Kevin's face, the two looked practically identical, from their reddish hair to the farmer tans they both maintained from hours in the sun. Kevin, much like a sheepdog, wore a thick head of hair until the beginning of spring, then shaved it almost to military length to keep cool in the heat and humidity every spring, as it was now.

Of the five brothers, they were the only two who looked remotely alike, and they shared the most in common.

"We'll check on them after this," Kevin assured his younger brother, speaking of the people trapped in their cars.

He knew other emergency units were on the way, and most of the people had been using their cellular phones to call for help.

Kevin had taken their father's death especially hard. He seldom spoke to Greg, holding Mike's twin partly responsible, even though he hadn't been at the farmhouse scene, or mustered courage enough to visit the burned hull that took his father's life afterward.

The incident took a toll on the lieutenant, and he saw no need to visit where, in essence, his father died.

Each of the brothers saw part of his life die with John Sheridan, but they moved forward, knowing they could presently make the difference their father had during his four decades of public safety.

"I wonder how Wade is holding up?" Kevin questioned from the front seat as the incident commander dismissed them from their current assignment.

"I'm sure he's doing fine," Mike said. "We just need to beef that boy up so he can carry his own weight."

Kevin acknowledged the call from dispatch that they were finished there.

"You doing anything with Sandi this weekend?" Kevin asked of Mike's fiancee, now that Mike had finally popped the question.

"Nothing real exciting. We're going to a horse race, I think."

Before Mike could elaborate, the tones came through the truck's radio, preparing them for the incoming report of whatever their next destination might be.

"Four Squad, we have report of a residential structure fire, possible entrapment," the dispatcher said over the line.

Immediately Kevin wondered why they were the only truck dispatched to such an important call, then realized every other truck was likely preoccupied with the flood calls.

"Shit," he commented as the driver started the large red truck toward the address the dispatcher went on to report.

Until other trucks broke free to help, the four men in Four Squad would be on their own. Mike struggled to get his pack on fast enough as the truck sped down a main street toward the fire. He noticed Sam Conley, the other firefighter in back with him, wrestling with one of the air tank's straps on his own pack.

The glance was fleeting, because Mike had to make certain his radio was on the right frequency, his pack was secure, his mask was looped over his neck, and his helmet was strapped over his face mask and protective hood.

All before they reached the scene.

He always waited until they reached the address to turn on his air tank, in order to preserve as much air as possible. Mike would put his gloves on after that, or his fingers would be too thick and fumbling as he tried to screw the connections together.

A few minutes later, he found himself pulling a hose line off the truck as his older brother sized up the scene. From somewhere, he heard a woman stating she thought the neighbors were gone, but their little girl was inside with a babysitter.

Usually, one truck would take the hose line inside, once charged with water, to extinguish the fire, while another crew scurried past the suppression crew to initiate the search.

From the few glances he took, Mike noticed gray smoke billowing from the side of the house, but no flames were showing. To this point, things didn't look overly dangerous.

"I hate to do this to you, Sam," Kevin said as both of firefighters drew near him, "but you've got the line while Mike and I search the house."

Conley nodded in understanding as the truck's driver scrambled to turn knobs and pull levers, once he had the truck in pump gear. Darrell Thomas thought of himself as little more than an overgrown farm boy, but few other drivers did as solid a job as the import from Kentucky.

Technically, the lieutenant was disobeying two basic rules, since no firefighter was supposed to enter any scene alone, and the officer in charge was always to remain outside, to command his scene, until relieved. Kevin was leaving the nozzle man by himself, and allowing his brother to search separately from him, since he had opted to come inside and neglect his command.

Realistically, it had to be that way.

A minute later, Mike pushed his way past Conley, and made his way upstairs, hearing the crackle of fire and wood between the noisy exhales of his air mask. Just a small orange glow was visible downstairs, but he soon found three rooms awaiting him atop the staircase. From experience, Mike knew this wasn't a large fire, or he would be feeling searing heat through his gear. Any fire could generate lots of smoke within a confined space, but it took fire growth to truly generate a thermal layer and flashover conditions.

Luckily, he could see through the hazy smoke, but barely. His brother had the thermal camera, for a quick search of people and hidden fire in the lower levels, where the fire originated. Mike had to check quickly, and maintain his bearings so he didn't become a victim himself.

Daytime fires were definitely preferable to Mike, not because they offered any more visibility in a smoke-filled building, but because they gave a beacon at the end of a tunnel for firefighters when they were lucky enough to find a window or vented opening. They also helped save time in setup and cleanup because no additional lighting was needed inside once ventilation was complete. During the day, sunlight streamed inside any ventilated building once holes were punched or cut into it, adding vastly more visibility.

He immediately heard noises to his right, which sounded like a little girl talking or whimpering from behind a closed door, but as he opened the wooden door, he found a sight more eerie than he expected.

Across the floor sat dolls and toys, several of which were activated by the fire and heat beneath them. An infant doll kept calling for its mother in a baby voice, which Mike had mistaken for the little girl's voice. A nearby toy piano chimed out several tunes, distracting the veteran firefighter once more.

This is creepy, Mike thought as the toys chattered around him. He accidentally pressed his hand down on a toy monkey, which clanged its cymbals together excitedly.

Beneath him, Mike could hear water furiously hitting the ceiling and walls as Conley did his job. Luckily, the fire was small, but the amount of thick smoke would still overcome a person not equipped with an air tank.

Especially a child.

By the time his warning bell sounded from the air tank strapped to his back, Mike had all three rooms thoroughly searched with negative results, and he stammered outside to find three other departmental trucks, all with red lights flashing, lining the street.

He had passed Kevin on his way out, and with assurance his brother was safe, Mike made his way outside, tossing his helmet atop a patch of soft grass, spying the babysitter and the little girl sitting near some paramedics, apparently oblivious to the fact the house was on fire until they returned home from wherever they had been.

Thank God, Mike thought, starting to remove the rest of his heavy gear.

His head and face were dripping with sweat as he watched his brother emerge from the house, say something to the officer now in charge, and make his way over.

"You okay?" he asked when he reached Mike.

"Fine. That upstairs was freaky."

Kevin gave a questioning stare.

"The toys were all talking because of the heat," Mike explained.

"Ah," Kevin said, understanding because he had seen such things before. "I guess they went out to the store for a minute and something got left on the stove."

"I love preventable fires," Mike said sarcastically. "I guess it can happen to anyone, though."

"We're lucky Sam stopped it at the kitchen, or you might just as well have been crawling on a frying pan."

"Kind of felt like I was already."

"You did fine," Kevin assured him. "I, however, might be taking some heat for my actions."

"What?" Mike asked, raising his voice intentionally so the officer in charge would hear. "Splitting us up?"

Kevin nodded.

"You had no choice," Mike exclaimed. "We go in there, and at least we've got some protection, and some experience. Anyone trapped in there doesn't have that luxury. If they blame you for that, that's bullshit."

"I'm not real worried," the lieutenant admitted. "They've called me in for worse stuff. You know Pat's not going to write me up or anything."

Mike looked up to the sky, noticing the clouds were moving east, and out of town. At least until the next front moved in.

"Not quite what I expected this morning," Mike admitted.

"Me neither. I figured the rain was the worst of it."

"I guess we were both wrong then."

Kevin nodded before walking off, his gear drenched from the water Conley had sprayed everywhere on the first floor. He had a few things to do before they headed back to the station, or to the grocery store to pick up supplies.

Hopefully the worst of their day was over.

CHAPTER 3

A week later, Mike was dripping wet from a shower, towel around his waist, looking for some fresh clothes to put on before his department's union meeting that night.

Some recent changes in the city of Carvers Grove made members of the fire department rather uneasy. Tonight's meeting would focus on some of those changes, and what could be done about a new volunteer department working in a territory they once covered.

"What are you looking for?" Sandi Linton, his girlfriend of two years, asked as she walked upstairs in the old farmhouse the two had bought as part of their engagement's solidification.

It needed renovation, but they figured that was half the fun.

"Have you seen my old department T-shirts?" he asked.

"They're in the black dresser, second drawer," she answered, seeing him in just a towel for the first time in quite awhile.

She eyed him up and down, as though something frisky crossed her mind.

Mike caught the glance and grinned.

"I don't have time for that, if that's what you're thinking."

"I didn't say a thing," Sandi defended herself. "You're the one always wanting sex around here."

He felt his face flush a bit after her straightforward outburst.

"We share that responsibility," he said, turning to look in the dresser for his shirts.

Soon after the holidays, when it was all but confirmed his father would not recover from the heart attack, Mike officially proposed to Sandi, despite the strange timing.

Some thought it was entirely inappropriate to propose when his father was lying in the hospital, but Mike knew the circumstances better than anyone, and wanted to make certain his father knew he was going to be married, before he passed away.

Mike recalled seeing a bit of a gleam in his father's eye the day he revealed the news, after his father told him, and him alone, that he knew he would not make it past the spring, and that he wanted all of his children to move on quickly once he died.

"I don't know what I'm going to do without you, Dad," Mike said after his father made the statement.

"You'll be fine," his father replied with as much strength as he could muster from the hospital bed, stuck inside a drab room. "I just wish you and Greg would put aside your differences and act like brothers."

"We've tried," Mike said. "We're just too different. I've gotten along with total strangers better than Greg."

"For me," John Sheridan pleaded of his son. "When I'm gone, I want you to keep the family together, Michael. Without each other, you'll have nothing. I know it's not easy, but we've always depended on one another, and that was our strength."

"No," Mike said. "You were our strength, Dad. I don't know what I'd do without you."

"You'll do fine. Just keep everyone together, Michael. You're the centerpiece of the family now. Patrick is too uptight, and Kevin is too busy to keep up with everyone. You're the one who's always made time for everyone else."

By this time, doctors had informed the father of seven his heart was too far gone to operate without serious risk of him dying on the operating table. Too much irreparable damage had been done to his heart between blockage and weakened vessels. His only chance of survival would be a donor, and he refused to take a heart that would give him such limited life compared to the younger people who might need it.

"I wish you'd reconsider the donor program, Dad," Mike said quietly, which was his way of pleading with his father so no one else would hear.

"No," John Sheridan said wearily, but with resolve. "I'm a waste of time to save. I don't have that much left in me."

"I don't want to see you die in here," Mike said, a tear forming in his eye.

Of all of the children, he was definitely the most attached to his father, and probably the closest thing to a clone of his father anyone could ask for. He and Kevin were both close to their father, but Mike made more of a point in showing it.

"You'll be fine, Michael. It's not like I haven't accomplished anything in seventy years. I've got seven great kids, and maybe I've saved a life or two."

The old man rolled to one side, though any movement seemed to pain him now that he was placed indefinitely in the hospital.

"I just want you to marry that girl of yours someday," he confessed. "I'll feel better leaving this world if I know you're happy."

Mike forced a grin.

"I asked her to marry me yesterday, Dad."

"Great," the retired captain said with a smile, trying not to strain himself.

Any strenuous activity or emotion worked his heart all the harder, and John Sheridan had no intention of dying any sooner than necessary.

Mike realized this was one of the last times he would ever see his father alive, and knew deep down the man would die with some happiness. The burden of keeping the family together was now his to undertake, which meant keeping Greg from feeling alienated after his alleged screw-up at the fire scene.

No one dared vocally blame Greg for anything, but Mike's twin brother felt alienated nonetheless, and made it worse on himself by avoiding his own family.

"There's one more thing I want from you, Michael," John said as he tried to position himself comfortably in the bed that had already left sores across his backside.

"Name it," his son said.

"No matter what, don't let the department slip away," John ordered. "It took us years to build it up and get a union in there. Don't be letting that alderman, or trustee, or whatever the fuck he is, take it away from you by moving some scab department in there."

"You're talking about that new volunteer department?"

"I am. And I know I've worked as a chief for a volunteer department for years, but I never took over someone's territory or livelihood. Don't let that asshole Malovich move his goofy bunch inside city limits, no matter how many protests, letters to the editor, and meetings you have to go through."

"I promise, Dad," Mike vowed, knowing how hard his father, and those like him, had worked over the years to get the men on his current department where they were. "I'll do everything I can."

He only saw his father two more times after that visit before the call came one rainy night that his father had passed away.

Though he knew for months it was coming, Mike still shed tears, and still felt hurt knowing the man he looked up to for so many years wasn't going to be there any longer to offer him advice, or tell him how proud he was. Little things like that meant everything to Mike, but he hoped to someday have little ones of his own to oversee.

"You okay?" Sandi asked, bringing him back to present day and the problems at hand.

"I'm fine," Mike answered, rummaging through the dresser drawers to find a particular shirt. "I was just thinking about what Dad would think of this meeting."

"Are you worried?"

"Yeah, a little bit. That scab department is already in action because that dickhead Malovich says he's saving the city money."

Mike was ready to jump on his soapbox now.

"He brings them in, it costs more to fund his district than he promised the public it would, and now they say they're going to start doing first responder runs because our department isn't equipped to. They've already gone over their budget setting their shit up, and maintaining that junk equipment they bought is going to cost more in the long run than paying the city for our fire protection."

"So it's all one big lie?" Sandi asked.

"So to speak. I think the mayor and Malovich are in cahoots, because our illustrious mayor doesn't like professional firefighters anyway. I think this is their plan to slowly put us out of business."

Sandi smirked.

"You're into conspiracy theories, aren't you?"

"Do the math, dear. They're spending more money creating this volunteer unit of yahoos than it would cost to just pay the city. Now the newspaper has named Malovich man of the year, so they won't let us publish anything negative against him or his *ingenious* department. This new contract negotiation might be the only way to fight them."

"They won't let you say anything in the paper?"

"No. It's a republican paper, and they don't want democrats telling them what to do, or badmouthing their politicians."

"Even if you write the truth?"

"Even if we write just the facts. They don't want to hear any of it."

Sandi watched him get dressed for a moment.

"But if they're covering the outskirts of town, isn't that less work for you guys?"

"Sure, but that's not what we're after," Mike said. "What stops other outlying parts of town from getting this department's protection? And what happens with annexation if they have a choice between departments? These people think they're getting good protection for a cheaper rate, and they aren't getting either."

Sandi had little desire to dig further into this can of worms she'd started with her fiancee, but his logic didn't make full sense to her.

Basically, the city had asked for too much money to cover the outlying industrial areas of Carvers Grove, according to Malovich. His alternative was finding, or building, a different source of fire protection by law, so he chose the latter.

Since the death of his father, Mike had seemed preoccupied with fire department business, much more than before. He attended more meetings, went drinking with the guys afterward, and struggled to make time for Sandi, almost to the point that he lost sleep.

Still, she understood this was his livelihood he was dealing with, and most of the firefighters felt threatened by this new volunteer department moving into the territory they once covered.

In her eyes, men tended to be much more possessive about their turf, and relationships, than women.

"Are you going out with the boys after the meeting?" Sandi asked with a hint of jealousy, indicating he might be better suited to come home after the meeting.

Mike sighed lightly, rolling his blue eyes.

"I'll be a good boy and come home to you tonight."

"Maybe you'll be rewarded for your trouble," she said, rubbing his chin with her index finger while he tried to imagine what he would tell his fellow firefighters to get out of a night on the town.

"I've been neglecting you a little bit lately, haven't I?" Mike asked, realizing his tough choices weren't always correct.

"A little bit."

He planted a soft kiss on her lips as his hands rubbed her body on down to her thighs.

"I'm sorry," he said as his hands returned to gently cup her chin. "I swear I'll be home as soon as the meeting is over."

"Promise?"

"I swear," he said, giving her another quick kiss. "And hopefully I'll bring some good news home for a change."

He looked at her a moment, finding her strawberry blonde hair glistening around her shoulders from the afternoon sunlight. She was soft in every good way, but especially in her heart. He had never met someone so caring of others, much like himself.

She struggled to fit in among the beehive-like structure of the prosecutor's office at work, but she was easily intelligent enough to make the grade as a clerical supervisor. Sandi thought of herself as a simple farmer's daughter, but she was absolutely everything Mike had ever wanted in a wife.

And more.

As Sandi started organizing the upstairs, Mike realized he was running late, then darted down the old stairs of the farmhouse. A familiar creak, almost like that of old bedsprings, came with each step on the way down.

"Love you," Mike called from the base of the stairs.

"Love you too," Sandi called back, wondering what had taken so long for him to say it.

Nestling a departmental baseball cap atop his head, Mike grinned to himself as he walked out the front door, ready to walk into a lion's den.

Within the half hour, Mike found himself walking inside the headquarters fire station, seeing an abundant number of cars in the parking lot, and across the street.

He also noticed some cars with blue lights planted on their tops. A feeling of rage seethed throughout his body a moment as he figured Washington Township volunteers were allowed to show up. He then remembered this was also the night fire chiefs from across the county met with the EMS director to discuss safety issues and their mutual aid agreements.

This group included the chief from Washington Township, the new volunteer department moving into city limits.

Mike shot Tom Ellis, the opposing chief, a dirty stare as he entered the station.

Ellis knew Mike from several encounters, since Mike had served on several boards on his department, some of which the volunteer chief was privy to.

"Take it easy," Kevin warned as Mike walked through the door.

"I'd love to beat his ass," Mike said.

"That wouldn't accomplish anything."

"But I'd feel a whole lot better."

Mike looked around, seeing quite a few of the younger department members present, including some who seldom attended union meetings. He wondered if the union board had put in some phone calls to make sure the vote would go their way. With enough of the young guys present, the veterans would be outnumbered, and the new contract would likely be passed on the first vote.

The board members made no secret of the fact they wanted the first responder issue to go through, and Mike wondered how many of them were the chief's pets, doing his bidding. He also suspected they were slanting the truth, because he didn't believe the city could force the department to make first responder runs. Mike had no problem with doing the runs, but he had a problem with the union board if its members were simply fulfilling their own agendas.

He recalled reading several reports of fire departments wanting to get out of first responder runs after trying it a year or two. The cost of buying medical supplies and maintaining their vehicles overwhelmed these departments, and he saw little difference between his own department and those wanting to rid themselves of the first responder albatross.

When the meeting finally came to order, the union representatives said they had negotiated a new contract with the city, and felt they had the best deal they could get from the city's representatives on the first try.

Further attempts to negotiate with the city could possibly get them a better contract, or cost them some of the key points they had already fought to acquire.

In other words, it was a gamble to turn this first contract down.

Though veteran members of the department vehemently argued against the first responder issue, the union board members pointed out that almost every other fire department in the state was making first responder runs, and that the city had threatened to bring in outside sources if the fire department refused.

"Who the fuck would they hire *just* to do first responder runs?" Mike asked Kevin, his voice barely above a whisper.

Kevin shrugged, seeing truth his brother's logic.

"You know there's someone out there dumb enough to do it."

The Carvers Grove Fire Department was being offered specialty pay, and an opportunity to help create the program if they accepted the contract. If they declined, the pay and the input might very well be thrown to the wayside the second time around.

Perhaps partly from fear of the unknown, and possibly from complete trust of the union board members by the younger members of the department, the vote went heavily in favor of approving the contract, which meant the department as a whole would be moving forward.

Many of the younger department members looked at doing first responder runs as job security. With fewer fires, thanks to technology and fire codes, and few other tasks firefighters could do to earn their wages, this would give them good publicity and keep them busier in the public eye.

"You okay with this?" Kevin asked of his younger brother once the meeting was adjourned.

"I'm fine with it. I sure as hell don't want those pricks from Washington Township in here."

"That was a crock of shit anyway," Kevin stated. "Like they're going to bring those guys in just to assist the EMS. And those guys wouldn't want the job anyway. Not for free."

"You never know. They brag about how they keep those two stations manned around the clock."

"Sure, with one or two guys. When have you ever seen two guys put out a house fire by themselves?"

Mike chuckled.

He knew two firefighters inside a house could do it, but common sense told him he would want an officer outside calling the shots, and he would certainly want someone operating the truck's pumping system.

"You know, I worry about Wade's future with the department," he commented.

"How so?"

"If this Washington Township thing takes off, what's to stop them from moving further into city limits and taking our jobs? That mayor isn't going to back us in the least, and he and Malovich are probably working together."

A few of the guys sauntered by before Kevin could reply, apparently ready to start their night of drinking at whichever pub they deemed suitable.

"You going, Mike?" one of the guys asked in passing.

"Uh, I can't make it," was Mike's reply, trying to avoid giving reasons why.

"Ah, come on, Mike," another firefighter urged, wearing a golf shirt and floppy straw hat, indicative of the fact he'd been on the golf course all day.

"Really, guys, I can't. The ol' lady has plans for me."

"Come on, ya big sissy," one of them prompted, drawing a resigned grin from Mike. "She'll never know if you have a beer or two. Just tell her the meeting ran over."

Mike knew from the experience of those around him that their wives and girlfriends always found things out in due time. He figured there was no harm in having a beer with the guys, but he was not about to break any promises to Sandi this early in their relationship.

Not if he expected it to last.

Mike shook his head negatively.

"I can't go tonight, guys. Maybe next week."

Apparently satisfied with the answer, the other firefighters shrugged before heading for the door. Kevin patted his younger brother on the back before following them.

"You going too?" Mike asked, feeling a bit more disappointed if he would miss his brother's company.

"Of course. You stay married as long as I have, you learn to appreciate the time you get away from home."

Mike sighed, half tempted to change his mind and tell Sandi the meeting took quite a while because of the debate, but he slumped his shoulders and walked toward the door. He could only hope whatever his fiancee had in mind would make his missed night out worthwhile.

CHAPTER 4

While the first week in May proved to be moderately hot, the second week was nearly blistering.

Without a single drop of rain the entire month, the city of Carvers Grove looked somewhat like the Texas plains with tan, dead grass, and small pools of motor oil being the only liquid the sun could find to shimmer from.

Nighttime brought little relief from the heat and humidity, but at least the blistering sun was gone, and the outdoors could be tolerated. No one dared open up the fire hydrants during the day, for fear what little water the city had might be needed at any time.

A lone figure crept along an old apartment building's exterior. Vacated of college students for the summer, and filled with components that made it ripe for a good burn, the building was virtually defenseless.

No smell of rain entered the air, and the building stood on the outskirts of town, putting it in the territory of the new Washington Township Volunteer Fire Department, which meant it would have a long time to burn before a single drop of water ever touched it.

The location meant nothing to the man ducking into the front door after unlocking it, and the padlock securing it. He was hired to do a job, and this was the target.

Pure and simple.

This particular job needed to look accidental, but in a very specific way. Assignments with clear directions made his job all the easier.

In the north end's older section, the building was surrounded by other apartments that were almost equally vacant. During the summer when kids left school for their hometowns, such buildings made the area look like a ghost town.

Most of the apartments in this area were older buildings, further away from campus. Because of the higher crime risk, and higher utility bills, the rent was typically cheaper. When the security students inadvertently provided for one another left in the summer, very few tenants stuck around.

The building had both electric and gas utilities turned on, which made the job even easier. Turning his large, square flashlight on, the intruder refused to turn on any main lights, fearful of attracting attention to himself.

He scurried through the musty smell of the old building, taking in the remnants of stale pizza and beer through his nostrils, left from the week before, when students were up late every night studying for finals or partying.

In one room he found everything he needed for a homegrown arson fire. Pulling a modified nightlight from his back pocket, the shadowy figure cut the building's power through the fuse box, then plugged the nightlight into an electrical outlet near the floor.

He found the water heater across the small room, and set to work loosening one of its gas line couplings. Any punctures or dents would look intentional, so he loosened a connection just enough to make it look like time, and perhaps the settling of the old building, had taken its toll on the gas line.

Satisfied the pipe was leaking, but not overwhelmingly obvious in doing so, he pulled a carbon monoxide detector from another pocket, finding the levels of the invisible gas already rising within the room.

Loosely stuffing a cloth up the aluminum ventilation pipe that took excess gas fumes up and outside, he knew this would ensure that no gas escaped the room, since the windows were sealed tight, and all of the doors would be closed on every floor.

Next, he blew out the pilot light, ensuring nothing caught fire or blew up early. The gas needed to fill the room, then the rest of the building, without interruption.

He set the flashlight in front of the light-sensitive nightlight, confirming the beam went straight into the sensor. This would make certain the nightlight would not kick on until the flashlight's battery died enough to trigger it.

Thorough testing had gone into this job, several times over, and he felt reasonably certain the batteries would die a few hours before daybreak, giving him ample time to make his way home and assure himself an alibi.

Not that he ever expected to need one.

Before the gas levels got too high, he switched the power back on, finding the nightlight inactive, and the flashlight's beam still strong. He gave himself a satisfied grunt and left through the same door he had entered, making sure to seal it as tightly as he could, so no gas could escape.

Careful to lock the door before he left, the shadowy figure knew any lock or door out of place, or left undone, would be a sign of a break-in. Following his orders, he wanted absolutely everything to point to this being an accidental explosion when the investigators examined it.

If everything went according to plan, the nightlight would kick itself on when the flashlight died, the modified wiring would spark, and the sparks would ignite the gaseous vapors leaking throughout the apartment building, either setting it ablaze, or more than likely, blowing it to kingdom come.

He walked away at a hurried pace toward his car, parked several blocks away. Everything about this crime would be perfect. No one would ever suspect anything of a leaky gas line, an old nightlight breaking down, or a flashlight just inside the fuse room.

If it wasn't perfect, it was damn close.

Wade yawned as he watched the end of a movie on one of the satellite dish's movie channels. He had given up trying to sleep after the tones went off the second time that night.

That was an hour ago, and dawn was closing in, so he saw little point in trying to sleep. Unlike the other guys on duty, he was young and full of energy.

Besides, he had no second job to worry about in the morning like they did. He could simply go home and sleep as he pleased.

Still, the cushioned easy chair was relaxing. Wade felt his head fall back against the plush headrest, and his eyes begin to heavily close as the tones sounded once more.

"Figures," he commented to himself, leaping out of the isolated television room toward the truck room floor.

He had been on duty over two weeks now, and the largest thing he had seen was a car fire, and a small one at that. Many a restless night could be attributed to waiting anxiously for his first "real" fire. Gaining acceptance from his peers would be incredibly tough until he weathered the interiors of a few burning buildings.

As Wade pulled up the straps to his night pants, he tried to listen to what the dispatcher said through the sound system. He missed the address, but the report was a working fire, and it was on the west end of town, obviously in their territory.

He had no idea how many trucks would beat them to the scene, but he was guessing someone else would catch the plug, which meant hooking the large water supply hose up to the fire hydrant. Wade tried to envision what he would need to do once he was off the truck.

"Always listen to your officer," his grandfather had told him when he first discovered Wade would be joining the department, after placing so high on the recruit list. "That's what they're there for."

Wade trusted his captain, and thanked his lucky stars he wasn't working directly under one of his uncles. He had enough pressure without having to worry about any of his rookie blunders being archived forever in fire department and family reunion lore.

A few minutes later, his air tank was strapped to his back as the smell of burning wood entered his captain's open window.

They were close, and he could feel his stomach tense. He tried to control his breathing and remain focused, but he was nervous, a bit scared, and excited all at the same time.

He wondered what was going on when the truck pulled to a stop, simply waiting there as the captain looked forward, listening for radio communication.

Why aren't we going over yet? Wade wondered, seeing the reflection of the orange flames dance against the metal backing of the truck where he was seated. Both jump seats faced the rear of the truck, which meant Wade and the other back-end firefighter could not fully turn to see what the driver and captain saw, unless they pulled their air tanks from the harnesses in the seats.

Wade stretched his neck like an upended turtle, struggling to see around his shoulder, because he could hear very little, and the radio was silent as his uncle, the battalion chief, made rounds to decide how best to attack the fire.

Across the lot, Patrick Sheridan looked to the smoldering pile of debris, seeing only the remains of the building piled floor by floor on top of one another. Though there were a few isolated fires, they were nothing a few small hose lines wouldn't take care of.

Like dominos, most of the piles were spread out enough that he could see spaces between the boards and sections of floor. He saw very little burned, or damaged, across the remains of the wood and concrete, which meant the source of the building's collapse wasn't fire, but it was something very intense.

"What have we got?" Kevin asked as he stepped up to his older brother, Sam Conley and Mike right behind him.

"An explosion," Patrick answered hesitantly. "I'm assuming."

Before he could elaborate, a neighbor informed him the building was abandoned for the summer, and that the front door had been padlocked for days, supporting the notion no one would be living there.

"You want us to put those out?" Kevin inquired, nodding toward the small sets of flames, "or are you calling an investigator first?"

Patrick thought a moment.

"I'm definitely calling Mason in, but go ahead and put those out without destroying anything. You know he'll throw a bitch fit if we destroy his evidence."

Mason Gray was the department's seasoned investigator, but he was still a young man in his mid-thirties, and seemed to think he knew absolutely everything. More than once, Patrick had shown the investigator otherwise, but Gray was too hardheaded to ever admit he was wrong.

"He'll make a great chief someday," Patrick had commented on more than one occasion in a sarcastic manner, since failure to admit fault was a trait he had seen in several fire chiefs over the years.

After calling the dispatchers to notify Gray that he was needed, Patrick grinned as he saw his nephew step from the truck, allowed to do little more than shift debris so that Mike and Conley could spray water into the crevices, where it needed to be to douse the flames hiding underneath.

Once again, Wade had been deprived of his first big fire, but barely.

Thinking of what a close call this had been, and feeling fairly reassured no one had been inside, the battalion chief removed his white helmet, running a hand through his sweaty black hair.

He considered a full-scale search of the building for potential trapped survivors, but without heavy equipment to move the concrete and wooden frames aside, the fire department ran the risk of harming, rather than helping anyone inside by knocking debris on top of them, or cutting off an air pocket.

Since it seemed highly unlikely there was anyone inside the building when it toppled, he would consult with Gray to decide what should be done.

"You don't see this every day," Gray commented a few minutes later as he strolled up to the battalion chief, flashlight and shovel in hand.

"I think it's going to take more than that," Patrick commented, referring to the shovel.

"So it would seem," Gray said. "Any chance of survivors?"

"Doubtful, since there was little chance of occupancy."

Gray grunted to himself, walking up to the edge of the disaster. He noticed the same traits of the building the battalion chief spotted moments earlier. Evidence of an explosion was overwhelming, and he would assume it was natural, unless he found indications otherwise.

If people wanted a building to the ground, they usually torched it, both men figured. That way, there was no chance of people being inside, or any chance of failure. It took a bit of knowledge to create an explosion that went off without a hitch.

Though handsome and intelligent, the arson investigator's personality offset his good traits. He was known to spend time with the town's elite, including doctors, lawyers, and city council members, on the golf course. Seldom did he attend functions with his fellow firefighters, and those he did, he always had a new young lady with him.

"What else are you going to need from me?" Patrick asked the investigator as Mike and Conley put out the last of the flames, finding no indications of people trapped inside the rubble.

If the explosion hadn't done any occupants in, the collapse certainly would have.

"I'll need a couple guys to stay behind and monitor the scene until I can get a crane down here."

"One Pump can stay until shift change," Patrick said. "Any idea who owns the building?"

"Not yet. Hopefully I can dig up some neighbors who know. I'll have to go looking for witnesses anyway, in case anyone saw anything before the explosion."

Gray paused to look through his business card collection for the right contacts, before continuing the conversation.

"I'll probably call the state boys in, so they can help me comb the area."

Gray took a peek at some of the damage on one of the bottom layers, finding several areas with heavy char, where the blast originated. He could see the remains of a water heater partly crushed beneath the walls of the building, wondering if it was the cause of his problems.

Patrick walked up behind him, taking in the same view, thinking along the same lines. Both knew the debris would have to be moved before they could analyze the source of the explosion further.

Gray knew of instances where relief valves had caused steam pressure and excessive temperatures to blow water heaters across rooms, but those were a different type of explosion. He was determined to figure out what had caused this one, hopefully without the state marshals hogging all of his glory.

"If you need anything else, just holler," the battalion chief said before leaving, not wanting Gray's company any longer than necessary.

Simply giving a dismissing wave, his attention on the debris, Gray knelt down to further examine his latest casualty.

Across the decimated lot, Greg had pulled up to the scene, near the end of his midnight shift. Word of the fallen building crossed city police scanners, but Greg had been busy at a traffic wreck when he heard about the incident.

Knowing his brothers were on duty, and would likely respond, he headed that way, despite their lack of attention to him since the holiday season.

He had given up trimming his fringe, and decided to shave his hair to stubble. As he stepped from the car, he cleaned his glasses, then walked over to his two brothers, wearing black leather gloves, despite the hot weather.

"Good morning, gentlemen," he said as he found Kevin and Mike resting a short distance from the wreckage.

"What's up, Greg?" Mike asked.

"Nothing much. Heard the news, so I thought I'd stop and see what you guys found."

"I've got to check with the captain before we take off," Kevin said to Mike, excusing himself with barely more than a glance in Greg's direction.

Greg felt certain his older brother was trying to avoid him. They had barely spoken two words to one another since their father's funeral.

"What's up, evil twin?" he asked Mike anyway.

"I'm not the one who carries a gun for a living," Mike replied. "You might want to rethink your title for me."

"It's amazing how none of you guys want to talk to me lately," Greg said, wondering why even his twin brother seemed to have no sense of humor anymore.

"You haven't exactly made yourself available. I leave you messages and I get a message back two days later because you never call when I'm at home."

Greg shrugged.

"I'm a busy guy."

"You could drop by the station once in a while. Contrary to what you think, I don't mind catching up with you occasionally."

Greg exhaled uneasily through his nose, looking away.

"Kevin doesn't want a thing to do with me, Mike. Every time I get within ten feet of him, he finds some reason to leave."

"It's going to take some time for him to heal. Dad's death hit him pretty hard."

"That doesn't mean he has to hold me responsible."

"I know, I know."

Greg gave his brother a quizzical stare for a few seconds.

"Do you hold me responsible?"

"No, of course not. If you hadn't been there, things might have been a hell of a lot worse."

Greg nodded quietly, hoping his brother was being truthful.

"How's Wade been doing?" he asked.

"Pretty good, but he's still waiting for his first big one."

Both looked over to their nephew, who was standing beside the rubble, chatting with a few other firefighters as he waited for his next set of orders.

He can have it, Greg thought, hoping he never had to enter another burning building again.

"Think you might have time to work on my car next time you're at the station?" Greg inquired, since Mike was a sideline mechanic, who charged little or nothing for his work.

He enjoyed working on vehicles at work just to pass the time.

"Still got that piece of shit Mustang of yours?"

"Yeah, I've still got ol' red."

"Bring her by."

Mike noticed Kevin waving him over to leave. Evidently they had been dismissed from the scene by the battalion chief.

"Take care, Greg," he said as he walked away.

"You too," the cop replied, unsure of where he stood with his family these days.

CHAPTER 5

Three days later, Mike was getting ready for work when Sandi found him making toast and frying eggs in the kitchen.

"Have you come up with a date yet?" he asked first thing.

"And good morning to you, too," Sandi replied. "I take it you mean our wedding date?"

She took a seat beside her fiancé, who was trying to wolf down breakfast so he wouldn't be late in relieving another firefighter at work.

"Of course I mean the wedding date."

"Well, I've been checking availability on reception halls and churches, and it looks like it's going to be at least October."

Mike winced at the notion. Typical of most men, he left the planning to his wife-to-be, but forgot just how long things could take in the planning stage. His married friends often warned him about the details of a wedding, and how long it took everything to fall together. He figured women just dragged things out on purpose, but he wasn't going to argue.

Arguing would just serve to get him further involved.

"How about December when the snow is three feet deep?" he kidded, standing to pour himself some more orange juice.

"I gave that some thought. A winter wonderland theme would be kind of nice."

Mike's look soured.

"I was kidding."

"But I'm not," Sandi said, a smile crossing her face. "I want you to be my husband as soon as possible."

He sat down, took a gulp of juice, then took hold of her hand.

"Sometime we need to have a talk about what could happen to me on this job, and what we need to do to prepare for it."

"No," Sandi objected. "I really don't want to have that talk."

She had always been squeamish on issues about death and gore. Mike learned early in their relationship to never discuss his job with her, or to skim over certain details if he did.

"There could come a morning when I don't make it home," Mike said realistically. "Statistically, there's little chance of me ever getting seriously hurt, or dying, but you never know in this line of work."

Sandi still shook her head.

"You would bring this up right before you leave for work," she commented negatively. "Now you're going to have me worried all day."

"Don't worry about me," Mike said, quickly kissing her forehead as he stood again with a grin. "I'm like a big dumb brick. Nothing ever hurts me."

"That's not what you said a minute ago."

"Yeah, well, I'm trying to leave on a good note."

"Then don't tell me we're going to have talks like that."

He forced a strange grin, thinking of what had happened to his father.

"Okay," he lied, knowing he would have to bring it up again at some point, just for her understanding of his job, if nothing else.

Sandi recalled her uncle having a strange accident on a tractor when she was a young girl. Unprepared for such horrors, she recalled seeing his mangled, bloody hand when the medics untangled it from the bailing system attached to the tractor. Dripping blood, only three fingers dangled from his stumpy hand, the others written off as losses. Taking time to look for them only ruined her uncle's chances of keeping what he had, and Sandi turned away from the gory scene, never expecting to see such sights as a naive child.

That, coupled with the untimely death of her older brother in New York City when he was robbed and murdered by a street gang, left her constantly worried about everyone in her family. There had been no justice for her brother, and her other brother worked on the Chicago Police Department, which she knew was dangerous work.

In her everyday life, Sandi functioned just fine, and shut out the thoughts of negativity, and worries about her family, until someone brought up the dangerous aspects of public safety, or she relived the day police from New York called regarding her brother's death. Sandi had answered the phone, and the words still haunted her.

Even as she kissed Mike before he left, she wondered just how long she would stay worried about him before she could distract herself with something more positive. Hopefully her own workday would keep her busy enough to forget this conversation.

🍁 🍁 🍁

"I appreciate you doing this," Greg said as he stood over the open hood of his Mustang, watching Mike change spark plug wires and the plugs themselves.

It was mid-morning at Station Four, and the firefighters were done with their training. Kevin was on a personal day, taking his kids fishing, so Greg had no worries about sticking around the station while his brother fixed up his old car.

All three bay doors were open in the front and back of the four-man station, letting sunlight and humidity stream in. Outside, noise from children playing echoed through the street as they rode bikes, shot basketballs, or ran through sprinkler systems in their yards.

Traffic sounded as it passed in front of the station, and several city smells, mostly like diesel fumes, passed through the extensive garage with the breeze.

Though nothing much to look at, the garage held basic essentials like a toolbox, a map of the city, and some exercise equipment. A giant heater ran from the center bay's front to back, overhead. It made noise enough to drown out any sound from the pumper truck's engine during the winter months, whenever it kicked on.

"Goddamn, when was the last time you had this thing serviced?" Mike's muffled voice came from under the hood, his face almost down inside the engine.

"It's been awhile."

Mike pulled himself out from under the hood a moment to face his fraternal twin.

"Well, you're looking at a bunch of tuneup maintenance, basically. I can order the parts and have them delivered pretty quick. You got time?"

"Yeah."

"You got money with you?"

Greg let a smile slip across his face. He had gone to the bank to withdraw a few hundred dollars, just in case it was worse than he thought.

"I've got it covered. I'll even buy you lunch, if that helps."

"Not necessary. We've already been to the store."

Mike was driving the truck, since the regular driver was covering Kevin's lieutenant position, and Mike had seniority over Sam Conley. Driving large vehicles was another thing Greg didn't envy his brothers for doing. He had seen several wrecks involving delivery trucks, fire trucks, and tractor trailers, knowing all too well they were like missiles when they hit smaller vehicles.

"So how's life as a beat cop?" Mike inquired, ducking under the hood to further examine the engine's contents.

"It may be short-lived."

"Oh?"

"I might be getting placed in the investigative unit, finally."

"Well, congratulations," Mike said, emerging once more to shake his brother's hand with a genuine smile, leaving several black streaks across Greg's palm. "Sorry," he quickly apologized.

"Not a problem," Greg replied, finding a paper towel to wipe his hand on.

"Does this involve a raise or anything?"

"Just a lot more training, and it'll give me a better background if I ever decide to instruct someday, or move into another division."

"You sure you want to go through all of that?" Mike asked, adjusting one of the plug wires.

"Sure. I've waited my whole life to be an investigator, and I've put in ten years on the force. I think I deserve it."

"I think you do, too," Mike said, his head still buried under the hood. "It's about time we all had some happiness in our lives."

Greg wondered if his brother's statement had a double meaning, but decided not to pursue it.

"Got a date on the wedding yet?" he asked instead.

"Ironically, I asked Sandi that this morning, and *she* doesn't even have an answer yet. I'm guessing the end of the year."

"Think she'll want something big?"

"Oh, yeah," Mike said, coming up for air once more, in a tone that hinted the wedding would be costing him a small fortune.

"Am I going to need a tux for this one?" Greg inquired, knowing from the other weddings in the family not every brother or sister was in everyone else's wedding party.

"Actually, I'm glad you brought that up. I was going to ask you later, but I don't see any point in waiting."

Mike walked to grab a paper towel, so he could wipe the excess grease from his hands.

"I want you to be my best man, Greg."

"You sure?" his brother asked, almost taken aback. "I thought you'd ask Kevin for sure."

Mike bobbed his head in thought a few seconds.

"I considered it, but you asked me to stand up for you when you got married, and I thought maybe this was a way we could finally get along once and for all."

Greg grinned.

"Remember when you used to throw my army toys in the driveway so Dad would run over them?"

"Oh, no," Mike said, firing back with a smile, recalling the situation with a different point of view. "That was only after you lit firecrackers in my model cars to give them a 'weathered' look."

Both burst out laughing simultaneously.

Sam Conley stepped into the truck bay from the kitchen wanting a cigarette, took one look at them, and stepped back inside. More than likely, he thought they were conspiring to do something devious toward him, because he had heard Greg was an assistant on more than one firehouse prank.

"I thought those cars were always too pristine," Greg admitted. "Old cars aren't supposed to look shiny new."

"You didn't even wait for the paint to dry before you blew them up," Mike said, trying not to laugh. "And you knew how much I loved those cars."

"Remember when I blamed it on the neighbor kid and you went chasing after them with that stick?" Greg asked, sending them both into hysterical laughter, so much so, that Mike fell back on a sofa resting against one wall, the side of his stomach aching from the outburst.

"Dad was ready to kill me until you took my side," Mike recalled. "I got blamed for so much of your shit, it's not funny," he added, still grinning.

"At least I stopped the firecracker thing when you started buying real cars."

"Well that's because you've got your own to beat up," Mike said, standing to greet the parts store delivery man, who was wondering what the laughter he'd heard a moment before was all about.

Mike paid him, not noticing the man's cautious look, as though the two might perpetrate some practical joke on him at any second. He left the station, still looking behind him every few steps.

Being separated by seven years from the next oldest brother, the twins had grown up having only one another to play with, and learn from.

Both settled down after their fits of laughter, letting the reality of the moment sink in. It was the first time they had really had any kind of discussion since their father passed away, and it felt both good and awkward at the same time.

"So," Mike said, breaking the ice first, "does this transfer to the investigative division mean you'll have a more normal schedule?"

"If it goes through, I'll probably be on the afternoon shift. They only have morning and afternoon shifts for the detectives."

"Good. Maybe I'll finally be able to call you without worrying about waking you up all the time."

Greg grinned, knowing how everyone could never keep up with his strange slumbering hours. He felt like a vampire, working the midnight shift on patrol, but it couldn't be helped.

Mike was about to say something else when the tones sounded for a business alarm in the center of town.

"Don't go anywhere," Mike told his brother, holding up a foreboding finger. "We should be right back."

Greg watched them all suit up and jump on the truck, ready for action.

"Like I haven't heard that before," he said to himself, thinking of all the times his father had said that, only to be gone for hours at a time because a simple alarm turned out to be an inferno in the middle of town.

Firefighters were a breed he could not, and would not ever understand, which was why he wasn't among their ranks. He hoped somewhere above, his father was proud of him, regardless.

Greg kicked a wadded paper towel across the floor and seated himself on the front of his car, taking in the view of the old station. Its nostalgia had never quite worked on him, and somehow he figured it never would.

Taking in the view of the kids playing across the street, he smirked and wondered exactly when his childhood had ended.

Perhaps, in a few ways, it hadn't.

CHAPTER 6

A week later, Wade was still waiting for his first real fire and it wasn't very forthcoming.

He had performed most of his rookie firefighter duties flawlessly, though little skill was required to clean toilets, scrub sinks, cook an occasional meal, and clean tools repeatedly from the pumper truck.

"You might go your whole first year and see nothing," one of the firefighters commented as Wade helped peel potatoes in the early morning hours for a lunch stew.

"That's not so bad," Wade said.

"What? You scared of fire or something?"

Wade made a sour face at the notion. The last thing he needed was any kind of rumor started that he was fearful of fire. Rumors spread fast, and reputations were sometimes built from them. And they weren't always accurate.

"Nah," Wade said easily, trying not to show his anger at the comment.

Showing emotion was another sign of weakness to the guys. Certain unwritten rules had to be obeyed by firefighters, and Wade had been lucky enough to be privy to them before joining the department. He knew when certain firefighters let jokes get to them, the other guys only teased them more. There were any number of guys on the department who could tease their colleagues, but didn't take retaliatory jokes very well.

Though he was closest in age to the twins, Wade was closer to Patrick than any other uncle. The battalion chief had a reputation as being gruff with his firefighters, but he softened up a little bit toward Wade. He tried not to make it too obvious, fearing Wade would catch hell from the other guys.

"I just don't like the fact that I have to get experience at someone else's expense," Wade said. "Every time there's a fire, someone's losing their house."

"Yeah, but it's fun as hell to get in there," another firefighter added.

Wade wasn't certain if the guys were as macho as they appeared, or if it was just an act to test him. He knew he would feel relieved after besting his first big fire, but the wait was painstaking.

"You guys better watch what you wish for," Patrick warned, stepping into the kitchen.

When he wasn't busy in his office filling out reports, making out a roster for the coming week, or reporting to the front office, he spent his time watching history shows on the television or reading books.

Usually, he kept his distance from his firefighters, never wanting to be too chummy with them. He had a fear of breaking the chain of command by doing so, and never wanted to lose an ounce of their respect by fraternizing with the guys.

In some ways, they considered him too old-school, but they certainly had respect for him because he never wavered, and never showed favoritism like some officers did.

Working with his uncles left Wade feeling a bit uncomfortable because he never knew how to take comments from the other guys. Were they picking on him more than most rookies because he had family there? Or was the teasing a usual amount of hazing?

Either way, Wade chose to play it cool and take every comment, joke, and prank with a grain of salt.

Already, the crew had made two fire runs that morning, but they were typical false alarms. Wade had to fight complacency after so many runs of nothing but brush fires, trash fires, and faulty security alarms.

"You believe that shit about not having anything for the longest time, then getting the big one?" Wade asked his uncle as they left the kitchen, once the beef stew was on the stove.

"Ah, it comes and goes," Patrick said with an airy wave of his hand. "You might go months without any real fires, then get two or three in one week."

"Just like that?"

"Yeah. Sometimes it's a weather-related thing, and sometimes we get an arsonist in the area, but it's kind of like a sport. Real streaky."

"How long has this drought been going on?" Wade inquired.

"Since just before you came aboard."

"Great," Wade said sarcastically.

The city had seen its share of big fires before. There were factories burned to the ground in years past, a few churches destroyed, and even a city block had burned in the middle of winter when nearby houses passed the fire to one another like torches on the beach.

Patrick had been there to witness the water freezing as soon as it made contact with anything but fire. Icicles hung from houses, fire trucks, and hose lines. When it was all said and done, the buildings looked like igloos, completely blanketed in ice.

With advents in fire codes and fire safety, Wade hoped to never see the likes of such fires during his career. Those were adventures that lasted all night, with lots of cleanup, after lots of hard work.

From the few small attic fires Wade had seen, he knew putting the fire out was just the beginning. Firefighters had to search for hot spots behind walls, which involved pulling out paneling or ceilings. Once that was finished, they had to overhaul, which meant sometimes clearing out rooms and determining if all of the fire was out. Finally, they had to bring equipment out to the truck, clean it, and pick up vast amounts of hose, once all of that was done. After that, they cleaned personal gear like their air masks at the station.

Most of their time was spent doing menial tasks around the station, but when they worked, they really earned their salaries.

"Like I said up there," Patrick warned, "be careful what you wish for. You might just get a lot more than you're hoping for. I've seen guys kid around about getting a big one, and sure enough, we get one that night worse than we could possibly imagine."

"I'm not hoping for anything," Wade confessed. "I just take it as it comes."

"Don't worry. You don't have to stay up nights waiting for that first big alarm. It's going to come. Maybe not today, maybe not this month, but it'll come."

Leaving to speak with one of the inspectors, Patrick gave Wade a pat on the back before Wade approached the front of the open truck bay.

Greg Stephens, one of the other firefighters stationed with Wade, stood beside the probationary firefighter at one of the front garage doors, which was open to let the late morning sun stream inside.

A bit more bold and opinionated than most of the firefighters, and a second-generation fireman himself, Stephens was still young, but seemed to think he could do no wrong.

He chose his friends and enemies carefully, but there seemed little distinction between the two when he spoke of any one person, save a few. Very few people measured up to his voiced standards, though Wade had seen him do little more than jump on the recliner in the television room for action.

"What do you think of this first responder stuff?" Stephens asked, raising Wade's suspicion of him digging for information.

The man was notorious for taking whatever a person told him, and turning it against that same person in a conversation behind his back later. Wade made it a point to answer as impartially as possible.

Wade had no ambitions to be in any certain cliques, and Stephens was one of those people who needed acceptance on a daily basis to survive.

"It should be a good step forward," Wade finally said of the first responder question. "If it keeps us in business, all the better."

"We've been needing this for a long time," Stephens said, making his opinion known.

"I suppose," Wade said, being too new to truly know.

"If we hadn't voted it through, Washington Township would have jumped on it and made us look even worse. They've been trying to push their way into our turf since they got started."

Wade felt uncomfortable around Stephens, as though the only thing the man wanted from him was information to use against him. It was Stephens who picked on him the most about not proving his worth, because he hadn't seen a "real fire" yet.

Still, Wade could not simply push away from anyone in the main group, or he risked alienating himself completely. In a line of work where one's safety, and life, was in the hands of others, he didn't need enemies.

"Didn't you used to be a volunteer?" Wade asked of Stephens, since the man incessantly berated the new local volunteer department.

"Yeah, but I wasn't a scab trying to move in on someone's job. These guys are mostly rejects from real volunteer departments, trying to make a name for themselves. They aren't properly trained, and they're scared to death of actually getting inside a burning building."

Wade wanted a reprieve from this conversation, and ironically, it came in the form of a Washington Township pumper truck, coming down the street in their direction.

"I'll be damned," Stephens said just above a whisper.

As it passed, the men inside the truck waved, finding indifferent stares from Stephens and Wade as they passed. Often, in transit to the store or training, the firefighters from the city department would flip anyone from Washington Township the middle finger instead, but with traffic, or the chief's office around, they simply chose to passively stare.

"Mother fuckers," Stephens commented to himself, walking away from the door, most likely to tell the other guys how he had heroically faced down the enemy department.

Wade smirked to himself, hearing the familiar sound of a Harley-Davidson pull into the parking lot beside the station.

Since he knew most of the guys on the department who owned motorcycles, and his father had ridden a Harley as long as he could remember, the rookie firefighter decided to see who was out riding on a such a beautiful morning.

As he rounded the corner, he looked the man on the bike over from head to toe, noticing the jet-black hair like his Uncle Patrick's, the tattered blue jeans, the white T-shirt drenched with sweat, covered by a black leather vest, and the treaded black boots.

With a full head of hair, and a full beard to match, the man was the epitome of a Harley rider. And though he had never joined the ranks of the fire department like his brothers, no one would ever question John Sheridan, Jr. about his courage, since the man climbed beyond the tops of skyscrapers for a living.

"Hi, Dad," Wade said as his father put the kick stand down with his booted foot.

"What's new?" Jay Sheridan asked his son in a throaty, deep voice.

He had been labeled 'Jay' since he was a toddler, and everyone in the family called him by that name, so as not to confuse him with his late father.

Since his late teenage years, Jay had worn a ponytail that reached halfway down his back. Finally respecting his father's wishes, Jay cut the trademark of his independence immediately after his father died, for the funeral. The move shocked his family, but he decided to honor his father the only way he knew how.

Since that time, his hair had remained perfectly trimmed and short. Jay would not go back on his silent word to his father.

"Nothing new here," Wade reported, kicking a pebble across the parking lot. "I thought you were in Chicago or something, hanging antennas this week."

"We got done early, so I came home for a few days."

Shortly after Wade was born, Jay started the commercial antenna business with a partner, eventually bought the man out of his shares, and the rest was history. He would supervise the construction of the mammoth antennas when he was home, then take trips to install them for his buyers.

In the past five years, Jay had seen every major city from Seattle to New York, Tampa to Los Angeles. By no means did he have to do so much work himself, but he loved traveling, meeting new women, and talking to fellow motorcycle fanatics.

"Your Uncle Pat treating you okay?"

"Oh, yeah. It's been pretty quiet around here."

Jay sat sideways on his bike, looking toward the station. Being the first child gave him the choice of doing whatever career he wanted without fear of reprimand. When he chose to follow his heart and join his friends in the factory right after high school, John Sheridan never said a word.

Perhaps the old man didn't really mind, but Jay had to do things his own way, and following in his father's footsteps wasn't for him, especially since he knew Patrick and Kevin were almost certain to.

"You free next weekend?" he asked Wade.

"More than likely."

"A bunch of us are taking our bikes down to Nashville for a rally if you want to tag along."

Wade knew most of his father's friends, and most of them were conservative in nature. They worked a regular week and went riding on the weekends for fun. Nice people, but most were considerably older than the rookie firefighter.

After all, Wade had friends his own age to run around with.

"I'll let you know," Wade answered. "You going to be in town all this week?"

Jay grinned, certain his son knew better than to ask such a question.

"Well, I'm making a run to Louisville tomorrow, but I should be around after that."

Wade felt certain his father had been in a mid-life crisis for several years, and now that he was only a few years from the half century mark in age, it seemed even more apparent.

"So, how's your mother?" he asked, as he did every so often.

"Doing well. She took a trip to Disney World with Allisa and the kids," Wade said of his older sister.

"I heard you guys passed a new contract," Jay noted.

"Yeah. First attempt, no less."

"Does any of that first responder stuff make you nervous?"

"Nah. It's a glorified first-aid class. We'll be running with the city's EMS providers anyway. We'll be more manpower than anything else."

Jay pulled his sweaty T-shirt away from his chest a second, realizing just how soaked he was from the sun's morning rays.

"Your bike holding up?" he asked his son.

"It runs, if that's what you mean. I haven't had much time to take it out, but I'm going to ride it here one day to give it a full inspection."

Wade was no mechanic, but he knew the basics of his own bike, and what usually went wrong with older models like his.

In the meantime, Mason Gray pulled into the lot with his fully-equipped van, parked, and headed for the front office.

"Any word on what caused that explosion the other night?" Wade casually asked the investigator as he walked past.

"Leak in the water heater's gas line," Gray answered. "We think a nightlight may have sparked and set off the gas, but it was a model that was recalled about a year ago, so we're not sure if it's intentional or not."

Wade nodded.

"Hell of a way to lose a building."

"Yeah, it is," Gray agreed, stepping inside after giving Jay a brief nod and a wave.

"I see he's still a friendly chap," Jay noted.

"That was more than you'll usually get from him," Wade said. "Most times he walks on by and doesn't say a word."

Wade was about to excuse himself to check on lunch across the truck bay floor when he heard the tones sound from inside the building for a fire run.

"I'll call," he simply told his father before dashing inside to get dressed for whatever call needed their attention.

Jay smirked to himself. He understood, and he'd been watching firemen come and go from the station since he was old enough to walk.

He just hoped his son knew what he was doing.

CHAPTER 7

On their next workday, Mike and Kevin sat across from one another at the kitchen table, trying to avoid the muggy air outside as the heat and humidity mercilessly hammered the state of Illinois, with no relief in sight.

Their morning had consisted of a few menial calls, but with the afternoon heat, they barely had the ambition to cross the truck room floor.

Sam Conley had been in the truck bay all day, watching television, and casually smoking cigarettes between runs, seated on a ragged recliner.

"How can he stand being out there like that?" Mike asked.

"He's a skinny fuck," Kevin answered. "By nature, he probably can't sweat, or he'll lose half of his body weight."

Mike chuckled.

Already, the group had gone uptown to get supplies, bought groceries, and ate lunch. By all accounts, they hoped their day was done.

Kevin flipped through television channels until he found a show with women cavorting around a beach with little more than two-piece bikinis. Anything with breasts seemed to distract the lieutenant, and Mike sometimes wondered what would happen on a fire scene if a half-naked woman passed in front of Kevin.

"Wade said they ruled the cause of that explosion undetermined," Mike said, trying to make conversation, and break Kevin away from mentally undressing the unsuspecting ladies on the screen.

"Maybe it was," Kevin replied, looking away from the screen just a split-second. "I've heard of malfunctioning water heaters, and that's what Gray said he thought it was at the scene."

"Yeah, but that's different. Usually, they explode from within because of steam buildup. You saw how charred that building was on the lower levels."

Kevin shot him a strange look.

"You after Gray's job or something?"

"No. I'm just saying."

Mike was about to defend himself further when a knock came to the kitchen door, and the two firefighters spied Sandi standing outside, peeking in at Mike.

"I wonder what she's doing here?" Mike asked himself.

"It'll only get worse once you're married," Kevin warned as Mike rose from his seat to see his fiancee.

He stepped into the truck bay to speak with her, and the muggy heat hit him like some of the fires he sometimes found himself in the middle of.

"Why aren't you at work?" he asked, obviously glad to see her, but somewhat concerned.

"I was out running a few errands for my boss, and decided to stop in."

"Everything okay?"

"Well, I woke up after you left this morning, feeling a little strange."

Mike gave her a quizzical look.

"You sick?"

"No, but I felt this way yesterday, too. I thought about going to the doctor's office, and then I decided not to, because maybe it would pass."

"You sure you're okay?" Mike asked as they walked to one of the garage doors on the rear side, that overlooked part of a city park to their left, and a flowing river straight back.

"Everything's fine," she said, as though she had now discovered something.

"What are you trying to say?" Mike asked, drawing an easy smile, wondering what had made his fiancee stop by, despite her usual strictly business attitude.

Before he could receive an answer, Mike saw several kids down the hill, beside the river, frantically looking in the water for something.

Or someone.

At first, the fireman thought perhaps they had lost something in the water, or maybe they were after a turtle. He hesitated, staring a moment, as Sandi looked to the same spot.

When they turned and saw Mike standing there, the kids urgently motioned for him to come down.

"Shit," he said, knowing Sandi was seeing all of this unfold as well.

He turned to Conley, who was oblivious to the scene, sitting in his easy chair across the garage.

"Sam!" Mike called. "Get Kevin and come down to the river!"

That said, Mike took off in a dead sprint toward the river, hoping his worst fear wasn't about to come true.

Rains from west of the state had bypassed Illinois, but they managed to fill the river on their way through neighboring states. Now the water flowed at a rapid pace, and higher than usual.

As Mike dashed toward the river, he thought of how many close calls he had as a kid, playing at the river with Greg. He respected the water, even as an accomplished swimmer, and felt reluctant about having to dive in there alone if it came to that.

He reached the kids, finding four of them about middle school age, standing there, looking into the water.

"It's Tommy," one said quickly. "He's been under there a long time."

Goddamn it, Mike thought, trying to remember what he was supposed to do, or how he was supposed to do it. Technically he was supposed to do nothing by himself, especially without some sort of rope or lifeline.

Instinct took over, and he would risk his own life, but he needed to know where to look.

"Where did he go in?" he asked.

"Over there," one of the kids said, pointing upstream.

"And where did you last see him?"

"There," another kid said of where Tommy had last bobbed to the surface.

Mike judged the current, figuring he was already well behind the teenager, but he had to get in the water, or Tommy would certainly be a goner.

Without another word, Mike stepped back, took off his duty shoes, and performed a flawless running dive into the water, immediately finding himself grabbed by the current.

Sandi watched to this point, then decided she needed to return to work. The station's other three firefighters sprinted down the hill toward Mike, but the excitement of their job didn't rub off on Sandi like it did so many others. She would have to wait until the time was right to tell Mike he would be a father, sooner than expected.

"I'm pregnant," she said the words to herself that she was about to tell him, as she turned to leave.

She needed to return to work, and she had come to learn that Mike always made it home from work. He always did. Somehow she just knew he would be safe, as though Mike was guided by the Lord's hands. Maybe that special something about him could help her put the past behind her, like her older brother and her uncle, along with the misfortunes they suffered.

Leaving the past behind was easy until Mike tried to suggest his job was dangerous.

Perhaps Mike was divinely protected in some way, Sandi figured. He was too good of a soul not to be, even though he never noticed his unseen protection.

In the meantime, Kevin cursed his brother's name as he reached the edge of the river with Sam Conley and Darrell Thomas, wishing Mike wasn't so excitable sometimes. He had already called for EMS, the fire department's rescue team, and several police divers.

"We need to get downstream," Kevin noted aloud, knowing the river would get worse before it flowed to the calmer reservoir. "Darrell, get the truck and meet us where the river drops off about half a mile upstream. Hopefully we can pull him out of there."

In the meantime, Mike had flowed with the current, occasionally taking a peek under the water, barely able to see more than a few feet in front of him, despite the water being fairly clear.

Bubbles and small floating objects impeded his vision from the current's flow, but he felt reasonably certain he would see the boy if he neared Tommy's body.

Realistically, he had only a few more minutes to find the boy, or resuscitation efforts would be worthless.

Though the water was deeper than usual, the river was never very deep in this particular area to begin with. Several jagged rocks, and discarded trash along the bottom of the river, had already cut into Mike's pants, and his legs. He felt several gashes bleeding, but he would worry about those later.

During one underwater peek, Mike barely saved his head from being pummeled by a large rock along the bottom by deflecting his body away from it with his hands. Accidentally taking in some water through his nose, he bobbed to the surface sputtering and coughing, which delayed more searches beneath the surface.

Once he recovered enough, he plunged himself under the surface again, trying to find the boy, but the current skimmed him along the bottom like a skipping stone. He bounced once, managed to get a good look ahead of him, and fought to surface for air, unaware that he had traveled to a deeper part of the river momentarily.

His head poked through the surface, and Mike immediately filled his lungs with air, seeing the reservoir come into view.

A moment later, Mike found himself dumped over a two-foot embankment, into calmer waters. He wasted little time in diving beneath the surface, looking for the lost child, but he could see little in the murky water.

The crash of the water over the embankment stirred up dirt and water plants for half a mile downstream. Mike had no chance of finding the boy short of bumping into him, and as he searched, he began to give up hope of bringing Tommy back to the living, even if he found him.

Like it had been with his father, things became a strange slow-motion blur soon thereafter.

He saw the dive team comprised of police and fire personnel show up and begin diving, then drag the water with a large net, once all hope was gone. Police dogs walked along the banks in hope of picking up any human scent from the water. Ahead, he saw city officials dam the river, to ensure that if the body was still in this reservoir, it would remain there until found, because another small stream continued on the other end of the large pond.

Tommy's parents showed up, only to break down once they learned that the last time they would see their son was as a bloated, drowned body, if he was recovered at all.

Mike found himself sitting on the bank as the latter events unfolded, watching the aftermath of his dive unfold as the sun began to set behind him. He was forbidden to help in the effort, but refused to go anywhere until the situation saw a conclusion of some sort.

His legs ached from the scratches and bloody slits left from the jagged rocks, but he didn't care. The water had cleaned them, and he could bandage them later, when he changed clothes.

"How are you feeling?" Kevin asked, sitting beside him on the grassy bank.

"Helpless. Like I'm useless, because I can't save a little boy."

"You did everything you could, Mike," the lieutenant assured him. "Not all of these stories have happy endings."

"I don't know, Kev. I just wish there was something else I could have done."

"You knew when you jumped in that water you were wishing on a hope and a prayer, trying to catch up with him."

Mike stared at the dusk sky a moment, wishing he had the answers for things he could never understand. Why his God would take some children at such an early age and spare so many others was beyond his comprehension.

Why does it have to be the kid I'm trying to save? he wondered.

"He shouldn't have been that far ahead of me," Mike commented.

"You don't know that. Those kids didn't know that. That river was flying, Mike. There's no way you were going to catch him unless he snagged on something, and even at that, he was probably too far gone to save."

"I know, but I just feel like I failed."

Mike looked over to the parents, who were being consoled by various police officers and medical personnel on the scene. They had arrived in a hysterical state, and now the realization of their son's death was setting in.

"That could've been one of your kids today, Kev. What if I couldn't save one of them?"

Kevin nervously licked his upper lip. He began to wonder if his little brother was fit to return to duty for the rest of their shift.

"Mike, it wasn't one of my kids, and you did everything you could. No one is going to blame you, or say otherwise."

He let himself stretch out in the cool grass, looking directly at his younger brother.

"You know, life isn't always fair, and things happen for a reason. Maybe this will somehow help, by keeping other kids away from the river, or maybe they'll put more protection around the sides of it. Shit, I don't know it all, but you can't go on letting this eat you up inside, or you might fuck up the next call we go on."

Kevin made sure his brother looked at him before he continued.

"I need you with me, Mike. You gonna be okay?"

Mike nodded slowly, swallowing back the pain of defeat.

He was aggressive on the job, which usually meant getting the results he wanted. Usually, saving lives was easier than it had been today.

"I know you don't want to hear this, but I'm proud of you," Kevin told his younger brother. "There isn't anyone on this department I'd rather have working with me. And that goes beyond us being kin. There aren't that many guys on here who think as selflessly as you did today, risking your life for that kid."

"Thanks," Mike said with little enthusiasm.

"Anytime."

Kevin looked at the scene across the river bank. The divers had yet to pull the teenager's body from the water, and he certainly didn't want Mike around when they did. With the heat and humidity, it would not be a pleasant sight, and the boy's parents would likely break down even worse than before.

"We've got to get back on station," he told Mike, knowing they really didn't *have* to.

With growing coverage from the television and print media, he decided it best to get Mike out of there. His brother was in no condition to be speaking publically, and there was a good possibility he would say something regrettable for the department and himself, even though Patrick had already made efforts to keep the media from talking to any of his men.

Any number of people had shook Mike's hand, or patted him on the back for his efforts, but none of that seemed to matter to him. Deep down, only one thing mattered.

He wanted that boy alive.

As they walked back to the truck, which Thomas had brought down hours before, just in case they had a call, none of them looked back. The four men had seen enough trauma in one day to last them the rest of the year, even if they hadn't seen a dead body.

Little could they know their tumultuous summer was just beginning.

CHAPTER 8

By the next week, Wade found himself in the middle of a dull workweek, still waiting for his first big fire, when he found himself having to pick sides in a practical joke war at the station.

Basically, his choice came down to who would be the nicest to him when it came time for revenge. Some of the guys were intellectual jokers, who might set up a phony lawsuit, or create fake divorce papers, and go so far as to bring in a fake attorney.

Others would just fill shoes with shaving cream, or leave a stack of empty pop cans in front of someone's bunk, so that the unsuspecting firefighter would knock them over in the middle of the night, trying to find his way to his bunk in the sheer darkness of the bedroom.

As battalion chief, Patrick stayed out of the practical joke battles. The men never targeted him, and so long as they never did, he would let them do as they pleased in their jokes.

Today, a bunch of toys for the local Toys for Tots program had been donated, which included a mammoth assortment of water guns. Since any type of plastic gun, knife, or sword, was prohibited from distribution around the holiday season, the firefighters found a new use for the water guns, filling them up, and chasing one another around the station house.

Wade found himself beside Bobby Pratt, another young firefighter, ducked behind several storage boxes on one end of the truck bay, as three of the other guys stalked them, not knowing where the two rookies were.

"Well, we either shoot them in the back and run, or we sit here and get pasted," Pratt said their options aloud.

"They just walked into my uncle's office looking for us," Wade noted. "I don't know about you, but I ain't getting *him* wet."

Pratt nodded.

"Then we wait until they come out."

They sat motionless a moment, simply staring at the door, hearing conversation from within, realizing they would probably be waiting a little while.

"How did Mike take that boy's drowning?" Pratt asked to pass the time.

"Not too well, I guess. At least he wasn't there when they pulled the boy from the water the next day. I guess that kid was a bloated mess."

"They found him past that dam they made, didn't they?"

"Yeah," Wade answered. "He was quite a ways down from where Mike ended up. There was no way he could've found that kid in time."

"We'll be seeing a lot more of that shit once we start doing first responder runs," Pratt noted.

"It won't be so bad. A few more runs a day to help EMS out."

"You'll think that until you go on your first vehicle crushed by a train, picking up gray matter and ligaments half a mile down the tracks."

By gray matter, Pratt meant pieces of someone's brain.

"I forgot you were an EMT, Bobby."

"Yeah, and I thought I'd gotten away from it."

Wade grunted silently to himself, then listened for activity in his uncle's office.

A few minutes passed before the group finished whatever discussion they were having with the battalion chief, leading Wade to believe they were giving up the hunt, or they were trying to lure Pratt and himself into some sort of water pistol trap.

When the three men emerged from the battalion chief's office, Pratt and Wade waited for them to step through the open door, then opened fire.

All three men ducked, and as luck would have it, Patrick had started to walk out behind them to file some paperwork with the chief's office. Most of his badge shirt was soaked with water, and he simply looked slowly down at his drenched chest, then to his nephew.

"We need to have a talk about horseplay, son," he said to no one but Wade after a moment, despite Pratt's involvement.

"Sorry," Wade said with as much voice as he could muster, noticing none of the other three firefighters still had their water guns.

He had been set up from the beginning.

"It can wait until later," Patrick said, knowing his retaliation would be a thin layer of baby powder in his nephew's bed, right after supper was finished that evening.

The group waited until the battalion chief had walked into the chief's office before breaking out in laughter.

"Fuck you guys!" Wade said. "That ain't cool, making me get the battalion chief wet."

"We didn't make you do anything," one of them commented.

Pratt cracked a grin.

"I suppose you were in on this, too," Wade accused him.

"No way," Pratt said, maintaining his innocence. "And I didn't hit the chief either if he asks me."

Turncoats, Wade thought. He didn't much like being the brunt of their joke, but at least he was breaking the ice with the guys by getting into trouble with his uncle. The less they thought of him as the battalion chief's nephew, the better.

Perhaps, in a roundabout way, things were looking up.

Across town at the alderman's office, Benjamin Malovich read a newspaper article concerning the city fire department's new policy on first responder runs. He realized the city had beat his new volunteer department to the punch on this policy, which would make him look bad if the media brought the issue to public attention.

Malovich had other issues to worry about, in keeping his high tax dollar district happy with his progress. Much of his area was in danger of being annexed by the city, which meant less people loyal to him, because they would be forced into the city's terrible septic systems, trash collection policy, and a considerable tax hike.

The more land the industrial areas lost to the city, the less area his fire department had to cover, and the less need there might be for the department.

Or himself.

Though nearly forty, Malovich looked the part of a young, confident politician, though he never ran for any office until he was several years into a career as a bank chairman. Now, he found himself in the middle of a multi-year plan for his campaign ladder, and he liked it.

His hair was perfectly combed, his suit perfectly pressed, and he walked with confidence, no matter what his mood was. He was up for reelection the following year, and he would be damned if the public saw him miss one step, or appear worried in the least.

He peered through his window just as the volunteer fire chief's Ford Bronco pulled into its designated spot.

Though Tom Ellis was never his first choice for chief, the man was the only one willing to commit against the city department, and its union. Ellis had several beefs with a few of the department's members, and Malovich spent countless hours coaching Ellis on how to refrain from saying anything stupid in public.

Ellis had left an agricultural business with his father and grandfather, making good money no less, to become chief further upstate. Finally, his chance to come home and stir up trouble in the community that had once scorned him three times during his testing to become a professional firefighter, brought him back.

"Good morning, Ben," Ellis said as he walked casually into the office, wearing EMT tech pants, with pockets from his waistline to his ankles.

He wore a golf shirt with his department's emblem, and his name and title stitched on the other side. Until his appointment as chief, Ellis had always worn a bushy beard, but shaved it clean for the National Fire Protection Agency mandate about facial hair, and how it broke the seal in the air masks, and never looked back.

It was ruled unsafe to have any facial hair that broke the mask's seal, and even though he would probably never have to wear a mask unless he chose to, Ellis complied to set an example.

"What's on your plate today, Chief?" Malovich asked, giving Ellis his usual compliment by using the man's title.

"Oh, not a whole lot. I was wanting to take the Quint up for some repairs, but the guys at the shop said I had to clear it with you first."

Ellis was referring to the shorter of his two aerial ladder trucks, which had been nothing but a pain in the ass since the day his department bought it at a nearby city auction, despite its sharp looks and the pretense under which it was purchased. Apparently the auctioneers had a different definition of what 'barely used' meant than the chief.

"Something about a funding issue," Ellis noted, revealing the nature of his visit.

"Well, our funds are running a little dry," Malovich said in a straightforward manner. "It took most of this year's budget to keep the trucks up and running to this point, and the rest of the money is already designated into the accounts you and I discussed at the first of the year."

Ellis smirked, settling uneasily into a chair across from Malovich's desk.

"So you're telling me I can't get any funding to get my shit fixed the rest of the year?"

"You're a volunteer department," Malovich pointed out. "Volunteer departments usually solicit funds, Tom."

Ellis let his smirk turn upside down.

"We're already raising money for our first responder program, and I'm catching all kinds of hell from the city about where I can and can't have the boys collect."

"What exactly is wrong with the truck?" Malovich inquired, already forgetting the name of the truck in question.

"It's the aerial ladder itself," the chief replied. "When you raise it over fifty feet, she buckles back a couple of inches. In other words, it slips."

"How big a deal is that? Just don't raise it that high, Tom."

"We're talking about a safety issue for Christ's sake, Ben."

"You've got another ladder. Just don't use that truck for anything but manpower until we can find a way to get it fixed."

Ellis sighed to himself, unhappy with the way things were turning out.

At first, taking over a brand new department was fantastic on his end, but he was beginning to see where the paved road ended, and the hard gravel trail began on the time line of his career as chief.

"Look, Tom, right now we have the newspaper in our back pocket. I know it's not easy, but if we play our cards right, I'll get the opportunity to run for mayor in two years, and I'll need a chief to run that professional department."

"We've had this talk," Ellis stated. "You know I'm behind you all the way, but I'm trying to keep us from getting sued before we have our chance to run this city."

"And I appreciate that," Malovich said. "I'm asking you to make a minor concession until things come our way."

The chief's eyes showed a reluctant acceptance.

"Understood."

Though his loyalties stayed with whoever paid his salary, Ellis had a few doubts about Malovich's intents.

First, it was the lack of funds to train new firefighters, then a lack of funds to send his veterans to state schools, just for a weekend. Now their equipment budget appeared to be shot, and he was worried about the safety of his firefighters volunteering their time to a community most of them didn't even live in.

If not for the notion that the mayor might step down, allowing for Malovich to run in the next major election, Ellis might have begun looking for employment with a different fire department.

There was no way he would do anything else for a career now. He had turned his back on his family's business years ago, then forsook marriage and any sort of normal life to pursue his dream as a firefighter, then as a chief. Ellis had never reached the lofty goals he originally set for himself, but he could still see gold at the end of the rainbow if he tolerated Malovich a bit longer.

Now entering middle-age, he had little to show for his life *except* being chief of two departments. He had little choice but to stick by Malovich, in the hope things worked to his advantage. If they didn't, and Malovich was voted out of office this year, there was a good chance his department would be disbanded, and his job liquidated, if the outlying areas of the township went back to the city's fire protection.

Ellis had never really worked his way up through the ranks like most volunteer and professional firefighters had to. He spent only a year fighting fire as a back-end man, then jumped to the rank of lieutenant on his first department.

City firefighters had no respect for him, because they knew his background, though he would never have his men believe he was anything less than a brilliant strategist when it came to doing any aspect of his job.

In some respects, perhaps he was a fraud, but Ellis was never called upon to prove himself. He could talk a good game, and train his men to the best of his ability, but even he lacked the luxury of extensive training beyond the basic requirements for any new firefighter.

He did what he could, but limited funding on his previous departments, and now Malovich's stingy nature, forced the chief to work with what he had, and like it.

Or else.

"Is there anything else I can do for you, Tom?" Malovich asked from behind his desk, hands on his lap, fingers neatly pressed together, as though he was a mafia godfather figure.

"No," Ellis said, standing to leave. "I've got to make sure my stations are staffed for the week."

He started toward the door, but the alderman's voice halted him as he opened it.

"What we discussed stays between us, Tom," Malovich said evenly. "We have everything going our way right now, so we can't go spending money left and right. Be patient, Chief, and everything will work out."

"Okay," Ellis said quietly with a nod before heading out.

He certainly hoped things worked out, or his whole life's work would be swirling down the drain.

CHAPTER 9

As he had promised his father, Mike attempted to keep the family together. During the first weekend in June, he threw a cookout at the farmhouse for his family, and a few close friends from the fire department.

By this time, he knew Sandi was carrying his child, and the couple doubled their efforts to find a wedding date, which was part of the reason for having the entire family over.

Whenever the Sheridan family had a reunion of any sort, it usually meant there was an announcement to be made, and that was understood.

Everyone attended, figuring the couple would simply be announcing their wedding date, since the formal engagement was somewhat bypassed with John Sheridan's passing.

Being a Saturday night, Greg was off-duty from his new position. Since all of the firefighters in the family worked the same shift, it was easy to get them together.

Even Jay managed to attend, only a day removed from a trip to Pennsylvania to repair a broken antenna atop a thirty-two story building. He was dressed in his usual garb, except he had ditched the leather vest for the remainder of the summer, since the heat was sweltering on a daily basis.

"Yeah, you just strap yourself in, and hope the line doesn't break," he told Kevin's wife, Julia, about his job. "It gets weird up there sometimes if you've got fog and patchy clouds floating by. The wind gets awful turbulent, too."

"I'll bet," Julia commented. "Ever had any close calls?"

"Once my safety line snapped, but I already had my foot wrapped in the antenna's permanent ladder. I fell back, heard my ankle break, and realized I was up there alone, with no chance of anyone finding me."

"Must have been scary."

"A little, but I got it together, and hobbled my way down. If I'd fallen, I probably would have done a few bounces off the building before plummeting to the sidewalk," Jay commented as though it might be a daily occurrence.

Julia grimaced at the thought.

"He tells that bullshit to everyone," Kevin said to Julia, walking by. "We think he just takes the elevator up and makes his workers do all the work."

"Hey, little brother," Jay replied, "I've got videotape proof, now. The news did a segment on me a few weeks back."

"I must have missed that," Kevin kidded, knowing the entire family had taped it.

Across the extensive back patio Mike had just finished building, he and Greg stood by the grill, watching the hamburgers and hot-dogs carefully as they chatted.

"So, how's life in the detective division?" Mike asked him.

"Shitty. They have me working every piece of shit leftover case they can think of," Greg said with a frustrated wave of his arms. "All in the name of gaining experience."

"Maybe our worlds aren't that different."

Greg took a swig from the bottle of beer he'd been holding.

"That, and the sergeant doesn't like me because I arrested his nephew a few years ago."

"Ah, politics," Mike said as though he was above all of that.

"You should talk, the way you attend every union and contract meeting possible."

"Yeah, and your police contract committee jumps right on our coattails every three years when we negotiate contracts, don't they?"

Greg said nothing, opting to tip the beer bottle to his lips once more.

Everyone else had brought their wives, or in Wade's case, a date, to the cookout. Greg came stag, figuring no one cared. He certainly didn't care, and even his initial excitement about the move to investigations had diminished quickly. The cop didn't mind living the life of a bachelor in a state of depression, but he felt himself slipping further and further into the void he called life every day.

Figuring the reunion would help him feel better, he attended, but in reality he felt worse. Maybe being alone was his best option. He wouldn't be a burden to his family, and Kevin wouldn't have to make an effort to avoid him.

"He still hasn't gotten past blaming me, has he?" Greg asked his twin.

Mike stared at Kevin, like his twin had been.

"You're reading too much into it, Greg."

"Am I? He hasn't said two words to me in months, and he makes it a point to avoid me whenever we cross paths."

"I don't know what to say to you anymore, brother," Mike said.

"Maybe there isn't anything to say," Greg replied, setting the beer bottle on the table behind him. "Maybe there isn't room for me in this family anymore."

Greg walked away, and Mike sensed the alcohol had been talking for him. After five drinks in that short a time, he probably would have been feeling a bit loopy too.

Kevin took notice of their conversation, then walked over once he saw Greg go talk with Casey, their youngest sister.

"What's wrong with him?" Kevin inquired as his brother flipped burgers on the grill.

"You," Mike answered without looking up from his work.

Kevin looked stunned when Mike finally looked up a moment later, the smell of grilled meat lingering under his nose.

"What's that supposed to mean?"

Mike shook his head.

"You know, when Greg first told me you were dodging him, I just kind of shrugged it off and thought he was overreacting."

"And now you think I'm being a complete bastard for real?"

"I wasn't going to say that," Mike chimed in quickly.

"But you were going to imply that I haven't been giving your brother much attention," Kevin said in such a way that implied Greg wasn't his own brother.

Mike drew a strange grin.

"Well, you waited until he left before walking over here."

"What do you want me to say? That I forgive him for being an inadequate fireman and leaving Dad by himself in that house?"

"He didn't leave Dad-"

"He certainly didn't help," Kevin said, noticing Mike looking out from the patio toward the rest of the family, who were beginning to take notice of their animated conversation.

Mike took a deep breath, realizing it was past time for him to take a stand for Greg's sake. His twin was losing a sense of purpose, and Kevin was not helping the least little bit.

"You weren't there, Kev," Mike stated. "Even I don't know exactly what happened up there, but I know he tried his damnedest to help Dad."

"Okay," Kevin said, conceding a little. "I'll try and lighten up a bit."

The last thing he wanted was to ruin the family gathering, especially since it was Mike who had the good news to share. He gave a quick look to Greg, who had stopped conversing with Casey to hear what was being said.

"Maybe it's time I go," he said to her, beginning to wonder why he had come in the first place.

For Mike, he thought the answer to himself.

"You sure?" Casey asked with the naive nature of a girl only two years removed from high school graduation.

"Yeah. I just remembered a few things I've gotta take care of."

"You'll miss their announcement," Casey prompted, trying to lure him into staying.

"I think I already know."

Greg gave her a quick kiss on the cheek, hoping to sneak out before anyone else could try talking him out of it.

"I'll talk to you later."

Before anyone else knew it, Greg was gone, left to drive home somewhat intoxicated, to escape into his own depressing world once more.

He needed help, maybe even therapy, but didn't want the hassle. The more he was alone, the better he seemed to feel.

Greg missed it as everyone else heard the shocking news about the pregnancy, once Mike and Sandi confirmed their wedding date would be in the middle of October.

As bad a night as he was having, he took comfort in the fact that someone, somewhere, was probably doing worse.

Now well past dark, Tom Ellis found himself cruising some of the old county roads he once served as a volunteer, before becoming chief.

He often watched how other local departments performed, almost to the point that they were uncomfortable whenever he was at their scenes, as though he might have started the fires for his own benefit.

Though he could never let on about his department's problems with Malovich, there *were* problems.

What was once a cinch to get people to sign up for volunteer time at the two stations was now a hassle, and no one seemed to have the time. He threatened their memberships on the department, and a few quit, while a few took up more shifts.

Most of the time, he was lucky to have one or two people at the stations, prepared for calls, outside of the few paid staff he maintained, which included himself. He got the necessary hours out of them, but their salaries were considerably less than his own, meaning most of them had second jobs.

This also meant they came to work dead tired, and sometimes slept when they needed to be working with the firefighters or the trucks.

With new state and national mandates coming out, and those he was just now discovering through the Internet and code books, Ellis discovered his department was further behind than he expected. They needed a lot more new equipment than his budget called for, and he realized the city was out of code on certain things as well, but ratting them out meant making himself look bad in the process.

Malovich was right.

The press, and the public, were on their side. If they waited, good things would continue to come. So what if a few rules were bent or broken for the ultimate betterment of the department?

Eventually, Ellis could weed out the deadbeats on his staff and build a strong department. He just needed to play this political card game with Malovich a little longer.

Though technically out of his district, Ellis heard a call over his scanner, indicating a small country house had smoke showing. A neighbor had called in the problem, and the local volunteers were now being dispatched.

"I'm just a few miles from that," Ellis told himself, wondering how it would look if he showed up first.

He had gear in the back of his vehicle, but without water, he doubted he would be able to enter the building and remain safe. And if he arrived first, it would certainly look suspicious, but it would look worse if people saw him driving *away* from the scene.

Ellis flipped his master light switch up, firing up all of the red and white flashing and rotating lights atop and around his vehicle. He started toward the fire, knowing there was only one stop sign between him and the house.

He found himself nearing the scene less than a minute later, just as one of the volunteers radioed back that he was en route to the station.

"It'll take them fucking forever to get out here," Ellis said to himself.

As he pulled closer to the house, the chief could see there were flames emitting from somewhere in the middle to the back of the residence.

He jumped out of his vehicle, put on his turnout gear and air pack, and did a quick walk around the house to see what he was against.

"Help me!" he heard a voice scream from inside before letting out a horrifying shriek more realistic than any he'd ever heard in a horror movie.

Ellis ran to the front of the house, realizing this was where the scream had come from. He peered through the picture window, seeing little aside from black smoke inside. There was no power from what he could tell, and his flashlight failed to penetrate the thick smoke inside, through the picture window.

"Shit!" Ellis said to himself, unaware of the volunteer department's hardship in stirring enough of their men from bed to rush to the fire.

He quickly tried the front door, but a storm door left from winter impeded his path, since it was locked. Ellis had little doubt the steel door behind it was locked too. He had a pry bar in his vehicle, but it was small, and the second door had a deadbolt.

Prying it would take too long, and might require another person's help. None of the neighbors who reportedly called dispatchers were anywhere to be found, so Ellis was definitely on his own.

Since the fire was centered in the house, smashing any window would draw it toward him in its hunger for oxygen, he figured. He felt reasonably certain the woman he'd heard was right in front of him, but he could not enter from the back and charge through the fire to save her, and smashing the window would possibly trap him before he could get to her, and get her free.

The only sound piercing the unearthly quiet was the crackle of the flames making their way across the roof as they drew closer to the front of the house.

No sirens, no gathering crowd behind him.

Just him, the fire, and this scream from within.

Ellis looked at his air mask dangling around his neck as it bounced up and down on his chest. Putting it on would only require seconds, but he wondered what good he could do.

He wanted to get in there and make a difference, but the truth was, Ellis had only been inside two fiery structures.

Ever.

He knew the science, and the strategy, but actually getting inside without the benefit of a hose line worried him.

Scared him.

Once more, he heard a blood-curdling scream from within, but he could only pace the front of the house, wondering what he should do.

Yes, he had protective gear, and yes, he had air, but the fire was growing now. Ellis knew the first rule of firefighter safety was never to endanger one's self, and he now felt threatened by this intense monster.

He heard one final scream diminish into a horrifying combination of a moan and gurgle from within the house, and he shuttered.

"My God," he muttered, realizing he had failed.

In more ways than one.

🍁   🍁   🍁

An hour later, the flames had long since been extinguished, though the house itself was in ruins. Only the smoldering remains of its wooden structure remained intact, and firefighters were exhausted after pounding thousands of gallons of water on the fire.

Luckily, a nearby pond gave the county firefighters a source of water to draft from, and the job was rudimentary after that.

"So you happened to be driving in the area, and heard our dispatch go off?" Chief Brad Barrett of the Garrison Volunteer Fire Department asked Ellis.

Ellis was seated on the back of his own vehicle's open tailgate, while Barrett stood before him, pen and pad in hand.

"I was about two miles away, heard the call, and got over here as quick as I could, but the building was already too far gone," Ellis reported.

"Did you see any neighbors?"

"None."

The closest neighbors were half a mile in either direction, so it was a wonder anyone had seen anything in the darkness to report in the first place.

Barrett began to wonder if someone might have set the fire, then called it in. He also wondered why a fellow volunteer chief was driving county roads so late at night.

"We had reports that there were people inside," Barrett said, glancing over to his men, who were sifting through the collapsed debris for any bodies or evidence.

A state fire marshal had driven to the scene, and now directed the volunteers on how to conduct their search without lousing up his crime scene.

"Did you see any evidence of anyone around here, or inside the house?" Barrett prompted, thinking Ellis might be of help in the investigation.

"No. I didn't see or hear anyone," the chief said, fighting the demons inside himself.

"You're sure?"

"Positive. Like I said, it was pretty much gone when I got here."

Barrett nodded, as though he had nothing else to ask.

"Thanks, Tom. If I need anything else, I'll call."

"Okay, Brad," Ellis said, hoping to slink away before the body in the living room was discovered.

Luck was not on his side as the firefighters called out to Barrett, and he made his way over to the scene. Ellis stood a moment, unable to see the charred corpse he knew they would find, but it turned out they had found two small corpses, the woman's children, right beside the back door, who perished trying to find their way out.

"Oh, God," Ellis told himself, realizing his failure was worse than he had imagined. "If only I would've gone in there, or tried to."

No one else was near him, so his grief and guilt went unheard, but Ellis knew the men of Carvers Grove, the men he was looking to replace or command, would have gone in there. Of course, they would have had the luxury of water and immediate backup, but they would have entered nonetheless. Those guys were fearless family men, or at least they left nothing but courageous images in the public eye.

Ellis rubbed his head and decided to sleep at home tonight, instead of the fire station. He had a lot of things to think about.

CHAPTER 10

Based on the evidence at the fire scene, it didn't take long for members of the Carvers Grove Fire Department, and firefighters from surrounding counties, to begin suspecting Ellis hadn't made much of an effort at the fire to save the children, or their mother.

It mattered little.

There was really nothing anyone could do, and the only harm done to Ellis was that of his reputation, locally anyway.

"I think he killed those people," Mike said to Kevin as they waited their turn to do CPR on the medical dummy in the headquarters station truck bay.

Despite his comments at the party, Kevin had forgiven his younger brother, and they were still talking.

Though Kevin still hadn't spoken with Greg.

"You don't have any proof. You weren't there," Kevin replied, echoing the words his brother had used at the party.

"I didn't have to be to know Tom Ellis is a piece of shit who won't go into a burning building for anything. He trains his men the same way, you know. Every time they're in the newspaper, you see them sticking a hose inside a window, or trying to put the fire out with a PPV fan from the outside."

"You trying to imply our good neighbors are pussies?" Kevin questioned.

"I'm not implying anything. I'll straight up say they are. And what the fuck was he doing out there anyway?"

Kevin shrugged.

"The man has little else to do. He was probably on fire patrol."

Mike chuckled.

"Yeah, sure."

Standing amongst a group of firefighters who had nothing else to do but chat while they waited their turns to pass their CPR practical test, the brothers took a moment to watch one of their colleagues finish his turn.

Several trucks were temporarily out-of-service so the firefighters could watch videos, practice, watch more videos, then test out by using their CPR skills on the dummy. For most of them, this was just an update to the training they had received three years earlier.

"Your turn, Mike," the CPR instructor said, knowing most of the firefighters by name after several recent classes.

Remembering the videos, and having been through the CPR process several times, Mike dropped to a kneeling position, went through the motions of checking the dummy for breathing, pulse, and consciousness, then set to delivering quick breaths. He watched to see if the chest rose upward, which it did, so he followed with chest compressions.

Within a moment he was finished, and stood up to face the instructor.

"You killed your patient," the instructor commented, as though he was going to let it pass anyway.

Mike grinned. He had done the compressions a bit too hard, which pushed the sternum too far into the chest on real patients, and actually did more damage than good.

"I guess I was taking out a few frustrations on him. Sorry."

"Just watch yourself on the real thing."

"Will do."

The instructor didn't have time to wait for Mike to do it again, since he was on a tight schedule, and he didn't want to make a big scene over something he knew the firefighter had long since mastered.

"You doing okay, kid?" Kevin asked as they walked up to Wade, who had already done his CPR training earlier.

"Pretty good," Wade answered quickly. "I can't wait until they start shipping me to some other stations so I can work with you guys."

"Give it a couple months," Mike said. "Get a couple fires behind you, and they'll set you free."

"At this rate I'll never get to leave," Wade scoffed.

"I keep hearing you're a good luck charm around here," Kevin remarked. "Maybe they won't let you go."

"Think we could trade Sam for him?" Mike asked in almost a whisper to his older brother.

"I don't think Patrick would go for having three of us on the same truck," Kevin replied, half-serious. "We'd cause way too much trouble for him."

"You know, you guys are going to jinx me talking like this," Wade said.

"You wish, kid," Mike replied. "You might go years without seeing any real fire."

※　　　※　　　※

"I hate them," Wade said to himself that afternoon as he fumbled with his air pack, nervous as could be, on their way to a reported blaze not far from their station.

He couldn't believe his uncles had jinxed him like that, and though he didn't really hate them, he had to admit he was caught off-guard when the call came soon after lunch.

As he struggled to get his equipment on, he heard the dispatcher relaying information over the radio about how kids might be trapped inside, and the house was reportedly rolling with flames, according to several neighbors.

Before he knew it, they were at the scene, and he still didn't have everything strapped and placed the way it should be. Wade stepped from the truck, trying to pull the straps tight, and make sure his air tank was working, as he breathed in the compressed air from the tank, unsure of where to go next.

Fire was shooting out the front, and over the eaves of the porch, but the fire only seemed to be in the front. Smoke was pouring out of every vent of the house, but the rookie didn't notice. He was focused on the hungry flames, wondering why on earth he had signed on for this job.

He saw Bobby Pratt yanking hose from the side of the truck bed, and the pumper truck driver was helping him. Once he had the connections on his mask and air tank secure, he helped them pull hose line until his captain gave him a different order.

"Pull the hose that way," he ordered, and Wade complied, taking the length of the hose down the street, away from the truck.

That way, the hose wouldn't crumple into a messy pile. If that happened, it would be nearly impossible to inch the line further into the house as the firefighters made their way through.

Wade kept pulling the hose until the captain urged him to follow Pratt into the house.

In there? he thought, wondering how it was possible to enter a house so engulfed in flames from the front, but Pratt showed him the way. Wade simply kept himself practically attached to Pratt's backside as he was trained to do.

Pratt took them right under the front door, found it already open, or missing, and positioned himself under the flames before opening up the line, moving the nozzle up and down, back and forth, as he killed the flames.

Shit, this is hot, Wade thought, not wanting to say anything aloud. He certainly didn't need to appear timid on his first real fire. Things like that became rumors around the station houses, and it didn't take long for the veterans to think less of him based on hearsay.

No matter how low he crouched, the heat felt intense on all sides, like sitting in the middle of an oven, despite the door being just a few feet away. Even the protective gear could not protect him fully from the radiant heat. Luckily the water cooled the area down, and Pratt was smart enough to use a straight-stream on the flames, rather than a fog pattern. A fog stream would create steam, and push even more heat back on them. Even Wade knew how steam could penetrate their gear and boil them like lobsters.

In the old days, numerous departments used nozzles that penetrated solid walls, then used fog patterns to put out the fires without risking firefighters. It was later discovered, however, that those patterns may have created intense steam inside, and possibly killed residents who were still alive before the water was applied.

Like anything else, firefighting proved to be a science, and pioneers discovered better ways to get the job done effectively.

"Get me more line," Pratt ordered, unable to tug the hose any further into the structure, because it was snagged on something outside.

Since they were only a few feet inside, Wade stepped back out to pull the hose, since his officer was still sizing up the scene, and the driver was occupied at the control panel of the truck. As he tugged the line, several other firefighters rushed past him, brushing past Pratt, to search the house for any victims, although it looked hopeless with so much fire inside.

Wade hated leaving Pratt's side, because that was one of the first things he learned in his mandatory training.

Never leave the side of your fellow firefighter.

Two in, two out.

Yet, here he was, pulling the line, instead of helping put out the fire. Wade felt guilty, but it was Pratt's wish to begin with, and his partner was still in plain sight. Falsely assuming anyone actually had time to monitor his activity, Wade also wanted to appear busy, so no one could say he was lazy on a fire scene.

In what seemed mere seconds to Wade, the fire was out. He had returned to Pratt's backside, and they fought their way inside, unable to see past the dense smoke, which seemed worse when water was applied to the flames.

The search yielded no results, which was good news. Neighbors always seemed to think there was the possibility of kids inside, and usually they were somewhere else with parents, or a babysitter, particularly during the daytime when people weren't in bed.

Wade felt a wave of relief when he was able to strip down to his night pants, removing his helmet, air pack, and heavy coat.

"Good job, man," Pratt said.

"You did all the work."

"You were right there with me, and you got my line free so I could get inside. No one else was out there tugging it for me."

Wade shrugged.

He still didn't feel as though he had done his part, and he felt bad for taking so long to suit up in the first place.

A wave of fresh firefighters pulled apart the walls and ceiling inside, while Pratt and Wade rested a few minutes. Everything seemed to be out, and only then did Wade feel somewhat assured he had done something right.

He always remembered hearing stories about the old days, when guys didn't wear air packs, and they got inside to find the fire no matter how hot it was, and stayed there until it was out. His training officer had informed him to be smarter than that, and told him being macho only got guys hurt or killed.

Still, Wade measured himself against those men of lore, and wanted to see if he had what it took to endure the same situations they had.

His answers would be coming sooner than he expected.

CHAPTER 11

During the next few weeks, Wade found himself in fire after fire, blaming his uncles for initially cursing him.

He bailed out of one fire due to an air tank problem, which he found was his own fault for not turning the air value fully open. He also got tangled up in a misplaced piece of equipment on the truck, which delayed his getting into a house fire with Pratt as quickly as he should have.

Wade also forgot his radio one time, in hooking up to a hydrant, which resulted in a mishap, because the horn was blown three times to evacuate firefighters from the house fire they were already in the midst of.

One blast was the department's signal to turn on the water flow to the large five-inch hoses, and Wade did so, when he wasn't supposed to during a three blast segment. This delayed efforts as water gushed everywhere, since the hose was not yet hooked to the back of the truck at the fire scene.

Wade felt terrible, and though some of his mistakes were just attributed to inexperience, he took a lot of heat from the guys, who made fun of him. He knew most of his mistakes were something they had all done wrong at one time, and shrugged it off, but it was getting to the point that he felt like he was doing more wrong than right.

"Give it time," Mike told him one day during a training film about their department's rescue truck. "You can't expect to run in there and be Superman every time. You haven't made the same mistakes twice, have you?"

"Well, no."

"There you go. If you're not making mistakes here, it means you're not working. Don't let these guys get to you, Wade. You're doing fine."

Wade had been sandwiched between Kevin and Mike during the training, and recently, he felt they were the only people sticking up for him at all, aside from Bobby Pratt.

Kevin had remained rather stoic most of the morning, as though something was preoccupying him.

"What's up with him?" Wade whispered to Mike.

"He had a fight with Julia about their family trip," Mike replied quickly, not wanting Kevin to overhear them.

Wade wondered how couples could quarrel over such trivial issues, but then again, he wasn't married with kids.

He watched some more of the video before the senior officers began to look their way. Even Mike had very little pull with some of them, because they were such hard-ass characters, including Patrick. Wade had done enough to screw things up lately, so he kept quiet until the video concluded.

As the group stood to disperse and talk amongst themselves, as was customary after mass training sessions, the tones sounded through several portable radios, sending almost half the trucks, including the one Kevin and Mike rode, to a local school for a bomb threat.

Usually, bomb threats were immediately blown off as pranks by the firefighters. The local police would take dogs in to sniff the entire school, and over a dozen firefighters would sit idly in their trucks for an hour or so and pass the time.

Sometimes they looked at the good-looking teachers with binoculars from the ambiguity of the truck, or talked to people they knew from the police department to get the scoop on what was happening inside.

Most of the time, students called in bomb threats to get out of class for a little while, or to break the monotony of their day. This call, however, was made by an adult in the middle of summer.

When there was no school in session.

Virtually every public safety facet had cars, trucks, and personnel around the scene. When the call came in a few minutes later that a bank across town had just been robbed, it was no shock to anyone, and finally the police realized they were duped into staging near the potential bomb.

Most of the police broke away from the scene, and soon enough, firefighters and EMS were allowed to leave. It seemed the bomb scare was simply a major decoy for the bank robbery, and worse yet, the robbers got away.

"Have a look at this," Kevin said, handing the binoculars to Mike in the back jump seat.

He pointed the direction to his younger brother, and Mike could tell Kevin was eyeing a young woman with shapely hips crossing the street to a jewelry store.

"You are such a pervert," Mike commented. "No wonder Julia doesn't want to take you on any trips."

"She caught me looking the other day, brother," Kevin said with a chuckle.

"Did you try and talk your way out of it?"

"For about three seconds until she told me to forget it."

Mike grinned, taking in the view as the lady dropped something on the sidewalk, bending over to pick it up.

"Holy," he commented to himself as Kevin snatched the binoculars away from him.

"Damn," Kevin said, mesmerized by the scene across the street.

"Julia needs to kick your ass," Mike said, offering a solution to his brother's wandering eyes.

"We tried that, but it didn't help."

"In foreign countries they cut your dick off for that stuff, you know."

"Now *that* might be deterrent enough for me," Kevin said, putting the binoculars back in the glove compartment. "Home, Darrell," he said to his driver, who was all too happy to comply.

He had a bed with his sheets on it just dying to be slept in.

On the way back to the station, Wade overheard a call on the radio involving a man trapped in a city dump area at the sanitation department's headquarters.

Because he had never seen the facility, the rookie firefighter had no idea how a man could get trapped in a pit of trash, but his uncles were all familiar with it, and they were the men being dispatched along with the rescue truck to help get the man out of the pit.

Smirking to himself as he stepped from the truck, Mike walked over to the edge of the pit, taking in the smells of rotten food and baby diapers, among others, as he peered into the deep pit. A wickedly intense sun served to further bake the rotten ingredients of this trash pie, and the smell would soon become unbearable.

Only halfway filled, the pit was a hazard if someone fell over the edge, because there was no way out, except for the entrance used by trucks and dozers at the other end. Usually a person could walk to the other end, or pull himself up to the edge if there was enough solid trash to stand on.

This man, however, had evidently broken his leg when it hit the hard corner of an old desk at the bottom of the pit. He was lying very still now, though complaining about being in the midst of trash, and the fire department's sluggish ability to get him free of the pit.

"Settle down," Kevin said, being somewhat informal with the man, since they both worked for the city.

He looked like an older man, who had probably dedicated a few decades of his life to working for the city, and probably never had any problems until this fateful day. His clothes were all tattered, but that came with the territory of his work, and he had several small bloody slits along his arms from pieces of trash cutting him, such as can lids and discarded knives.

"Hope he doesn't get lockjaw from all those cuts," Mike commented.

"If he's had his shots, he won't," Kevin replied, noticing a variety of expressions from the sanitation workers standing around.

All of them were concerned, but a few were amused. Kevin figured he would find some humor in the situation later, but he had to put forth his game face in public.

All of the firefighters were standing atop the pit, looking over, as they decided the best way to pull the man free, without harming him, or endangering themselves and equipment.

None of the trucks could enter the dozer entrance, because the trash piles would quickly halt them, so they needed to bring the man up to them.

Two of the men on the rescue truck were certified as emergency medical technicians, so their input was valuable.

Kevin was technically in charge since his truck was first on the scene, but he would not interfere with any decisions made by the rescue truck's crew, since they were specialized in traumatic situations.

"Are you going to use the basket?" he asked the lieutenant on the rescue truck.

"Yeah, but it's a question of how to get him back up here."

Named the Goody Basket, the rescue basket was basically a wooden board encased in what looked to be thick chicken wire. It was named for Barry Goodspeed, a retired firefighter who reportedly had several mishaps with the basket during his career.

Considering Goodspeed had retired shortly after Patrick Sheridan joined the fire department, the basket was rather dated. Still, it did the job, and several modifications, including straps to secure patients, kept it in business.

Kevin looked over the side, realizing the combination of trash piles and a slight slope beneath the edge of the wall made using a rope rather risky. There was only one other realistic way to pull the basket up the embankment once they had the sanitation worker secured.

"Ladder?" he asked the rescue lieutenant, who seemed to be thinking the same thing.

While Conley and Mike went about getting a ladder from their pumper truck, the rescue crew readied the basket.

Soon enough the ladder was laid against the edge of the pit, and the bottom was placed near the injured man. The rescue crew fought the horrid stench of the pit as they reached the sanitation worker, securing his leg with splints since it wasn't a compound fracture.

"How the hell did you fall in here anyway?" one of the rescue truck's men asked the fallen worker.

"You won't believe me if I tell you," the man replied sourly.

"Try us," the second firefighter said as Mike and Conley held the ladder steady from above, waiting for the signal to send down ropes, which would be used to pull, and guide, the basket up the ladder as one of the rescue men pushed and steadied from behind.

"I was walking around, doing inventory on our trucks, and I slipped."

"On what?"

The man simply pointed to the culprit, but the firefighters could not decipher what he was pointing to in the massive pile.

"What?" they asked.

"That banana peel."

Looking to one another, the firefighters each cracked a grin.

"Oh, laugh it up," the older man complained as they finished strapping him securely inside the basket.

As they pulled him toward the ladder, one of the firefighters slipped, accidentally setting his hand down on the man's injured leg to steady himself. In response, the man let out a painful yowl matching the best of coyotes, which set his colleagues above into fits of laughter.

"You son-of-a-bitch," the man stammered. "That's my injured leg."

"Sorry," the firefighter quickly apologized. "If you guys would clean this pit out, it would probably help."

"Strap the basket," Kevin ordered, realizing how ugly the situation was getting from several perspectives.

Though the man complained the entire trip up the ladder, Kevin managed to get things under control by moving the sanitation workers back, who would most likely have a field day teasing this poor fellow once he was back to work.

Kevin knew firefighters all did a few dumb things over the course of their careers, but he had never stepped on, or braced himself against someone's broken limb before. This would also likely result in some departmental teasing for the rescue firefighter.

"This is a first," Mike commented once the firefighters had transferred the man to the emergency medical technicians on the scene.

"Definitely," Kevin replied.

"We going out for lunch?"

"With you being a perspective dad and all, can you afford that?"

"I'm not a dad yet, so I can still squeeze it into the budget."

Five minutes later, the two continued their conversation, seated inside a local sub shop.

"I can't believe you two are having a kid already."

"It's kind of a surprise to me too," Mike confessed.

Conley sat with Thomas as the two brothers talked.

He never really conversed much with anyone, and usually kept to himself. Conley never seemed to have a steady girlfriend, lived by himself in the country, and had only farm animals as pets, even though he really didn't live on a farm.

Some of his brother firefighters wondered if he was the next big serial bomber, so they kept on his good side.

"Is Greg still pissed at me?" Kevin asked between bites of a meatball sub.

"He was never pissed at you. You're the one making *him* feel alienated, remember?"

"Well, then maybe it's time I had a chat with my little brother."

Mike paused from eating a moment.

"You know, you and I might have the most in common, but he looked up to you a lot as a kid. Jay and Patrick were too old, and you were all we had. You not talking to him is eating him up inside, and the way he's been lately, I'm getting a little worried."

"How so?" Kevin inquired, pausing as well.

"He doesn't return calls, he hasn't been on a date in months, and I think he's miserable in his new division. You talking to him could help."

"I suppose," the lieutenant said, as though coming to a sudden realization of how much he was hurting his brother.

Mike thought about what he wanted to say, knowing Kevin didn't want to hear it, but decided it needed stating nonetheless.

"You know, if that fire hadn't taken Dad, he wouldn't have lasted that much longer, Kev. You can't blame Greg for anything that happened that day. I was there too, and it's just as much my fault if you're going to lay blame."

He noticed Conley and Thomas getting a bit uncomfortable at their nearby table, despite him trying to keep his voice down.

Mike leaned in a bit more to keep the conversation private.

"Maybe if I had gone upstairs, I could've done more, or maybe if more of the volunteers had shown up, they could have gotten him out of there quicker."

Kevin had now lost any appetite he walked into the restaurant with.

"So what exactly are you saying, Mike?"

"I'm just saying there were a lot of people who didn't pull their weight, and at least Greg had balls enough to get in there with us and contribute. Up until that day you were on good terms with him, and every day you go on ignoring him and his life gets a little more miserable from the other shit he's dealing with, the more I worry about our family staying together like Dad wanted us to."

"Is that what this is about? Us all staying together? It's not the same, Mike. We're all grown up with kids of our own. We had a perfect Christmas together, and that was probably the last one we'll ever have. Don't go burying yourself by trying to keep this family together. Things aren't going to be the same. Ever."

"I'm not asking us to be the Brady Bunch, but we're damn lucky we all live around here, and we never take advantage of it. What are our kids going to think when they grow up? That it's okay to have no family ties whatsoever?"

"I don't know, but I will talk to Greg. Soon."

"Good. He probably needs all the support he can get."

Kevin nodded. He had failed in his responsibility as an older brother the past few months, but he would make it up to Greg.

He didn't recall Mike overwhelming their brother with attention either, but he wasn't about to open another can of worms by bringing up the subject.

The lieutenant simply wanted to finish out his day and go home.

CHAPTER 12

When it came across his scanner in the middle of the night that an apartment fire in his district had just been reported, Tom Ellis wasted no time in racing to the scene.

He discovered two of his trucks were already on the way, but when he arrived, the volunteer chief discovered the old building was already a complete loss.

An old city block with three remnants of unsavory apartment buildings had recently been purchased by a local man, who knew from inside sources, that a national retail chain wanted the land to build a new store.

Local people figured he had bought the land simply to increase his profit margin when he resold to the retail chain. Now one of the buildings was completely ablaze, and the other two were in considerable danger of joining it.

Ellis simply emerged from his truck, staring at the completely engulfed building before him, wondering how such an isolated patch of buildings had caught fire, and how he was going to stop it, with the closest major water supply almost a mile away.

The tallest of the three buildings was showing flames through every door and window. Fire destroyed and fed on every organic material available in the old wooden frame. He could feel radiant heat, even from a distance, and everything around him showed how dry the entire summer had been.

From the dusty ground to the unbearably humid air, evidence of perfect fire conditions lingered everywhere.

Along with the slight easterly breeze came an odor of gas, and Ellis felt reasonably certain nothing had been stored inside the buildings. So far as he knew, they were both completely vacant of people and belongings, and had been for years. The odor was likely a cause in the fire spreading so quickly, and he wondered why someone would want these three buildings gone.

Occasionally, fiery embers flew from the building as the crackle of the doomed wood filled the chief's ears. He closed his eyes a few seconds, but the intense orange glow still penetrated his eyelids.

This was no ordinary fire, and he definitely suspected it had an unnatural origin.

He thought about looking for an evidence trail left behind by the arsonist, but he had no camera, and none of the necessary equipment to measure or cast footprints or tire tracks.

"Ah, fuck," he said hopelessly to himself, radioing to the incoming trucks to lay down the supply lines as they came to the fire scene.

He wondered if he had enough men coming to adequately man the hose lines and trucks. If not, he was in for one long night.

※　　　　　※　　　　　※

By the time Mason Gray pulled into the area two hours later, all three buildings were lying in smoldering heaps.

He stepped from his marked vehicle, a strange smirk on his face as he saw only four firefighters, Tom Ellis, and a mess of hose lines around the two trucks that had made the scene.

"I guess the paper won't be hearing about this one, eh, Tom?" he asked the chief when he walked up.

"You don't see any reporters here, do you?" Ellis retorted.

He didn't.

"Must be nice to selectively use the press to your advantage," Gray said.

"You know, Mason, I don't recall asking for an investigator to be dispatched."

"Well, you know, Tom, I think you're technically closer to Carvers Grove than any other community. So, unless you want the state boys down here to see what a great job you and the boys did on this fire, you're stuck with me."

Ellis grunted to himself.

Playing politics with Malovich was bad enough. Now he found himself dealing with Gray as well.

He watched a moment as the investigator retrieved his necessary tools from his vehicle, then went about putting on his night pants.

"I suppose you could've investigated this yourself?" Gray asked the chief, as though to imply the chief was inadequately trained to do anything outside of his primary duties.

Which he was.

"I've got some training in arson investigations," Ellis said with a confident tone.

"Like one basic class?"

"Two. And what makes you such an expert anyway?"

"The fact that I've been investigating half of my career, and seen almost a hundred fires. I've done this on the side too, you know, for an insurance company. But, of course, that was before I got paid substantial amounts of money on my weekends to lecture at state and national fire conventions about my expertise in the field. Pretty good gig, wouldn't you say?"

Ellis waved his hand toward the rubble past his two trucks, cussing Gray's name under his breath.

"Have at it."

Gray wanted to comply, but he felt a war of words was necessary, because Ellis usually skipped on by their stations, protected from the wrath of the city's professional department.

"So, did you guys even get water on the flames before all three buildings fell?" he asked in an almost taunting manner.

Gray was arrogant, and not just around his fellow firefighters. His reputation followed him throughout the county, and even a little beyond.

"By the time the guys got water from the hydrant, the third building was already involved," Ellis reported, ignoring the investigator's tone.

"I thought you had an entire platoon of guys ready to go at the drop of a hat," Gray said. "Did they already head home?" he asked, looking around as though expecting to see dozens of hardworking volunteers.

Ellis drew his face into a scowl.

"At least we didn't call your department for mutual aid."

"Of course not. You might have saved something with a department that has a response time under ten minutes."

"My department doesn't ask the public for too much money, unlike yours."

"No, Malovich just charges the industrial areas double what the city was asking for in taxes, after stating his plan will save them money. Secretly, no less."

"Taxes are public records."

"Public records no one sees, because the newspaper certainly won't print it, even if an individual discovers the discrepancy."

Ellis grinned, despite the dire circumstances surrounding him.

"You know the paper only prints the truth, Gray."

"Their truth, not my truth."

"Well, if your department was a good product, we wouldn't exist."

Gray drew a strange smirk for a few seconds before replying.

"If I had my way, *you* wouldn't exist at all."

"Wishful thinking isn't going to help you, and unless you get a new alderman and mayor in the hot seat, your department might be in big trouble."

"Actually, the public is the one that'll be in trouble. I've seen your handiwork several times now, and I don't see how they stand for it."

Ellis rubbed his thumb against his two forefingers on one hand.

"Money. The only thing they care about is how much they're paying in taxes, if their roads are paved, and that crime isn't a daily occurrence in their neighborhood. We service them just fine in all three, and they aren't going to see any need to change."

Gray shook his head.

"You're a piece of work, Tom. I can investigate the loss of these buildings, but I already know you're the one responsible."

"I didn't set no fire," the chief said, defending himself.

"No, but you didn't do much to stop it, either."

Gray walked off with that said, and Ellis didn't bother to reply, because he knew it was somewhat true. His department wasn't everything it was made out to be, and if the word got out, he and Malovich would be in serious trouble just before the big election.

"Fuck you," Ellis said once the investigator was out of earshot, knowing Gray wasn't that much different.

After all, he was rumored to be running in the next coroner's election.

As Gray walked around the scene, he noticed very little left of the buildings in solid form. Most everything was ashes and embers, with only a few feet of framework left from each building. Like grotesquely tragic Roman statues reaching for the heavens, the structural skeletons were charred and black. The first two buildings provided the investigator a full view inside, without even having to stand on his toes.

The third had a little bit more framework left to it, since Ellis and his crew had finally gotten water on it. Gray knew the fire had burned quick and hot, which implied it had help of some sort.

He knew which building was on fire first, based on the damage, and set to finding samples from its origin. Gray had several sealed evidence cans with him, and tools for prying up part of the floor. He knew what made for cases in court, and how to prepare for them.

Taking one last look toward the firefighters, who were picking up a virtual ton of hose lines, he started sizing up his scene, seeing how this old, decrepit city block was a distance away from the rest of town. This area had long since fallen in upon itself, neglected by the city and its ownership for far too long.

Either way, it was about to start anew, as retailers brought it back into the city's mainstream.

Collecting the evidence would be the easy part. For Gray, this was routine. Already, he found himself wondering why someone would burn it, because he seemed to recall the buildings being condemned, which practically voided any property insurance on them. Also, the land had just been bought for resale.

Everyone knew that.

There would be motive in burning the buildings down *and* collecting insurance, so Gray made a mental note to check into the new owner's insurance policy, if one existed.

From a distance, Ellis seemed to size him up, as though grading him on how he carried out the investigation. Gray simply smiled to himself, wondering how Ellis even kept his job after some of the bone-headed things the man had done.

Gray finished up before the chief and his men had even cleaned up their mess. He brushed past Ellis on the way out, as though to show the man who was boss.

Simply clenching his teeth to himself, Ellis chose not to make any trouble for himself or his department. Gray was out for himself, and as long as Ellis didn't make waves, they would probably both have what they wanted.

CHAPTER 13

A few nights later, the Sheridan boys found themselves outside a biker bar they visited infrequently. When Jay was in town, they sometimes got together for a bite to eat and a guys night out.

This time, however, the wives were invited, which was fine, since the establishment served alcohol and good food, as well as some unusual forms of entertainment, which often ended up mimicking the circus more than anything.

While Mike and Kevin took Sandi and Julia inside to reserve a fairly large area to sit, Wade and Greg waited outside, by themselves. It seemed to be their usual routine lately, to travel alone.

"I thought firefighters got all kinds of pussy," Wade confessed to Greg as they stood outside the bar, waiting for Jay. "I haven't gotten laid since I got this job."

Greg put a hand to his face, shaking his head. Perhaps being a police officer had softened any blunt nature he once had, or maturity had aged him, but he found Wade's comments a bit brash.

"Do you talk like that around the firehouse?"

"All the time. I thought you cops were dirty-minded too."

"We are, but we don't talk about it as much."

"Some role model you turned out to be."

Greg rolled his eyes.

"You've got a lot to learn, kid."

"Now I see why you're a cop."

"Why's that?"

"You're too damn serious, Uncle Greg. You act like you're still married or something."

Greg shrugged indifferently.

"I still feel like I am. Don't ever get married unless you plan to live with her forever, or kill her before you break up. Divorce sucks."

I'll keep that in mind, Wade thought.

A moment later, his father pulled up on his motorcycle with an attractive blonde's arms wrapped around his stomach. Being a fairly cool evening for a change, Jay wore his leather jacket and sunglasses, looking the part for the setting they were all about the enter.

"Hi, fellas," he said in his usual throaty deep voice. "Everyone make it?"

"Everyone but Patrick," Wade said, as though it was preposterous to expect the battalion chief to attend such a flamboyant event.

"Guys, this is Candi," Jay said of his new fling.

Both gave the usual casual wave, expecting Candi to be yesterday's news, literally by the next morning.

Inside, Mike and Kevin had seated themselves as far away from the bar as possible, knowing all too well what the atmosphere of the tavern was like. Their original intent was to leave Julia and Sandi at home, but the girls had ganged up on them, wondering why it always had to be a guys night out at Jay's favorite bar.

"You really want to find out?" Mike had asked with a foreboding tone in his voice.

"We do," they answered, so the two firefighters decided to enlighten them on how Jay spent a night on the town.

Surrounded by virtual darkness, except for a few candles and dim overhead lights, the four waited for the others to arrive, taking in the atmosphere.

"This place seems kind of dingy," Julia noted, seeing mounted animal heads along several walls, and Indian artifacts along another.

By no means was it a typical biker bar. It had a touch of historical value, even if it lacked class in other areas.

"What are those?" Sandi questioned of a net holding two unusual round objects, just beneath a bison's mounted head.

"Buffalo testicles," Mike answered flatly.

Sandi gave him an incredulous stare.

"You're kidding, right?"

"No. I'm not."

Sandi twisted her face into a disgusted look, unaware that the worst of this environment had yet to appear. Though Mike and Kevin had shielded the women from the bar, it would come to life momentarily, once more people filtered into the tavern.

They had just ordered drinks when Jay and the others made their way through the sea of picnic tables, which served as eating areas toward the back of the tavern. His new fling, however, split from the group about halfway through their walk, heading for the bar counter.

"Where's she going?" Julia asked when the guys all made their way to the table, then sat down.

"She's got to perform," Jay replied, straddling the seat for a better view of the bar.

Mike and Kevin each shot one another alarmed stares.

Though the bar usually had some bizarre forms of entertainment, there was one night reserved for amateurs to show their stuff.

All of their stuff.

Unfortunately the guys had forgotten tonight was amateur night, and that meant there would soon be lots of cleavage bouncing atop the bar. It never occurred to them that Jay would invite them on amateur night, because they usually just went whenever their schedules allowed them to meet up.

Seeing naked women only served to get them in trouble, and the two realized just how much hot water they were about to get into.

Kevin leaned over the table for a private word with Jay.

"You didn't tell us tonight was amateur night."

"You didn't ask," Jay replied in a hushed voice.

"And now your girlfriend is going up there?"

"Ah," Jay said with an airy wave, "the girls will love it."

"Bullshit. They'll never let us out with you again."

Jay grinned. Somehow Kevin suspected his older brother had set them up, or maybe he was just being his usual quirky self.

"I'll smooth it over with 'em," Jay assured both of his brothers, as though the women would take anything he spoke as gospel.

In the meantime, Julia and Sandi had taken notice of Jay's new fling climbing the bar, with several other women lining up for their turn. Jay was quite accustomed to the atmosphere, and enjoyed women who didn't mind flaunting their bodies.

"Do they dance up there?" Sandi asked, still not expecting her fiancé to expose her to anything more than harmless fun.

"Oh, they do more than that," Jay chimed in with a chuckle.

Kevin smacked him on the arm, but his older brother barely felt it through the leather jacket. He was frantically thinking of any excuse to leave the bar, because even the distance they were sitting from the bar wasn't far enough to keep the women from seeing naked flesh momentarily.

He could tell Mike was thinking the same thing, but Greg and Wade made their way back from the bar, carrying drinks. The two brothers sat at the edge of the table, basically trapping everyone else inside.

Shit, Kevin thought. Julia's about to see a mound of tits, and now I'm stuck with Greg.

He was definitely between a rock and a hard place.

Julia already knew he was a pervert, so he was more concerned about Mike and Sandi, considering the show about to start. Whether he wanted to or not, he would have to speak with Greg to appear oblivious to the activities at the bar.

As much as it pained him to keep his eyes to himself.

"So, what's new?" he asked his younger brother, who appeared unsure of how to react once Kevin finally spoke to him.

"Not much," Greg answered, seeing Jay's new girl slowly peeling her top from her chest in a very seductive manner.

Kevin had to fight to keep his eyes to himself, or aimed toward Greg, with Candi dancing atop the bar counter, now removing her bra. He failed to notice Sandi's expression as she watched in amazement, wondering why she and Julia had asked to tag along, and why the guys would choose amateur night to attend this establishment.

"Is this what you guys usually do?" Sandi asked her fiancé.

"No," Mike answered bluntly. "We just kind of meet here when Jay wants to."

He bent over closer to Sandi, so only she would hear his next statement.

"I had no idea this was going on tonight."

"And you've never been here with women stripping?" she asked with an accusatory tone.

Mike shrugged casually.

"Maybe once. It's Jay's thing. He just buys us beers and we talk. No big deal."

Sandi didn't look pleased, but it was her idea for the girls to tag along this time. She felt positive Mike would have worked harder at talking her out of it, had he known biker women would be taking their clothes off for everyone to see.

Even the biker women who weren't on the bar seemed to enjoy the show. Sandi found the whole situation strange, but said nothing more about it.

"Congratulations on the move to detectives," Kevin said to Greg, trying to ignore Julia's occasional stare his way.

Apparently her opinion of the evening entertainment wasn't very different from Sandi's.

"Thanks," Greg replied uneasily. "I heard about that boy who drowned a couple weeks ago. Sorry to hear he didn't make it."

"It wasn't for lack of effort," Kevin said, sure Mike wasn't overhearing their conversation with the chatter and music in the background. "Mike did everything he could've done to find that boy."

"That's Mike."

Kevin nodded. They both knew their brother was as aggressive as firefighters came. He took everything personally on the job, and berated himself heavily if he felt he had screwed up, or failed at something.

Both noticed Mike doing his best to keep Sandi's attention, assuring her he had no idea what the night was going to hold. Truthfully, he didn't, but she now knew all of their guys nights out weren't so innocent.

"Have you forgiven me?" Greg decided to ask.

Kevin gave him a strange look, then understood what he was being asked.

"I never really blamed you, Greg," he said casually, as though such a thought never crossed his mind. "I guess I just didn't take Dad's death real well."

"I see. If I would've followed the family line like the rest of you did, maybe things would have turned out differently."

Kevin suddenly felt uneasy.

"You know, I wasn't there, so I can't judge what you did as right or wrong. I know you would never let anything happen to Dad, and you haven't done any firefighting in years. Greg, I'm sorry if I wasn't as chummy as I should've been the past few months. You forgive me?"

Greg smirked as the shiny center of his head glimmered in the candlelight.

"Yeah, I suppose," he said, though thinking Kevin wasn't being entirely sincere.

He suspected Mike had prompted Kevin to talk with him, even though the twins hadn't really spoken much the past few months themselves.

By this time, the group was ready to order some food, and everyone except Jay did their best to ignore the bouncing flesh on the top of the bar. At least three girls stood up there at a time, pulling off their tops. And some, their lingerie.

"Holy shit," Wade said to himself, taking in the view.

He had avoided talking to his uncles altogether, just to see the view.

"Nice choice, Dad," he said to Jay, who had only missed the action when he blinked.

"She's not bad. A nurse out of Chicago."

"A nurse?"

"Yeah. She likes to live it up on the weekends."

"I'd say."

Virtually everyone sitting at the table had begun to feel a bit uncomfortable, except for Jay, who was right in the middle of his element. His brothers noticed his actions, and when he took off his jacket to stammer up to the bar to dance a jig in front of everyone present, they knew he had taken in a few too many beers.

Jay was gyrating his hips and elbows, the likes of which his brothers had never seen before. When intoxicated, their oldest brother was a completely different person from the reserved intellectual they knew and loved.

He could also be a mean drunk if they didn't control him.

"Growing up with him must have been a chore," Mike commented to Wade.

"It was a trip."

"Hey, Wade, that isn't the girl he came with, is it?" Mike asked, noticing his older brother now getting very close and personal with one of the other dancing women.

Someone else's companion.

"Uh oh."

Before Mike and Wade could even stand up, to attempt fetching Jay from the bar, another biker had already taken exception to Jay's intimate moves toward his girlfriend. Even though bikers usually seem a bit more liberal than most people when it comes to exposing body parts and temporarily swapping their girls, this particular biker didn't like it one bit.

Luckily the brothers beat the man to the front of the bar, and made an excuse for Jay to come back to the table with them. Thinking it was unwise to attack three men, without friends of his own to back him up, the man simply gave his girlfriend a quick kiss and seated himself a bit closer to the bar this time.

"Are you about ready?" Sandi questioned Mike soon after the food was gone.

He wasn't about to ask why she wanted to go, because he knew all too well Sandi and Julia were not accustomed to this environment.

A few minutes later, the couple walked outside, toward Mike's car, leaving the noise and smells of good food behind them.

"So you really didn't know this was going to happen tonight?" Sandi asked of the stripping biker women inside.

"Do you really think I would've brought you if I did?"

"No, but who's to say how many times you've come to watch these women show their stuff without me?"

Mike was not about to start an argument, but he wouldn't buckle under his fiancee's questioning either.

"We've seen it once, and that was only because Jay picked the day. He's the one who throws this stuff together, and we don't always come to this place. I'm sorry if you were offended by that stuff, but by the time I found out, it was too late."

Sandi stopped at the car, allowing Mike to open the passenger side door for her.

"I'm starting to think you Sheridan boys are a little strange."

"We're not that different," Mike replied. "There's just more of us."

Mike waited until they were on the road before continuing the conversation.

"I wish you would've said something sooner, Sandi. We could've left anytime, and Jay wouldn't have cared. When he gets drunk, he's in his own little world."

"It's okay," she said half-heartedly. "You guys hardly ever get together, so I didn't want to ruin your night."

"Yeah, but Jay should've known better, and he should have told us what night it was."

Sandi was a bit more upset than she would state, but Mike seemed genuinely innocent of knowing it was amateur night at the tavern.

"For brothers, you guys don't really seem that close," she said instead.

"Well, Dad was always kind of standoffish, so I guess he rubbed off on us." Mike paused a moment to a make a turn. "We all get along, even though we're each a little unique."

"It's not like that with you and Kevin," his fiancee pointed out.

"Well, we've got a lot in common. Jay was always the wild child, Patrick always thought he was a little bit better than the rest of us, and Greg, well, Greg had to make a statement by being everything I wasn't."

"I heard you strived to be the different one," Sandi said, trying to pry for information since Mike was in a talking mood.

"Nah. Don't let Greg fill your head with that shit."

"It wasn't Greg who told me."

Mike grinned to himself and shrugged as he kept an eye on the speedometer.

"You've got to keep in mind, Jay was about to graduate high school when the two of us were born, and aside from Greg, Kevin was all I ever had as a kid. Dad was always working, Mom was doing things around the house, and we just grew up the best we could."

"Did you ever have any big fights?"

"Not really," Mike said, thinking back. "We've always been pretty protective of one another, but it was kind of strange having brothers so much older. It always felt more like they were uncles, because we hardly ever saw them. Kevin was always the one who took us out places, and took us on vacations. I think he took it kind of hard when he found out Greg wasn't going to try out for the fire department. That's when he and I grew a little closer and found out we had a lot in common."

"And your sisters? Did they ever try out for the fire department?"

Mike shook his head.

"Dad told Missy and Casey early in their lives not to follow in his footsteps. Maybe he was sexist, but he didn't think women belonged in our line of work."

"What do you think?" Sandi asked, testing him.

"I don't have a problem with it, and there's going to come a day when we get our first female firefighter. I'll be okay with it."

"Don't you guys ever worry about one another, going into all of these fires?"

"Yeah, a little, but we just worry about doing our jobs right. That way everyone comes out alive."

"When was the last time someone was killed on your department?"

Mike rapped his knuckles twice against the car dash before answering.

"We've never had one."

"Never?"

"Pretty lucky, eh?"

"I'd say," Sandi commented.

She waited a moment before continuing the conversation.

"You think Jay will be okay to get home? He was pretty trashed."

"Jay always finds his way home, and it's usually with one of us driving him."

❧   ❧   ❧

A short time later, the remaining brothers decided to get Jay home, and informed his date that they would give her a lift to wherever she needed to be.

"You sure he'll be okay?" Candi asked Kevin, who had taken a leadership position concerning Jay's safety.

"Oh, he'll be fine."

"We're used to this," Greg commented.

The brothers had already decided Wade would ride his father's motorcycle back to Jay's house, while Greg would drive his intoxicated brother in his car.

Jay knew better than to insist otherwise, because Greg had threatened to arrest him before, and once drew out his handcuffs to prove his point. This time, Jay was barely conscious after downing enough beers that his brothers lost count.

He reeked of alcohol, and almost forgot his gloves, sunglasses, and jacket when he got ready to leave. Greg and Kevin both helped him outside, and made sure everything was paid up.

"Is he usually like this?" Candi asked Greg in parting.

"Oh, not this bad. He just has bad spells like everyone else from time to time."

She quickly took out a pad and pen, jotting something down, before handing it to Greg. He looked, finding a phone number and her name on the scrap paper.

"If he wants to, he can call anytime," Candi said before stepping into Kevin's truck, so he could take her to her hotel.

Greg gave a brief wave, wondering how anyone could still be attracted to his brother after seeing him act so stupidly while drunk. Then again, Jay had a healthy checking account from his business, and a lot of good companionship to offer when he wasn't drinking.

"You ready, big boy?" Greg asked when he slid into the driver's seat, seeing Jay already buckled up beside him.

"I remembered," Jay announced with a slur. "Click it or ticket," he said the police slogan he'd read while traveling through Indiana.

Greg sighed aloud. He pulled out of the parking lot, followed by Kevin, then Wade, who had no trouble handling his father's motorcycle. Wade would get a lift back to the bar to retrieve his car later.

"You're a piece of work sometimes. I can't believe you brought the guys here on amateur night when they were bringing the girls."

"I didn't know they were bringing the wives," Jay said, his eyes glassy, and his breath stronger than cheap cologne.

"And how do you consider it a guys night out when you're bringing your own women to these things?"

"Hey, I like to have fun," Jay defended himself. "And you guys aren't always that much fun."

The alcohol was making him blatantly honest, and Greg wasn't enjoying much of the conversation. Reasoning with Jay when he was drunk was equivalent to throwing a rock at a brick wall in the hopes of toppling it.

"You ever gettin' married again?" Jay almost spat forth, a moment later.

"Maybe," Greg answered evenly. "If I ever find the right girl."

"Just whore around like I do. It's a hell of a lot more fun."

Sure, Greg thought sarcastically. A different sleeping partner every weekend no longer suited him, because he liked stability, and he enjoyed his routine. His life wasn't as perfectly stable as Kevin's, or Mike's, and he knew everyone loved firemen, and disliked cops. Anytime he had a date, he seemed to have one strike against him from the beginning.

At the moment, he was wishing Jay would pass out.

They got within a mile of Jay's house before his older brother spoke again.

"It's times like this I miss Dad," he said. "He was always real strict with us, but he was the glue that held this family together. Look at us now, Greg. We're nothing like we were before."

Greg wanted to let the statement go, but somehow he couldn't.

"How can you say that? We've always gone out together and got together on holidays."

"Yeah, but it ain't the same. Hell, Mom's gone downhill since he died, and here you are chauffeuring me around like I'm some invalid or something."

"You're drunk, Jay."

"Ah, I'm just coping."

"With what?"

No answer. Now Greg could spy his brother's driveway through the windshield.

"Do you have any regrets?" Jay asked with an almost deliberate tone through the grogginess of his voice.

"About what?"

"You know, about letting Dad die."

Greg turned into the driveway, too stunned to bring himself to answer the question. He wanted to let it pass, because Jay was drunk, expressing himself much more heavily than usual, but this was already something plaguing Greg every waking day.

He wanted to know what Jay was implying.

Memories of his father writhing in pain at that fire, accompanied by the screams of the woman he could not save years ago, rushed through his mind like a speeding freight train.

"What the hell do you mean by that?"

"Well, Kevin says you let him die. I don't know if I believe that or not."

Greg pulled the car to a stop near the house, his blood boiling, his muscles tensing, and his breaths coming in heavy, audible exhales. Jay was too wasted beside him to notice the damage he'd done, and Kevin was going to be the recipient of Greg's wrath, not his incognizant oldest brother.

Jay said nothing more, as though even through his drunken state, he realized he had said something he should not have.

Headlights reflected from the windows of Greg's car as their brother pulled into the driveway behind them.

From the way Greg virtually leaped from his car and marched down to Kevin's, his older brother should have known something was wrong, but he simply stepped out, finding two fists clenched around the collar of his shirt.

Greg was fuming at this point. Even his glasses had steamed up from the heat and sweat his face produced in his rage.

His face, and even the bald area atop his head were nearly as red as a fire engine, and he threw Kevin back against his car for added effect. Greg's muscles were like rocks, with furious blood pumping through them. It was very much unlike him to lose his cool over anything, and Kevin was oblivious to why he was being manhandled like a common criminal.

"You mother fucker," Greg stammered, still too angry to decide what action he wanted to take next. "You go around telling our own family I'm the reason Dad died? How the fuck could you?"

"Greg, I-"

"Save it! I've got Jay doing a tell-all in my car on the way over here, and he says you think I'm the reason Dad is gone."

By this time, involuntarily moisture reached Greg's eye. He couldn't remember the last time he had even shed a tear, but the hurt Kevin had caused, coupled with their father's death shortly after Christmas, was too much for him to shoulder anymore.

"Maybe I believed it once," Kevin tried to explain, "but I know better now."

By this time, Wade had pulled up on the motorcycle, unsure of what to think about his two uncles arguing like this. He had never seen any of them come to blows, but he felt almost certain Greg was about to pound Kevin like a jackhammer on concrete.

Against the detective's thick arms, there was little Wade or his intoxicated father could do to stop him if his fists went flying.

"It's a little fucking late, Kev," Greg stated. "Now everyone else thinks I fucked up. You know, I didn't love the man any less than any of you, and I damn sure made the best of a shitty situation Christmas night."

Kevin was now on the defensive.

"No one said you di-"

"Yeah, you did," Greg cut off Kevin once more.

It seemed apparent to Wade that Kevin was beginning to fear for his safety. Comparatively speaking, Greg was a trained killer to the skills any of the firefighters had. Greg also had a firearm tucked in his backside.

Jay had pulled himself from the car, sobering up a bit more quickly in the fresh air. He had enough of his wits to attempt to break up this heated debate between his younger brothers.

"Greg, I never meant to hurt you like that," he said, knowing it was a bit late, after the fact.

"No, Jay, but you sure as hell did. You basically said you both think I'm the reason Dad is dead. Fuck the both of you," he said, shoving Kevin aside, nearly hard enough to send his brother to the ground.

Kevin simply regained his balance and watched in stunned silence as Greg stomped toward his car. Jay backed off, realizing Greg was ready to leave, and snatched his belongings from the back seat just before Greg reached the driver's side door.

"Greg, I'm sorry," he said quickly, trying to ebb the rift he had accidentally caused between the three of them.

"No, fuck you," Greg said, stepping into the car, slamming the door shut behind him.

His window was still down, and he barely looked behind him to make sure everyone was out of the way before backing around Kevin's car.

"You know what," he said as he backed out, still steamed as a lobster in boiling water. "Fuck the whole lot of you. I don't need you."

That said, the three watched him speed down the road, none of them able to utter the first word. Really, there was nothing to say, because Greg had every right to be upset with them.

"Come on," Kevin finally said to Wade, his voice lacking its usual poise. "Let's go get your car."

Later that evening, close to midnight, Mike and Kevin laid atop the hood of Mike's old pickup truck, using the windshield as a backrest, simply staring up to the stars.

Since Kevin's teenage years, the brothers had come to this little stretch of road near downtown, just outside the old hardware store to park their vehicles, drink a bit of beer, and talk about things they couldn't talk about in school, or around the rest of the family.

Mike loved it downtown.

They were mere blocks away from the headquarters fire station, and as far back as he could recall, some of the best nights of his life were spent talking to Kevin about his problems, his dreams, and his social life, sprawled out across the hood of a car or truck.

Especially when he joined the fire department, the spot meant more to him, because it linked him to his memories, his new job, and his older brother.

"I guess I really pissed Greg off tonight," Kevin confessed, knowing he had to be to work early in the morning.

At this point, he didn't care. He held a beer in his right hand, but he was done drinking for the night, knowing he didn't need an excuse for Patrick to discipline him the next morning.

For years, just the two brothers had come to this spot. No Patrick, no Greg. It was the one sacred bond Mike held with his older brother that no one else came between, because no one else knew.

"Greg will be okay," Mike said. "He gets a little too sensitive about stuff like that."

"If you say so, but I thought for sure he was going to beat me into the dirt."

Mike breathed deeply, just taking in the night air as a red blinking light passed overhead. Several jets were leaving the Chicago area at the late hour, and he felt certain he could see constellations he'd never seen before in the clear sky.

Years before, their spot had been the primary hangout for high school students looking to get drunk or high, or even have sex, but there were new spots now, and Mike and Kevin had their patch of gravel, just off the old street, to themselves.

Everywhere around them, they could see city lights, and occasionally hear a truck go by. No cops patrolled this area, and if they did happen by, they were usually looking for troublesome kids. Most every officer knew the Sheridan brothers, because of Greg, and left them alone.

"You know, it sounds corny, but I love this city," Mike confessed. "And this area."

"Why's that?"

"I don't know. It's kind of a mix of loneliness and solitude, I guess. It feels like you're in the middle of nowhere with no one around, but you're not."

Kevin chuckled.

"I think you've had too much to drink."

"No, but I did have sex."

"And I'm sure Sandi was thrilled when I called, asking you to come back out with me."

"Actually, she didn't care. I think she trusts you a hell of a lot more than Jay."

Kevin laughed aloud.

"Yeah. I wonder why?" he asked a rhetorical question.

Though it wasn't the most direct route to the downtown station house, Mike often took the road by the old hardware store and granary just to recall the old days. For a time, he and Kevin worked the downtown station together, and they were a terror to the other guys, often playing jokes, or beating everyone at ping pong and basketball.

"I'm going to confess something to you," Mike finally said. "I don't want you telling this to anyone else, or thinking I'm some sort of mushy kid drooling all over you."

"Shoot," Kevin said.

Historically, everything said at their downtown patch stayed right there, and the two kept their conversations private, because some of them were deeply personal.

"There's never been anything more satisfying for me, than working this job with you."

Kevin looked at him with a smirk.

"Seriously," Mike insisted. "I always wanted to be a fireman like you and Dad, but I never knew if I would really like it or not."

"And?"

"It's the best thing that's ever happened to me, hands down. I honestly can't ask for anything more."

"Me too," Kevin admitted. "Fatherhood was something else that changed me in a good way, and I'm letting you know to enjoy everything you've got right now, because kids take up all your time and money."

"I still can't believe I'm going to be a dad," Mike said with an elated tone. "Everyone thinks it's way too soon, but I can't wait."

"Good for you," Kevin said.

He looked over to the old hardware store, which Mr. Randolph still opened at his convenience on a daily basis throughout the week. The store, and its no-nonsense owner, had been there since Kevin was in high school.

Some things never change, he decided.

"We've gotta work in the morning," he informed his younger brother, as though Mike might have forgotten.

"Yeah, but we can sleep if we have to."

"Sure, but I don't want to be in bed all day. You've got to get me home before Julia kicks my ass."

"All right," Mike agreed, only because he suspected Kevin was already in enough trouble with his wife.

Both brothers slid off the hood of the old truck, and Mike took one last look around them, taking in the nearby buildings of the city, thinking how little the old downtown had changed in two decades since he and Kevin first had personal talks that went deep into the night.

Some things weren't meant to change, he decided before stepping into the truck.

And he liked it that way.

CHAPTER 14

Almost a week had passed when Greg opted to take some overtime on a Saturday night for some additional income, and to keep the horrific thoughts of his failures from entering his mind.

Detectives didn't work midnight shifts or weekends, rotating the on-call investigator every week instead. When overtime came up in the uniform division, it was usually a scramble to snatch up hours, but on this particular weekend, there was a police convention of some sort in Chicago a lot of the officers were attending.

Greg chose to stay close to home, even though he hadn't spoken to any of his family, save his mother, during the past week.

Though Marie Sheridan urged him to open up to his brothers, she didn't know the entire story. She knew whatever slanted version Kevin and Jay cooked up for her. To hear her tell it, his brothers were worried because Greg felt responsible for their father's death.

The longer Greg was alone, the more positive he was that his brothers were set against him, and meant to keep him out of the family.

"I'm being a paranoid conspiracy theory freak," he told himself once more, patrolling the streets of the city shortly after dusk.

Surely his brothers weren't all plotting to alienate him.

Being alone with his thoughts seemed dangerous lately, so the chance to work and keep his mind off family problems, and his miserable transition to his new division, was more than welcome.

He was still getting every menial case possible in the investigative division. He considered it the equivalent of rescuing cats from trees on the fire department. His cases made for great public relations, but did little else in the scheme of actual police work, so far as clearing the real criminal element from the streets went.

All because his sergeant disliked him.

Despite trying to keep busy in his squad car, Greg's mind kept wandering. Once more, he found himself searching for reasons to go on with life.

He had no wife, no kids.

His brothers thought he had basically killed their father, even though he probably didn't do anything differently than they would have.

He saw his mother die a little more each day from within, even if the others didn't.

His job was becoming miserable, because it would take much longer than he had ever imagined to work on significant cases, despite his overall experience.

Greg saw little reason to go on with life, and his mind slipped further down the staircase it had created in its darkest caverns, that led to a dark, unknown place.

Greg had religion, but he felt certain God would never issue him this hard a test in life, and began doubting if there was any afterlife to look forward to if he survived these hardships. After all, life without friends and family was really no life at all.

He sat at a stoplight too long, thinking about his problems, but the driver in the car behind him didn't have the nerve to honk at a marked squad car.

Power had never meant that much to Greg, because he got into police work to serve, not to abuse his authority. Like his brothers, he had a strong sense of obligation to the public he worked for.

Why then, did everything have to be so wrong?

Toward the end of his shift, Greg drove past a set of apartment buildings being renovated during the summer for students to live in, once local college classes started in the fall.

The Brookshire Apartments were nothing more than a labyrinth of staircases and multi-room apartments made of more wood than the world's largest roller-coasters. Locally owned, they were practically abandoned for the summer, with the exception of a few rooms on the far end.

Though the rooms were still locked, the homeless, and occasional vagrant teenagers, found their way inside for a place to sleep, or to vandalize.

Greg saw an eerie flickering from one of the windows in the center of the complex, and knew no one was supposed to be in there. He pulled to the back of the building, shutting his lights off ahead of time, and stepped quietly from the car once he had called his location into his department's dispatchers.

He pulled a key from the departmental key ring on his belt to open a small metallic box mounted at the main entrance. Pulling out a master key from the box that would open any door in the building, short of the manager's office, Greg chose a door that would lead him straight to the source of the flickering light.

Such boxes were spread throughout the city at businesses, schools, and large apartments, and officers held one key that opened any of the boxes.

Allowing police and fire departments access to the building, while keeping it otherwise perfectly secure, the boxes were a fantastic tool for both departments. Both the fire and police departments were issued all kinds of keys to access such buildings in case of emergency quite regularly.

Having the universal boxes made their job just a bit easier, keeping their key collections to a minimum.

He turned his portable radio down before stepping inside the building, and made his way up the creaky wooden steps to the second of three floors. Old and dry, the wood was only half of the building's problem. A major lack of fire stops, combined with small windows, technically put the building out of code by modern standards, but it had been grandfathered as long as it could, before city officials forced the owner to renovate the building, or have it condemned.

Once the second floor's solid door closed behind him, Greg walked along the main hallway, apartments on either side of him, looking for a glow beneath one of the doors that would indicate the room he had spied from the road.

Listening intently for activity, or someone trying to flee from him after hearing the door clank shut behind him, Greg could hear nothing but the sound of his own heavy footsteps along the bare wooden floor.

Odors of cat urine and rotted food of some sort entered his nostrils, indicating the building had been vacated for several months, and obviously unattended in any way.

His eyes adjusted to the darkness of the upstairs, since the power was cut to most of the rooms, then he found the room in question. Greg slowly turned the knob, right hand perched atop his firearm and holster, and swung the door open, finding no one present in the living room.

Looking rather bare, the apartment had no carpet, no real ceiling, and only half of its walls in place. He knew the place was being renovated, but thought this looked a bit more excessive than a simple upgrade and facelift.

In the center, he saw a blanket spread out across the floor, and a candle burning beside it. There was a can opener and a few cans of basic food, like shelters sometimes gave out, as though someone was planning a makeshift picnic.

Greg quickly examined every room, closet, and corner, ensuring no one was inside the apartment before he blew out the candle, then locked the door before leaving.

When he reached his patrol car, he jotted a note in his personal notepad to tell the incoming midnight shift that people were still inhabiting the apartment, and to keep an eye on it.

"I wish the homeless would find someplace legal to stay," he muttered to himself as he replaced his pen and pad in his uniform shirt's breast pocket.

As Greg stepped into the vehicle, a man hiding under an awning, across the parking lot, grinned to himself in the darkness. The first phase of his next planned 'accident' for Carvers Grove was complete, and phase two would take place shortly.

※　　　　※　　　　※

Even at the midnight hour, the Washington Township Fire Department was still having a good time at their north station. Most of the men were spent, after cooking out all day, giving tours of their station to local kids, and swimming in the nearby reservoir.

Many of the men were still at the station, and most of them expected no action whatsoever on a Saturday night. The past few weeks had barely brought them any calls, and every fire run over the last month had been a false alarm except for the abandoned apartments. The four men that bothered to attend that alarm found little reason to save the three buildings, since they were already gutted.

Several firefighters reclined inside the station, settling in for the night within the living quarters, while a majority of the men sat or stood outside, telling stories, or taking in the stars over their heads on a calm summer night. It was considerably less humid than usual, and even the mosquitos were nowhere to be found.

Everything seemed almost too perfect.

Ellis stood with his men, but he wasn't doing much talking. He had been unusually silent most of the day, after Malovich chastised him for the lack of manpower at the fire that destroyed the three old apartments a few weeks back.

"I need you to make sure those stations are manned at all times," the alderman had boldly stated soon after the fire.

"They are," Ellis said, defending himself.

"Not enough. The few fires we've had in our district are always after dark, and your men seem to have a lack of commitment when it comes to their bedtimes."

Ellis took in a deep breath, both under the stars, and back in the conversation he was recalling.

"You're damn lucky Gray didn't blow the whistle on you for letting those burn like that," Malovich stated. "If his head wasn't so far up everyone's ass right now, trying to make his bid for the coroner's job, we'd be toast."

It was now confirmed Gray had thrown his name into the election ring for the coroner's position, since no one else in his political party seemed to want it. It was simply another way for the investigator to give himself power and leverage, and become part of the city's elite.

Of course, he had to win first. Stirring up trouble would not be in Gray's best interest if he wanted the support of certain contributors.

"I'll get the manpower," Ellis recalled promising.

He used threats to get the men to spend nights at the station, and made it mandatory that both stations were manned round the clock. At the same time, he created cookouts and other functions to raise public interest. He hoped to raise the morale of his men as well, and it looked as though he'd succeeded.

Training had been virtually nonexistent lately with the lack of funds. Ellis could barely afford gas for the trucks with the budget so tight, and about the only simulations he could pull off were around the station, trying to mimic the surroundings in a house fire by blinding the men with tape over their air masks, making them search for a dummy, which represented a victim.

Little did they know how quickly that training would be put to the test as the tones went off, stating there was a structure fire in a large apartment building at the edge of town.

He saw the eyes of his men light up, because they were thirsting for action, but the volunteer chief knew exactly what they were about to find themselves in the middle of.

"Holy," Ellis muttered to himself, knowing exactly which building the dispatcher was talking about.

As he climbed into his vehicle, switching on the red warning lights before he even started it, Ellis listened to more of the dispatcher's description, hearing police had already reported homeless people might have been inside earlier that evening, which meant there could be trapped victims.

Bad had gone to worse before Ellis even left the station, and he knew with the Carvers Grove Fire Department running mutual aid with them, it had the possibility of becoming a turf war, which was the last thing anyone needed.

Ellis sighed heavily to himself as he led the way toward the reported fire, seeing a small orange glow in the distance, the moment he left the station.

Despite heavy manpower, and the city fire department's assistance, Ellis could not envision any kind of noteworthy save on the building, considering it was basically one big, oversized matchbook.

His knuckles gripped the steering wheel tightly as he neared the orange glow. He wondered if he was ready for a test of such proportions, and with so many unusual factors.

Ellis would soon find out.

CHAPTER 15

Ellis arrived, finding things even worse than he expected, almost two minutes later.

From top to bottom, the center of the building looked like one big wall of monstrous flame, and the fire began moving in both directions for fresh food.

Though there was a breeze, it was not enough to help spread the fire any more quickly. Like everyone on the city police and fire department, Ellis knew there was an inhabited part of the long apartment building. It seemed to stretch an entire city block, though the backside faced a river, making it impossible to get any kind of vehicle behind it.

This is going to suck, Ellis thought, unable to envision how to stop the fire from spreading short of an interior attack.

Carvers Grove manned an interior attack department, but Ellis seldom sent his men inside on anything more than an isolated room fire. In the distance, he heard the sirens from the Carvers Grove trucks, and suspected they were probably sending at least two or three pieces of apparatus to a fire of this magnitude, even if they were just providing additional support.

"Richie, Luke," he called to two of his men.

They were younger, and not nearly as experienced as the others.

"Go down there and make sure everyone is out of the building," he ordered, pointing to the far end where a few people were staying for the summer.

Though they wanted to stay and contribute, the two young firefighters did as they were told, and marched down toward the end of the building, hoping to appear helpful to the public.

In the meantime, his other men had been stretching hose line out from the pumper trucks and hooking up to a nearby hydrant for a water supply. They were almost ready for further orders, but Ellis had yet to decide how to handle the blaze.

Like a dragon's head, it seemed to loom up and down, then lash out and swing from side to side, showing its power. Smoke plumed in the air from the dragon's nostrils, and without the benefit of full gear, Ellis could feel the radiant heat, even from a reasonably safe distance.

He could smell nothing but burning wood, and heard snaps and crackles as the old wood surrendered to the flames, buckling under the intense heat. Ellis locked his eyes into its form, wondering what kind of challenge it posed.

Deciding he needed to cut it off before sending his men in for a search, he had two teams work their way toward the building on either side of the fire, holding it at bay with streams from their nozzles. He then called for his last pair of firefighters, who were unsure of what to expect.

Ellis put a hand on each of their shoulders as he talked, looking into their eyes through the air masks they had already donned.

"I need you guys to go around back, and if at all possible, get inside and look for anyone trapped," he ordered, knowing the fire was mostly in the front apartments, possibly working its way to the sides, rather than the back. "Take the thermal imaging camera, stick together, and radio me with anything you find. Whatever you do, don't take any chances, and don't get lost."

Both nodded, gathered what they needed, and walked the shortest route possible toward the back of the building.

Ellis had a reputation of not being capable on a fire scene, but he knew what to do after reading numerous texts, and he was performing flawlessly, in his own estimation, on this scene. Experience was a key, he thought, and this certainly wasn't his first big fire.

He watched as his two crews kept the fire at bay, preventing it from moving further outward. Once his first two men evacuated the occupied area of the apartment building, he would set them to searching the non-engulfed areas of the building for stragglers.

Sirens drew closer until the Carvers Grove Fire Department arrived with two trucks and their battalion chief.

Patrick Sheridan had been dispatched just in case Ellis didn't make the call, or got delayed. With volunteers, dispatchers never knew if they were at home, the station, or in a different city. Their policy was dispatch first, ask questions later.

Stepping from his vehicle, the battalion chief knew there was no chance of getting a water supply around the back without going through the building. He wanted to see the deck guns set up for an exterior attack that would flow a greater volume of water inside, as well as the hose lines moved inward to kill the flames before they could do more damage and cause a collapse.

But then, he wasn't technically in charge.

"What have we got, Tom?" he asked Ellis instead, reluctantly submitting his knowledge and experience to the volunteer chief.

Ellis quickly explained where his men were, and what they were trying to accomplish. Until the last statement about the two men doing a search from the rear, Patrick found everything Ellis was doing to be satisfactory.

"You sent two men in the back without a charged line?"

"I had to," Ellis explained.

"Did you send them with a rope, or a line of any kind so they wouldn't get lost?"

"There wasn't time. I told them to use the camera and stick together. The boys out here should have the fire under control in no time."

"It's a fucking maze in there, Tom," Patrick said, raising his voice. "Any part of that roof, or any one of those floors could collapse any second."

Behind the battalion chief, Kevin, Mike, and Conley finished getting geared up and ready to help with an interior attack, or whatever they might be ordered to do. Kevin didn't particularly care for the setup Ellis had chosen, but he was in less of a position to make his point than Patrick.

Thomas helped the volunteer driver set up the deck gun on his truck, just in case it was ordered into use. Afterward, he would probably have to help set up another truck for pumping, possibly from a different hydrant if one was available.

Ellis stared at the front of the building a moment, thinking about the battalion chief's warning. A large eave made an eerie sound as its metallic frame twisted and contorted at the mercy of the flames, before it fell entirely off the front of the building, crashing to the ground with a thousand sparks that looked like fireworks as they sprayed into the air.

"Okay," Ellis said to Patrick. "I'll get them out of there."

If it's not too late, the battalion chief thought to himself, wondering if he would have risked his own men in that mess to begin with, even with proper technique. He would have trusted Kevin's judgment, and Kevin certainly would have entered the building from the back if possible. Ellis, however, didn't have the luxury of seasoned personnel, like the paid department.

"Do you have more people on the way?" Patrick asked the chief.

"Probably a dozen or so."

Patrick nodded. He would request dispatchers to send another truck just in case, but he worried about the personnel already committed to this blaze, and how on earth they were going to attack it without getting to its backside.

"Can you get one of your crews through the apartments with a line to hit the back?" he questioned Ellis, rather than tell the chief what he would do.

The apartment building was too thick to simply ignore its backside.

"I've got it under control," Ellis said with a tone indicating he didn't want any further input.

Patrick watched the chief's firefighters back down from the blaze a little bit, and it started moving out to both sides. They were hitting the center, then hitting the sides, but the fire was sneaking into the back of the building where they couldn't hit it at all.

What he didn't notice, was the old five-inch supply hose, which fed the old Washington Township pumper truck its essential water supply, had a small leak the size of a pin hole. While he was concentrating on the scene, the tiny hole was spurting water out at a high pressure. At the side of the truck, even the driver was oblivious to the leak, and everyone else was scrambling to get ready, or to help him.

Both the trucks and equipment for the volunteer department were bought used, and despite ample testing when the equipment came to the department, things were bound to break down.

And they were about to.

Both Sean Carson and Bill Jones were scared out of their minds as fire roared up around them, and they realized they were completely lost in the vast hallways and rooms throughout the apartment.

Their only defense was to crouch as low to the ground as possible, where the air was a bit cooler, and continue crawling to find an exit point.

With their camera's battery almost dead, and of little help in this funhouse of horrors where everything looked alike, no matter where they went, they felt certain they were about to die. What looked to be windows in the camera were nothing more than mirrors, and all of the doors seemed to just lead into other rooms.

Carson, the older and more experienced of the two, held the camera. By all accounts, it looked as though they were heading into fire no matter where they went, and he was simply trying to look for a dark spot in the camera lens, which indicated cooler areas. In the scope of the camera's grayscale, white was bad and black was good.

Everything looked like solar flares through the lens, except for one dark gray spot ahead, and to his right. He grasped Jones to make sure the chunky firefighter was still with him, and conscious, and started toward the spot. From there, he hoped to radio Ellis and relay their desperate situation to the chief.

As the two firefighters made their way into some sort of cubby hole, which Carson guessed was a closet, he plucked his radio from its clip on his heavy coat, then radioed Ellis.

"Chief, this is Carson," he said, trying to keep some calm in his voice so he could be understood. "We're trapped somewhere on the second floor and can't find our way out of here."

"Are you safe?" Ellis asked, everyone around him listening for some news.

Each of the fire departments used a different frequency with their dispatchers, so they could not use the same radios to communicate.

"We've got fire all around us," Carson reported. "We can't find our way out, and we're stuck up here."

"Stay calm, Sean," Ellis said. "We're sending up a team to find you."

Patrick had already gotten Kevin's attention, and now pulled him close.

"Take Sam and find those guys. Make sure you bring whatever you need to find your way back out," he said with stern resolve.

Kevin nodded, but Mike wasn't content with being left behind.

"Kev," he almost pleaded with his lieutenant through his face mask.

His brother.

"I've got more experience than Sam. Take me up there with you."

"No way," Kevin answered. "If something happens to me, I want you to come looking for me. I need you out here, Mike."

Though he understood his brother's point, Mike still wasn't pleased about being left behind. He took off his helmet and face mask, knowing they would not be necessary until Patrick ordered him inside, or to man a hose line. A look of concern crossed Mike's face while he observed his brother and Conley gathering up two rolled hose lines, some bags of rope, their own thermal camera, and a prying tool.

Within a moment, they disappeared into one side of the building, not yet touched by flames, and went through the back for the quickest response time possible to the trapped firefighters.

When they reached the access point, Kevin noticed the flames reaching dangerously close to the back end of the building. He ordered Conley to help him connect the two hose lines together, then tied a rope around the end of the line. Hose would not be destroyed in a fire, short of a flashover, unlike rope, so he hoped to have some realistic chance of finding his way back out, even if the rope started to burn.

The two finally hooked up their air lines to their packs, then turned everything on. Kevin made certain Conley's valve was open and working, then set to leading them inside.

He found a wrought iron fence to wrap one end of the hose line around, to serve as the anchor point, so they could make their way out in an emergency.

"Stay down," he told Conley as soon as they entered the building.

While Conley kept hold of his lieutenant's ankle, he let the hose unravel as they went, to serve as a breadcrumb trail for them to find their way to the back entrance. In the meantime, Kevin looked ahead with the camera, seeing nothing but flames drawing dangerously close.

Though visibility wasn't bad yet, it would soon grow worse as they moved further into the building, and the fire continued to spread.

He stopped a moment to use his radio once they reached the bottom of the stairway that would take them to the second floor.

"Patrick, have Chief Ellis get his men to yell for us, without using their radios, in about thirty seconds," Kevin requested, knowing it would take nearly that long to get settled atop the stairs. "And see if you can't get us some water back here, please. We're getting roasted."

"Clear," he heard the reply from his older brother, meaning Patrick would honor all of his requests.

As both men fought their way up the stairs, Kevin was relieved to see water stream inside, killing some of the flames, giving them a touch of relief from the intense heat. Conley ran out of hose line at the top of the stairs, and started to pull rope from the bag to continue his breadcrumb trail.

He hoped it wouldn't touch the flames, or its life span would be considerably short.

"Lieutenant Sheridan," Kevin heard his older brother say over the line, "this is Chief Sheridan."

"Go ahead," Kevin said, wanting to get on with the task at hand, rather than monkey around with the radio all night.

"One of the trapped firefighters is low on air," Patrick reported. "We can hear the tones in his pack going off through the radio."

Well, I can't, Kevin thought, realizing the firefighters had to be further from him than he'd originally hoped, or trapped behind several walls.

"Clear," the lieutenant answered, realizing it was more important than ever to find them quickly.

Kevin realized they were out of the durable hose line, and wanted to make certain he could make it back to a safe point. By now he could barely hear the men yelling from down the hall, as they were ordered to do by Ellis.

Little more than thickening smoke filled the hallway as Kevin stared down toward the origin point of the yelling. He knew the fire would be entering the rooms to his right, and the backside of the building was to his left. With danger closing in, he could ill afford to lose his bearings.

"Stay here and be my reference point," he ordered Conley with a muffled voice through the air mask.

Conley nodded in understanding, though he didn't like being left in the middle of a growing inferno.

"If I start yelling, you start yelling back until I find you," Kevin ordered. "Whatever you do, don't leave the end of this hose line or I'll beat you silly with it."

Kevin started crawling down the hall, rope trickling out of the bag as he went, to leave a trail. Within a matter of seconds, he was gone from Conley's view, swallowed by the thickening smoke.

"This sucks," Conley muttered to himself, hoping their packs held out long enough to rescue the two men.

CHAPTER 16

Regardless of what fire department he belonged to, each man on the scene was readily concerned about the lives of two trapped firefighters, who were now desperately low on air.

Patrick suspected the two men were probably a bit anxious and scared of such an unusual situation, and breathed a lot deeper, and more often, than usual. In turn, that would deplete the air in their tanks much faster.

From what few reports the two trapped firemen gave, they had gone deeper into the building than they intended to, and it seemed the flames were attempting to surround them. He had to trust that Kevin was taking the right steps in finding the men, and that his own decision to keep Mike out of the fray would prove correct.

It had taken every ounce of management control Patrick could muster to keep Mike busy enough to keep him from asking every few minutes if he could follow Kevin and Conley inside to help in the search. Since the two had left for the back of the building, Mike had been a Mexican jumping bean, hardly able to contain himself, he wanted action so badly.

Mike was aggressive, and he was one-hundred percent devoted to Kevin. He didn't fancy the idea of his lieutenant facing danger without him one bit.

At the moment, Patrick spied him checking one of the map books for another hydrant location, but there probably weren't any available. Using a siamese adapter, the firefighters could hook up another pumper truck to the same hydrant, using the two smaller coupling ends on the hydrant, but the result would probably be the same as dedicating the water to a single truck, unless they wanted more hand lines available.

Hydrants could only flow so many gallons per minute, no matter what.

"How much longer do you figure that framework is going to hold up?" Ellis asked the battalion chief.

"Not much longer," Patrick answered. "We need to get everyone away from there and contain the fire to that area once all of our guys are out."

Ellis nodded, then stared at the three stories in front of him. A section of about a dozen apartments was already destroyed, or soon would be. He suddenly regretted ever sending his men into such a dangerous situation, but knew the man beside him would have done the same exact thing, and actually just had.

He wasn't embarrassed yet, but Ellis was worried about his two firefighters. He didn't need the Carvers Grove Fire Department upstaging him, but politics were meaningless to him at the moment. Bad things happened to even the best departments, and he would tell Malovich to stick his media games up his ass when it was all said and done.

The orange glow could be see for miles around, and traffic was practically at a standstill as motorists watched the ensuing battle around the apartments.

Though it couldn't advance, the fire wasn't surrendering either.

Ellis turned to some of his fresh firefighters, who had just arrived at the scene in their personal vehicles.

"Go and relieve the guys on the lines," he ordered, pointing to the firefighters manning the hose lines near the apartment. "Keep a safe distance, and hit the rear side, too."

A moment passed, with each man wondering what was going on inside, each wanting to help, but ordered to stay out front by the two chiefs in command.

Each firefighter felt useless, just standing there, but everything that could be done was getting done. Adding additional hose lines from another truck meant shutting down the hydrant to add another supply line, and with the fire contained, Ellis wasn't about to risk running out of water in his current pumper for even a second.

Patrick tapped his foot nervously on the ground, wishing the two firefighters would radio something, anything, to their chief.

Almost a dozen men stood behind the chiefs, waiting for something to do, or just to hear some news. Each understood the sensation of being lost inside a building, though they had never experienced it on such a grand scale.

Finally, Jones radioed back to Ellis, and he sounded hoarse, as though he'd been breathing the smoky air, now on his last legs.

"Chief, this is Jones," he said. "Sean's out of air, and we're buddy breathing."

Ellis stood there a moment, just letting the words sink in. If they were buddy breathing, their air supply was almost completely gone, and there was no telling how far away help was. They had heard nothing from Kevin, and he would have no idea the two men were almost out of air, unless Patrick could radio him the information.

The chief's eyes stared at the ground as he breathed heavily, then looked skyward, as though for some kind of spiritual intervention.

"Don't talk, Bill," Ellis finally said into the radio. "Save your air. Help is on the way."

If the environment was as toxic and hot as Ellis suspected it was, they would last a minute at best without the benefit of their air tanks. His heart sunk at the thought of losing two men for nothing.

He saw no way the lieutenant could reach the two men and pull them both to safety if they were out of air. Even if Conley was with him, they would have a tremendously difficult time in any sort of rescue effort, since the men were trapped in the middle of the building, on the second floor, and apparently nowhere near an exit door.

Patrick quickly relayed the situation to Kevin, who wasted few words in his response.

"Clear," came the brief reply.

Just about the time Mike started to approach the battalion chief once more, he heard a strange noise from behind him.

Whirling to find the tiny leak spurting water upward, Mike saw the leak suddenly become a gash as the thick supply line's outer yellow jacket pulled apart like skin slit with a sharp blade. The old, rotted insides had finally given way, and let the water burst out through the weakened exterior layer, which already had a hole of its own.

"Oh, shit!" Mike exclaimed as water began to gush from the hose line, instantly cutting pressure to the pumper truck.

With two lines active from the truck, they had approximately two minutes of water supply from the truck's tank, at best. Mike and the others scrambled toward the useless supply hose as the driver shut down the truck's suction, so they could replace the damaged section with a good one.

Like a pit crew at a race, the firefighters worked in unison to get the truck a working water supply, because they both had firefighters at risk inside the dilapidating building.

Mike knew there would be a delay in switching supply hoses, because the water from the hydrant would have to be temporarily shut down. This action would probably leave them with no water for a minute or two once the truck's tank was exhausted, no matter how quickly they worked.

He hoped Kevin was out of harm's way, or he would soon find himself in the middle of a fiery oven.

❧   ❧   ❧

Following the occasional cries of the men down the hall, Kevin mentally noted where he was at all times, and to this point, he hadn't turned, or gone into any rooms.

His path was consistently straight, and he wanted to keep it that way.

A moment passed with no sound whatsoever, and the lieutenant decided to call out for the two men, needing to know if they were still alive.

"Are you guys there?" he called down the hallway, suspecting he was close. "I'm with Carvers Grove! Give me a holler if you can hear me!"

"Down here!" Jones yelled a reply, letting his partner suck down the last of their fresh air.

Until this moment, Jones had prepared himself for certain death. Whether he remained with his partner in this corner, or went scurrying desperately for a way out, he was sure they would run out of fresh air to breathe and succumb to the thick smoke before escaping the maze that ensnared them.

Jones had made peace with God, and even made some promises to the Lord he would carry through, if allowed to survive this ordeal.

Hearing someone else's voice, however, gave him new hope that he might live to see his wife and kids again.

Kevin quickly made his way down the hall, following the noise of the expiring air pack bells and warning alarms that went off when firefighters stood still for too long. Using the camera, still crawling beneath the most intensely heated areas, Kevin made his way into an apartment, then a bathroom secluded from most of the fire and smoke.

Fire crawled along the ceiling over him, as though it hadn't spotted him yet. Still, it had two prisoners, and seemed to be content just to corner the Washington Township firemen.

Thankful the two had been intelligent enough to find a safe spot and stay there, Kevin still had his own bearings, and figured he could get the two firemen to fresh air in time to save them both.

Crouched as low as they could get inside the room, the two firefighters wore every piece of protective equipment available, except their air masks. They had taken those off, since their air supply was mostly depleted, to share the remaining pack's air, until it expired as well. The firemen also needed to be heard when yelling for help, so they would call out for Kevin, then put their masks to their faces for protection from the intense heat.

"Strap your masks back on," Kevin ordered, not wasting a second of time. "Stick the air hoses down your coats, and you'll get some cleaner air."

Both were still cognizant enough to understand what he was asking of them, and complied. Their camera had long since died, which was part of the reason they stayed where they were.

"I've got a rope with me," Kevin stated with an air of confidence the two men were secretly relieved to hear. "I'm going to follow it back out to my partner, and I want you both to grab my ankles, or the rope. I won't leave you behind, and we'll be out of here in no time."

Ever the calm, collected officer, Kevin gained the trust of both men quickly, and led them down the hallway, following his rope, until he found it severed. He picked up the end, finding it burned, and flames quickly building all around him.

If not for the flames, he would still have found his way back to Conley at the stairway just crawling straight ahead, but it seemed a change in plan was needed.

"Sam?" he called, suddenly realizing the hissing sound of water destroying the flames was no longer present.

"Over here!" he heard a call, realizing a wall of flames separated him from his partner.

No chance of getting to Conley presented itself, and Kevin found his mind racing for a solution to this new problem. Getting out the way he entered was no longer an option.

"Get the fuck out of here and have them set up some ladders in the back," he called to his firefighter. "I'll have to get these guys out some other way."

"Okay," Conley simply said before obeying his orders, following the hose line back to the entrance they had used earlier.

"We're okay," Kevin assured the two men, despite the flames now dancing over their heads, arming themselves for a flashover, which almost always proved fatal to even the best equipped firemen.

Hot gases were mingling, raising the air temperature considerably, and Kevin needed to find a way outside immediately, even if it meant jumping from a second story window. Getting a few broken bones was considerably better than looking like a chicken breast left on the grill for too long.

He quickly crawled to his right, remembering which way was the back of the building.

"Come on," he said, staying low, shouldering an apartment door that would lead to an outside vantage point.

It was locked, but gave way rather easily, since it was already damaged from the heat and strenuous conditions around it.

Kevin wondered why the water had stopped spraying, having no idea of the supply line trouble his colleagues were experiencing outside. Still, if all went well, he would be a free man in a minute or two.

"Shut that door," he ordered one of the firefighters, once they were all inside the apartment.

Carson complied, but he had to jam the door into its frame to get it to stay put. The lieutenant had broken the lock mechanism by busting through, but by all accounts, things were looking up.

Kevin had no desire to let the fire in behind them, like a stray, rabid animal, meaning them harm. As long as the fire remained trapped in the hallway, it posed no threat to them.

Comparatively speaking, the room had less smoke than the three men had experienced across the hall. Kevin knew the heat vapors were building up as the fire moved in their direction, with no water to force it back. Each of the men still sweltered from the radiant heat, but at least they were away from the flames.

He quickly searched the apartment, using his camera to identify the back window above a table in the family room. Seeing it was barely large enough to let an average man through it, Kevin recalled part of the renovation being for safety, which was to include larger windows, fire escapes, and reinforced walls to block, or at least slow, fire from spreading.

To this point, he had seen none of those improvements.

"That fucking window is a tight fit," he said, standing halfway up to examine it. "We're going to have to take our packs off to fit through, then jump to the ground."

Both men shot him quizzical stares, as though this wasn't the rescue they were expecting.

"It's either that or we can hope they get the ladder to the right window, and I'm not hanging out in this shit any longer than I have to," the lieutenant said, answering their thoughts.

Reluctantly, both men stripped themselves of their air packs, despite more heat and smoke making its way inside the room. Jones stood at the window, ready to make the jump, and Kevin used a nearby hammer he had found lying on the floor to smash out the window, not seeing the apartment's entrance door buckle just a little.

Flames licked the bottom of the door from the hallway outside, sensing the new oxygen supply Kevin had just created.

And they wanted more.

"That's a long way," Jones complained, once seated on the window frame.

"Jump you moron," Kevin chided, "or we're all going to be crispy stiffs in a matter of seconds."

Jones forced himself to make the jump, especially with Carson pressing lightly against his back, wanting to get out of the building just as desperately. Jones heard a bone in his lower leg snap upon impact with the ground, but mostly because he was a bit overweight, and landed somewhat awkwardly.

He let out a cry of pain as Carson seated himself at the window. Kevin was removing his own air tank and helmet, to ensure he wouldn't get snagged on anything in his escape. He could hear the sound of water starting up again, and wondered what the holdup had been.

"Go!" he ordered Carson, taking his air mask off for added emphasis, failing to see the door bulge once more from the intense heat on the other side, and the fire pushing to reach the new source of oxygen.

Carson jumped, landing much more intact than his partner had, simply thankful to be alive.

Kevin took a few seconds to toss the thermal cameras to the ground below, then felt a burning tingle reach his ears through his protective hood as the heat in the room rose even more. Without his helmet or mask, he was more vulnerable to the heat, but decided it wouldn't matter in a few seconds.

As he started lifting his first leg toward the open sill, Kevin froze, hearing a strange moaning noise behind him. The noise, sounding almost distinctly human, got the lieutenant to turn fully around as his instinct to save lives kicked in once more.

The groaning apartment door gave way, letting a virtual stream of flame race for the open window, like a flamethrower aimed at a target.

Unfortunately, the lieutenant stood in its path of destruction.

A stream of fire burst through the door, hugging the ceiling for some sort of fuel source, as it reached the other side of the room in less than a second's time.

Less protected than usual, Kevin felt the raging flames pass through his turnout gear, searing him inside and out as the fire took any opening it could find. Pain shot through his body, the likes of which he had never experienced as he bounced off one wall, unable to steady himself against the force of the flames. He hit the wall hard, adding to the disorientation he already felt from the unbearable heat.

He let out a long, agonizing scream as his skin bubbled from the instant third degree burns, and the two firefighters on the ground below could only watch in horror as the fire retreated for a moment, then let loose its full wrath on the disarmed firefighter.

Without the benefit of his helmet or air pack, Kevin was far more exposed than usual, and the flames found their way into his gear through the smallest of crevices. His face, arms, and chest felt like hot grease was continuously being poured onto them, and he lost all collective thought as pain overtook every rational part of his brain.

The lieutenant stood helplessly, thinking briefly of Julia and the kids in his numbed state, as though he knew his body would be unable to survive the trauma it had already experienced.

He was so close to escape, yet too mentally and physically injured to comprehend it, as the force of the flames sprinting to the window knocked his head against the wall above its frame, rendering him unconscious, as the rest of the fire moved in for the kill.

"Oh, God," Carson muttered, fumbling for his radio, seeing flames now shooting out of the window they had just jumped from.

CHAPTER 17

As he sat on the top part of his couch, Greg thought about all of the wrongs in his life, trying to search for something positive.

Still dressed in his uniform, Greg had been off work for three hours now, oblivious to the fact that the area of the building he had inspected for homeless people earlier, was now little more than a pile of rubble.

He thought back to the Christmas fire, and even several years before that, to the fire that claimed the life of a woman after he had taken a wrong turn on an upstairs apartment floor, then got himself trapped behind a door that only opened one way.

It was a community apartment building that offered assisted living to the elderly, but Greg felt certain he had assisted no one that night. While most of the guys on the department knew where the one-way access doors were, and which ones not to go through, Greg didn't.

He had been busy studying for the police tests, and didn't memorize building layouts the way a volunteer firefighter probably should have.

As soon as the door closed behind him, Greg sensed he was trapped, and though he was right beside the door, its sturdy metallic frame forbid him reentry.

Electrical wires made it impossible to rescue the woman with a ladder, and by the time another crew got to her floor to rescue her, she had already jumped to her death to avoid the intense heat coming up from the fully engulfed floors below.

Greg had two dark nights in the back of his mind. Both mistakes were attributable to inexperience in the fire service, but he felt just as guilty, regardless.

At one time, he drew strength from his family.

Especially his brothers.

After the divorce, they were there for him. They took him out, took his mind off his problems, and even took turns giving him a place to stay while he went through countless court battles. At one of the lowest points in his life, they made it tolerable, and Greg drew strength from the bond he shared with his brothers.

His sisters were there for him too.

They tried to get him dates at their workplaces, but he was never quite ready to start a relationship again. There were a few times he went drinking and had meaningless sex on the weekends, but commitment was now something Greg was very much afraid of.

Giving full devotion to one person, only to have her tear apart every shred of what made him who he was, made Greg a hardened soul.

Now, after surviving all of those low points, he felt betrayed by those he held dearest, and began harboring serious doubts about his performance on Christmas Day. He despised Jay and Kevin for thinking he had failed their father, and even more so for voicing their opinions.

From his perch atop the couch, he saw his answering machine's red light blinking twice quickly, then pausing for a moment.

He had two messages.

For the past week, Jay and Mike had called, trying to make amends, though he had no beef with Mike.

Greg pressed the play button to get tonight's messages over with.

"Greg, this is Jay," the first began with his brother's throaty voice. "Look, I'm sorry about last week, and I wish to God you would call me back. I was drunker than shit and I didn't know what I was saying. So, please, just give me a call back. I'll be in town most of this week."

A beep separated it from the second message.

"Hey, Greg, this is Mike," his twin's voice said from the machine. "I know you're at work, but you really need to call Jay back. He feels terrible about what happened last week. Look, I know how you feel, and if you need someone to talk to, I'll be up late at the station tonight. Just give me a call whenever you get the chance."

Another beep, and the machine was finished.

Greg wondered how much his brothers would actually miss him when he was gone, and he looked to his service weapon lying on the coffee table before him. Its cold, steel barrel glistened from what little light emitted from the kitchen.

He felt a tear come to his eye once more, and he had found himself crying at home rather often during the past week. Emotionally, he was breaking down, going through various phases of depression, and he knew it.

But he didn't care.

Everything around him was in ruins. His former marriage, his family, and even the new house he was renting. His heart felt heavy in his chest, and his mind felt like mud trying to climb a hill. He couldn't see the top of the figurative hill, and there seemed to be no way out of the troubles plaguing his mind.

Greg reached for the gun, examined it, and pointed it at his head, just to see how ready he was to take his own life.

Ready enough, he decided, making sure the safety was off, and the gun had a bullet in the chamber.

Though he wasn't sobbing, a teardrop ran down his cheek, hitting the gun as he raised it to his mouth, opening wide for the barrel's easy access.

He wanted to make sure he did this right, because he had seen suicide victims who lived, and they were grotesque shadows of their former selves. A note sat on his kitchen table explaining everything, and who would receive what few possessions he still owned.

Greg had just positioned the gun correctly when his phone rang, acting as the rarest of signs in the middle of the night for him to stop what he was doing.

He didn't care.

He ignored the first five rings, but they were nuisance enough to distract him from finishing the task at hand. Greg finally decided he could kill himself later when it was a bit more peaceful. Perhaps, just perhaps, there was actually something good waiting for him on the other end of the line.

Snatching the phone from its receiver just before the answering machine would have kicked in, Greg swallowed hard, putting the phone to his ear.

"Hello?"

"Greg, it's Patrick," his older brother said from the other end.

Patrick *never* called him. He was the one brother Greg never seemed to have communication with, short of family gatherings.

So why was he calling in the middle of the night?

"What's going on?" Greg questioned, knowing his brother was at work, usually in a deep sleep at this time.

"We had a fire tonight," Patrick said, trying to soften the blow of what he was about to announce. "Kevin went inside to save two guys from the volunteer department, and, uh-"

Greg sat in shock as he heard his older brother's voice crack, certain he heard Patrick sniffle back some painful sobs. The one thing Greg and Patrick shared was their unemotional attachment to anything. They never cried, but ironically, they were both breaking down this evening.

"Kevin didn't make it back out," Patrick finished quickly between brief sobs.

"Oh, fuck," Greg heard himself say before he even knew it. "No," he added numbly, thinking Kevin couldn't be gone.

Kevin couldn't die without him getting an opportunity to apologize for the other night. It just didn't seem possible.

Not fair.

"Where are you?" Greg asked, trying to clear his mind.

"We're at the Brookshire Apartments, trying to dig out his body," Patrick said hesitantly.

Greg could hear commotion in the background, though it didn't sound very hectic. He expected it to sound more like a beehive if they were desperately trying to free someone.

"How can you be sure he's gone?" Greg had to ask.

A few seconds of silence.

"He's gone, Greg. If you could see what I'm looking at, you'd understand."

Greg sat in stunned silence a moment.

"I'll, uh, be down there in a little bit," Greg finally said, all of his problems vanquished within the span of two minutes.

"Okay," Patrick said before terminating the call on his cellular phone.

With everyone in the family contacted except his mother, Patrick looked to the pile of rubble before him, knowing there was no way anyone could have survived.

Taking a tremendous chance to begin with, his firefighters had set up a ladder at the window Jones and Carson indicated they leaped from, but the building began to crumble under its own weight shortly thereafter, crushing the ladder and everything in its path on the way down.

Patrick had witnessed heavy flames shooting from the room just before the collapse, and knew if his brother was inside, there was no way he was alive.

In a manner of speaking, the building had practically put itself out when major support beams on either side of the middle section gave way, sending that area of the building down upon itself. Charred debris brought down fresh wood from the neighboring sections with it, creating a potpourri of remains.

To an onlooker, it appeared as though someone had taken an eraser to one whole section of the long complex, leaving the eraser crumbs in the center, which were actually piles of ash and wooden remains.

Now, with the fire completely out, and the rest of the apartment building saved, the crews began the unenviable task of sifting through the charred remains, looking for a fallen firefighter.

Despite his broken leg, Jones made paramedics splint him up on the spot so he could see if there was any chance the man who had saved his life might be alive. He felt terrible, thinking if he had jumped a few seconds sooner, maybe the lieutenant might have made it out before the fire overtook the room.

Steam and wisps of smoke filtered upward from the piles of burnt debris, and the smell would linger for miles in any direction. Police, reporters, and all kinds of onlookers were huddled on the other side of the decimated building, hoping for some good news after hearing a fireman was missing.

Jay had volunteered to tell Marie Sheridan one of her children wasn't coming home again. He never stopped by the scene, and had no desire to. Jay simply took Patrick's word, woke their church's pastor, and started toward their mother's house after picking up the pastor on the way.

"It'll absolutely kill her," Patrick said to Mike, who wasn't in the mood to hear anything related to his brother's death.

"That should've been me in there," Mike muttered to himself, wanting to blame Patrick in some way for Kevin's demise. "You should have sent me with him."

Patrick took Mike aside, making certain no one else was around.

"If I had sent you, Kevin would have done the same thing he did with Sam, and nothing would've changed. I knew damn well how dangerous it was sending him up there without water, and I wasn't about to risk the both of you."

He paused a moment to check his emotions, keeping as stern a face as possible given the circumstances.

"I loved Kevin too, but there was no way I was going to put both of you at risk."

Mike shook his head, feeling his emotions begin to overwhelm him. He wanted to break down completely, but he was still on the scene, still in front of everyone. He wasn't about to disgrace Kevin by displaying open emotion in front of a crowd.

"The kids, Pat, the kids. And Julia, what is she going-"

Patrick shut his brother up by pulling him into a hug, before Mike went completely hysterical on him.

"We'll work it out," he said quietly, feeling Mike break down against his shoulder in heaved sobs. "We're family. We'll get through this."

He led Mike to a dark, quiet area, where the building was still safe to sit beneath. There, he let Mike vent his frustrations by himself, while he returned to see the progress of the sifting and digging.

"I'm sorry," Ellis said, approaching the battalion chief. "It never should have come to this."

"No, it shouldn't have," Patrick replied evenly, thinking of a hundred reasons he wanted to slug Ellis at that moment, but none of his reasons would bring Kevin back.

There never should have been an inexperienced volunteer department.

Tom Ellis never should have been chief.

Ellis never should have assumed command of this fire scene.

Kevin never should have gone upstairs to rescue two men from the volunteer department that never should have existed to begin with.

Everything added up, but Patrick hated the end result.

Now his department had suffered its first casualty ever, and his family would endure its second big loss in a year's time.

Gray had shown up, but chose to save his condolences until the body was found, preferring to start the daunting task of searching for a cause and origin. In the pile of ash and charred timbers laid before him, finding either would take some time, and some cooperation from local authorities.

He avoided most of the firefighters, working with police officers on the scene instead, trying to seal off the scene with yellow tape and a police guard. If he determined the fire was intentionally set, it would be nothing less than murder in the eyes of the courts and his own department.

Just as Greg made his way past the police at the front of the scene, the firefighters announced they had found Kevin's body, though none of them could bear to look at it for more than a second. The smell was horrendous, and most had to take a few steps back.

Mike took notice of the commotion from his resting area. All at once, he stood and charged the group of firefighters standing over the body.

"I want to see him," he said, trying to push past Patrick and several other firefighters who were holding him back. "I've got to see."

They restrained Mike while several other firefighters brought a body bag over to the area, and Gray was consulted about moving the body, since it was being treated as a crime scene.

Since Kevin's death was not directly related to the cause of the fire, and it would only add more pain and suffering if left there, he quickly told the inquiring firefighters to move it once they had the coroner's blessing, which they quickly received.

"You don't want to see it," Patrick said, still helping to hold Mike back.

He clasped his younger brother by the shoulders as Greg joined the group in making sure Mike didn't see his brother's body.

"Do you want to remember him like this?" Patrick asked in his older brother tone. "Do you want this to be your last memory of how Kevin looked?"

"No," Mike finally decided, hanging his head as he walked away from the group.

Greg had seen the worst possible dead bodies in his decade of law enforcement, but even he cringed a bit, catching a glimpse of Kevin's charred remains as the firefighters quickly worked to place his body inside the black bag, the smell escaping the contained area.

"God," Greg said to himself before walking over to the edge of the building and vomiting.

Like a nurse making rounds, Patrick walked up behind him, putting an arm on his shoulder, having seen their brother's body as well.

"You probably shouldn't have seen that either," he said, unsure of what else to say, or think, at the moment.

"What the hell happened?" Greg demanded, wanting to know why Kevin had to die.

"He saved two lives," Patrick said. "This whole fire was a goddamned catastrophe to begin with."

"But why? What the hell went wrong?"

Greg was feeling a bit bold, especially after almost taking his own life earlier. He wanted answers, and he didn't care how he got them.

"Two of the Washington Township guys got lost inside," Patrick started to explain. "We, uh, *I* sent Kevin and Sam Conley in there to find them, then the water supply died, and the building just deteriorated before we could get back there to pull Kevin out."

Greg shook his head negatively. He wasn't satisfied, and he now fully understood why his brothers detested the new volunteer department so much.

He looked over to the group of volunteers, who seemed to be huddled by themselves. They couldn't be happy about their performance, and certainly not about the death of a fire department's officer.

Ellis began assigning them cleanup tasks to keep their minds off the incident, in the hopes of getting them all out of there before the city police and fire departments started hammering them with questions.

Gray shot the chief an unfriendly stare, and Ellis felt certain they would be having a discussion about the events at the fire scene sooner than later.

While all of this was going on, Greg and Patrick looked to Mike, who was seated beside the stream, thinking about nothing aside from his loss.

To him, Kevin was much more than a brother. He was Mike's fishing buddy, his confidant, his role model, and his officer on the fire department. Mike felt certain he had let Kevin down, even if he had direct orders from both of his older brothers to stay put.

"What are we going to do with him?" Greg asked, more concerned about his twin than anything else at the moment.

"Watch him," Patrick said. "Very carefully."

Thinking his brother was a walking time bomb, Patrick observed Mike walk up to the ambulance as the emergency medical technicians loaded the body bag for transport to the morgue. He put his hand on the large box-shaped vehicle, looking through the back window until it pulled away, as though watching his best friend go away for the summer, like he did as a kid.

He turned finally, his stare burning a hole through Ellis, and his brothers saw Mike storm in the chief's direction, ready to get some retribution for his loss. A hoard of firefighters held him back before he could openly swing at the volunteer chief, and Ellis decided it was time for him to leave.

"You mother fucker!" Mike shouted from the half dozen arms restraining him. "If I get my hands on you, you're dead."

Ellis said nothing as an empathetic look crossed his face, and he turned to leave.

Mike wanted someone to blame, and the chief was as good a target as he could think of.

"That's it!" Mike continued as his fellow firemen kept him restrained. "Kill my brother, then take off like the chicken-shit you are!"

As Ellis pulled away, Mike was finally set free, and the others slowly parted from him, leaving him alone in the center of a grassy patch to stew in his own juices.

By this time, a captain from the Carvers Grove department had arrived with the uptown truck. He had already sent Wade home, and reworked the manpower schedule to accommodate the two remaining brothers, so they could also be sent home.

Greg approached Gray as the investigator studied the outside of the structure, working his way inward. He wanted some backup from the state fire marshal's office to help him comb through the wreckage before he dug too far inside.

"I was here earlier tonight," Greg said so calmly that Gray wasn't sure he believed him, or the cop was just talking to keep his mind off the terrible events of the evening.

Greg was still in his uniform, though it looked slept in.

"Oh?" Gray simply asked in reply.

Greg slowly showed signs his mind was in the right place as he looked the debris over, knowing exactly where he had entered. Where he had seen signs of the homeless getting a free night's stay, now stood as a pile of blackened boards and charred concrete.

"I saw some light from the second floor, so I went inside," Greg explained, officially catching Gray's attention. "There was a blanket, and a candle. And some cans of food."

"Cans of food?"

"Yeah, and a can opener, I think."

"Was there anyone inside?"

"No. I checked the entire apartment, and never saw anyone," Greg answered, his voice still steady, signs of shock still somewhat evident.

"Was there any sign of forced entry?"

"No," Greg said, finding it somewhat odd, all of the sudden. "The door was unlocked. I just walked right in."

Gray was afraid to press too far, considering Greg's state of mind, but the officer was willing to talk, so he decided to ask another question or two.

"How did you leave the apartment?"

"I locked the door and blew out the candle before I left," Greg said positively enough that the fire marshal didn't doubt him.

"Do you remember the apartment number?" Gray inquired, thinking he might be able to verify whether or not it was locked once he sifted through the debris and reconstructed the remains of the apartment.

"Twenty-six," Greg answered. "I remembered it because it was my baseball jersey number in high school."

"Nice number," Gray commented.

"No, it sucked. I got stuck with it my freshman year."

Gray simply nodded, thinking he had learned enough for one evening.

"I might be calling you in the next day or two for a formal interview," he told Greg, who was ready to get back to his family anyway. "Thanks. And I'm sorry about losing Kevin. He was a great guy."

"Yeah, sure."

Mike slowly settled down as Patrick talked with the captain about the arrangements. There would be dozens of things to plan for the services and funeral, and he wasn't even sure if someone had talked to Julia yet.

"No," Patrick replied when Mike finally asked. "The chief's office held off, thinking we might want to be there."

"I'll go," Mike volunteered, thinking Julia's grief couldn't bring him any further pain than he already felt.

"You sure you're up to it?" Greg questioned.

"Yeah, I'm sure."

"I'll drive you there."

Mike was about to object, but his mind was too scrambled to be driving, and he knew it. Still, he wasn't sure Greg would be in any better condition, but Greg was accustomed to dealing with strange situations every day, and driving distraught people where they needed to be.

"Okay."

CHAPTER 18

As the twins and the fire department's chief told Julia the tragic news, waking her up in the middle of the night, then finding her embracing them for support, the lights were on at every station, and every flag lowered to half mast.

Every firefighter stayed up, stunned by the news of Kevin's death. Some drank coffee, some watched television to pass the painful time until their shift ended, and others told stories about their time with the lieutenant.

Everyone had some story to tell about Kevin, whether it was the way he always conducted himself as someone who knew his job, or the practical jokes he played during his time at the headquarters station.

Some remembered how he would almost give himself whiplash, riding in the fire trucks, whenever a pretty woman walked past. He was good at his job, and professional, but he had a weakness when it came to observing a woman's features.

Most of the firefighters held up well, trying to keep their emotions in check, but this was a first for the entire department, and the chief's office would be scrambling in the morning to figure out how to handle their first departmental on-the-job death, and its funeral.

While everyone else in the family chose to meet at their mother's house, in part to console her, Mike wanted to be alone.

He sat on the edge of his porch, drinking a beer, looking up to the stars above, wondering if his brother's spirit was among them.

The image of Kevin's body haunted him, now burned into the far reaches of his mind like an old black and white photograph. He knew how different things were going to be, and he hated it.

Absolutely hated it.

His best friend was gone, and there was nothing he could ever do to replace Kevin. No one he knew was even a close second when it came to people he bonded with.

Things might have been, or at least *felt* differently if Mike had been in there with his brother. Knowing he was left behind, partly for his own safety, hurt him even more. Inside, he might have made a difference, or he might have been the one who went after the two trapped men.

Mike would have gladly given his life for his brother's. After all, Mike had no kids to come home to, and he wasn't even married yet. Some would say he had his whole life ahead of him, but he viewed his life as having few attachments.

Fewer people to mourn him if anything happened, unlike Kevin.

His head hurt from being up so long, and from crying in the dark, once he was away from everyone else.

Looking up to the stars, he thought of Kevin, and how brave his older brother had always been, setting an example for him, and for Greg. The reality that he would wake up in the morning and not see Kevin at work, or be able to call him, began to set in.

Mike looked upward, the agony of his loss eating away at his insides.

He had explained things to Sandi in brief when he arrived home, and she decided to give him time to himself. Now, as daybreak approached, she slowly stepped out on the porch, taking a seat beside him.

Though she seldom drank, she held a beer.

"I figured maybe you wanted someone to talk to," she said softly, touching his strong shoulder.

"I don't know," he said numbly. "I don't even know what to *think* yet."

"Say whatever you want," she assured him. "I'm just hear to listen."

Mike appreciated that. There were so many things he had never told Sandi about his work, and about his family.

"Kevin was everything a big brother should be," Mike explained. "God, I worshiped him from the time I could walk."

"Why?"

"He never did anything wrong. He was so straight-laced, and such a great example to us. He never had to do the things for Greg and me that he did, and even when he got married, he never forgot about us. He was the perfect big brother."

Mike thumbed his beer a few seconds, then took a big gulp.

"He was always a great officer to work for, too. He was better than Patrick at every aspect of our job, but he would never say that. Seniority was the only thing that kept Patrick ahead of him at work, but Kevin knew what he was doing, and he always put his interests behind those of everyone else."

"How did Julia take it?"

"Not too well. She wanted to rush to the hospital, but Greg talked her out of it. Greg took the kids up to Mom's house, and Julia said she had to make some calls, so I left. I told her to call me if she needed anything."

He took another drink.

"I guess now I understand why you never wanted to talk about me dying."

"Yeah," Sandi said, taking a drink from her own beer.

"It could've been me up there," Mike said anyway, knowing Sandi didn't want to hear this. "Kevin and Pat protected me. They kept me out of there. Kevin made up some bullshit excuse why he didn't want me to go, but I think he knew the danger."

"Would you have gone?"

"In a heartbeat."

Sandi closed her eyes. She knew the answer before asking, and Mike's willingness to jump into danger scared her, especially now. Her earlier beliefs about him being impervious to danger or injury vanished into the early morning air.

"Do you want to go to your Mom's?" she asked.

"No, not yet," he answered, simply staring upward.

"Do you want me to go?"

"No."

"I'm so sorry," she said, carefully placing a hand on his back, rubbing gently.

"Me too. He meant everything to me."

Both sat silently as the sun peeked over the horizon, thinking Kevin had been taken too soon, but died doing what he loved.

Mike would have given anything to have his brother back, or to go back in time and change the outcome. He would forever wonder why he hadn't stepped in and refused an order, but he knew if he had it to do over and over, he would listen to his brothers every single time. Like always, Kevin had protected him.

"You know," he said to Sandi, "my father wanted me to keep the family together after he died. He knew he was dying, and I accepted it. I cried, and moved on, but it hurt. This, this is just totally different."

He felt a tear rush to his eye once more.

"It just isn't fair for all of us to lose such a good man."

Mike paused a moment.

"When we were growing up, I wanted to be whatever Kevin was going to be. I figured he would join the fire department, but he could have been a cop, or a garbage man, and I still would have walked the ends of the earth to be like him."

He put his one set of knuckles up to his mouth, almost biting them to contain his emotions.

"I just can't believe he's gone."

"I know," Sandi said, trying to keep her promise to simply be a good listener.

"And Greg, I know he feels like shit. His last words to Kevin were something to the effect that he didn't need him anymore, and to fuck off. He doesn't show emotion, but I know Greg will be hurting."

"You all will, Mike. When you're ready, go to them. They all need you to keep this family together."

Mike forced a grin.

He knew Sandi was right, and he had to reach out to the others, rather than suffer alone. His mother would certainly want to see him, and he hoped the news wouldn't add to the slow torture she had undergone since her husband died.

"Let's go see the family," he finally decided aloud, ready to begin the healing process, even though he knew it would take a long time to complete.

CHAPTER 19

Kevin's funeral proved almost more than the city of Carvers Grove could bear, with firefighters flying and driving in from all over the country, and locals from Chicago pouring in, just to attend the proceedings.

Hotels were packed for miles around, and the local businesses were caught off-guard when so many firefighters and friends came to town, looking for places to eat, drink, or entertain themselves.

Perhaps it was how heroically Kevin had died that spurred such great interest, but four days after his death, the proceedings began for his funeral.

Calling hours seemed to linger on forever, with each of his siblings, and his mother beside the coffin, shaking hands, meeting people from all reaches of the country, and occasionally looking to the closed casket.

Everyone knew there was no chance of making Kevin presentable for the funeral, and it hurt Mike to think that everyone would only get to see his brother through the collage of photos the family had pasted to a billboard in remembrance of their fallen brother.

There were family pictures of all seven kids together, Kevin and his own family, and departmental pictures of all kinds that the firefighters had contributed. One entire wall was dedicated to displaying the dozens of flower arrangements people had sent.

"I've never seen anything like this," Casey, Mike's younger sister, commented.

"He was a special guy," Mike replied.

While Mike and Patrick dressed in their departmental dress uniforms, Greg and Jay stood by in dark suits. Their sisters each wore conservative dresses, as their mother had requested. None of the four brothers would act as a pall bearer, since so many men from the fire department had practically begged to do the honors.

Wade stood with Julia much of the time, because she felt overwhelmed seeing so many people turn out for Kevin's funeral, and she still wasn't coping with the idea of losing her husband so soon.

Her children were old enough to understand what happened to their father, and they certainly showed their anguish openly. Wade and the others had done everything they could to let the kids know they weren't alone, and that the family would always be there for them.

For Mike, he hoped this wouldn't be the one thing that would tear his family apart. Greg and Jay seemed to be getting along, though neither had spoken very much.

During a slow time, the twins stepped outside for a moment.

"How are you holding up?" Greg asked first, staring at all of the cars across the parking lot.

He noticed several blue lights mounted atop some of the cars, though he had yet to see anyone from Washington Township show up that he recognized.

Especially not Tom Ellis.

"I'm okay," Mike said, his open mourning long since over.

He would act as solid as a rock through the rest of the process.

"And you?"

"I keep playing that night over and over in my head," Greg stated.

"What? The fire?"

"No. The night I was such an asshole and told Kevin I didn't need him."

"You couldn't have known."

"No, but I could have forgiven him. Believed him."

"Well, we all make mistakes," Mike said. "I wished I had gone into that building with him. Patrick isn't right about everything. I could have refused him and gone inside with Kev."

Greg looked Mike in the eye, knowing better.

"You wouldn't do that any sooner than I would. Dad taught us better."

Mike grinned, then let it fade as quickly as it had come.

"Have you talked to Gray?" Greg inquired.

"No. Why?"

"I want to know who's responsible for that fire starting."

"What does it matter, Greg? Kevin's gone."

"I won't let the person responsible get away with it. If it was an accident, they're still guilty. Someone should have reported it a lot sooner."

Mike shrugged. He didn't share his twin's inquisitive nature, and his focus was on the family.

"Are you going on the hunt?" he asked.

"I won't stop until I know who did it," Greg said evenly. "And you shouldn't either. Because of someone out there, there are a whole lot of us who won't get to see our big brother again."

Mike saw Greg's point, but he wasn't ready to move on yet.

"You were there," Mike pointed out. "Didn't you say homeless people were up there?"

"I said the scene implied it," Greg corrected. "I never saw anyone, and I know that door was locked when I left."

Both let that thought plant itself in their minds, and decided almost simultaneously it was time to return inside.

※ ※ ※

Most of the family didn't say very much to one another before the casket was hoisted by pall bearers upon one of the pumper trucks to be carried down to the cemetery.

With the casket covered by a flag, the pumper truck was followed by scores of firefighters, family, and several men from the Chicago area playing bagpipes. Traffic would be held up nearly an hour as the procession passed through, but Mike was glad his brother was getting a bit of the spotlight in death, because he certainly never would have asked for it in life.

Mike marched closely behind, wearing white gloves, his rounded hat, and his pressed uniform, trying to make Kevin proud. He walked beside Sandi and Patrick, but the entire family stood near them.

As they crossed one corner on the sunny, almost perfect day, Mike spied someone he didn't want to see during the one chance they had to properly lay his brother to rest.

"Oh, shit," he said just loud enough that his brother and Sandi could hear.

Standing beside a bus stop shelter, Gladys, the local nutcase on the loose, was just waiting for a crowd to entertain.

A slightly obese black woman who rode the bus daily, shouting at passing traffic about God and how people were going to burn in hell who didn't believe, Gladys had a most unusual way of preaching the Lord's gospel.

And hundreds of people were about to discover a new kind of sermon.

Suffering from both mental illness and slight retardation, Gladys had been left to fend for herself since her teenage years, never receiving the help she needed in the form of hospitalization or a group home. In a group home, she would have received the medication, attention, and help she needed, but that cost money, and no one was willing to even claim her, much less pay for assisted living.

As usual, she wore black stretch pants, and a loose purple top, holding a tattered Bible in one hand. Her dark hair glistened with oil from a lack of washing, and appeared knotted and ragged. Whenever she walked, she waddled to and fro like a penguin, but she strode with a purpose.

"Stay calm," Patrick warned his younger brother, certain he saw one of Mike's hands form a fist.

On most workdays, the firefighters passed her at the bus stop, made a few witty remarks to themselves, and thought little more of Gladys. Mike was no exception, and he felt Gladys had every right to get back at him in some form or another for all of the jokes he had made of her around fellow firefighters, but not today.

Not at Kevin's funeral.

Sandi, like most everyone else around her, was unsure of what to expect, but the firefighters were accustomed to pulling out of their station and encountering Gladys.

All at once, the tirade of a sermon began.

"You mother fuckers better worship Him," she began. "God says you are for him, or you are on your fucking own!"

"Cool it," Patrick said again, knowing Mike was growing infuriated from the look on his face. "Stay in formation. It'll pass."

Mike felt his blood pressure and temperature all rise at once, and he was infuriated that anything would desecrate his brother's funeral. Kevin deserved a perfect burial, and this was not what anyone had in mind.

Luckily, Greg had the presence of mind to ask some of his fellow officers to escort Gladys aside, which they should have known to do in the first place.

"All you mother fuckers are going to burn in hell for not respecting the Lord," she called back as the officers took her aside. "The Lord says to repent, or forever be a piece of shit in his eyes."

Sandi gave Mike a strange look as the other firefighters within earshot of Gladys wondered exactly what they had just experienced.

Mike gave no reply to the stare, but simply kept walking, finishing out the ceremonial journey to Kevin's final resting place. All of these people here to show support and respect a fallen firefighter, Mike thought, and she has to be here causing a scene.

"You all belong to Satan," he heard her call from a distance.

At this point, he wished the police would club her. He knew it was wrong to think such a thing, but he didn't care.

Even as the preacher spoke, and the casket was finally lowered into the earth, with Amazing Grace gently echoing through bagpipes off to one side of the site, Mike barely felt any calmer. His anger wasn't just from Gladys, and it didn't stem from Kevin's death alone.

The culmination of events made him uneasy, and he still wondered why it was Kevin who had to die when no one had any business being in the building in the first place. Despite the information that homeless people might have been inside, it was extremely risky sending anyone inside, though Mike knew he would have been too blinded to realize it at the fire scene.

Like anyone else, he had a desire to be the hero while helping others, and he would gladly risk his life to save others every single time. He knew the two volunteer firefighters didn't belong in that building, especially with lives at stake. He wanted the city to know, but his department as a whole fought an uphill battle against the media.

They would never hear of the new fire department being weak in its leadership, its membership, and especially not from its founding father, Benjamin Malovich.

While Mike focused on the aspect that it never should have been Kevin risking his life, Greg thought of the party ultimately responsible. Someone had set that fire, intentionally or accidentally, and he wanted answers about the fire's origin, and why the building was so easily accessible.

He watched as firefighters and family dispersed slowly from the scene, once the casket was lowered, and saw his mother almost too devastated to cry. Her face was a blank slate, as though the death of her son was too much, too soon after her husband's passing.

"I'm worried," Patrick said to Jay as they walked away from the grave.

"About what?"

"Him," the battalion chief answered, looking to Mike, who still remained by the casket, despite the workers throwing dirt over it. "And her."

Jay noticed their mother being led away by his sisters, who had remained quite strong through the entire process. None of the seven expected to die, or lose one of their siblings this soon, so perhaps the shock still lingered.

He saw Casey ask her a question several times, receiving no response for her efforts.

"Things are going to be a lot different," Jay noted.

"Yeah, they sure are."

Reluctantly, the family filtered from the cemetery, and Greg finally had to be the one to fetch Mike so the workers could do their jobs. He took Sandi with him as backup.

Oblivious to their approach, Mike conversed with himself, hoping somewhere Kevin might hear his words. He looked at Kevin's tombstone, which had the usual information, and below it, a fire truck carved beside a custom image of his brother, which the entire family pitched in to have engraved on the stone. Taken from a recent photo, the image of the lieutenant showed his smiling face and the twinkle in his eyes perfectly. On the other side of the image sat the department's customized Maltese Cross, used on their shirts and trucks. Now the everyday symbol Kevin worked with would be resting with him for all time.

"I still can't believe it," Mike said, obviously more devastated than any of the other family members. "I never thought it would be this bad, but I miss you *so* much, Kev."

He had seen Kevin almost every day, even when he wasn't at work. All at once, he had lost his lieutenant, his brother, and his best friend.

"We're going to Mom's for a little bit," Greg said, putting a reassuring hand on his brother's shoulder. "She needs all of our support right now."

"Okay," Mike simply said with a nod.

He was so numb with emotional pain that it didn't matter where he went.

His healing process would begin, but none of the Sheridan family would be celebrating or cooking out anytime soon. They had learned to get by without their father, and they would learn a new family life once again, but it would take time.

CHAPTER 20

On Friday, Greg decided to pay a visit to Mason Gray's office at the headquarters fire station, unsatisfied with the results printed in the local newspaper about his brother's death.

Gray had left the fire's cause undetermined on paper because no accelerants were found, and because of Greg's own testimony that there was evidence of homeless people where the fire was believed to have begun. In his determination, there was nothing to gain financially, or otherwise, for the owners, because they were in the middle of renovating the apartment building to raise rates in the fall.

Several things didn't add up with Greg, including how a fire started within an hour after he left the apartment. He had blown out the candle before leaving, locked the door, and made sure no one was in the area.

Even the front and back doors were locked when he left, and he had run that entire night's events through his mind a thousand times over. He was positive the apartment was impregnable when he left.

Gray found no evidence of a break-in, and despite the lack of remains, the witness testimony from firefighters stated there were no broken doors or windows, except where the flames had blown them out from heat on the upper floors.

The investigator also revealed the fire had started on the second floor, both from witness testimony, and the damage done to the floor levels once they were sifted and examined.

Greg wondered if he could have done more, but he was spurned to discover why or how someone had regained access to the building after he made so certain it was secure.

Greg dressed casually before leaving his apartment. He would not return to work until the following Monday, which left him little time to dig up some of the information he was after. Most everything, including the fire department's front office, was closed on weekends.

Before he could reach the front door of the fire station just after lunchtime, his cellular phone rang at his side.

"Hello," he said, recognizing his twin brother's phone number on the phone's digital screen.

"Greg, it's Sandi."

"Hey, Sandi. What's up?"

"I'm getting worried about Mike," she confessed in a hushed voice, as though he might be sitting in the next room. "He's been sitting like a catatonic the past few days. He won't cry, won't move, won't eat. He's acting emotionless."

Greg paused a moment, trying to envision his brother being as depressed as Greg himself had been on Saturday night.

"Can you talk to him?"

"He nods, or mumbles something, but it's like he doesn't have any ambition to do anything."

"He'll get better," Greg assured her.

"That's what I thought, but I've taken the last two days off from work because I was so worried about him."

"Want me to drop by later?"

"Please. I'm getting very worried he's not going to come out of this funk he's put himself in."

"Okay. I'll be over in an hour or so."

"Thank you."

"Sure thing," Greg said before switching his phone off.

He walked into the fire station, finding no one around. Patrick was still on leave, but Wade had returned to work this morning. It seemed eerily quiet in the truck room, and noises from the living quarters barely made their way to Greg's ears.

He passed through the garage, reaching the front office to find equally silent quarters as the inspectors and chiefs walked around, doing their usual work, trying to keep their minds off the recent tragedy.

Greg said a few greetings, then reached Mason Gray's office, finding the arson investigator speaking with someone on the phone.

He shifted his eyes in the detective's direction, said a few quick words to excuse himself from the call, and hung up. To Greg, it appeared as though he might be speaking with someone he didn't want the young detective to know about.

"Hi, Greg," Gray said with more friendliness than usual. "What can I do for you?"

"You can start by telling me more than you've told the papers," Greg replied, straight to the point. "I want to know how you came to decide the start of that fire was undetermined."

"Because I had no evidence of foul play," Gray answered.

"So you're suggesting I lied, or had no idea what I was talking about when I said the building was secured when I left?"

"Greg, there are a hundred ways into that complex, and it's like a hotel with all of those floors winding everywhere, and no secured doors within. Anyone could have gotten in anywhere, and started that fire."

"In exactly the same spot I had just investigated?"

Gray forced a smile, along with an audible sigh.

"You may think I'm a dickhead, or some sort of hard-ass, but I'm just doing my job. From the remains I had, there wasn't really enough to tell if there had been forced entry or not, and I didn't find any tools, or much left of the locking mechanisms in that heap to work with. For all I know, it could have been an accident caused by one of the maintenance crew."

"That would be quite a coincidence," Greg noted, not convinced.

"It would be, but without any conclusive proof, I can't just pick a cause and fling it out to the papers in the hopes that they buy it. If it makes you feel any better, the state boys are looking over the samples I sent them as we speak."

Greg grunted to himself.

He looked around the office, finding filing cabinets, a large desk, several photos and certificates lining the walls, and several collectible statues. Most of the photos were of Gray with some of his friends from the elite community. They were the type of people Greg never met under normal circumstances, and when he had to meet them, they weren't happy to see him.

"What about the owners?" Greg asked. "Surely they had to make money from the insurance."

"Maybe a little, but they were already turning a profit renting out the apartments to college kids."

Greg figured they were making a profit, but when the city cracked down on the new codes, they were surely going to spend quite a bit to bring the building up to code.

"If you're looking for answers to why your brother died, I don't have them," Gray assured the detective. "I'm sorry about losing Kevin. We all are. But the fact remains, I don't have any evidence to even launch an investigation. The owners were out of town in Florida last week."

"How convenient," Greg said sarcastically, thinking things were a bit too perfectly arranged.

Perhaps arranged ahead of time.

"Any chance I can see your files?" Greg asked, unable to think of any other questions off the top of his head.

"Like I said, I don't really have anything," Gray answered.

"So I take that as a 'no'?"

"Unfortunately, no, you can't look at them unless you're officially assigned to the case, which I know your department isn't going to give you clearance to do."

Greg grinned, suspecting Gray was keeping something from him, whether it was for his own good, or Gray had some other aspect he couldn't talk about. At this point, Greg had nothing to go on, because the newspaper printed very little about the apartment building itself, focusing instead on Kevin's death.

Greg needed some shred of information to start with, and he knew the fire department kept all of their run files on computer for organization, and every member of each Carvers Grove department had access codes to call up any files that pertained to his department.

Mike had the access Greg needed, if the detective could convince his brother to help.

"Thanks for your time," he said to Gray before stepping out of the office.

"Anytime," Gray replied, though not very sincerely.

Greg walked away from the fire department headquarters, hoping to find more to Kevin's death than the sloppy undetermined result the fire marshal had labeled it with. Someone was responsible one way or another, and Greg wanted to know who.

No matter the cost.

For a moment, Greg had considered fetching Wade from the living quarters, but decided he didn't want to raise suspicion. If he could convince Mike to return to the land of the living, his twin would be a much better source of information, and could probably get him access to more places.

He pulled into his brother's driveway, unsure of how Mike would react to him showing up, if he reacted at all.

Greg stepped from his car, finding Sandi standing on the front porch, obviously relieved to see him. If she had taken two days off from the prosecutor's office, she probably had doubts about Mike's mental well-being.

"How's he doing?" Greg asked as he was pulled into an unexpected hug.

"Not good," Sandi said, her eyes glistening with moisture. "I've tried talking, leaving, even having people call him, but he won't talk to anyone, or even move."

"Has he spoken at all?"

"Oh, he'll answer me with a word or two, but I haven't had a conversation with him since right after the funeral."

Not good, Greg thought. He was starting from square one, or so it sounded. Mike was normally not an emotional introvert, so this was going to be a new challenge, especially since the twins had never been very close.

Sandi let him into the house, then pointed the way to where Mike was watching afternoon television, letting very little of his viewing actually soak into his brain.

"Hey, Mike," Greg said, stepping inside the living room.

"Hey," Mike simply answered, not removing his eyes from the television.

"You doing okay?"

"Fine," came the unenthusiastic answer.

Greg had no patience for his brother's apathetic nature, so he switched off the television, which seemed to be Mike's only friend.

He decided to waste no time in asking for the help he needed, hoping Mike would respond.

"Look, I need your help, and I know you're hurting, but we've got a chance to do one last good thing for Kevin."

Mike didn't seemed the least bit phased.

"What? Catch his killer? As if someone set that place on fire?"

"Someone did."

Mike seemed a bit more interested now, because his eyes actually glanced away from the blank television set.

"I read the paper," he said anyway. "The case is dead. Gray didn't find anything to indicate arson."

"Do you believe everything Gray tells you? Or everything the newspaper prints?"

Mike sat silently a moment, still not willing to simply give in to Greg's request.

"I guess not."

Mike felt too emotionally exhausted to carry on a conversation, but it was obvious Greg wasn't going to leave him alone.

"This isn't about us, or even Kevin," Greg stated. "This is about bringing a killer to justice before someone else loses a brother or sister."

Mike rubbed his head as though it hurt.

"Okay. Before I agree to help you track down this ghost, how can you be so sure it was arson, and not some homeless person having an accident?"

"It seems there have been a number of undetermined accidents in our city this year, starting with that explosion a few months back. Everyone I interviewed on that scene said the doors were locked, and the lab results said they were still locked, and that the door was actually blown off the hinges from the blast."

"So?"

"So it looked like a normal accident. No big deal. Then this fire comes along, and I get suckered into looking upstairs. I was damn quiet when I went inside, Mike. If there were homeless people staying up there, I doubt they would have been stupid enough to leave a candle burning and leave the apartment. There was no reason for them to leave the apartment to begin with, and I don't see why anyone would leave cans of food and a can opener lying around."

"What are you getting at?"

"It looked like it was set up, like someone was supposed to see it and notice there were homeless people taking shelter up there."

"Set up?"

"Yeah, like stage props or something. It was just *too* neatly placed."

Mike thought a moment. He knew Greg was being truthful, and that his brother didn't have a vivid imagination that might lead him to think beyond the scope of reality.

"And the door was unlocked?" he inquired.

"Yeah."

"Could they have just walked to the bathroom?"

"The bathrooms are in the apartments. I checked every inch of the apartment over."

"Oh, yeah," Mike said with a tone of realization.

He sat there a moment, seeing Sandi peek into the room, deciding he didn't want her knowing exactly what he was about to start with his brother. She wanted to see him heal, and he could fake it by saying he was going out with Greg for a little while.

Reluctantly, he leaned his head back, his mind still not ready to cope with reality. Somehow he would make it cope with the loss and move on.

"Okay. Where do we start, Greg?"

CHAPTER 21

When Wade received a call of a working house fire on the south end of town, it didn't excite him like it would have a week prior.

He was barely a few months into the job, but felt like a hardened veteran. Losing a fellow firefighter, especially a close relative, tended to do that to the best of men. Not that Wade possessed any more knowledge than before, but he felt more capable of handling situations, and he didn't have any fear of putting his life on the line.

After such situations, firefighters tend to go one of two ways. One, they can pull into a shell, be conservative, and never enter a burning structure again. Or, they decide that someone made the ultimate sacrifice for a reason, and aspire to be like that person.

Wade decided to be like his uncle, knowing Kevin's death was a tragic accident, that might have been altered by any number of minuscule changes.

Just an accident.

He strapped his air pack on with uncanny ease, because he felt no real nervousness. Perhaps he was still a bit numb from his uncle's death, but Wade felt completely in control.

As he stepped from the truck, finding flames shooting out the second story window of a house, he wondered if it looked anything like the apartment complex fire. Even as he helped pull the hose line from the truck, Wade felt nothing but a desire to get in there and kill the fire.

He took hold of the nozzle before Pratt could get to it, and had to wait a few seconds for his partner to finish fastening the connection between his mask's hose and the air tank. They finally stepped into the house, finding the downstairs eerily clear.

Not a wisp of smoke appeared from anywhere, meaning the fire was contained upstairs, and probably growing hotter and thicker by the second, now that it had an air supply from the busted window.

"See if you can find that staircase," Wade said, tired from dragging the line around several corners, finding no sign of a staircase in any of the downstairs rooms.

If the upstairs was only accessible through a hatch, or a fold-down ladder to the attic, they would find themselves in twice the battle they had originally planned on.

Pratt scurried through several other rooms, and Wade was about to take the line outside and fight it from the street, but his partner finally called from a tiny hallway in the back. Pratt had found a thin curtain disguising the staircase, or perhaps dividing living quarters in the house.

Wade dragged the hose line up the stairs with help from his partner, and took the lead, opening the door that had been masking the upstairs fire the entire time.

"Holy shit!" Wade shouted, the reality that he was mortal coming back to him as flames reached around the doorway, as though to grab him.

The door itself collapsed to the inside, leaving the two firefighters instantly singed by the heat. Hansel and Gretel had probably pushed the witch into a far lesser fire than this.

"Open that thing up!" Pratt almost begged.

Wade wasted no time in opening the nozzle, battling back the flames as he zigzagged the stream throughout the room, trying to bring the heat and the building thermal layer back to a tolerable temperature.

While they fought to make progress in the room, someone outside had set up a ladder, and now fired another stream of water through the window. The flames had little chance with two streams hitting them, using the fire's heat to change the water to steam, which forced the fire to help in combating itself.

As the smoke began to filter out the window, Wade could see the upstairs was completely gutted. Only mattress springs, a toilet, and the remains of an old storage chest remained. Wade couldn't tell if the upstairs was currently lived in, or just used for storage, but he sensed it would be some time before it could be used for anything again.

After another ten minutes or so, the two heard the tones from one of their packs signaling low air. With the fire pretty much dead, the two backed out, down the stairs, as a fresh crew readily took their place.

Wade took off his mask at the bottom of the stairs, spying an aquarium with a goldfish happily swimming from end to end, with the tank all to itself.

"At least we saved the fish," Pratt thought aloud.

"Better than nothing," Wade commented.

"You did pretty well up there. You almost got us cooked there for a second, but you're doing a whole lot better."

"Thanks," Wade said, though he didn't feel like he was doing anything different than before.

He had never been as close to Kevin as his father and uncles, but he still felt the loss. Somewhere, he figured the lieutenant would be looking down on him, and he wanted to make the man proud, even if that was the only thing he could do.

"Let's get some fucking water," Pratt suggested, leading the way through the living room, which dripped warm water from every part of the ceiling above.

As water from the hose lines the firefighters had just sprayed soaked its way through the floor joists and boards upstairs, it fell like rain into the downstairs.

"Good idea."

※ ※ ※

In the meantime, Greg and Mike were in the battalion chief's office where reports were filled out, and most of the shift business was conducted, from evaluations to roster changes.

"You do realize Patrick would probably report us both to your chief if he knew what we were doing, don't you?" Mike asked his twin.

"Probably, but he doesn't share our intuitive nature."

Mike typed his password into the computer, calling up the main menu, then hit another key to enter the filed reports section.

All firefighters were allowed to fill out reports, because sometimes officers, drivers, or even the guys on the back of the truck were the main witnesses to the incident. By the same token, they were all allowed to recall old reports for editing purposes.

Mike typed in the fateful date his brother had been killed, and both looked to the report, trying to find any kind of basic information that might launch an investigation outside of what the police and Mason Gray were attempting.

"If we don't get an owner's phone number and address, we use the neighbors," Mike revealed. "I'm hoping they got some actual information about the apartment's owner."

"I could probably get it myself, but I'd raise some eyebrows doing so," Greg said. "I want to keep this as low profile as possible."

"Agreed. If Patrick finds out any of this, he'll skin us alive."

Mike skimmed through the information, discovering the firefighters had spoken with one of the tenants, and the resident had every shred of information available about the building's owner. He was positive he spied a grin crossing his twin's lips, but when he turned to look, it quickly disappeared.

"What do you have in mind, Greg? Knocking on their door and asking if they torched their own place for profit?"

"Not exactly. That name rings a bell."

"Dirk Shelton? Isn't he that real estate tycoon with the videotapes about how to make your fortune overnight buying and reselling property?"

"Yeah, but it appears he knows some other ways to make money, too."

"If he's got so much cash flow, why would he bother burning his own place?"

"Maybe he's *not* responsible, but I intend to find out."

Greg started to jot down the information, but Mike discovered a way to print the entire report, and did so twice. He pocketed one after handing the other to his twin.

"Want some help?" Mike offered.

"No. Let me handle this myself to keep things quiet. I'll let you know when I find something out."

"You'd better. I'm not going to help you if it's on a part-time basis."

"I know. And you've already been more of a help than you know."

Mike heard the squeal of the pumper truck's air brakes outside, and knew it was time for them to get out of the station before someone saw both of them together.

"Let's go," he told Greg, leading his brother out of the office, toward the back door.

"I'll let you know what I find out," Greg promised as the two walked to their vehicles in the parking lot, just out of the view of the returning truck.

"You know where I'll be."

Greg looked at the printout, once seated in his car, wondering just what he would discover, and whether or not he would find any proof of arson that he could take to court, considering he was unofficially investigating the entire incident.

He knew no one had the right to access information about insurance policies or the number of properties owned, except the investigators assigned to a particular case. Stepping out of his assigned cases meant potentially stepping into a minefield. Greg had to make certain no one knew what he was investigating, which made his task an uphill battle from the start.

He had enough reliable sources to jumpstart an investigation, but those would soon run out. Greg needed to make the most of what little information he received. Starting the car, he thought of no better time than the present to begin his search.

CHAPTER 22

As much as it pained Greg, he needed an inside source to the world of insurance, so he could track any claims Dirk Shelton had made the past few years, and his best bet was an ex-girlfriend he was with less than a few years back.

Before and after his short-lived marriage, Greg had made himself quite available to women throughout the county, often frequenting bars, or dating women he met through his job. It wasn't until a year after the divorce that he learned his lesson, and discovered he was filling the emotional hole in his heart with nothing but temporary satisfaction.

By this time, most of his relationships were based on sex, and he had a reputation of being a user, so no respectable women came near him.

He learned the error of his ways, and simply dropped from the public scene altogether, throwing himself into his work.

Tasha Barnes was one of those women he knew before his marriage, and she was definitely the one who got away.

Intelligent, cute, and very witty, she had seen Greg's shallow nature before he did, and decided she wanted more from a man. She broke up with him, and he was too proud to pursue her, never knowing he could have proved his love by doing so.

His entire family told him he was bone-headed for letting Tasha go, but he would hear none of it, and quickly rebounded with the relationship that nearly ruined his life. Greg had made mistakes, but this might have been his biggest ever.

Still, that was the past, and things had changed. Greg could never change things between Tasha and himself, but perhaps she had enough concern about him to help him find his brother's killer.

Greg could think of no other way. Someone had set that fire, and that same person was a murderer, whether he knew it or not. If he saw Shelton's insurance claims, he could prove or disprove the man's innocence in his own mind.

Making his way through the growing offices of the insurance company known as the Carrington Group, Greg wondered how a local company had made it so big, but they had a reputation for serving businesses, and serving them well.

Literally under construction, the offices were a tangled mess of desks, phone lines, and ceiling tiles hanging from thin wires above as workers added in new lines, insulation, and climate controls.

"Can you tell me where I might find Tasha Barnes?" Greg asked the first friendly face he came across, in the form a of young lady who looked like the secretarial type.

"She's back there," the woman replied, pointing toward the main offices where the company's executive board resided.

"She is?" Greg had to ask, remembering when she had just worked her way up from answering phones to doing field work, finally taking claims and bringing in new clients.

Things certainly had changed.

He half expected her to be out with big clients to a late lunch, or talking on the phone with the president of a national bank, but he found Tasha sitting at her desk, reading a document before signing it, thorough as ever.

"Hello," he said as their eyes made contact, half expecting her to call security to escort him from the building.

"Hi," she said, as though trying to remember who he was, or perhaps why she was supposed to be upset with him. "Sorry to hear about your brother," she said sincerely, a few seconds later.

"Thanks," Greg said evenly.

"Long time, no see, Greg," Tasha said, standing to offer him a seat across from her desk, being far more cordial than he expected.

Greg took the seat uneasily, wondering just how far her hospitality would extend.

"I guess things have changed," he said, eyeing the office, which held every visible commendation she had ever received with her company.

Quite a few, he figured, considering most of them came after their relationship went sour.

He gave her a quick look, noticing her face was still as pretty as he recalled, though she seemed a little too tan. Greg could remember feeling so lucky being seen with her in public, and she was still one of the prettiest women he had ever dated.

"I'm now the vice-president of operations," Tasha said without a trace of arrogance. "Things just kind of fell into place, and I got moved up rather quickly."

"I see."

"And you?"

"Oh, I'm still beating the streets, but I'm an investigator now," Greg said, finding it hard to state his job description, considering how he was treated in his new division.

"That's great," Tasha said, though not overly impressed. "I take it you're not here to catch up on old times, though."

Greg cracked his knuckles nervously.

"I, uh, came to ask you a professional favor, but off the record."

"Oh?" Tasha asked curiously.

"It concerns my brother's death, which I'm not supposed to be investigating."

"I see. Then why are you?"

The detective paused a moment before answering.

"Well, I don't think its being investigated as thoroughly as possible," Greg admitted. "There have been several fire cases left undetermined this year, which had very suspicious origins."

"What exactly are you asking me to do?" Tasha asked, raising one leg over the other, giving Greg a perfect view of her silky smooth legs, including the insides, for the briefest of seconds.

Greg held his knuckles up to his mouth to cover his expression, realizing exactly how long it had been since he was on a date, much less in bed with a woman.

"I need to find out some information about the owner of the building that burned. What kind of claims he's had as an owner, and whether there was an investigation into those claims."

Tasha nodded slowly, as though he was asking for the world.

"Well, that's quite a tall order, starting with the fact that I would be violating several company codes of conduct, not to mention invading the man's right to privacy by asking his insurance company for information, since we don't have his business."

"Can't you fake a submission of some sort?"

"Yes, but those get traced if I submit anything over the computer, and a basic inquiry won't give us much information."

"*Any* information is better than what I have," Greg said, thinking he was starting to sound like he was pleading.

"Can I ask whom we're speaking of?"

Greg paused a moment, realizing he would eventually have to reveal the name anyway. He wanted to wait until he had confirmation of her decision to help, or not, before giving out too much critical information.

"We're talking about Dirk Shelton," he finally said.

"Oh, Dirk Shelton who owns Shelton Properties, which happens to be one of the largest real estate firms around?"

Her tone seemed laced with some cynicism.

"I suppose so, yes."

"Before we get into this any further, I have to know something, Greg," Tasha said, standing to close her office door before continuing the conversation.

She sat back down, in a less revealing position this time, placing her hands atop the desk in a cupped position.

"What happened to us?" she asked.

"You left me," Greg said bluntly, not thinking beyond the surface like she was implying he should.

"And why did I leave you?"

"Because you thought I lacked emotional attachment," Greg stated her parting words almost verbatim.

"And why, now, after all these years, are you coming to me for help?"

"Because no one else knows I'm doing this, and you might be the only link I have to finding out a history on this Shelton guy. Someone started that fire for a reason, and I want to know why."

Tasha didn't give an inch.

"So this is a revenge thing?"

"No, this is about justice."

She still didn't seem sold.

"I've got a good thing going here, Greg. I'm engaged," she added, holding up her left hand, a diamond gleaming from her ring finger.

"I wouldn't ask if it wasn't important," Greg insisted, trying to avoid being distracted by the ring, or the thought of his former girlfriend happy with someone else.

She looked around the small office, thinking it over.

"Even if I agree to help you, I can only access what kind of insurance rating he has, and whether or not he's a risk to insure. It's doubtful I'll get any specifics about the claims if he has any. Only his insurance company would know the specifics of the claims."

"And I'm sure you'd know someone over at his insurance company," Greg hinted.

Tasha said nothing for a moment, apparently thinking of the consequences of checking on Dirk Shelton, if there really were any. Greg had a feeling she was trying to make him squirm, liking the notion of having an advantage over him.

It worked.

"Most every fire claim is handled through the fire department's arson investigator, so you won't get much, even from his insurance company," Tasha claimed. "Sometimes, however, they hire out their own investigators privately, if there's something fishy."

Greg's hopes dwindled.

"Does this mean you're not helping me?"

"It means I'm giving you some alternatives while I see what I can do."

Greg let a smile cross his face, unable to contain his excitement at having an inside source to secretly help him.

"You don't call me, you don't drop by, and you leave me a card with the numbers I can use to get in touch with you," Tasha insisted. "I'll see what I can do, and let you know what I find out."

Greg stood, sliding one of his cards across the desk after scratching his alternate phone numbers on the back.

"Thank you," he said quietly before leaving.

Tasha watched him leave, wondering what she had just agreed to, and why. After all, she was in the middle of a new life, and it was partly thanks to the detective that she found the courage to start over again, and search for something better.

Still, she couldn't help but feel for him. If he was right, and no one else was doing his brother justice by investigating the case properly, she could understand where he came from.

Tasha shuffled a few papers on her desk, ready to sign a few more documents before heading out for the afternoon. She still had business of her own to attend to.

CHAPTER 23

Mike didn't like being asked to do his twin brother's line of work, but realized his obligation to finding the person responsible for the apartment fire would be no easy task.

He wanted access to Mason Gray's files, but knew asking for them would expose their secretive investigation, and probably put them further behind. Gray wasn't cooperative to begin with, and upsetting him in any way ruined their chances for future assistance.

Gray really had no boss to answer to, so far as his reports were concerned. He wrote them, kept them stored away, and brought them into court when necessary. There was no chance of Mike ever seeing those files, unless Gray conceded to let him.

Currently, he was putting in a shift of observing Dirk Shelton's estate from a distance, waiting to see who the man met with, where he went, and what he did at home. From his car, Mike could feel stubble along his face, because he had left in the morning without shaving, or even showering, to pick up where Greg left off.

He didn't see much point in monitoring Shelton, but Greg insisted they start somewhere, since his other leads were floundering. Mike had doubts about the investigation as a whole, but he was supposed to meet an arson investigator from the Rockford area, who was contracted to scope out suspicious fires throughout the state by Shelton's insurance company.

It was partly by chance that Mike had met the man the day before, investigating the Brookshire fire in the late afternoon. As luck would have it, the man would be in town today as well, after checking on another suspicious fire a few towns away.

He reluctantly agreed to meet Mike after he was finished, but only because Mike didn't tell him all of the reasons he wanted to meet.

"I could get in trouble for telling you any of the aspects I find," the investigator told Mike as the sun set behind them at the fire scene the previous evening.

"I won't tell anyone a thing, because I can't," Mike had assured him. "I just need to know if you think the fire was accidental or not, and why."

The man shook his head, his conclusion not quite reached.

"I've got another fire to investigate tomorrow afternoon when I meet with the landlord of another apartment complex. After that, I'll tell you what I can."

"I'll even buy you a beer," Mike offered.

"Sure. I'll call you when I'm finished."

That call had been placed half an hour earlier, and the man wanted to meet Mike at the scene of the fire first, to make some final decisions about his determination, and hopefully show Mike some of his findings.

As Mike pulled away from Shelton's house, ready to meet the investigator, he passed a gray car, which pulled into the real estate tycoon's driveway. Mike managed to turn around quickly enough to scribble most of the license plate on a leftover napkin, wondering if Greg would be able to trace it without detection.

Mike suspected it was probably no one special, since Shelton seemed to have few visitors, and most of them appeared to be family.

A few minutes later, Mike pulled up to the scene, finding the investigator already there.

A thin man with drawn cheeks and prematurely gray hair, he almost seemed to hate what he was doing, as though the business of investigating fires had caused him extensive grief. He wore no gun at his side, and had no clothes, other than his departmental baseball cap, to indicate he had anything to do with the fire service.

"Hello," Mike said as he approached the man, trying to make sure the meeting was still going to happen.

"I'm still not sure what to tell you," the man said, barely looking away from the pile of debris laid before him.

To Mike, it all looked like embers and junk, but apparently the investigator saw things differently, and perhaps with more detail.

Before they could continue their discussion, Greg pulled up, as he had promised Mike he would. He wanted to hear every bit of the conversation, so he could add the information to his own unofficial investigation.

"You're the one I talked to about the stuff inside the apartment," the arson investigator said, recognizing Greg.

"Yeah, and I'm really curious about what you found."

"Well," the man said, looking to the pile, "you were right about the room being stripped down. It seems kind of funny that this was the only area missing drywall, carpeting, and half of its closet doors."

"And your determination?" Mike prompted.

"I can't rule it intentional," the investigator said with a shrug. "There just isn't enough evidence to support that claim, since no accelerant was used."

"Shit."

"There were a couple things that were overlooked by your local guy, though," the investigator said, raising both of their interests.

They perked up like two dogs hearing dinner bells, though both knew Gray was secretive, and might have simply kept certain information to himself.

"Let's go get that beer you promised me first," the investigator said, looking to Mike.

Within a few minutes, the three men were seated at a local restaurant, and both brothers waited anxiously for some answers as the investigator sipped his beer.

"Your brother's death might have been more than a tragic accident," he finally revealed.

"What?" both Sheridan brothers asked at once.

"I found evidence of exposed gas lines," the man said. "They had that place gutted, as though it was primed for a fire."

"How could you tell they were exposed?" Mike asked.

"From what's still standing. Both sides show evidence of exposed lines and torn up materials, and it goes back to normal just a few feet in. Just that one section seemed to be naked."

"Even if they were exposed, how did the gas lines affect the fire?" Mike inquired, knowing gas lines usually weren't a factor unless they ruptured.

"What's your name again?" Greg quickly inquired of the investigator.

"Harrison. Ben Harrison."

Harrison paused a moment as the smells of steaks and barbequed chicken passed by, lingering in the air.

"To answer your question, Mike, I think one of the gas lines was damaged when part of the apartment began to fall in upon itself. If Kevin had been a few seconds quicker in getting out of there, he probably would have avoided the flames altogether. Of course, this is all theory on my part."

"Ben," Greg said, getting the investigator's attention. "What's more important, is what *caused* the fire?"

"Couldn't tell. I could tell where it started, but there was no way to know exactly what started it, because there wasn't any evidence left from the point of origin."

"Maybe a candle started it," Greg suggested bitterly.

All three men pondered the thought for a moment, knowing how easily a tipped candle could have started a fire that would roar through the exposed materials of the apartment, leaving no trace of it ever being there.

"I want your honest opinion, your gut feeling," Mike told Harrison. "Was this fire arson?"

Harrison carefully chose his words before speaking them.

"My instincts tell me this is an arson for profit, carefully plotted, and carefully designed. I can see your investigator keeping some of his information from the press, but he didn't disclose several things to me that people in his position usually do."

"Well, he's kind of an asshole," Mike explained.

"Still, he should have known I would find things out for myself, so there was no need to keep secrets, unless he figured I was incompetent enough to overlook some of the facts."

Harrison sipped his beer for a moment.

"Really, guys, I'm sorry about what happened to your brother. I wish I could help you more."

"We just want to make sure Kevin's death isn't blood on someone else's hands," Mike said. "If someone set that fire, they need to be held responsible."

"It's not always that easy," Harrison said.

"It can be."

"Don't do anything crazy," Harrison suggested. "I can give you my opinion on this stuff, but I ain't God. I don't know for sure what happened up there. I know you guys are hurting inside, but going on a witch hunt without proof isn't going to do a thing for your brother."

"Even if we catch the prick responsible?" Greg asked a rhetorical question.

"My guidance stops here," Harrison said. "What you guys do is your business, but someone could very well dislike this Shelton guy.

Unless you get some witnesses, or find something other than circumstantial evidence, you'll be wasting your time."

Mike thought a second, wanting to ask Harrison every conceivable question possible before the investigator went home.

"What about the doors?" he finally asked. "Weren't they locked?"

Harrison shrugged.

"Greg here says they were locked, and they all appeared to be, but I have to take your investigator's word on that. When you get a dozen firefighters doing their job and trampling everywhere, you can't really count on much of anything being like it was at the start of the fire. By the time I get to these things, I'm getting leftovers and information from sources I'm forced to trust."

He scooped a handful of pretzels from the bowl centered in the table before speaking again.

"Do you guys really mistrust the local investigators enough to take this upon yourselves?"

"I saw what I saw," Greg assured him. "That apartment was laid out like a movie set. Homeless people don't just get up and leave, even if they think the police are coming, because they know we'll just give them a ride to the shelter."

"So you're suggesting it was just a ruse to get you to testify that homeless people were present?"

"Yes, I do. And now that I made mention of it, everyone seems to think it could be nothing other than an accident."

"I don't know what to tell you guys," Harrison said, standing to leave, "but thanks for the beer."

"And thanks for the answers," Mike said.

"No problem."

As the brothers watched the fire investigator leave, they wondered how much closer they actually were to the truth, though both suspected they were in the right. If Shelton had anything to do with the fire, he would never have dirtied his own hands.

They could begin looking for locals who worked as arsonists for hire, or they could continue observing Shelton as they had been.

Either way, they weren't giving up, and each gave the other a look that indicated their desire to continue the hunt.

CHAPTER 24

Wade's workdays became less taxing on his mind with every day that passed. He could go to work without worries about screwing up on a fire scene by the time August rolled around, and the death of his uncle was ebbing a bit from his mind.

He had no idea about Greg and Mike's plan to pursue the alleged arsonist, and his life was a bit simpler than theirs, even though he had to work with Patrick at the headquarters station.

No matter what anyone said, the battalion chief seemed to blame himself for sending Kevin inside, even though another firefighter might have been killed sooner, gotten lost, or perhaps, gotten everyone out alive. Everyone knew Kevin was the best available person to send inside that mess, and no matter what he thought, Patrick had made the best choice possible, given the circumstances.

Everyone else said so.

Wade realized his job had no right or wrong answers, and he tried consoling his uncle a few times when they were by themselves, but Patrick pulled himself inside a figurative shell, letting the outside world pass by.

On this particular morning, he had another chance to speak with his uncle, since everyone else was outside playing a quick game of basketball before lunch. Wade promised to join them momentarily, but he needed to ask his uncle something first.

"Got a minute?" he asked the battalion chief after giving the office door a quick knock, then pulling it open.

"Sure," Patrick answered, looking up from his roster sheet.

It looked strange not having Kevin's name inside the Station Four square. Both of them gave it a glance before returning to their conversation.

"Julia asked me if I'd take the kids on a small vacation so she could see her folks up north," Wade said, wasting little time. "Dad and I are going to take them to a theme park for a few days, but I need a personal day for one of them."

"You've got two coming," Patrick said, slightly offended that Julia wouldn't ask him to take care of the kids.

"It's two weeks from tomorrow."

Patrick looked to the vacation sheet, finding the date booked.

"Two guys already have it," he said, "but I might be able to talk Jim out of it. He said he was just taking it to have a day off."

"I'd appreciate it," Wade said.

"I'll let you know by suppertime."

"Thanks," Wade said.

He paused a moment, but not long enough to let his uncle get back to work.

"So, how are you holding up?"

Patrick shrugged, trying to act stoic as usual.

"Ah, things are okay. My kids have been keeping me busy. They're both home from college, and they're always wanting to go somewhere, so it's been hard keeping them around long enough to do anything together."

"How's Mike been doing?" Wade decided to ask, hoping to get a roundabout answer to his first family inquiry.

"Well, he's back to work, but I don't think he's ever going to be used to having a different lieutenant. I think he had visions of retiring with Kevin so they could spend their golden years ditching their wives for a week at a time to go fishing."

"I talked to Sandi the other day. She says he's been spending a lot of time with Greg."

Patrick raised an eyebrow at the notion.

"That's odd. Those two are polar opposites. I wonder what has them running around together."

"I don't know, but she thought it was good therapy for Mike."

"Maybe it is."

Again, Patrick had been dumped by his family members for other people. Perhaps so many years of leaving himself unavailable to others had caused a role reversal.

"You know, I worry about Mom," Patrick confessed to the only person he seemed to have left as a listener in his family. "I thought she was going downhill after Dad died, but now with Kevin, it's like she has no will left at all."

"Dad's been taking a lot of time off work to be with her, but he says it's not helping."

"When someone loses their will to live, their body dies just a little bit each day," Patrick stated almost blankly of what he believed in his heart. "I think the sooner Mom sees Dad in the afterlife, the happier she'll be. Hell, after fifty years of marriage, I guess I would feel the same way."

Wade nodded in understanding. It had to be devastating to wake up one morning and realize life as one knew it for half a century was vastly different.

Scary, perhaps.

"It's hard to be around her like that," Patrick admitted. "It hurts to see someone break down when she raised all seven of us so right. I don't want to remember her like this, Wade."

"Dad says the same thing, but I guess he feels obligated to stay by her side because he's the oldest."

Patrick sat back in his chair for a moment, pondering his role in his mother's care.

He helped, but Jay took lots of time off work to help their mother along. Of course, Jay could afford to be away from work whenever he wanted, but Patrick had two out of every three days off.

"I'll have to give Jay a call in a little bit," he decided aloud. "He shouldn't be shouldering all of this alone."

Wade nodded.

"And maybe I can get you that personal day, kid. I'll let you know in a little bit."

"Thanks again," Wade said before heading out of the office to play ball with his fellow firefighters.

As his nephew left, Patrick scooped up the morning paper, reviewing an article about how quick the new volunteer department's response times were. It ate him alive, knowing the public actually believed the stats were legitimate, thinking the Washington Township Fire Department would gloriously show up to any scene with two or three trucks, ready to battle raging fires in a whim.

In reality, their chief usually patrolled the city half the night in a vehicle some city residents were paying for with their tax dollars. He often happened to be the first on the scene because he was already out and about.

It only took *one* person to be on scene, and report it, and the dispatcher's log would show that time as the initial response time, even if it took another ten or twenty minutes for the other firefighters to show up.

While the city department had a quick response time with adequate personnel, the volunteer department didn't appear that far off, and they were winning the media war. Patrick folded the paper, setting it to the side of his desk.

He had better things to do than worry about someone else's job at the moment.

"I really didn't expect you to call me back," Greg confessed as he sat beside Tasha on a park bench, occasionally throwing bread chunks from his turkey sub to the nearby pigeons.

"It took some time to dig up information without making it obvious," his ex-girlfriend revealed. "I could easily get fired for some of the things I did to get this."

She handed him a small packet of papers, held together by a rubber band.

"I appreciate it," Greg said sincerely. "We haven't had a whole lot to go on so far."

"It wasn't easy, and I didn't get as many details as I wanted to, but I'm afraid you're going to have a hard time proving anything, Greg."

Greg thumbed through the papers, finding several key points of interest.

"One of Shelton's apartments caught fire a few years ago," Tasha stated, "but it was minimal in damage, and they didn't think it was intentionally set. He reported a burglary last year in a different complex, in which a number of his valuables were stolen."

"Kind of a strange coincidence," Greg deduced.

"One would think, but he apparently claimed he was storing items in his apartment building while he and his wife moved into their new house."

Greg tossed a piece of bread out to the birds.

"So the first fire was dismissed as well?"

"Well, it was minimal. Maybe a few thousand in damages, tops."

"Was it investigated by an outside source?"

"I doubt it."

Damn, Greg thought.

"That's not to say he wouldn't have reason to burn his own building down," Tasha said. "I got a bit of his credit history, and he's not exactly filthy rich. Shelton's tied up in loans, including three rather nice cars, a lavish house, and his expanding property business."

"So he might have motive?"

"He might. He also might have enemies."

Greg decided he would glance through the papers later. Both sat silently a moment before he tossed another piece of bread to the birds, who drew closer each time he fed them, hoping for an early jump on the next piece of food.

Overhead, the skies threatened thunderstorms, so he decided to ask some questions that had plagued him since seeing Tasha again.

"So what's his name?"

"Who?" Tasha asked.

"Your fiancé."

"Blaine," she answered cautiously. "Blaine Emerson. Why do you want to know?"

"No reason. What's he do?"

Tasha laughed slightly, thinking Greg was jealous.

"He's a lawyer."

Greg shook his head. Her taste in men had changed drastically with the new promotion.

"And I suppose he makes you happy in every way?"

Tasha drew a look of exasperation.

"That's really none of your business, Greg. You walked out of my life a long time ago, and what I do now is my business."

He paused a moment.

"Sorry. I shouldn't be asking you all these personal questions."

"Look, I appreciate the concern, and I don't mind helping you, but maybe we should just leave it right here."

Greg felt his heart slump in his chest, even though he had never truly expected her to feel anything for him again. Still, being rejected twice was a bit rough on him, considering his recent emotional turbulence.

Particularly his recent decision to put a bullet in his head, which was only thwarted by a phone call.

"I managed to get copies of the police and fire reports in each incident," Tasha assured him, noticing his glum expression. "It should give you a little bit more to work with."

"I wish I could interview the man," Greg thought aloud.

"Why's that?"

"Just some strange things about the apartment building. Like why the gas was left on when most of the electricity was cut for the summer."

Tasha hummed a moment in thought.

"That *is* weird. Both would require a service charge to turn on again, so it seems pointless to turn either one off, actually."

"Of course, but electricity doesn't really help a building burn. Gas would."

"You're really after this arson thing, aren't you?" she asked.

"Only because I'm sure it's arson. I want to know who lit the match, or rigged it to burn. If only I had access to Shelton, or even Mason Gray's records," Greg concluded, letting the notion linger.

Tasha giggled to herself, then laughed, upsetting Greg all the more.

"What's so funny?"

"You keep talking about interviewing Shelton, like he keeps his own apartment buildings. Someone like that doesn't own three luxury cars, vacation in the Bahamas, and watch over his own apartments. He hires a manager."

Greg thought a moment about this new revelation. Interviewing Shelton's landlord or manager, whichever the case might be, would only result in the owner hearing about the interview later. He would be no better off than he would speaking with Shelton himself.

"I don't know about that," Greg said. "Maybe I can come up with some way to interview him without him knowing he's being questioned."

"I'm sure you'll come up with something," Tasha said before looking around the park, as though expecting someone to catch her with her ex-boyfriend. "Look, I've gotta go, Greg."

"Okay."

"Best of luck to you," she said, standing from the bench.

"Thanks," he said. "For everything."

"You're welcome," she said, almost forcing a grin, as though it pained her to leave him this way.

Greg watched her walk away, wondering why he had to be alone when she seemed to have found happiness in every way.

Maybe once he settled the matter at hand, he could begin piecing his own life back together, and just maybe he could find true love someday.

Perhaps.

CHAPTER 25

By the next morning, Mike was more than ready to go home as the sun rose in the horizon, bringing a warmth to the otherwise cool garage bay at Station Four.

Every bay door was open, and a humid breeze passed through, while Mike waited for the firefighter relieving him to show up. He leaned against the side of one of the open doors, watching the occasional early morning factory worker drive by, coffee in hand. Before, he never envied the men and women who slaved away in the unbearable heat and stench factories offered, but now their job seemed so much simpler. There weren't very many line of duty deaths in factories.

Another night of little sleep had come and gone. He could close his eyes, but images of the apartment fire and the glimpse of Kevin's charred corpse would forever haunt him.

At least to this point they had.

Life with a new lieutenant was almost more than he could tolerate.

Granted, the man was good at his job, and had more seniority than Mike and Sam Conley put together, but he wasn't Kevin. He didn't know the intricacies of burning buildings, or how quickly weakened structures could become dangerous as well as Kevin had.

Mike had no question the man knew his business, but Kevin was the best lieutenant he had ever worked with, and that wasn't just because the man was his brother.

By this time, his new lieutenant was probably almost home, while Mike would have to wait for his terribly slow relief to show up. Almost daily, he had to wait almost half an hour to leave the station.

Firefighters were given a thirty minute grace period to relieve one another in the morning, and some took advantage of every minute.

As the tones went off, Mike rolled his eyes and thought about ways to get back at the man who was taking his sweet time coming to work, leaving him to go on a run with firefighters from a completely different shift than his own.

Mike had nothing against the incoming shift, but he always felt awkward running with them, because each shift had its own way of doing things.

Still, he put on his gear, listening for the incoming dispatch.

"Four Squad, we have a possible kitchen fire at the Temple Baptist Church on Edgewood Road," the dispatcher said over the loudspeakers as the four men suited up for action.

By itself, a kitchen fire was no big deal, but given time to spread, then feed on the environment, it could become a raging basement inferno in no time. Most churches keep their kitchens down below, and whether or not windows are present is always a question for firefighters.

Mike had his turnout gear on within half a minute, then set to putting on his air pack. He wanted everything ready to go the moment he stepped from the pumper truck.

He overheard the radio stating Washington Township would also be en route, but expected to beat them there, since their reported response times were a farce. This would be Mike's first fire of any kind since Kevin's death, but he felt no different in responding, except for the lack of his brother in the front seat.

Usually there was no need to communicate with Kevin because they understood one another, and shared similar styles in how they approached scenes.

This turn would likely be apprehensive about working with Mike, since he was the odd man out. They also had no idea how he would react to scenes without Kevin, much like his own shift wondered.

As the church came into the lieutenant's view, he heard the dispatcher come over the radio once more.

"Four Squad, Washington Township advises a Signal-9."

In other words, the volunteer department had beaten them there and needed no further assistance.

As the truck grew closer, however, the lieutenant and driver noticed there was no fire truck of any kind in sight.

"Keep going," the officer ordered his driver.

He keyed the radio.

"Dispatch, we have no Washington Township truck visible. We're proceeding to get information."

As the pumper truck pulled into the parking lot, the lieutenant noticed light smoke filtering out of the building and a small car parked out front. Beside a Volkswagen Beetle stood a man dressed only in swimming trunks and a pair of floppy sandals, who looked to be a patron nice enough to stop at the sign of trouble.

"I've got it," the man reported to the lieutenant as the pumper truck pulled up.

"Got what?" the officer inquired.

"The situation. I gave you guys a Signal-9 through dispatch."

Everyone in the pumper truck widened their eyes, looking from this nearly naked man to the smoke billowing from the church.

"How do you have this under control when you're not even dressed to fight fire?" the lieutenant asked. "And you don't even have a truck here yet."

"It's nothing," the man insisted. "Just heavy smoke."

"I'll be the judge of that," the lieutenant said, stepping from the truck, all three of his firefighters following suit.

He walked toward the church with the Washington Township firefighter following only a few steps before the volunteer realized his chance to seize the glory for his department was fading quickly. Mike and the other back-end firefighter turned on their air packs, pulling the hose from the truck as the lieutenant tried to size up the scene.

He walked inside without benefit of an air tank, only to rush back out a few seconds later.

"There's flame," he reported in brief.

Wasting no time, Mike pulled the hose inside as water coursed through it, bringing it to life. Mike tried pulling the line around some steps leading down to the basement, but the line quickly got snagged around the railing.

"Get me some more line," he yelled back to his newfound partner.

"We were getting ready for our bake sale, and the oven caught fire," he overheard an older woman report to his lieutenant from the top of the stairs.

He missed the rest of the conversation as he opened the line on the flames across the room from the entrance. Barely visible through the smoke, the flames didn't immediately die when water hit them, which Mike guessed would be the result of grease, or gas, fueling the fire.

Even as he began doing his job, just as he had a hundred times before, Mike wondered exactly why he was there, and what kept him performing his job day after day. There was no rush, no excitement, and really, no happiness.

He suddenly wondered if his job was even worth doing any longer. Mike could perform his duty flawlessly, but the desire that once got him up at the break of dawn to get into work was no longer in him.

A few minutes later he numbly walked up the church stairs, took off his helmet and stripped the air mask from his face, feeling sweat drip down his cheeks and neck. He stumbled over to the truck, thinking of nothing but Kevin's death and the apartment fire.

"He left me down there," the other firefighter said quietly to the officer as he reached the top of the stairs. "We pretty much got the fire out, and he just left without saying a word."

Both looked to Mike, who leaned one arm against the truck, then walked around it to throw up. Thoughts of his brother, compounded with his rush to get back to work and prove he was ready to perform, had pushed him to physical and mental fatigue after so many restless nights of little or no sleep.

All three fellow firefighters saw him puke several times, feeling uneasy about having him back to work.

The volunteer firefighter also saw Mike's actions, thinking along completely different lines.

"He the new guy?" he inquired. "Can't handle it?"

"Not quite," the lieutenant said, pointing his finger in a somewhat threatening manner toward the young volunteer, armed with the knowledge that Tom Ellis wasn't the only one helping to manipulate the run times.

"He just lost his brother, and maybe he's not sleeping well these days. And I suggest you start worrying about falsifying your reports, because I don't know what the fuck you thought you were going to do to that fire down there."

"I was-"

"You were going to take a garden hose to it?"

"But I-"

"I don't give a shit what you were going to do. You don't ever put someone's property or life in danger by calling off your backup when you don't have adequate equipment to handle the situation. Hell, you *still* don't have a truck here, and we've already got the fire out."

Unsure of what to say, the firefighter stepped back, nervously touching his swimming trunks.

"I'll be telling my chief about this."

"You better hope you beat me to it, because I'll definitely have some words for him."

By this time, Mike was berating himself to the point that he was sobbing, his mind far too tired and clouded with a variety of emotions, including failure. He distanced himself from the group, trying to collect himself before letting them see him.

"What are we going to do with him?" one of the firefighters asked the lieutenant.

"Let him get himself together, guys. We've got some cleanup to do."

With that, the three reluctantly turned, seeing Mike clench his fists, angrily talking to himself as he walked aimlessly away from the truck.

༺ ༺ ༺

Greg discovered he had several more avenues to pursue after speaking with his ex-girlfriend. Though he discovered little of use toward Shelton, Greg was beginning to piece together some roundabout ways to discover the man's motives, and more about his holdings.

He found himself outside the office of the contractors scheduled to renovate Shelton's apartment over the summer. They were likely down one job for the season, but he doubted it would hurt their business in any way, with homeowners everywhere wanting jobs done.

Stepping inside, Greg found a woman his age dressed rather ruggedly, as though she had just come in from a work site.

Her dark hair reached her shoulders, and a thin layer of dust covered the flannel shirt and heavy utility vest she wore, and it appeared as though her morning had gotten the best of her. Greg wondered if she was the owner's working wife, but he didn't have time to ask warmup questions.

"Is the owner in?" he asked, though no one else appeared present in the small building that housed the construction company's business dealings.

"Yes, I am," the woman answered quickly, as though she had little time for inquiries herself.

"I have a few questions about the Brookshire Apartments, since you were the company slated to do the renovation."

"You with the police?" she asked skeptically.

Greg fished his wallet from his back pocket, quickly flipping it open to reveal the badge. As he replaced the wallet, his eyes met hers, and he felt certain the look of weary determination scrawled across his face did little to phase her.

"I'm a detective for Carvers Grove," Greg informed her. "Greg Sheridan."

The two shook hands briefly.

"Cassie Jones," she replied. "I assume you're here to inquire about the fire?"

"Yes."

He decided not to reveal the nature of his investigation, because most people would never call the police back, and that was the only way they would ever discover he was sleuthing in an unofficial capacity.

"I can't say a whole lot about it," Cassie said. "Though I own this company, I wasn't the one overseeing the daily operations at that site."

"Who can I talk to then?"

"Bob Tolbert is the man in charge of operations over there. He's currently overseeing the renovation of the old middle school into an assisted living facility on Tally Street."

"Would I be able to find him today?"

Cassie searched her mind for a moment, her expression one of momentary lapse, considering she had a dozen foremen to account for on a daily basis.

"Well, he should be *here* any minute," she finally said. "He's supposed to give me some figures on what materials he'll need for the next phase of his new project. Obviously the apartment job has been put on hold."

Greg nodded, figuring as much.

"Mind if I wait?"

"Not at all," Cassie replied, pouring herself a cup of coffee. "Want a cup?"

"Sure."

Greg looked over her features as she poured the coffee into disposable cups.

She appeared attractive, but in a weathered, tough girl kind of way. Wearing no makeup, Cassie seemed to believe appearances were entirely pretentious, and totally unnecessary in her line of work. Her throaty voice reminded Greg of his older brother, Jay, but with her it seemed rather sexy, like some female radio announcers he remembered listening to.

"We've already had the police question us about the fire," Cassie said, handing him a steaming cup. "What exactly brings you out here?"

Greg sensed she already knew something more than she was telling, so he decided to be honest, rather than risk her catching him in a lie and blowing his entire investigation.

"My brother died in that fire," he confessed, reaching for a sugar packet.

"Oh," she said with a sudden realization of how personal the nature of his search must have been. "I'm so sorry."

"Well, I'm not allowed to investigate through my department, but I want some answers about what happened that night."

"When Bob gets here we can explain everything-"

"No, please," Greg requested, cutting her off. "The fewer people who know how I'm going about this investigation, the better."

Cassie's face showed her confusion, so Greg decided to elaborate.

"I can't risk anyone else knowing I don't have my department's blessing on this, and as long as people think I'm here on official business, the better my chances of getting answers will be."

"And what makes you so sure I won't contact your department?"

Greg shrugged uneasily.

"Because I think you know I'm right, and someone is responsible for my brother's death. Whether it's the property owner, or someone else, I intend to find him."

"And then what would you do?"

"It depends."

"On what?"

"On how I get my answers, and if they can be used in a court of law."

"And if they can't?" Cassie asked, raising an eyebrow.

She seemed to be testing him.

"Then maybe I'll have to take care of things myself."

"And what would that solve?"

Greg stopped for a moment, wondering how this whole conversation blossomed into a visit to the psychologist's office. Here he was searching for answers, and he was being mentally probed by someone he didn't even know.

"Not to be rude, but what do you care how I go about solving my brother's murder?" he finally asked.

"Well, you are on my property, asking to see my foreman. And the newspaper said the fire department reached no conclusion on whether the fire was even arson, so how do you conclude someone is responsible for your brother's death?"

"If you had seen what I have, and talked to a third party who knows more about these things than the fire department's investigator, you would understand. Hell, I shouldn't even be telling you all of this."

Greg threw his hands up in frustration, then took a sip of coffee as he chuckled to himself for throwing such a fit. After all, he was still a detective by nature and description.

"Maybe it's good therapy," Cassie suggested.

"The only good therapy I can get is finding out what caused that fire," Greg said with grim determination. "I was there an hour before it started, and there was no sign of anyone, or any materials. I don't see any way that fire started on its own."

"Well, Bob is here, so I'll turn him over to you. First thing."

"Thanks," Greg said.

A minute later, Cassie introduced the detective to her foreman, and the two took a seat at a picnic table just outside the building in a break area.

"How can I help you?" Tolbert asked after taking a seat on the table's bench.

"I need to know why you had part of the Brookshire Apartments building torn apart in the middle."

"Torn apart?" Tolbert asked, corkscrewing his face in confusion.

"You had the middle gutted of carpeting and wall coverings, and there were gas lines exposed. Why was that?"

"Not to be a sarcastic asshole, but that's why they call it renovation."

"I understand that, but you chose the middle. Why not one of the ends? Both ends still had everything in them, needing to be upgraded too."

"Well, we wanted to get those done first, because the property manager said they were getting rented out first, before school started."

Greg made a mental note of the statement.

"And who is the property manager?"

"Scott Gustin."

"And why were you starting the renovation so close to the start of the school year? Didn't that need to be started in the spring, right after students left?"

Tolbert thought a second or two.

"Well, my understanding was that we were delayed with other projects, but I suppose they probably didn't want the construction done that soon, or Cassie would have had someone over there starting the work. We got there, and had to start everything from scratch. Sometimes they at least subcontract a company to gut the place for us."

"This Gustin fellow," Greg said, writing the name down, then airily waving a finger in thought. "Where do I find him?"

"He comes around every so often, but he works for a variety of people as a property manager. I think he has an office uptown."

"So he's probably not even hands-on with the everyday affairs?"

"Nah. He deals with the big money, insurance, industrial contracts. Stuff like that."

"I see."

Greg shook Tolbert's hand.

"Thanks for your time."

"No problem, detective."

Greg walked away, thinking he had some new leads to check. He felt like he was getting spread too thin with so much information, and hoped Mike might be able to help him track down some answers.

Then again, Mike was no detective, so Greg needed to filter what information his brother received.

CHAPTER 26

After almost a full day of sleep on his first day off, Mike spent his second day on his father's old tractor, tilling the ground in preparation for a garden the following spring.

One of his agreements with Sandi was to work a garden together the following year, and he knew from watching his parents for years that tilling it would be easier after the winter thaw if he stirred up the ground first, killing any grass and weeds, while raising some of the better soil from beneath.

Mike had inherited his father's tractor by default. It was too old to sell for any real worth, and it ran well enough that he could start using it on his own new farm. If it broke down, he would usually be able to fix it.

Humidity and hot temperatures caused him to sweat from head to toe, but the baseball cap he wore kept the sun from burning him too badly. Dressed in tattered jeans and a faded button shirt, he looked the part of a farmer. He even had a piece of straw dangling from the corner of one lip as his blue eyes squinted against the sunlight.

"How long has he been out there?" Greg asked Sandi as he walked from his car to the front porch.

"A couple hours," she replied. "I thought he was getting better, but he's not doing too well. Wade called and said a few of the guys were worried about him."

"Why?"

"I guess he broke down on a fire scene yesterday and started crying for no reason. He also left another firefighter alone in the building."

Both of them knew Mike well enough to know neither action was characteristic of the fireman. If he was cracking because of Kevin's death, they needed to act quickly, because things would only get worse, and someone might get hurt.

"How's he been acting around here?" Greg inquired.

"Fine. He'll talk some, then want to be alone for awhile."

She took a moment to stare out to the field as Mike rounded a corner for another pass with the tiller. As the blades spun, turning and spitting up the chunks of ground, small puffs of dust rose from behind the tractor and the tiller it towed behind it.

"Everything still okay with the wedding?"

"We really haven't talked about it."

"I don't think I've congratulated you on the baby yet, have I?" Greg asked, remembering one of his brothers informing him of such, shortly after the cookout.

"No, but thanks," Sandi said with a smile. "It just seems like terrible timing, because Mike can't even enjoy it."

"He will. And he'll be a great dad, too."

"Yeah, he will. It'll be so peaceful out here in the country with nothing to worry about, raising our little one. I just can't wait for Mike to get himself back on track."

Greg paced the front of the porch a moment. His own life wasn't getting any better either. His sergeant continued to ensure he would work nothing but light cases, and his personal investigation was at a standstill unless he could get Mike back on track to help him.

"Can you help him?" Sandi asked, as though Greg might be her last hope to get Mike back to normal.

"I can try. I thought I had him going in the right direction, but maybe I was wrong."

"I've got to go pick up a few groceries. Can you stay with him until I get back?"

"Sure."

Greg stuck around long enough to see Sandi leave, then waited a few more minutes until Mike grew weary of sitting on the tractor. He finally brought it to a stop at the edge of the field and sauntered over to see his twin brother.

"What's new?" Greg asked.

"Just doing some plowing," Mike replied, thrusting a cup beneath a water jug at the edge of the porch to get some lemonade. "What brings you out here?"

"I was a little worried about you, since I haven't seen you in a few days."

Mike shrugged.

"Nothing new with me."

"I've been carrying on my search without you, and I might have some answers."

Mike looked to the sky, as though trying to avoid the subject, or perhaps any subject at the moment.

"What's wrong with you?" Greg felt compelled to ask.

"I don't know," Mike said uneasily, instead of trying to make up some lie. "I guess I thought I could cope with everything, but maybe I can't."

"I heard about your breakdown on the fire scene yesterday."

"I'm sure everyone has by now, and honestly, I don't give two shits."

Greg looked his brother in the eyes, even if Mike wouldn't return his stare.

"You need to start giving a shit about yourself, Mike. If you don't want to help me find who set that fire, that's fine, but you need to start thinking about you."

They stepped onto the open porch, taking seats in two wicker rocking chairs.

"When Dad died, I got over it," Mike said. "We had a few months to prepare for it, and it wasn't a big shock. When Kev died, though, it crushed me. Being as hardheaded as I am, I thought I could get through it, then I went back to work and realized it wasn't the same. Goddamn, it'll never be the same, Greg, and I don't know if I can put in another twenty years feeling like this."

"I know what you mean, and even though it gets a little easier every morning, I still think about Dad and Kevin a lot, every single day."

"It hasn't gotten easier for me," Mike admitted. "Not this time."

Greg sat back a moment as they both enjoyed the light breeze passing them by, rocking away part of their day.

"I go to work, and there's a new lieutenant there," Mike said. "He's a great guy, and he knows his job, but he's not Kev. Everyone at work touches me with kid gloves now. No one wants to talk about it, like it never happened."

"Put yourself in their shoes, Mike. How often would you bring up such a touchy subject?"

"I suppose you're right."

For a moment, they lost themselves in a world of rocking wicker chairs, no cares around them. Neither had taken a moment since Kevin's death to truly reflect.

Or relax.

"Look, I know how you're feeling, but I need your help if I'm going to find out who's behind that apartment fire," Greg said. "I'd bet my life that it was arson, and I'm narrowing the list of suspects rather quickly."

"Oh?"

"I've been talking to certain people connected to the apartment's renovation, and it seems there are a few fishy moves the construction team made, that were under the direction of the apartment's manager."

Mike perked up a bit.

"Have you talked to him yet?"

"No, but I have been checking a few things out. I went to his office and got some information under the pretense I was looking for a place to stay. He runs several apartment buildings for several different owners."

"That's odd."

"That's what I thought, until I discovered there's a trio of owners who comprise a little unofficial group. You'd never know it, because they each have their own holdings, but they stick together as kind of a secretive monopoly in Carvers Grove."

"Have you checked their insurance claims, or looked for discrepancies in their taxes?"

"I'm getting started on the insurance thing. I could give a crap less about their taxes, because I'm sure their attorneys keep their paperwork in perfect order. Besides, what they're doing isn't illegal, but it could put a cloud around their empire so authorities don't find the real source of their big bucks."

"But why torch their own places?"

"Buy cheap, spend as they go on the renovation, and take out monstrous insurance policies on their property. They rotate the fires among their properties to avoid suspicion, hire a professional to make it look accidental, and share the profits in the end."

"But don't the insurance companies check that they rebuild their buildings, to keep them insured?"

"Maybe. It doesn't matter, though, because one of our trio owns a construction company that rebuilds the stuff at a fraction of the estimated cost."

"So he shops around, takes the highest possible bid, and gets the money," Mike surmised. "I'm surprised they haven't been caught yet."

"Well, they don't leave much of a trail, and your arson investigator seems to have some ties to the higher elite in our city, so maybe things get brushed aside rather quickly."

Mike appeared stunned.

"Are you suggesting Gray would cover up for these people?"

"Maybe he just wasn't looking real hard," Greg replied with a shrug.

"He's a prick, but I can't believe he would do something like that."

"And just imagine if he did it on the fire that killed Kevin."

"How could you even think that?" Mike retorted, insulted at his twin's words.

"You heard it yourself when the outside investigator suggested Gray hadn't been real cooperative, and hadn't mentioned the exposed gas lines to him. Do you really think Gray is that much of an asshole, or do you think he might be falsifying his reports?"

Mike thought a moment.

"My God, what if he did omit stuff from his reports?" he finally asked, more to himself than his brother.

"You know he keeps that stuff under lock and key. Even your chief doesn't get to it. Maybe you can find a way to get inside and look through his files."

"If I get caught, it could be my job," Mike said. "I can't break and enter into the main office."

"You might not have to do either," Greg suggested.

"What do you have in mind?" Mike asked, a quirky smile crossing his lips.

🍁　　　🍁　　　🍁

I'm killing Greg when I get out of here, Mike thought nervously from the closet of Mason Gray's office, shut behind a door.

He had to wait about five more minutes before every room in the chief's front office would close, and everyone would go home.

Gaining access to the offices was easy, as Mike walked through the front door, stating he was going to visit some of the guys in the firehouse itself. He simply waited until the coast was clear when Gray walked to the bathroom, to sneak into the office undetected, and close himself into the investigator's closet.

Everything seemed fine until he heard Gray return to the office, shuffle some papers, and make a call to someone on the police department with little relevance to anything. He tried holding his breath, completely fearful Gray would open the door to fetch a spare shirt, or hear him breathing behind the door.

Mike could feel his legs trembling slightly from the fear of being caught, because he had never done anything quite like this before.

He felt certain Greg had set him up with the hardest job either of them could possibly have done in their search for the truth. Gray was just enough of a prick to have Mike arrested and fired from his job if he caught the firefighter inside his closet.

Mike had no excuse ready, because there was no excuse to be hiding in someone's closet so close to closing time.

A practical joke, Mike quickly thought.

No, Gray has no sense of humor, he decided.

Shit, I have no excuse, he thought as the light outside the office clicked off, and he heard the door shut and lock as Gray and the other officers went home for the evening.

Mike breathed a sigh of relief, but still waited a few minutes to make certain no stragglers would see him inside the office.

None of the regular firefighters would have access to the front offices, so once all of the white shirts left, he would have free run of the place, but no real way to get out. At least no way out without leaving some evidence that someone had been there, he deduced.

All of the doors had deadbolt locks, and though he could let himself out, there would be no way to cover his tracks. Gray would know someone was in his office, and likely cover his tracks if he was responsible for any kind of coverup.

"I'm fucked," Mike told himself, opening the closet door to begin his search.

❦   ❦   ❦

Tasha Barnes finished her day on a positive note, having landed several new clients in lunch meetings.

Often she had three or four lunches a day with clients, and seldom ate more than a tiny salad at each, to ensure her figure remained exactly as it was.

She felt it would be impolite to refuse lunch altogether, so she limited her intake, focusing more on talks with her clients. Tasha had to give clients the impression they were the *only* people she would speak to that day, even if it wasn't true.

As she approached her car in the nearly full parking lot, Tasha was startled when someone spoke to her from a car parked in an adjacent parking spot.

"Tasha," Greg said. "I need your help one more time."

Quickly over her initial shock, she turned to unlock her door, ignoring him as best she could.

"I can't help you anymore," she replied, trying to escape the situation.

"Why? Because your future husband might be connected to my brother's death?"

She turned around, a mix of anger and ignorance of what he was saying, written across her face.

"How dare you!"

"How dare me? You've been protecting him all this time, thinking I wouldn't find out?"

"I don't know what you're talking about," she stammered.

"Give me five minutes, and I'll explain everything to you."

"How do I know this isn't some trick to lure me back to you?"

Greg rolled his eyes.

"Because I don't have time for anything but solving an arson right now, and you're keeping me from finding the man ultimately responsible."

Tasha weighed her options.

Thinking it preposterous her fiancé could be involved with an arson fire in any way, she wanted to hear what Greg had to say, to disprove him if nothing else.

"Okay," she finally agreed. "I'll hear you out if you promise to leave me alone when we're through."

"Fair enough," Greg said, thinking she would either be insulted enough to never want to be near him again, or she would go the opposite way and want him to protect her, if she believed Blaine Emerson was capable of helping the trio who had probably helped themselves to millions of dollars.

Either way, Tasha was in for an earful.

※　　　※　　　※

Odors of air-fresheners lingered in the room as Mike began searching through the desk first, finding just a few files of interest.

He set them on the desk, for later reading, and set to trying the filing cabinets, which were all locked except for one on the bottom. It held little more than trophies and trinkets, which Gray lacked room to display in his already heavily decorated office.

"This sucks," Mike commented under his breath, wondering why the investigator would be paranoid enough to lock his filing cabinet, even when his office door was locked.

Maybe because of people like me, he deduced.

Despite lacking the time to search for keys, Mike knew he needed to get into the cabinets somehow, and looked through the desk once more, positive he had seen several small sets of keys throughout several of the drawers.

Gray seemed very protective of his work, speaking to no one about his investigations, keeping his files locked up, and never showing anyone the results unless necessary in a court of law. Even so, Mike now wondered if the investigator always disclosed the full truth under oath.

In his search, Mike found a key for the investigator's office, which he guessed was a spare. He could use it to lock this office when he left, but he would probably have to leave through the front or back door of the main office, leaving one unlocked, since this was no master key.

Still, he was better off than a minute ago.

Moving like legs on a caterpillar, his fingers sorted through papers and assorted junk inside the remaining desk drawers, looking for keys that might fit the filing cabinet.

Finding no other keys inside the desk, he turned to look at the small refrigerator stuffed into a corner beside the closet, a sudden thought crossing his mind.

In several of the fire stations, firefighters locked their refrigerators so the other shifts couldn't access them when they were gone, and in doing so, locked keys that fit other cabinets and cupboards inside the appliances as well.

If luck was on his side, Gray was a creature of similar habit.

He pulled the door to the fridge open, searched a flip-up hatch, and found a small set of keys sitting inside.

"Oh, please," he begged no particular spirit as he swiped the keys from their spot, stopping a few seconds as a bumping noise caught his attention from somewhere in, or near, the office.

He listened until he heard a toilet flush from an adjoining room, and sighed relief before taking the keys over to the cabinet, careful to insert and turn them quietly.

They worked, and he was able to gain access to everything Mason Gray had ever worked on since taking the investigator position for the Carvers Grove Fire Department.

"Sweet," Mike said to himself, looking over the folders like a kid who finds an Easter basket flowing with goodies.

"I can't believe you would even imply Blaine is involved in arson," Tasha said in an exasperated tone as they both stepped from their cars inside Jackson Park.

"Well, it's speculation on my part," Greg said, leading the way to the nearby riverbank, "but I'm almost positive his brother is involved in some kind of conspiracy to reap profits from insurance companies."

"That's insane," Tasha said, raising her hands against the idea. "His brother runs a legitimate construction company."

"And owns several apartment buildings."

"So?"

"They all share a common general manager named Scott Gustin," Greg revealed. "And that's just the beginning of their ties."

"What are you talking about?"

Both simultaneously seated themselves at a picnic table.

"Dirk Shelton is connected in a trio with Ronnie Emerson and some Bryan Boyce guy. They're all connected through Gustin, and I've been checking up on them. Somehow they're friends or partners, but I haven't had time to research their connection yet. I have reason to believe they're in a scheme to make money from insurance companies, but it would take some investigating to make sure."

Tasha shot him a look of complete disbelief, as though he might have just informed her she was adopted.

"You are asking me to investigate my future brother-in-law on a hunch?" she demanded. "I can't just go searching insurance records at will and stake my future on some jealous hunch you might have."

"Jealous? I'm trying to figure out who killed my brother, and the only thing you can think about is your future family matters?"

"Well, it is going to seem funny around Thanksgiving, sitting around the table, having my brother-in-law bring up the time I tried to prove he was part of a major insurance scam. Oh, I'm sure we'll just laugh it off and eat some cranberries."

Greg didn't find the statement the least bit funny.

"I'm only asking you to look into their insurance statements if you choose to. If I'm wrong, you never need to speak to me again. If I'm right, I'd at least appreciate a phone call."

"I just can't do what you're asking," Tasha insisted. "If Blaine ever found out…"

Greg saw her let the notion hang in the air, like she had their relationship several years before.

"Okay," Greg said, slapping his hands against his knees as he stood to leave. "I can see I'm going to have to find my answers elsewhere."

"Yes," Tasha said, a mist coming to her eyes, entirely unable to look at her ex-boyfriend. "You are."

Greg wanted to say any number of things, but most would leave them both feeling worse and more awkward than they already were.

"Bye," he simply said, walking toward his car.

Tasha sat a moment, looking at the ducks gliding across the calm waters before her. She wondered if he was telling the truth about her fiancé's brother. Of course he was, she decided. He wasn't the type to make up stories for attention, or to ruin her relationships maliciously.

Deciding what to do would take some time, because she had everything to lose by cooperating with Greg's secret investigation. If she did opt to help, Greg would owe it all to her conscience.

The one thing he truly loved about her when they dated.

She wished Greg all the luck in the world, but Tasha felt unsure about throwing her career and her future away for a man she openly denied feeling anything for.

Life had been good to her, and she wasn't about to throw it away so easily.

Making himself at home in the office, Mike propped his feet on the desk as the sun set outside, leaving little light across any of the offices.

He turned on a desk lamp to read by, knowing Gray's office was nestled too far inside the front office chambers for anyone from the outside to notice. Half an hour alone inside the office had already made him overly comfortable in the surroundings.

As he thumbed through several files, Mike noticed two different columns of paperwork. Anything clipped to the left side of the folders was Gray's true, honest opinion. They usually came in the form of handwritten notes scrawled messily on whatever scrap paper the investigator unearthed from his vehicle at the fire scene.

Everything secured with a paperclip on the right was typically his official report, which he used for courtroom purposes. Sometimes these reports didn't completely match the scribbles on the left.

Part of it could have been Mike's ignorance of how arson reports were completed, some of it could have been amendments Gray made before filling out the official report, and in some cases, Mike felt certain the report itself had been completed to fill an agenda.

"Goddamn him," Mike muttered, discovering the explosion a few months back had conflicting conclusions from the left page to the right.

On the right stood the facade Gray had fed the media about how the explosion was accidental, caused by a faulty gas line, then triggered by an electrical short. Everything seemed feasible, especially the way it was presented in the official report.

Mike's eyes returned to the left side of the page, and he read some of the notes as he flipped through the scrap sheets of paper.

He read the choppy notes aloud as they appeared.

"Evidence of small dents in the gas line indicates possible tampering, doors still locked from the outside, no evidence of breaking and entering. Inside job? Why is a nightlight in the storage closet? Possible blockage of vent pipes."

In Mike's opinion, there was too much evidence to rule the explosion accidental, especially so soon. He looked further into the papers, then stopped as he found something interesting.

"Boyce Realty," he muttered the name aloud, thinking he knew it from somewhere.

They owned the property, so he made a mental note of the find. He closed the file, already suspicious of Gray's work ethic, and decided he had wasted enough time. Mike needed to check the Brookshire fire report, and see if Gray was truly crooked or not. And, if his brother's death was accidental, or murder.

Gray officially ruled the fire inconclusive, since there were no accelerants found inside the ruins, which Mike now knew was the truth. Still, there were conflicts again on the left page in comparison to the official report.

Again, Mike read them to himself as he saw them.

"Gas lines evident…exposed before the fire. No electric, but gas is on. Fire started on second floor, probably around room twenty-five to twenty-eight. All exterior and interior doors appear locked. Inside job? Witnesses? Bare-bones section of apartment, ripe for a burn. Lack of fire stops and open walls allowed fire to travel fast."

Mike paused a second.

"No shit," he commented to himself.

He stood for a moment, looking at some of the accolades along the walls and shelves of the office, noticing photos of Gray with various prominent members of the local society, few of which Mike could identify.

Wishing he and his brother would exchange information more often, Mike felt positive he was probably staring at more clues than he realized.

As he returned to the pages after a brief break, a scribbled piece of information caught his attention.

"Security tape removed from recorder," he mumbled the line aloud. "Well, if that doesn't look strange as hell."

He finally looked through several other cases, finding the investigator extremely proficient and consistent in his job, with the exception of only a few files. As he compared the files, Mike discovered they were usually close to a year apart, and the discrepancies were eerily similar.

Using the investigator's computer, he checked the run reports from those dates, finding his hunch of foul play was more real than he could have imagined.

"Holy shit," Mike said, looking at the files, noticing the ownership of the buildings was spread between three different people, and each of the names popped up more than once in the various reports.

More than likely, the fires had been spread far enough apart that fire officers would have forgotten about the ownership, and they were likely spread between the three fire department shifts, so no one had ever taken notice.

Except one person.

"What the hell is Gray's connection to these men?" Mike wondered aloud.

Positive he had seen enough, and risked trouble with the law in doing so, he decided to make copies for proof. Stepping into the hallway, Mike took the incriminating files with him, setting the first one carefully on the copy machine, only to have the copier demand a code before it would perform in any way.

"Fuck."

Mike lightly kicked the machine, then realized the danger of doing so, and quickly gathered the files together. He paced the floor a moment, realizing he had proof toward an incredible break in the case, knowing it was useless if he took it with him.

Walking along the hallway containing the copier and Gray's office door, Mike let his mind wander for ideas of how to leave with the proof. He had no camera, he couldn't call anyone, there was no fax machine available, and writing every detail down would take hours.

Leaving with only his new knowledge of Gray's activities seemed worthless, because it would be useless in a court of law, but he had little choice.

Papers obtained by illegally entering the man's office would also be worthless. Either way, Mike was no further than he had been from a legal standpoint.

Greg would not be happy.

"Dammit," he muttered, deciding to put the files back where they belonged, to fight again another day from an investigative standpoint.

Mike jotted down a few of the key names and notes, careful not to leave any evidence of his writing through the pad he used, by taking the top three sheets with him.

He carefully locked Gray's door, slid the key underneath, so it would look like it accidentally fell out of the main desk drawer to the floor, and exited through a back door that required no lock from the inside. He felt lucky about his exit, but irritated he had nothing to show for his trouble.

Perhaps his brother had something to show for their troubles.

CHAPTER 27

Mike returned to work the next morning, feeling horrible from a lack of sleep the night before.

After failing to retrieve anything from Gray's office, he tossed and turned all night, thinking of ways to gather proof. The one time he did fall asleep, he had a dream that Gray discovered him inside his office, and Mike had to come up with a quick lie about why he was there.

Gray bought it, and Mike escaped the office, only to find Kevin outside with a disapproving look across his face. Mike tried to approach his older brother, but woke up just before he could actually speak to Kevin. He wondered why things happened in dreams that would never occur in reality. If he was caught in Gray's office for real, he would probably be beaten and tortured by the investigator until he told the truth about why he was there.

Kevin's image bothered him a bit more, because it seemed real, and just like in real life, he failed to communicate with his older brother the way he wanted. Maybe not getting the chance to speak with Kevin in the dream was a way of stating he should give up his search for the arsonist, or that he just needed to remain patient, and he would make contact with his brother again.

Trying to shake off the avalanche of terrible events from the night before, Mike watched a mid-morning game show on television inside the station's second living quarters, hoping to fall asleep in the recliner before the show grasped his attention.

A stream of light entered the room as the door opened behind him, and Mike knew his prayers for an overdue rest would go unanswered.

"Hi, Greg," Mike said almost sourly from the recliner as his brother took a seat on a nearby couch.

"Sorry we didn't meet up last night, but I was doing some searching of my own," Greg explained. "Did you find anything good?"

"Only the mother lode," Mike stated.

"What does that mean?"

Mike looked around to make sure none of the other firefighters were within earshot, even if they weren't in the room.

"I found evidence linking several fires to Shelton and Emerson."

"Anything about a Bryan Boyce?"

"Yeah, him too."

"So, what do you have for me?"

"Nothing."

Mike quickly explained his problems with the copier.

"That stinks," Greg commented. "Not that any of it would be useful in court, but I would have felt more secure seeing something on paper."

"Gray is covering up a lot more than we ever might have thought, Greg. He has all kinds of scribbled notes of ideas and facts, but when it comes to the official report, he changes his story."

"That's not unusual."

"It is when he changes his story completely, or leaves out facts."

Greg sighed to himself.

"We need something really incriminating here, Mike. Does he mention ownership of the burned properties in his reports, or anything that links the property owners to each other, maybe indicating he has an idea of what's going on?"

"No, he never mentions the owners. I had to dig that up from our run reports."

Greg sat silently a moment, trying to think of any way Mike's find might be useful.

"What is it?" Mike finally asked.

"I just don't see any way this is going to help us without hard evidence, Mike. Everything you found in there is circumstantial."

"Bullshit. I conclusively linked Gray to those fires. There's no way he could not have known about the ownership."

"You know that, and I know that, but unless you plan on going vigilante on me, we need to find some real proof we can turn in to the proper authorities if we're going to get anywhere."

"And just who are we going to give this information to, Greg?" Mike questioned, realizing Greg had never stated where he might go with hard evidence. "You think your department is going to just up and take over the case when you hand it to them? And the state police are worse than anyone about having something thrown in their lap. We'd be damn lucky if they didn't come after us."

Greg took in the words, but they didn't phase him one bit.

"We prove the insurance angle, we work the arson investigator angle, and we watch Scott Gustin, because he's the one link to all three of these men," Greg stated with a solid voice that knew no other course of action.

"I don't know," Mike said, shaking his head. "I risked my career last night to get you some information, and you say we can't use a bit of it. Kevin deserves better than us beating around the bush, trying to legally pinpoint who's behind this."

"And what would you do?" Greg fired back, realizing too late he was raising his voice enough to send it ringing through the station. "We can't go banging heads trying to find the arsonist, or we might blow it."

Mike disagreed.

"We wait too long to nail him, our trail might get cold, or maybe he splits town."

"And if we go beating the information out of people, or make too much noise, we put people into hiding, and they cover up our evidence. Mike, if we play this cool and build a case, we have a chance of getting these men convicted. All of them."

He leaned forward.

"We *have* to keep quiet about this. I appreciate everything you did last night, don't get me wrong, but let me handle things from here. If I'm real lucky, I may have a great source of information falling into my lap this week."

Luck, Mike thought sarcastically.

Maybe he was too ambitious, or too impatient, but Greg wasn't exactly presenting him with any overwhelming leads toward bringing the men responsible for Kevin's death to justice.

"Okay," Mike finally said. "You go about your investigation, and see what you can do."

"You sure you're okay with that?"

"Yeah," Mike lied, putting on his best content face.

"Great. I'll keep you posted about whatever I find."

Both sat a few moments, pretending to watch the game show. Greg thought about what avenues he had left to pursue, and interviewing Scott Gustin, he decided, was not one of them.

Following the man, perhaps, but no interviews. Gustin would be dangerous since he worked for all three men involved in the arson-for-profit conspiracy. Perhaps he was privy to the plan, or worse, the arsonist.

No, Greg decided about any interviews. That was too risky.

"You doing okay around here?" Greg finally asked.

"Yeah, I'm doing better."

"I can tell by the way you mope around by yourself," Greg said sarcastically.

"I'm coping."

Greg smelled lunch from the next room as the new lieutenant cooked with Conley and Thomas, trying to promote unity with his new group.

"Smells like you're about to eat," the detective noted.

"Probably," Mike said as though uninterested. "Ollie's trying to win us over by cooking for us every day."

"And that's bad?"

"No, but he needs to understand I don't hate him, and I'll adapt over time, but it's not going to happen overnight."

"I see. Sounds like you're about as miserable as I've been."

"Detective work not suit you?" Mike asked, perking up a bit.

"Not when it involves tracking down internal theft at the local pizza parlor, or checking cold cases older than I am."

"No wonder you have to investigate on your own. You must get bored up there."

"Sometimes."

Greg stood to leave, having a few things to check before he went into work that afternoon.

"I appreciate you leaving this in my hands," he told Mike.

"No problem. You'd better get some results, though, or I'll be carrying out my own ideas of justice."

"It could take awhile, but I'll get us some proof," Greg promised. "And a way to use it in court if we can get it there."

Mike nodded, and Greg gave a brief wave before leaving the room.

Waiting until his brother left the station, Mike sat down with a pad and pen, thinking of every way he could begin to pursue his brother's killer without Greg's bureaucratic nonsense. He might be forever waiting for evidence to come their way, and even if something went to court, it sounded like any of the three conspirators would have ample funds to buy an attorney who would get them off the hook.

If Gustin went to court for anything, they would sell him up the creek, and no real justice would be served.

Unless, of course, he was the arsonist.

"I have to know who's lighting the match," Mike said to himself.

Only then would he begin to understand who the real guilty parties were, and to what extent they were involved.

Fault could be found in quite a few places, but Mike had a good idea who the real people to blame were.

He knew Patrick had tried to convince their mother to sue the Washington Township Fire Department, to give them bad publicity if nothing else. She refused, despite support from the family, and nothing would come of it.

Few avenues of retribution remained, leaving Mike more and more convinced the job of finding the ultimate party responsible for killing Kevin was his undertaking.

And his alone.

He jotted down a few more ideas, and decided he would put some of his plans into action the very next morning.

※　　　　※　　　　※

Sitting nervously at his desk with his chin resting on his clasped hands, Scott Gustin could not rest easily of late.

By all accounts, the Brookshire fire could be summed up as accidental, but he felt certain someone would begin to piece together the information. Those people would then likely turn their attention to him.

He knew Mason Gray was no factor, because the informal conglomerate had already given major contributions to his recent bid for coroner, just as they had helped his cause several times before.

Still, a firefighter was killed, and regardless of whether or not Gray pieced together the scenario, he wasn't going to try very hard. Gustin knew there were other investigators, however, and an entire community, distraught over Kevin Sheridan's death.

Hopefully blame would fall on the new volunteer department, but Gustin wasn't counting on it.

His three employers had told him to keep quiet about everything. If he put on a business as usual front, everything would be fine.

Gustin originally went to work for Ronnie Emerson, but soon found himself working for Boyce and Shelton as well. With added raises came added responsibility, but Gustin had no problem being their errand boy for what they paid him.

Even when he was approached about finding a suitable fire setter to keep their hands clean, he had no objections. No one would get hurt, and he would be given a fair share of the insurance money. Everything seemed flawless at the time.

Lately, things had been a bit more hectic, and keeping a low profile grew more difficult by the day. State fire marshals had spoken with him, along with the private insurance investigator. Shelton would see no financial gain if the private investigator found any evidence of arson.

Worse yet, the arsonist himself had been in touch with Gustin, trying to get the remainder of his fee.

Half up front, half after the job, was the standard deal, and usually Gustin had no trouble in paying promptly, but the firefighter's death had put a lot of attention on Shelton Properties, and Gustin himself.

"What's wrong with you?" Ronnie Emerson asked as he strolled through the property manager's office, noticing Gustin's nervous fidgeting.

"Nothing," Gustin lied.

Paying the arsonist was strictly his responsibility, and his bosses never wanted to hear another word about it, so telling the truth was technically prohibited. They were excessively careful never to mention a word directly about the scheme at work, home, or play, and expected the same of him.

"Have you dealt with the business at hand?" Emerson asked, skirting around the topic of the arsonist.

"Not yet. Our client has yet to receive payment," Gustin said, encrypting his words.

"You should take care of it," Emerson said assuredly. "There's no heat. No one knows about us."

"Are you sure?"

"Of course I am. We need to keep good business practices, Scotty."

He paused to pour himself a cup of coffee, looking around the drab office as he tested it for the necessary amount of sweetener.

"We've got to watch ourselves," Gustin said out of nowhere.

"What's that supposed to mean?"

"We're doing too much too fast."

Suddenly Emerson was annoyed about Gustin speaking of their less than legitimate business.

"Shut the fuck up, Scott. If you don't want any part of this, you can walk out anytime and we'll happily pay your salary to someone else."

Gustin put up a defensive hand.

"I'll deal with our boy," he said. "Sorry I doubted your judgment."

"You'd better. Tell him to lay low and keep his mouth shut, and everything will work out just fine," Emerson said with a smug grin. "There's nothing stopping us now, Scotty, unless you decide to go shoot your mouth off."

Gustin shook his head negatively.

"You can count on me, boss."

"I hope so, because it would be a shame to use our boy's talents on you. We both know he does exactly what he's paid to do."

Swallowing hard, Gustin reached into the desk drawer for an envelope stuffed with cash. As Emerson casually sauntered out, he picked up the phone to contact his hired hand through a third party.

The time to finish the business at hand had long since passed.

᙮ ᙮ ᙮

After supper that evening, Patrick sent Wade to one of the outlying stations, where he was to ride the rescue truck. One of the other firefighters was making a quick trip to the hospital to see his daughter through a minor surgery. Rather than call in someone for overtime, the battalion chief decided to cut the manpower of the headquarters truck for two hours.

Certain firefighters have superstitions about everything from which bed they sleep in, to never breaking their morning routine. They fear any change from one day to another might lead them into a raging fire that day. Never, under any circumstances, do those firefighters ever say they expect 'the big one' that night, or sure enough, they get it.

"Be careful what you wish for," Wade heard his Uncle Patrick say every so often, inside his mind.

Wade's superstition was based on a few experiences in the past when his uncle had sent him out to cover for a few hours. He hated packing up his gear and leaving his home station, but he was the low man on the shift in terms of seniority, so he had little choice.

Two out of the three times he had covered someone before, Wade found himself in a working house fire, and an assist on a car accident, which proved to be little more than a fender bender. Still, Wade looked at the few hours he was asked to cover another station, and how those few hours were burned into the archives of his memory.

So, when the alarms went off, and dispatchers notified the rescue crew that they had a vehicle accident with entrapment, it didn't surprise Wade in the least. His two truck mates didn't seem shaken either, but they had probably done this about a hundred times before.

When Wade first arrived at the station, the two men showed him some basics about the truck and the hydraulic tools, but they all knew a person needed to be stationed with the rescue truck for a few weeks or more to truly understand how the tools worked. Just learning where items were throughout the twenty-two storage compartments required uncanny memorization ability, and the checklist used in the morning to inventory every piece of equipment could barely keep up with the changes each shift made to the truck.

It seemed every week or two they added more new equipment, and the truck ran out of places to store everything. A few things would be removed here and there as their newer, more effective counterparts were delivered, but the shifts often failed to communicate the changes to one another, making an already tough truck all the more difficult to learn.

Even as he rode in the back of the truck, getting his full gear on, as he knew he was supposed to, even on a non-fire run, Wade wondered what on earth he was supposed to do once they got there.

He refused to fake his way through anything, so he decided just to stay out of the way and fetch anything the two veterans needed.

"Entrapment means jaws," he muttered to himself, trying to think of what they would need. "Or maybe the shears."

He knew both pieces of apparatus by name and appearance, but he had never actually used them.

Both were hydraulic monsters that could tear apart, or cut, through any fiberglass and metal conventional vehicles challenged them with. Just before Wade had come on the department, all of the younger members were allowed to test the hydraulic tools on a locally donated car.

Figures, he thought as the large rescue truck pulled to a stop, it's box shape impeding most of the road, which police hard cordoned off anyway.

"You need anything?" Wade asked the driver, who started plugging air hoses into the right slots on the miniature air compressor along the backside of the truck, knowing exactly what they needed.

Both men had performed a quick evaluation before the rescue truck even stopped, and knew they would simply need the jaws of life to pry the door from the car frame, enabling EMS to get their patient out of the car.

"Stay with Joe and see what he needs," the driver said. "And take this."

He stuffed a rescue blanket into the rookie firefighter's hand, which looked shiny and silverish, like spacesuits from television shows in the 60's. Wade took it, following Joe West over to the car where technicians had already packaged the victim for transport, using a cervical collar to stabilize the neck, with a backboard ready to go once the door was removed.

Wade watched as West used a center punch in one lower corner of the window, creating a spider web effect across the glass. Reaching a hand through the small hole in the lower corner he had just used the punch on, West brushed the glass out toward himself, away from the patient, while one of the paramedics shielded the injured driver.

Lieutenant Joe West was from the old-school of firefighting. Very respected, and liked by everyone, because he seemed to fear nothing, West took every situation like a bull by the horns. He never lost control, never gave up, and always had something good to say about everyone, even though the department had a few known jerks within its ranks.

His hair was graying with age, but he held a rookie-like spark in his eyes on every run he made. To him, the job never got old, and it was about helping others above all else.

"Thanks," West simply said, taking the blanket from Wade as the driver brought the jaws of life over to the them, setting the tool down behind West.

Freed up for a moment, Wade finally surveyed the scene, seeing several cops standing around, a few doing work. Several citizens stared from behind the police line around the car, which had wrapped its passenger side around an electrical pole.

The car itself was somewhat of a horseshoe shape, and the door's usual method of opening or closing was ruined. Parts of the frame jutted outward, and the door was stuck by shards of metal. In some ways, it looked as though West's job might be easier, since some of the inner workings were exposed, but the job seemed to take as much time as anything Wade recalled seeing in training videotapes.

Being a smaller foreign car, perhaps West wasn't accustomed to the make and model, or maybe he was being extremely cautious because of the patient's condition, leaving nothing to chance. Wade heard the grinding and cracking of metal as the jaws opened outward, widening the gap between the door and its frame, forcing it to open against its will.

Luckily the pole had stood its ground, and no wires had come undone, or the rescue would not yet be taking place. The electric company would need to be called to shut down the hot wires, and they weren't always speedy in their arrival.

Wade figured the woman in the driver's seat would be fortunate if her back wasn't broken in several places, and extremely fortunate if it wasn't fractured at all. Any passengers would surely have been killed, and no sign of anyone else was evident in the car, or in the open field behind the electrical pole.

Listening to the purr of the rescue truck's generator, and the hum of the jaws, Wade watched West work with extraordinary proficiency as he and the driver communicated, knowing what one another wanted, and how to conduct themselves in this type of scenario.

Wade knew he could handle the job with proper training, but he wasn't ready yet. After all, he had barely seen any working fires. Before he drove any of the trucks, did rescue work, or got in the frame of mind to do first responder work, he wanted to make sure he knew his first and most primary job in every aspect.

Fighting fires.

Wade felt somewhat useless in this situation, but once West had the door open, and EMS began pulling their patient through the opening on a stretcher, West put him in a playful headlock away from the onlookers.

"You did good, kid," West said.

"I didn't do anything though."

"You stayed clear and did what you were told. And you were assertive enough to ask Jerry what we needed."

"Like I said, I didn't do anything."

West chuckled as they packed their tools away.

"One of these days you'll get some time on this truck, kid, and we'll be happy to have you."

Wade forced a grin, wondering how long it would take to get such kinship and respect from everyone else on his shift.

Only time would tell.

CHAPTER 28

As things worked out, the arsonist in question didn't want to meet until the next day, because he had some other clients to deal with.

Gustin didn't bother asking what sort of business the man had going, aside from setting fires, but in the morning's pouring rain, he parked his car in a neglected area of town. Few other cars were around at this hour, or anytime, because people typically didn't frequent this end of town unless it was absolutely necessary.

Walking through the heavy rain, Gustin instantly felt wetness soak into his clothes. He suddenly regretted having to do this business with such terrible timing, but he wanted it over with.

No matter what it took.

He ducked into an alley, which led to the back door of a local bar on the south end of town.

Inside, he would conclude his business with the man, and sleep much easier at night. Gustin knocked three times, paused, and knocked a fourth time. A few seconds later the door opened just long enough for him to slip inside.

From inside a nearby car, one man had seen all of Gustin's activities that morning, until the man slipped inside the bar. He was dead tired from another night of incomplete slumber, but Mike was functional enough to monitor the property manager, picking up where Greg had left off to pursue his own legitimate investigation.

Mike grunted to himself at the thought of Greg's pursuits, thinking it a complete waste of time to investigate three men who were already above the law. If they had power enough to bribe Gray, as he suspected, there would be little they could get done on a local level.

He waited patiently, listening to the radio to pass the time. Approaching the bar would only alert someone to his presence, and Mike's photo had been in the newspaper several times as the firefighter who lost a brother in the tragic fire.

As he watched Gustin emerge from the bar a few minutes later, Mike suspected he was very close to the source of his search. Gustin had no reason to visit this end of town in the course of his everyday business.

Of that, Mike was certain.

Cracked sidewalks, trash strewn across lawns, and buildings literally falling apart in the old district served as little more than eyesores, though a few seedy businesses, such as this bar, seemed to survive.

Mike himself would never be able to enter such a place and figure out who was in there, or what Gray's business might have been with the person inside, but he knew someone who could probably pull off such a feat.

Every other place he had followed Gustin to that morning was an apartment, a legitimate business, or an insurance company. This seemed much more personal, and that fact alone prompted Mike to pick up his cellular phone and dial the number of someone who might be able to help.

"You've got to be fucking kidding me," Jay said as he stood a block away from the bar with Mike, going over the plan an hour later.

"You've got your phone on you in case anything goes wrong, Jay," Mike assured him, knowing his older brother was probably the only person who could possibly fit in with the bar's clientele.

"People who run these places just use them as fronts," Jay stated, his voice a bit more raspy than usual, as though suffering the effects of a cold. "They don't like strangers, and they don't invite new business."

He pointed to the front of the building, which held no sign or neon light stating it was open.

"See? They aren't open to the public."

"Bullshit. Quit being such a pussy and think of a cover story for you to be here."

"Maybe I'm looking to get killed," Jay said with some sarcasm. "They'll believe that, and probably help me out."

"The way I see it, our arsonist is in there, and we owe it to Kevin to find out who he is."

"*Probably* in there," Jay stated with some doubt. "And what's this about 'we' when I'm the one risking his ass?"

Mike pulled a gun from the backside of his jeans, holding it for Jay to see.

"If anything goes wrong, you speed dial me with your phone, and I come running in to bail you out."

"Since when do you own a gun?" Jay questioned, an unusual hint of surprise crossing his face.

"Since two days ago when I got it from one of Dad's old boxes of stuff."

Jay thought a gun would be trouble, feeling certain Mike was not in the right frame of mind lately to be carrying any kind of weapon.

"Greg is going to kill us if he finds out about this," he said, rather than follow up on the gun issue.

"Only if you get arrested or squeal to him," Mike replied. "Greg's way is going to take forever, and even you don't want to see someone go to trial and get off the hook by hiring some crooked lawyer."

Looking concerned, Jay knew he was no more of a vigilante thug than his younger brother, but Mike's words echoed some truth.

"I hope you have something planned if we actually find this guy."

"Oh, I do," Mike said with a devious smile that almost made Jay cringe.

Whatever Mike had in mind, he probably wanted no part of it. Jay looked the part of a roughhouse biker, but didn't care much for trouble. At least when he was sober.

"You sure no one's left the building since you saw Gustin leave?" he asked.

Jay was looking for any excuse to back out, now that he knew what Mike's desperate plea of help was about.

Per Mike's request, Jay had worn his usual riding clothes, including his black leather vest and treaded boots. He looked like a gruff Harley rider, and that was his only chance of fitting in with the bar's crowd, assuming anyone was even there at this early hour.

"You walk in and you're lost," Mike suggested. "You're biking and lost your way or something."

"Oh, that'll fly, little brother. They'll think I'm a homo looking for a date, or I'm a complete idiot."

Mike waved his hands in circles as he struggled to find a more realistic story.

"Your bike broke down, and you want to know if you can use the phone."

"We carry tools. We fix our own bikes."

"But you need a part," Mike quickly improvised.

Jay soured at the idea, but the excuses were getting a bit more realistic.

He looked to the bar, noticing the place had an upstairs above it, which probably served as makeshift apartments. Getting a peek at all of them would probably be impossible, so he needed to make his one opportunity count.

"God, I hate you sometimes," he said, resolved to at least try it for Kevin's sake. "If I get shot, you better tell Wade everything's his, 'cause I never filled out no will."

"You'll be fine," Mike said, turning his older brother in the right direction. "Besides, you don't have anything Wade would want anyway."

"Bullshit," Jay said, starting toward the bar. "My motorcycle and my dog."

Mike grinned as Jay made his way toward the front of the bar, but worried how far this farce would get them. He had some doubt Jay would even make his way inside, but if anyone could do it, Jay could. Thanks to his job, Jay had unmatched people skills compared to his family and friends, and he was capable of working almost any angle to get the results he wanted.

He also had more street smarts than the rest of his family, making him the obvious candidate for such an unusual task.

Hopefully, he would be at his best as the late morning sun began to make its way through the clouds.

"I'm going to kill him," Jay mumbled to himself as he knocked on the front door of the bar, which appeared almost useless.

Weeds and trash littered the sidewalk leading up the door, and several rusted deadbolts and hinges made the old wooden door appear useless, as though it would be trapped in the same spot until the entire building came down around it.

Jay had a plan of action worked out in his head, but executing it would be altogether different if he made it inside.

Taking a deep breath, he knocked on the old door, wondering just how much effort he dared put into the act conjured up in his mind.

A few seconds passed, and he wondered if he was mentally exaggerating how dangerous the situation might be. After all, arsonists were often everyday people with a gift for setting things on fire. Maybe the man would be halfway friendly, or perhaps he wouldn't see the man at all. Possibilities of all kinds ran through his mind before he heard footsteps heavily tread toward the door from inside.

"Go around back," a voice simply boomed through the door. "That door doesn't work anymore."

At least the person wasn't telling him to go away, so Jay figured he was halfway to getting inside and finding some answers.

He stepped around back, but an ominous large man opened the door, startling him a bit, before he could even reach it.

"What's your business?" the man asked, as though Jay needed an appointment to be there.

His white T-shirt was dotted with several different stains, and he smelled like the type who did any number of things to stain his clothes, never washing them afterwards. His curly hair appeared matted, as though he hadn't seen the likes of a shower in some time.

"Well, uh, my bike broke down about a block from here," Jay started to explain, "and I need a couple parts to fix it up. I was wondering if I might use your phone and get a drink."

"It's not even noon," the man half-heartedly objected about the drink.

"That's never stopped me before," Jay said, trying his best to be casual about the whole situation.

Standing a moment in judgment of the biker before him, the man looked down the street, spying a Harley-Davidson at the side of the road, strategically placed there by Jay upon Mike's urging.

"Come on," the large man finally said with a quick wave of his hand.

Jay stepped into a world of perpetual darkness, with only a few neon signs guiding him to the bar. The bright morning sun left his eyes unprepared for the virtual cave he was now walking through.

Quickly enough, his eyes adjusted, and he made his way to the bar. Shoving a large phone down to him as he slid atop a bar stool, the man pulled out a frosted mug.

"What'll it be?"

"A fuckin' beer would be great," Jay said, reaching for his wallet. "I've been on the road two days and haven't seen a girl worth fucking, or a beer any colder than my own piss."

Jay was in his element now, and he was the only person other than the bartender inside the place. He hated fighting to keep his tongue in check around family, and at his job, because he preferred saying what he wanted, when he wanted. That was half the fun about being a biker, even if it was only on the weekends.

He tried looking around for access to the upstairs, or to at least memorize the layout of the place for Mike, but his new host was keeping watch, so he dared not let his eyes stray too far for too long.

A cockroach darted across the bar, but he pretended to ignore it, even though it confirmed what he already suspected. This place would win honorable mention in his list of least sanitary places to socialize.

Nowhere could he find any sign of mints, or peanuts, and doubted he would partake in any kind of snack food if he saw it lying upon the bar. Even the worst of biker bars failed to measure up to the level of disarray this place displayed.

"I'm not from around here," Jay lied with uncanny cool. "Got a phone book?"

A moment later he flipped through the yellow pages, found several businesses specializing in bike parts, and pretended to dial the number for one, even though it was just to Mike. Jay spent a few minutes faking an order, even asking the bartender the address so he could meet the delivery driver outside. He explained in detail what was the matter with his bike, as though the person on the other end of the line thought he might know bikes well enough to confirm what parts he needed.

"Everyone's a know-it-all," Jay said as he hung up the phone. "The prick tries to tell me he thinks it's in the transmission when I know fuckin' well it's in the engine, then tells me it might be half an hour before he can get someone over here."

"Welcome to Carvers Grove," the large man said, finally breaking a smile.

He seemed to be buying Jay's act, so it would soon be time to take his plan to the next level, even though Jay had nothing plotted that far ahead, because he never expected to get inside the bar to begin with.

"I try getting away from the wife for a few days because we had this big fight, and it figures I'd break down on my way back."

"Where you from?"

"Just outside Aurora. You know, it might be just as well, because I don't want to face that bitch this soon anyway."

The bartender smiled, as though he could sympathize.

"I married her partly for the money, because her dad left her this big sum when he died, but do you think I get to see any of it? No way."

Jay shook his head with a sneer. He took a few gulps of the beer, acting as though he was contemplating whether he wanted to say something personal or not. He paused about half a minute before speaking again.

"She keeps all of it in a bank. Says it'll benefit us both in the long run if we just let it collect interest or some shit like that," Jay said easily. "There's only one way I'll ever see any of that money."

Perking up a bit, the bartender had to ask.

"How's that?"

"If she's dead, my friend."

The man pulled back, but not enough to indicate he was horrified at the notion.

"Oh, I've thought about some kind of poison, or putting a match to the place while she's in bed and letting it burn to the ground, but you know who the fuckin' cops are gonna come after."

Jay pointed straight to his own chest.

"I can't stand her, and she sure as hell can't stand me. She thought she was marrying a businessman with a passion for bikes on the side. Thing is, she got it backwards, and found out too late."

"So you didn't marry her for the money then?"

"Fuck yeah I married her for the money. That's why I'm so miserable. Sure, I do okay, but I'm talking about enough to get me the fuck out of Illinois for the rest of my life, and to the Bahamas or overseas."

Taking another drink of beer, Jay decided he had laid about enough bait if he was going to ensnare an arsonist. Too much more information, and the bartender would get suspicious. Men didn't ramble on and on about killing their wives, especially to complete strangers.

Jay wondered if he had played it cool enough to this point.

He quickly finished the beer, slid a five on the counter, and pushed himself away from the bar.

"Guess I'd better wait for the parts guy so I can get back to hell before the day's over with," he said with a smirk.

Before he could turn, the bartender held up a finger, indicating he should wait a moment.

"Were you serious about offing the wife?" he asked with a tone, trying to sound halfway skeptical.

Jay rubbed his head, as though trying to think of the correct response in such an awkward line of questioning.

"You know, a year ago, things were pretty tolerable, bud. These days, I expect a lawyer to come walking up with divorce papers any day. You do the math."

Jay gave a cynical grin, then opened the back door.

"Thanks for the beer," he said before stepping outside with a quick wave.

Saying nothing, the bartender watched him step outside, then ran upstairs for an overhead view of what the strange biker he had just met might be doing.

He peered from a window, watching Jay for a moment. When he discovered the biker wasn't going to do anything but wait for bike parts, he knocked on one of the upstairs apartment doors.

"Who is it?" a voice asked gruffly from inside.

"Hey, Spiff, it's Arnie."

"What do you want?"

"I think I might have a job for you," the bartender said with a hint of excitement in his voice. "And it might pay you a hell of a lot more than those creeps from the north end."

A moment passed, then the door opened just enough to reveal a green eye from inside the dark apartment.

"This better be good, Arnie."

CHAPTER 29

Jay stood outside almost ten minutes, wondering if his charade was working in any way, shape, or form.

As promised, Mike was keeping a safe distance away, completely out of sight. There was no contingency plan if this failed, and Mike was counting on his older brother's charm and easygoing nature to fool whomever he encountered.

If nothing else, Mike planned to learn the layout of the place to try examining it himself, but Jay could see no other way upstairs, except through the bar itself.

Living in that type of apartment was like having a free security system so long as patrons from the bar never made their way upstairs.

"You sure he's not a cop?" Spiff asked the bartender as they stared through the upstairs window toward Jay, who took off his vest and settled in for a longer wait.

His white shirt was drenched with sweat, and they saw no visible wires, weapons, or identification hanging out of his back pocket that indicated he might be a law enforcement officer.

"He doesn't act like a cop, and his motorcycle is just up the road," Arnie said, pointing toward the stranded bike. "He called some parts store, and they're supposed to be on the way."

"Let's just see if his parts show up," Spiff said skeptically. "How long is it supposed to take?"

"Half an hour, I guess."

Arnie had already informed Spiff of the biker's statements, but the arsonist for hire was incredibly wary of cops, especially after the Brookshire fire. Killing a firefighter was not part of the plan, and virtually guaranteed to bring heat down on him if the wrong people started looking for the source of the inferno.

Known only as Spiff to the locals, he preferred no one know his real name. Arnie wasn't so much of a friend as he was a business partner. He gave Spiff a place to live, and Spiff provided a form of security to his bar, because no one dared mess with a man capable of destroying their house overnight, leaving no proof in the aftermath.

His reputation stayed on the tattered streets he lived on, and went no further.

As a kid, Spiff took an interest in science, especially in chemical reactions. He used a chemistry kit his parents bought him one Christmas to mix chemicals that reacted, or sometimes exploded with a few secret ingredients mixed into the batch.

Later, he learned about electricity from his father, and took several fire science classes at his local tech school. He never took an interest in conforming to the rules of the real world, much less working in such an environment.

He left home after quitting high school, finding odd jobs to get him by. It wasn't until a few years back that he began doing arson jobs for businessmen. They took such a liking to his undeterminable style that they paid him larger cash sums for harder jobs. Making fires and explosions look like accidents was his calling, and having an investigator who had overlooked several key clues helped all the more.

Spiff had no direct contact with anyone except Gustin, but he knew about some of the ties between Shelton, Emerson, and the arson investigator. Even on the low end, information drifted down when it was important enough. Information from the low end never filtered back, however, because no one cared about that part of town.

Both men kept careful watch over Jay, who had little choice but to wait, hoping his brother had something in mind. Jay suspected he was being watched, but put his faith in Mike to come up with a way to keep his cover looking legitimate.

Mike had about another ten minutes to think of something, or their best lead would be null and void.

Using his computer at work, which linked every public safety department in the city, Greg used his brother's user name and password to look into old fire reports, searching for the cases Mike swore he'd seen in Gray's office.

If Tasha wasn't going to help him, he would have to do whatever it took to gather enough evidence against Shelton and his cronies to take them to court.

Speaking with Gustin wasn't prudent, and any sort of contact with the three property owners would be a major mistake, so he stuck to low-level investigation, piecing together likely scenarios.

Greg tried to think of people with enough balls to submit such a case to the prosecutor's office if he got all of the facts. His fellow detectives would resent him handing them a case if it meant he had done their work, and the state fire marshals probably wouldn't touch it because of Gray's possible involvement.

Using keyword searches, Greg easily found the cases, printing them after he read each one. Even this information was little more than a building block, because the real proof remained tied up in insurance reports and Gray's investigation records.

A thought suddenly crossed Greg's mind, that lately the fires were all at the outskirts of town, which put them in Washington Township's territory. Surely the department hadn't been around during all of the insurance scam fires.

Or had it?

Greg quickly skimmed through the reports, finding about one or two mishaps per year between the three men. They went too far back to fully include Washington Township, since it was new within the last year.

Amazed at how the links between these fires could go on undetected so long, he began to suspect Gray had a lot more knowledge than he let anyone know. His bid for coroner, among other things, had put a high price tag on his necessary campaign funds, and perhaps, on his services.

"His election," Greg muttered to himself, wondering if he had just come up with a new piece of evidence.

Within his county, and most of the state, if not all of it, all donations made to any candidate's campaign had to be recorded, and could be accessed inside the county building.

Logging out of Mike's account, he snatched up the papers, stuffed them inside a leather tote bag he'd brought, and headed out the door. If all went well, he would be one step closer to proving Gray's involvement in the coverup of the arson fires, and he would have someone to start looking at more closely.

Regardless, he needed to watch his step, but Greg felt certain he would be able to legitimately bring the wrongful parties to justice.

Soon.

Spiff and Arnie were somewhat surprised when a car pulled up to the stranded biker below, and a shirtless driver emerged from the car, partly covered in grease.

They stared through a window long since dotted with fly droppings, dried spit, and old chewing gum. The smell alone would deter most people from getting anywhere near the window, but the two men began to smell money above all else.

Watching as the delivery man handed the biker a box full of something, and a receipt which he had to sign, they felt convinced the biker was exactly who he said he was, and perhaps it was because he never said very much about who he was.

Police tended to overdo their acting, but this biker talked at random, giving just bits of information.

Like a normal guy passing through town.

"What do you think?" Arnie asked his partner.

"I don't know. I'd want to talk to the guy myself."

"I swear, he's real," Arnie stated. "No cop is gonna come up here, and no one even knows where the fuck you live, or about any of the shit you've done."

Spiff rubbed his chin. He focused on the rest of the transaction below, wanting to take in every detail before he made a final decision.

"Very clever," Jay said to his younger brother sarcastically as they faked the exchange of parts for money. "I especially like the grease," he added, glancing at Mike's belly and neck where the smears were most visible.

Mike had handed him two sheets of formerly crumpled paper that looked like a carbon receipt. Jay signed the top sheet, handing Mike one copy. The box contained nothing more than trinkets found in the back seat of his car.

"What the fuck do I do with these?" Jay asked, peeking inside the box.

"I don't know," Mike said quickly. "Act like you're putting something on your bike. From a distance, they'll never know what you're doing. Oh, and pay me."

Jay looked the fake receipt over, pulled out his wallet, and acted as though searching for the correct bill to give his delivery driver. He pulled two twenty dollar bills out, folding them before handing them over to Mike.

"If we live through this, I'm killing you. Get out of here before you make them suspicious in there."

Mike fought back a smile as he stepped into the car.

"And I want my money back later," Jay stated. "That way I can buy something to beat you with."

As Mike drove off, Jay sauntered up the road toward his bike, his box of junk in hand. Luckily, his bike had a few tools mounted to it, so he could fake putting on some parts. From a distance, the men inside the bar would never know the difference.

"Ah, hell, they probably aren't even falling for it," Jay mumbled to himself. "They're probably the wrong people anyway."

Though Mike felt positive Gustin had stopped in to make a payment, Jay wasn't privy to witness the event, so he had doubts. Still, the bartender hadn't seemed shocked in the least by his comments about killing his imaginary wife for her money.

He made his way up to the bike, knelt down, and began disconnecting several parts of the underside, figuring he was wasting the last bit of his morning in the hopes of someone soliciting illegal work from him.

Trying his hardest not to look back toward the bar very often, Jay put off completing his forged repair as long as he could, realizing no one was going to speak with him. All morning, traffic filtered by, and several local gang members checked him over as they passed with their rap music blaring, but the leather vest laying beside Jay might have held any number of things for all they knew.

Including a gun.

He tightened down the last part he had taken off, stood up, and almost bumped into someone larger than himself who had approached without his knowledge.

"Did I forget to leave a tip?" he asked the bartender, who had strolled up the road.

Jay tried to act as though he was ready to go.

"When you were talking back there, how serious were you?"

"About what?"

"You know, your wife."

Jay cracked a grin, sighed, and let his expression turn a bit more serious.

"Like I said, it's a lot of money, but there's no way I'd ever do it, because I can't get away with anything. I'd be the only suspect, man."

Jay climbed onto his bike.

"That's twice you've asked me that. How come?"

Arnie drew back a bit, nervously touching his chin.

"Well, I've got someone who might be able to help you out, if you're interested in obtaining that money you talked about."

Jay stared at him, then cracked a grin.

"I was just talking, partner," he said, trying not to appear too easy. "She's a bitch, but I don't know if I could have that on my conscience."

He started the bike, acting ready to ride away. It roared to life, them hummed at the side of the road as Jay let it warm up.

"What kind of help are you talking about?" he asked, as though curiosity had gotten the better of him.

"The kind of help that could get you your money, and get rid of your wife while you go set up a perfect alibi."

Jay sat on his bike a moment, thinking of how to play this, while Arnie figured he might have a potential client.

"Got a number where I can call you?" Jay asked, deciding not to push his luck.

Arnie pulled out a scrap piece of paper, scribbling down a phone number.

"That's the bar's number," he said.

"Okay. I'll think about it, friend. I've got some time to kill on the way to Aurora, and I'll see how things are when I get home."

Jay flashed a mischievous grin.

"Maybe we'll do some business."

Greg stepped inside the county building, overwhelmed by how clean it looked. From sparkling tile floors to new wooden doors with gleaming name plates identifying each room, it was spotless. Even the building directory looked brand new, even though the detective recalled seeing it the past three years.

He knew exactly where he was going, and the records office would be the place that held a majority of the reports and paperwork. Greg had no idea how often the records about campaign contributions were updated, but he figured it was as good a place as any to start.

For such an occasion, he wore his slacks and tie. He was due to start his shift within the hour, so he decided to look fairly formal. Greg would use any advantage he could to obtain the information he needed.

Stepping inside the office, he spied three women behind the counter, all looking as though they were busy with something, scurrying from place to place, filing papers, and speaking to unknown city residents on the phone lines.

He chose to wait patiently a moment, looking up to the ceilings that seemed far too high to maintain decent heating and cooling bills. Finding little of interest to keep him occupied on the counter, he simply strolled around the informal lobby area until one of the ladies managed to break free from her duties.

"How can I help you?" she offered.

An older lady with a grandmother type of charm about her, she smiled as she waited for his response.

"I need to know if you have fairly current campaign contributions on file," Greg said, unsure of whether or not he had made a wise decision in coming to the county building.

Perhaps he would have been better suited going straight to the party headquarters to ask the chairman for the records. Surely they kept better updated records.

"They're computerized," the woman answered. "They get updated daily."

She paused to punch a key on her computer's keyboard, bringing the system back to life from its sleep mode.

"Any particular person you're looking for?"

"I need to know what contributions have been made for Mason Gray's bid for coroner," Greg answered quietly enough that only she could hear.

He still felt paranoid asking anyone a single thing about the arson investigator. If anyone discovered his unofficial investigation, it would instantly be a dead issue.

"He's a new candidate, but he has a fairly lengthy list already. Care to narrow it down at all?"

"No. I need a complete list, no matter how many trees have to die to print it out."

"Okay," the woman said, souring a bit for the first time.

Greg immediately thought he might arouse her suspicion, so he decided to say something else to take her mind off of his last statement.

"I've got some friends who said they gave, and I'm just trying to make sure they're telling the truth."

"I see," the woman said, though she really didn't know what he meant, or seem to care.

Nonetheless, Greg had his printout a few minutes later, once the old dot matrix printer finished spitting out the green and white lined paper. He glanced it over on his way out of the building, peeking over the edge of the paper just long enough to spy the man he least wanted to see at the moment.

Mason Gray.

Walking toward the county building with some official business on his mind, Gray ignored the detective altogether, like he did most people.

Greg quickly returned to scanning the list, and found what he needed before even reaching his car, because the three largest contributions easily caught his eye. They weren't disguised very well, because Shelton Properties, Emerson Construction, and Boyce Realty had readily made donations to the man's campaign for more money than Greg would spend on a good used car.

"Holy shit," he commented, stepping into his car.

His circle of damning evidence was closing in around the arson investigator, and soon he would be confronting Gray with his find.

❦   ❦   ❦

Mike drove through town shortly after dusk to pick up his paycheck from the headquarters fire station, as he had for years, but as he drew near the spot he and Kevin had shared for years, talking after hours about their personal lives, he stopped the truck and stared.

He pulled to the side of the road so cars could pass him, but he refused to enter their sacred spot by himself. It would never be the same.

Not without Kevin.

"I hope you can forgive me for what I'm going to do," he said, hoping somewhere his older brother would hear. "I don't know if I'm doing it for all the right reasons, but I plan to stop anyone else's brother or sister from dying."

His words of finding nothing more satisfying than working his job with Kevin haunted him from that night, earlier in the summer. Now Mike felt completely alone, and he had no one to tell his personal problems to. Kevin always understood, always listened.

Sandi tried, but she didn't want to hear certain things, and there was never editing of content when Mike spoke to his brother.

He wanted to cry, but he couldn't. The time for mourning was past, and Mike's body felt emotionally and physically drained. He could only sit numbly for a minute, watching memories pass through his mind like old movies.

Mike remembered being downtown and *doing* his job, and how much he and Kevin enjoyed working together, being downtown. At the time, everything was fun, and Mike had nothing else to ask for in life.

Now, parked just before the strip he and Kevin shared, Mike knew his job would never be fun again, and if he had one thing to ask for, it would be to have Kevin back. He really didn't care if he ever worked downtown again, or saw another fire.

The two men who made his life what it was had died during the past year, and Mike saw little reason to continue the path he was on, except to do them justice. If he could make them proud, maybe he would find a purpose to enjoy life again, or at least try.

In the distance a lone trumpet played a slow dirge of some sort, probably for a high school football game, or a local music show. Somehow the tune struck Mike oddly, because it sounded so lonely and sad, much like he felt at the moment.

Turning his truck around, Mike decided he would take a different route to the fire station. He just couldn't bear passing the old hardware store and his spot this soon.

Or perhaps ever.

CHAPTER 30

As time passed, the guys grew more accustomed to Wade, and they slowly talked the way they were accustomed to, realizing what they said stayed in the room, and Wade would not rat them out to his uncle.

During their training that morning, he spoke with Mike, but his uncle seemed on edge. Perhaps Kevin's death still weighed on his mind, but Wade figured it was something more. They conversed briefly, but their talk had little substance to it.

Now the headquarters group washed dishes, having just finished lunch, and Wade was privy to a type of conversation he'd never heard before. He knew of the other shifts talking a bit dirty about their home lives, but his own shift was just now getting to trust him enough to bring up such things.

Wade knew firefighters talked about strange things, but today's conversation started at lunch when one of the men talked about manners at the fire station compared to manners at home. Somehow, the talk went from actions in the bedroom to things done in the bathroom.

"You ever fart on your wife?" one of the men asked the pumper truck driver as the group washed dishes in the kitchen.

"Yeah, but only because she does it to me."

Their battalion chief had left immediately after the meal to do paperwork, leaving the men to carry their conversation to new extremes.

"Jill doesn't pass gas in front of me, so I'm nice and don't do it to her," one of the guys said.

Ted Gilman, or 'Gilly' as some called him, often liked to brag about all of the sexual positions he and his wife tried out on the weekends their kids were gone, including things his fellow firemen didn't want to hear about.

"Darlena doesn't ever fart in the house," Gilman said, putting his two cents into the conversation.

"Even after you plank her in the ass?" one of the other guys asked, referring to one of the sexual positions mentioned in previous conversations.

Though the comment would seem offensive to most normal people in the community, the firefighters roused laughter enough to be heard by the front office, and their battalion chief, though no one walked in to inquire about the noise.

Gilman's face flushed red, and he tried to avoid saying anything, knowing he would only make it worse for himself. He could talk up a storm, or dish out derogatory remarks about other people, but Gilman didn't particularly like being teased.

For Wade, this was the first time he heard such things from the crew surrounding him. He knew he worked with some perverted people, but this was a bit unusual. Still, he laughed with the guys and rolled his eyes as the thought of Gilman and his wife in bed galloped through his mind.

"I can't stand being farted on," one of the other guys said. "My kids do that shit all the time around the house."

Wade shook his head as he swept the floor beneath the table, unsure of whether he regretted not being part of these conversations before. There were times when the guys would have fairly intellectual conversations about their other jobs, or about politics and regional news, then there were times they talked about sex, passing gas, and who snored the loudest at night.

Soon the conversation moved to comments other guys on the department had made about the idea of sleeping with celebrity women, and what they would all do if the chance presented itself. While this went on, Wade finished sweeping and mopping the floor, then walked out back, where a picnic table sat.

He wondered why his father hadn't been in touch lately, because Jay usually called him every few days to let him know where he was, or what new project kept him busy. Wade understood his father took charge in caring for his grandmother, so perhaps he was too busy with her to call.

Either way, Wade wasn't concerned, but just a little curious.

Deciding to keep himself occupied, he fetched parts for a motorcycle he was trying to rebuild in his spare time from his truck. Putting the bucket up on the table, he took out some cleaning spray for motorized parts, then set the can beside the bucket.

Prepared to spend his afternoon passing the time by cleaning parts, Wade was caught off-guard when a wall of water hit his head and shoulders squarely from above, soaking him with its cold texture. A chill ran down his spine, and his body snapped to a rigid standing position like a soldier saluting a commanding officer as he heard laughter from above.

"Hey, Wade, it's supposed to rain today if you didn't already hear," one of the guys chided, though all of them had ducked back from the station's roof ledge.

None of them wanted him to know who was responsible, because there would certainly be a measure of revenge taken against the wrongful party later, and because it was half the fun making him wonder. They would all deny throwing a bucket of water on the rookie, but Wade would find out one way or another.

"You guys are so dead," Wade shouted before running inside to snatch one of the garden hoses from the wall.

If he was quick enough, he would soak them all before they could make it down the roof access ladder in the back of the living quarters. He would have to clean up a wet mess, but it would certainly be worth it.

Unlike the rest of his family, Wade was getting on with his life.

🍁 　　　🍁　　　🍁

Later that evening, after supper, the firefighters decided it was time to further initiate Wade into their clan by giving him the usual public humiliation all new recruits during the past five years or so had been through.

"You've got to be kidding," Wade said when they dangled the Sparky the Firedog suit in front of him.

Wade figured it couldn't be that terrible to dress up for a few minutes so the guys would get their entertainment value from it.

"Nah, we ain't kidding," one of the firemen said in reply. "And guess what, you get to stand in front of the station for the late rush traffic."

"Oh, no," Wade said defensively. "No way."

"Ah, come on. Everyone does it," they teased.

Wade sighed, shaking his head. Much of his acceptance was enduring the rookie hazing, so he would do what they asked, or risk being alienated.

"What do I have to do?"

"Just put it on and wave to everyone going by."

Wade looked the suit over, finding no mask. He eyed the costume suspiciously, wondering what they had in store for him.

It smelled musty, as though stored in a cellar for years. Perhaps that was part of the joke, Wade figured, starting to put it on anyway.

"Is there a mask or anything?" he asked the three firefighters who stood around him.

"We lost it," one said with a straight face, although Wade was positive they were all laughing on the inside.

"Lost it?"

"Yeah, lost it," another firefighter chimed in.

Bullshit, Wade thought.

One of the three ran off to gather the other firefighters, so everyone could watch Wade make a fool of himself, all for the sake of comradery.

Most of them had been inside that costume, so they figured it was only fair for Wade to do the same.

He was about to be humiliated in front of the city, and he could only pray that his father, or anyone else he knew, didn't drive by. He could picture his father being devious enough to videotape such a scene, and Wade wanted no lasting proof of this spectacle.

"Ready?" they asked him.

"As I'll ever be," Wade said, zipping up the last of the dog suit, ready to get this over with.

If he was lucky, they would leave him out there half an hour tops. And if not, this would be one of the longest days of his life.

CHAPTER 31

Sandi got up for work the next morning, expecting Mike to already be in the kitchen, fixing her breakfast like he often did.

No smell of eggs, bacon, or toast filled the air, however, as she got out of bed. Throwing on a bathrobe, she headed down the hallway, wondering where her fiancé might be. As she reached the end of the hall, one of her three cats rubbed against her shins, wanting to be fed.

"Mike?" she called, receiving no answer.

He always came straight home after work in the morning, or at least called if something would delay him. Lately, he acted a bit more strangely, but she dismissed it as some sort of post-traumatic stress syndrome from Kevin's death.

Looking out the back window, she almost expected him to be doing something related to their future garden on the tractor, or perhaps cutting down the straw that reached her waist when she tried wading through it, along the nearby fields.

No sound of a tractor reached her ears, and she saw nothing moving out back. Out front, she saw no sign of Mike's car, and her mind raced, wondering where he might be.

Perhaps his relief was late at work, or maybe he had something to help Greg with. After all, the twins had been spending more time with one another lately, though Sandi couldn't recall seeing Greg during the past week, as though their relationship was returning to normal.

She called the fire station, where someone picked up after two rings.

"Number Four Fire Station," the man answered.

"Hello. Is Mike still there?"

"No, ma'am. He left about an hour ago."

"Okay, thanks."

Sandi held down the receiver with one finger, wondering who to call next.

"Maybe I'm just overreacting," she thought aloud.

Still, Mike *never* came home late, or he called to tell her. He was very devoted to Sandi that way, and she worried about his state of mind. It wasn't good if he brooded by himself, and it was even worse if no one knew how to find him.

She saw him changing by the day, becoming a bit less caring and lovable. Once, he was willing to do anything for anyone, but the death of his father, the boy he couldn't save from drowning, and now Kevin's death, had taken their toll on him.

Sandi saw it in his eyes. An emptiness sometimes crossed his blue eyes, and they seemed to darken just a bit to match the empty void he felt in his soul. She felt as though Mike struggled for a reason to go on with life, and perhaps she wasn't enough, no matter how hard she tried.

Questioning how long she could go on supporting someone who slipped further and further away from the everyday world, Sandi knew she couldn't give up easily. After all, Mike was a good man who had already saved any number of lives through his work. He might also have saved countless lives through the time he spent doing lectures at schools and churches with kids about fire safety.

At the moment, he walked a dark path, but she felt certain he would not stray too far from the love and comfort his family provided.

Still, she picked up the phone, dialing Greg's number.

"Hello?" a voice said groggily from the other end, and she knew immediately she had woke Greg from bed.

"Greg, it's Sandi."

"Hi there. Everything okay?" he asked, starting to perk up a bit.

"Mike didn't come right home this morning, and he didn't call. Do you have any idea where he might be?"

"No. I haven't seen him in about a week myself."

Sandi paused a moment.

"Am I being paranoid? It's just that he's been acting strange lately."

"I thought you said he was doing better."

"Well, he was. He was staying home, or around you, but now he's gone a lot, gets calls from someone all the time, and always seems to be writing down things he won't let me see."

Greg propped himself on one elbow in his bed as he began to figure out what Mike was probably up to.

"Who's he on the phone with, Sandi?"

"Jay, I think."

What the fuck would he want with Jay? Greg wondered.

"Am I being paranoid?" Sandi asked him. "Ever since he stopped going out with you, he's been acting really strange."

"I have an idea what's going on," Greg replied. "I wouldn't worry about him just yet."

At least not until I get my hands on him, he thought after the statement.

"Thanks, Greg. I'm sorry if I woke you up."

"Oh, that's okay. I'll call you later to make sure he got home."

"Thanks."

Greg hung up the phone, suspicious of what Mike was trying to accomplish on his own. He had no idea their conversation a week prior would spur Mike to carry out actions of his own, trying to discover who was behind the fire.

Little did he know just how far his twin brother had gotten, or exactly how far he might go to avenge Kevin's death.

He decided he needed to find out, and jumped out of bed to get dressed.

※　　　　※　　　　※

By late morning, the sun was creating a heat wave across the city, but that mattered little to Mike, as he sat beside his older brother in Jay's red Corvette, which would help them pull off the ruse that Jay had substantial money, but wanted more.

Or so they hoped.

"You still haven't told me what we're going to do if I get this guy to identify himself," Jay stated from behind the steering wheel.

Everything was already arranged.

Jay had called the day before, while Mike was at work, to give a story about how his wife was filing for divorce within the week, and this was the only way he knew to get what he had coming to him. Arnie arranged a meeting time with his mysterious friend after Jay said he could be in town the next morning.

Currently, they sat several blocks away from the bar, and a briefcase full of cash sat in the back seat, which would serve to lure the arsonist out of hiding, and into Mike's next phase of the plan.

"If we get him out of hiding and identify him, I'll deal with him," Mike assured his older brother. "You won't have to stick around if you don't want to."

"You better not kill him, 'cause I don't want any part of that," Jay said. "You're just going to rough him up a little bit and get some information, right?"

"If that's what you want to call it," Mike said with such a calm demeanor that it scared Jay in a way no family member had ever worried him before.

Dressed a bit better, in a polo shirt and dark jeans, Jay wore a western belt and black lizard skin cowboy boots. He wasn't about to change his appearance drastically, nor was he going to be completely fake and wear a suit and tie.

Dress clothes were definitely not Jay's style.

"They're gonna think you're *Walker, Texas Ranger,* or something," Mike commented about his brother's appearance.

"Fuck you. I don't see you going above and beyond for this little operation of yours."

Jay's trademark 'fuck you' had little effect on his brothers, since he used it so often. He never meant it anyway, so it was water off a duck's back when they heard his typical retaliatory remark.

Jay glanced behind him.

"And what's with me having to front the cash for this? What if you don't get it back from that little son-of-a-bitch once you have him?"

Mike grinned.

"Oh, I plan to get whatever I want from him, once we have him to ourselves."

"But, if nothing else, you just want me to identify him?"

"Name, description, anything," Mike said. "He's the key to finding out exactly who's behind this whole scam of theirs, and who ordered that arson fire that killed Kev."

Jay didn't like the idea of losing several thousand dollars in cash, but if anyone in the family had that kind of money to begin with, it was him. He never disclosed his annual income with family members, but they suspected he made a fair amount with several classic, restored cars sitting in a garage large enough to hold at least ten more just like them.

Now that Wade was old enough, Jay no longer paid child support, and whatever money he made was entirely his.

"You sure you're ready to do this?" Mike asked, still having conscience enough to offer Jay a way out of their plan.

"I didn't come this far to drop the whole thing now," Jay replied as straightforward as ever.

Mike climbed out of the car, standing there a moment.

"You know I don't mind helping you," Jay said, "but what turned you from a caring firefighter who saved lives to someone who acts bent on taking one?"

"I never said I wanted to kill anyone," Mike replied. "One way or another, though, I will see some justice served."

"And you think Kevin would want that?"

"If the same thing happened to me, yes."

"And when this is all over with, are you going to be the same old Mike we love and care about?"

Mike stood there a moment, unsure of how to answer, because he knew nothing would ever be the same again.

"I'll be what this whole process makes me into," he finally said. "Like Greg said, we can't get Kevin back, but maybe we can stop someone else's brother or sister from getting killed. In a roundabout way, maybe that's my way of still being a caring firefighter."

Nodding to himself, Jay sighed as he exhaled, ready to carry out the plan. He wanted some form of retribution too, but he was willing to play along only so far.

"If you have any trouble, you give me a signal," Mike said. "I won't be far away."

"I'm probably going to meet some pimple-faced kid," Jay said with a chuckle. "And I've got some protection of my own under the seat."

He patted a revolver taped under the seat to make sure it was still fastened by the gray duct tape, which it was.

"Good luck," Mike said, walking to his own car.

"Yeah," Jay said under his breath, thinking he needed every bit of luck he could get, walking into an unknown situation.

Within a few minutes, Jay pulled up to the bar, took out the briefcase full of money, and quickly placed it in the trunk. There, it would be safe, and he wouldn't look too anxious to pay for the job.

Play it cool, he kept thinking to himself, even as he stepped inside the bar through the back door in the alley.

"I see you've got a full house again," he commented to Arnie, who wiped down some shot glasses behind the bar.

Every chair was turned up on the tables, and the only sound inside the bar was Jay's footsteps as he walked toward the bar.

"We do a lot of late business, if you get my drift," Arnie said with an easy smile. "A lot of our clients don't get off work very early."

"I know the feeling," Jay said almost to himself.

"Can I get you anything before my friend gets here?"

"A beer wouldn't hurt."

Jay slid onto a bar stool, accepting the drink straight from the bottle. He tried to put a five dollar bill on the counter, but Arnie waved him off.

"On the house."

"Thanks."

Evidently, things were going according to plan. Jay took a few sips of beer, hearing footsteps come down from the stairs he was positive led to the upstairs apartments.

At last, he was going to meet this mysterious arsonist, unsure of what to expect.

As large a man as the bartender was, the young man emerging from the stairway had to be his complete opposite. If ever Jay had met a Laurel and Hardy combination in person, this was it.

At the base of the stairs, he was barely more than a shadow, but Jay could see a few details.

"I understand you want to do some business," the younger man said, his frame about as thin as some fence rails Jay had pounded into the ground as a teenager on his father's farm.

"That depends," Jay answered.

He studied the man's features carefully as they began to converse.

Everything about him made Jay certain the kid had gone through a rough four years of high school, if he finished all four. From the skinny frame to the acne scars dotting his face, this young man had probably turned to creating explosions and fires to empower himself, and though Jay was no investigator, he knew enough to draw a basic profile.

Still, his objective was simply to get some details for Mike, and hopefully prove beyond a shadow of a doubt this was the person responsible for Kevin's death.

Though most of the details were worked out, through Arnie, there would be a period of each party feeling out the other.

"Did you bring the requested funds?" Spiff asked, trying too hard to sound intelligent.

"I've got the money. Before we do anything, I want some proof of what you can do."

"And I want some proof you're not a cop."

Spiff finally stepped from the shadows, revealing his entire form. Though Jay didn't yet know the man's name, or even his nickname, he could now see the young man was dressed rather plainly, but he was clean.

For someone who probably made good money torching buildings, he didn't look like he spent much of it on his appearance, Jay figured. Then again, that was probably to keep his cover intact. If people on this end of town knew he had money, Spiff would be looking over his shoulder every other minute for fear of being mugged.

Jay gave an annoyed look, stood from the bar stool, and took his shirt off to reveal he had no wire.

"Want me to drop my pants too?"

"That won't be necessary," Spiff said, walking over to pat Jay's legs and waist down, satisfied he felt nothing out of the ordinary.

Jay tucked his shirt into his pants, then gave Arnie a look, as though to ask if all of this was necessary.

Arnie just returned a helpless shrug, the simple guy he was.

"I want to see some money, then I'll give you a demonstration of what I can do," Spiff said.

Jay smirked at the notion.

"If I'm going to hand you a wad of cash, I want a little more than a demonstration," Jay said, deciding to push his luck. "We're going for a ride so you can give me some references."

"I take it you mean *show* you some references?"

"Whatever floats your boat. I'm not taking your word for it that you can bring a house to the ground without a trace."

Spiff thought about it a moment.

Based on everything Arnie told him, combined with Jay's actions, he felt reasonably sure Jay wasn't a cop. Everything about him, from the Corvette and the motorcycle, to his full beard, indicated he wasn't a regular cop anyway, and he doubted they would send an older man such as this undercover.

Besides, no one knew about Spiff's talents except Arnie and Scott Gustin, and neither of them were making such information available to anyone else.

"You driving?" Spiff asked.

"Yeah. That way you can just point the way and tell me about how well each building burned."

Spiff had never been able to relate his stories of creating fires and explosions to anyone but Arnie before this, and figured it would an ample opportunity to do some bragging about his exploits.

He decided to test Jay once more, to determine the man's motives for certain.

"I'll show you, but I don't know how much narration you're going to get from me."

"Fair enough," Jay answered the correct response. "I just want to see what you're capable of to make sure *I* don't get burned on this deal, if you get my drift."

"We have an agreement," Spiff noted. "Half now, and half when the job is complete. When it comes to money, I don't fall short on my end."

Jay scuffed one boot against the floor as he grinned.

"You do what you promise, and neither one of us will fall short on finances, kid."

A few minutes later, the Corvette left the parking lot with Jay and Spiff inside. Mike could only watch and wonder if everything was going according to plan, because he dared not follow. Gaining Spiff's trust was the only way to make certain they got proof of his past actions.

He waited a few minutes, until the car was completely out of sight, then started his own vehicle. If everything was going as they planned, Jay would basically bring Spiff right to him, once he had the proof they needed.

Since Jay hadn't used his cellular phone, Mike figured everything was okay.

He couldn't bear to lose another brother, and tried not to think about the possibility. After all, they had taken every precaution, figured the plan down to the minute, and knew once they got the arsonist away from the bar, he would be away from the only true safety he knew.

Mike was about to discover if all of his planning would pay off.

CHAPTER 32

What Spiff could not have known was that Jay was recording the entire conversation through a recorder in his glove compartment. A small microphone hung out of the bottom, completely out of sight.

Both brothers doubted the recording would ever come to be used in a court of law, but they needed insurance that Spiff wouldn't come after them once Mike carried out his plans on the arsonist.

Jay knew Mike's actions wouldn't be pleasant, but he still didn't know exactly what his younger brother had in mind once they reached their destination.

He also had no idea Greg was searching feverishly for them, beginning to understand what type of plan Mike had devised. Greg didn't need anyone endangering his own investigation, and he certainly didn't want his brothers trying to do his type of work without proper training.

By this time, Spiff had shown Jay two sites he burned to the ground, and Jay made a mental note of the addresses to inform Mike later. Both seemed like buildings Mike had warned him might be former target areas, but Jay wasn't positive.

"So are you convinced I can get the job done?" Spiff asked once they were away from the second site.

Jay was still overwhelmed by how much detail the man revealed about how he took both buildings down without detection of arson, and realized how easy it would be to trick the insurance company.

Even without the help of a shady arson investigator.

"I think you can get the job done, but I still want you to have an idea of my house's layout."

"So we're taking a trip to Aurora?"

"Yup."

"And you don't mind losing your house in the process?"

"You kidding?" Jay asked, flashing a smile. "With that bitch gone, I'll be able to collect the insurance and everything else. There's nothing in there I need, so it'll just help my alibi when everything I own goes up in flames."

Jay turned onto an exit that led to the Aurora area.

By this time, Jay had turned over the briefcase, ensuring Spiff he wasn't being duped in any way. Jay had the young man's trust, and planned on meeting Mike at the designated spot within the hour to finish out their plan.

"So what kind of name is Spiff, anyway?" Jay had to ask, now that he knew the nickname.

"I'd rather not talk about how I came to get called that," the young man said quickly. "Hell, I don't even know your name yet."

"Jay."

Deciding he would figure out who he and Mike were by the end of the day anyway, Jay saw no point in hiding his identity, or his first name at the very least.

"I got my nickname when I was a kid, and people just call me that now," the young man revealed as Jay turned onto a country road.

Jay noticed a bit of concern in Spiff's eyes, so he decided to explain himself.

"Got to pick up a few things from my vacation cottage," he said. "I do a lot of fishing during the summer, but I need some of my gear for a trip next weekend."

Spiff nodded, but didn't seem convinced. His strictly-business attitude made him suspicious of everything people did, except for Arnie.

Jay almost felt bad about leading the young man to the angry lion, his younger brother in this case, but he now felt relatively certain Spiff was responsible for several key fires, including the one that claimed Kevin.

"How far is this place?" Spiff asked when Jay turned on another road, lined as far as he could see with trees and shrubs, and no other houses in sight, indicating they were getting far away from civilization as they knew it.

"Not much further."

"I don't particularly like detours," Spiff said, his right hand slowly easing down the right side of his pants, as though perhaps reaching for a weapon.

Jay caught the movement from the corner of his eye, but knew he was too far along to break away from the plan. Besides, there was no house in Aurora, and he would be caught in the middle of his lie. Better to chance the remaining half mile to the cottage his friend let him use in the summertime and meet up with Mike, than have his head blown off, and his car stolen by the young arsonist, he decided.

His own firearm remained taped beneath the seat, too far to be of any use to him.

"This'll just take a second," Jay assured his passenger. "You can come inside if you want to."

"And you couldn't have done this after you took me back to Carvers Grove?"

"Ah, shit," Jay said easily. "It'll be dark by then, and this place doesn't have electricity half the fuckin' time."

Spiff nodded, but still didn't seem convinced. He let Jay pull up to the cabin with a lakeside view behind it, and trees surrounding the other three sides. Completely embedded in shade, the cabin was an ideal fishing or camping spot, and a mosquito haven as well during the humid summer months.

Smells of fresh pine trees and grilled meat from cabins around the lake lingered through the woods as Jay stepped out, finding no other vehicles around. If Mike was nowhere to be found, he had no idea how to carry out the next phase of the plan, or even if he could.

He suspected Spiff was armed, and taking too long inside the cabin would not be in his best interest. Stepping toward the locked door, Jay fished a key ring from his pocket, which actually contained the key to the door that his friend had given him several years back.

Certain his friend would not be at the cabin this week, Jay told Mike it would be a perfect spot to lure Spiff and attain information from the young man. Still clueless of what exactly his younger brother had in store for Spiff, Jay simply walked up, put the key into the lock, and let himself inside.

The darkness outside the cabin in the shaded areas held little comparison to the dim interior. Because all of the blinds were closed, and there were few windows built into the cabin, Jay found his hand fumbling blindly for the light switch he was certain sat along the wall to the right of the door.

"Shit," he muttered, finding the switch a few seconds later, as Spiff walked up from behind.

As the interior illuminated from several overhead chandeliers containing candle-like bulbs, Jay could see the wooden floors, and smell the stale air from inside the cabin that seldom saw visitation. Every time he entered the old building he felt like an intruder, because the cabin almost seemed to reject inhabitants by putting up a haunted front.

From its covered furniture and stale odor, to the mounted animal heads along several walls, the cabin looked as though it preferred its own company.

"For someone who owns this place, you don't seem overly familiar with it," Spiff commented, acting more suspicious by the second.

"Yeah, well, it's hard to see without any light, and I don't dare leave the blinds up, because vagrants might see something they like in here, and break in," Jay replied in his own defense. "There aren't exactly a lot of neighbors around to have a neighborhood watch, either."

Jay turned, unexpectedly finding a gun pointed straight at his face, confirming his suspicions.

"I don't like games," Spiff said, "so why don't we just part ways here and call it even. When you walk your ass back to Carvers Grove you can ask about your car, but I'm afraid it'll be in a million pieces, and found in about a hundred chop shops by then."

Jay swallowed hard, knowing he had underestimated the arsonist's need for money, and his ability to lead the young man on. Whether Spiff believed him or not was irrelevant, because a gun was pointed at a spot that would kill any man instantly.

"You're making a big mistake," Jay said, seeing the slightest movement behind the younger man.

"You had me sold, but I think you've taken up enough of my time," Spiff said. "I don't like doing business with distractions, and I don't think you're being very sincere. If you were serious about killing your wife, you'd have the balls to do it yourself, and you wouldn't be dragging me out here to pick up fishing tackle. So what gives?"

"You do," a voice behind Spiff said, causing the young man to whirl around.

As quickly as Spiff swung around, gun in hand, Mike's two hands were already in motion, swinging a baseball bat that connected with the young man's head before he even made a half turn, rendering him unconscious as his body slumped to the floor in a loud heap.

"About fuckin' time," Jay commented, his breathing a bit labored after his close encounter with death.

"I was here the whole time," Mike said. "I just wanted you to sweat it out a bit."

"Why don't you hand me that baseball bat so I can see how well your knees take a direct hit?" Jay suggested.

"I think not," Mike said with a smile, kicking Spiff's gun away from his limp hand. "I've got some pretty creative ideas about how his body is going to take some direct hits, and I think we're going to enjoy it a lot more than our young friend here."

Jay raised a skeptical eyebrow.

"What exactly do you have in mind, little brother?"

He saw a sinister squint from Mike's eyes.

"Just you wait and see."

Great, Jay thought sarcastically as he picked up the loaded firearm.

He had a brother bent on revenge, holding a baseball bat. Not that he much cared, after having a gun pointed at his forehead, but Jay figured Spiff had one hell of a beating coming his way.

CHAPTER 33

Jay could barely stand the screams and wails from Spiff as Mike laid into him with the baseball bat, almost half an hour after Spiff had originally been rendered unconscious.

At first, Mike started slowly, whacking the backside of the chair, or the meaty parts of the young man's body, but now things were getting a bit more serious.

Taking time enough to check his recording, which proved incredibly clear, and to make certain all of his cash was still inside the briefcase, Jay returned to the inside of the cabin. From the doorway he heard Spiff's arm snap after Mike took a swing that mirrored Mickey Mantle, hitting the humerous bone, square between the elbow joint and the shoulder.

Jay winced as Spiff let out a painful yowl.

"I tried reasoning with you," Mike said to the young man, who was helplessly strapped into a chair with enough rope to scale a small skyscraper. "We can do this the hard way, but if I hit you in just the right spot, or miss my mark, I might hit a major artery, and you could bleed to death internally."

Jay shuttered, shook his head, and turned to go outside, already having seen enough.

If even a possibility of blood spilling existed, Jay had to leave. On the exterior, he was the most rugged of the five brothers, but Jay had always been squeamish around blood.

On two different occasions he had lacerated his forearms at a vein while more than twenty stories above the ground. On both occasions, when blood abundantly showed, he nearly passed out from a lightheaded feeling. Not from a lack of blood, but the sight of it.

"If your artery busts," Mike continued, "you bleed internally, and the blood runs out of places to go. As your muscles harden from the blood pools, you'll begin to feel really cold as you slowly die from the lack of blood to and from your heart."

"Fuck you," Spiff fired back. "If I tell you anything, you're going straight to the cops."

"I can't go to the cops," Mike assured him. "If I do, they're going to wonder how I got my information, then I'll get in trouble for beating you senseless."

Mike drew in close enough for just Spiff to hear him.

"I want to know who's been paying you to start those fires. That's the *only* thing I want from you."

Before Spiff had regained consciousness from his first baseball bat encounter, Mike and Jay took time enough to converse about the locations Spiff had revealed. Mike immediately knew them as properties belonging to the insurance scam trio, but he wanted to hear it from Spiff himself.

They searched the young man for any form of identification, but came up short. They found nothing but a twenty dollar bill in one of his pockets.

"You know I can't tell you who I work for," Spiff insisted with a sneer.

"I already know," Mike revealed. "I just want you to tell me which one of those sons-of-bitches paid you to set the fire that killed my brother."

Realization showed in Spiff's eyes, and he knew he wasn't in for just a simple beating if he failed to cooperate. Mike's interest in this was extremely personal, and a few broken bones to an arsonist thug would make no dent in his conscience.

"I didn't know," Spiff said, his words sputtering in fear as his lips quivered.

"I know," Mike said with a tone of understanding, obviously faked, since he was raising the baseball bat once again.

Before Spiff could beg for mercy, the bat cracked against the front of his left shin, splintering it from within as pain seemed to pass through every nerve ending the young man had in his body.

"That's going to make for a long walk home," Mike stated casually, as though he had been beating people up for a living a long time. "Of course, I could toss you into the lake down there and see how many breast strokes you get in before that arm and leg fail, sending you straight to the bottom."

"You wouldn't do that," Spiff insisted.

In reply, Mike let an eerie smile cross his lips.

"Try me."

❦   ❦   ❦

As his brother toyed with the arsonist inside, Jay used his cellular phone to call Greg, who had been searching for his brothers all morning.

"Hello?"

"Greg, it's Jay."

"Where the hell are you? I've been trying to find you and Mike all morning."

"What makes you think I'm with Mike?"

"I had a little conversation with Sandi this morning, and she seems to think you two are spending an awful lot of time together."

Jay paused, taking cover beneath several of the overgrown trees so Mike wouldn't spot him from inside.

"Where are you two?" Greg insisted on asking.

"Uh, we're checking on a few things."

"Well you two need to quit playing hero and let me handle this. I'm getting some answers, legally, and that's the way I want to keep it."

Jay smirked, thinking Greg's investigation was no more legitimate than their own.

"Well, you might try finding out the real name of a guy they call Spiff," Jay informed his younger brother. "He's our arsonist, but we don't know his real name."

"And how the fuck did you come across this little piece of information?"

A long, drawn out painful scream echoed from the cabin, and Jay tried to cover the phone's mouthpiece too late.

"What was that?" Greg asked in shock.

"Better that you don't know, little brother."

Greg looked skyward on his end, positive his knowing would not be to his benefit later on. He would likely be an accessory to some crime if he knew, so he decided not to press the issue.

"I don't know what you two are trying to accomplish, but I'm getting very close on my end," Greg stated. "A little more evidence, and I can turn this over to the state authorities, since this conspiracy goes deeper than any of us originally thought."

"I could just play dumb and pretend I don't know what you're talking about."

"And I could play dumb and pretend I believe you, but that won't do any of us any good. I don't know what Mike has cooked up, but tell him to quit before it's too late."

Another scream boomed from inside the cabin, followed by an agonizing, lingering moan, and Jay made no attempt to shield it this time.

"Yeah, I'll see what I can do," he said before terminating the call.

As he walked inside the cabin, he saw blood streaming from several areas on the arsonist's body, and wondered how much further he dared let his brother go.

"Still not talking?" he asked Mike, trying his hardest to keep his eyes off the battered arsonist.

And the blood.

"He's not saying what I want to hear, and if he waits too long, he'll be unconscious, then I'll *really* be mad."

Spiff was sobbing uncontrollably from the pain, and his words came much harder now. The difficult choice to confess, or to take immeasurable pain was his to make, and he had no idea how far the fireman would go in getting the answers he wanted.

"He's about had it," Jay whispered to his younger brother. "You go too much further, you might end up killing him."

"It'd be a shame," Mike sneered.

"I told you, I'm not going to be a part of murder, and I don't like the way you're doing this, so hurry the fuck up and be done with it."

Jay thought he heard a vehicle outside, so he walked to the door to check.

"Okay, I'll tell you," Spiff mumbled through his pain.

Mike leaned in, not wanting Jay to hear, because he wanted to keep Jay as innocent as he could from this point on. Jay amazed him by going along with the plan this far, but his older brother lacked the killer instinct to carry out the final phase of the plan Mike had in mind for the one person who held the power.

As Spiff whispered the name Mike wanted to hear, with assurance that the man was the one behind everything, Mike nodded.

"So he's the ringleader?"

Spiff bobbed his head heavily.

Mike undid the bonds, carrying Spiff outside before dumping him on the hard dirt.

"If you make your way down to the dock someone might see you and get you to a hospital," Mike said to the virtually crippled Spiff.

"There aren't any phones around here, and hardly anyone uses this road, so it's your best chance if you don't want to freeze to death overnight."

"You can't just leave me here like this," Spiff pleaded.

"Can you tell me something that might change my mind?"

"There's…there's a job that I'm supposed to do in the middle of the night. I guess they're getting pretty hard up for money, because they've had me do a lot of work this summer, but Gustin usually calls me to confirm everything through the bar."

Damn it, Mike thought, realizing the situation was worse than he thought.

"Where's this job?"

"In the old Dayton Hotel," Spiff answered, instantly bringing the image of the old, dilapidated, seven story hotel into Mike's mind.

Listed as a historical landmark, scheduled to be renovated the following spring, the hotel was a ghastly chamber of dust, asbestos, lead paint, and falling chunks of ceiling. The firefighters toured it early in the summer to see the hazards of the old building for themselves, and though no one officially resided there, it held potential for homeless and stragglers on a nightly basis.

"But if he can't reach you, he won't burn it, will he?" Mike asked.

"I don't know. He said something about an insurance change, and getting it done by the end of the week."

"Fuck," Mike said to himself, Jay just now walking toward him.

"I thought there was a car coming, but it was just a jet passing overhead," Jay commented.

He saw the look on Mike's face.

"What's wrong?"

"The Dayton Hotel is scheduled to be burned overnight."

"Tonight?"

Mike nodded.

"This is getting worse by the minute."

"What about me?" Spiff begged. "I told you what you wanted to know."

"Like I said, try and get down to the dock," Mike insisted, showing no remorse for his earlier actions. "If I see you anywhere near Carvers Grove again, I'm putting a bullet in your head myself."

Jay held up the tiny tape recorder, waving it for Spiff to see.

"We've got an interesting conversation on here, and the police will be checking over your apartment within the hour, so it wouldn't be in your best interest to return. Ever."

"But you can't-"

Mike held up a foreboding finger.

"The alternative is another beating, son. You can limp your gimpy ass down to the dock, or I can take out some more body parts for you."

He held up the bat, now smeared with blood, as provocation.

"I'll limp," Spiff said, starting to drag himself toward the winding wooden steps that would eventually get him down to the dock.

Though he didn't trust either brother, he knew they were right about the lack of traffic, and the phones, because there were no phone lines, or cable television lines, or even running water this far out.

"I called Greg," Jay revealed as they stepped into the Corvette.

"You did what?"

"I didn't tell him anything, but he suspects what we're doing."

"How?"

"He talked to your fiancee."

Mike cursed beneath his breath, because Greg stood to ruin everything he had planned. He saw little choice but to dodge his twin, or reveal everything in the hopes that Greg would help, because another building stood to burst into a ball of flame if he didn't.

"You were lying about the police raiding his apartment, right?" Mike inquired.

"Yeah, of course."

"Good, because I'm going to raid it. I want to know who that little prick really is."

Jay started the car, saying nothing. He sensed this was the end of his partnership with Mike, because his brother had clammed up entirely about Spiff, so he must have discovered something he wanted to know, and he wasn't about to share.

As for Mike, several tough choices were his to make, because he didn't want to trust anyone else, or take it for granted Greg's investigation would pan out. Still, he needed to decide if the Dayton Hotel was really in danger, or if Spiff was the group's only hope of accurately setting a fire that looked accidental, as he had so many times before.

"You sure Spiff's apartment is above that bar?" he asked Jay as the Corvette sped away from the cabin.

"Positive."

"Think it's the only one?"

"Probably, unless the bartender has one too."

"I may need one more favor from you big brother."

"Oh, God," Jay muttered, knowing what Mike was about to ask.

CHAPTER 34

"What do you mean you can't find him?" Ronnie Emerson demanded angrily over the phone in front of his two business partners.

The dark part in his hair appeared disheveled as he twisted and turned with the phone at every utterance from the other end of the line.

All three partners sat in a suite along the top floor of the Star Building, which housed Shelton Properties, among other businesses.

A rather large room, the suite was basically a meeting room with variable lighting, an excellent view of the parking lot below, and plenty of chairs around a long rectangular table. On either side it held doors to the secretary's office, or Dirk Shelton's private office.

Each of the three had very accommodating spaces to meet, but they rotated to keep the public unaware of their partnership as much as possible. The less people knew about their business relationship, the less chance anyone would piece together the scattered clues of arson fires and insurance fraud.

Had they known two different groups were already cornering the necessary information to make their lives miserable, they might have reconsidered the plan of action they were about to execute, and forego the largest sum of insurance money they had ever attempted to claim.

"I don't want excuses, Scott," his partners heard Emerson state. "If you can't find him, you're going to have to carry through the plan yourself."

Obvious objection came through the line loud enough for everyone to hear.

"You've watched him work, and you know his techniques," Emerson continued without falter. "Make it look like an accident, pure and simple, and we all walk away from this with a lot of money. Understand?"

Though Gustin didn't sound happy on the other end, he apparently agreed, because he had little choice.

"You've got the keys to the place, so get in there and make it look accidental, just like Spiff does," Emerson said, trying to evoke confidence in his property manager. "Set a slow burn, then get somewhere public, so a hundred people can say you were there when the fire started."

Gustin said a few more words, indicating he would carry out Emerson's wishes.

"You'll do fine, Scott."

Emerson slammed the phone down when he was done.

"I don't think Scott shares our sense of urgency," he stated. "If that building doesn't go down tonight, we're fucked."

While Emerson and Boyce dressed in full suits, Shelton wore casual clothes, since he had just come from the golf course with Mason Gray.

"Everything went fine on my end," he reported of his meeting with Gray.

"Once the Historic Society gets that paperwork signed, the insurance falls partly into their hands for contributing funds to the project, so to speak," Boyce said. "After that, there's no way to avoid rebuilding the hotel, even if it's a complete loss."

A slender man with thinning blond hair, a trimmed mustache, and thin wire glasses, Boyce was an expert on nearly every facet of property ownership, whether it was private, public, or government owned. He looked like the scientist nerd type, but his intellect in property was unparalleled, which made him invaluable to the trio.

"This could have been avoided by keeping the Historic Society out of the picture completely," Shelton debated.

"And we would have had no cover when the hotel burned," Boyce countered. "This way it looks like my company made every conceivable effort to rebuild and reopen the hotel."

Emerson shook his head.

"I wished we could have waited, because it's risky doing another fire this soon."

"It was your idea," Boyce reminded him.

"I know, but this is going to be pushing it."

Though he put on a good front, Emerson needed the money to pay several major outstanding debts. After putting up every imaginable excuse why they needed to burn the hotel so soon, he contacted the Illinois Historic Society to put pressure on Boyce, without his partner ever knowing it.

"We don't have a thing to worry about," Shelton assured them. "If Gray can keep the state off his back, and Gustin does his job right, we're going to be sitting on a gold mine."

"Did Gustin have trouble locating our firebug?" Boyce inquired.

"Apparently," Emerson answered, "but Scott knows what needs to be done. No matter what it takes, the Dayton Hotel will be ashes by tomorrow. Gentlemen, I suggest you start planning your alibis for tonight, and make them good."

All three men looked to one another, then smiled openly, thinking their plan was foolproof, and no one would know the better when they split well over a million dollars between them. The Historic Society would openly cry at the loss in public, and everyone would think what a shame it was how the old hotel burned down before new life could be breathed into it.

In truth, the trio had bought up all sorts of similar properties. Some they refinished, others they left alone, some they rented out, and occasionally one burned to the ground. They knew their business, and they had the right people in their corner. The Washington Township Fire Department was little more than a blessing in disguise, because some of their properties were on the outskirts of town, where it would take volunteer firefighters ten minutes to half an hour to respond to any emergency.

Legally, as the owner, Boyce controlled how the insurance money was spent if anything happened to the Dayton Hotel, but once he let the Historic Society donate funds, part of the responsibility became theirs, and legal matters became much more complicated concerning the insurance, since some of the construction would be funded by the state.

His agreement to allow the Society to help forced his hand much quicker than he figured, and Emerson used this to his personal advantage, telling his partner to let Spiff take care of the hotel before the lawyers got involved.

Emerson considered the death of Kevin Sheridan a tragedy, but thought of it as little more than collateral damage in his quest for money and power. To him, it was more of an unfortunate incident because it put his plans in jeopardy, not because a family was mourning. Emerson now needed to exercise extra caution in every phase of his plans, because the risks were higher, and authorities beyond Mason Gray's level might possibly be called in more often.

Now the stage was set for their largest profit of the year if everything went according to plan. None of them knew where Spiff was, and none of them really cared. He knew better than to turn against them, or he would be buried with the remains of the buildings he so carefully burned.

Their evening plans simply included separating, then joining clusters of people to establish their alibis, while the culmination of their profit scheme took shape. One way or another, they planned to wake up rich men in the morning.

On paper at least.

※ ※ ※

Mike crawled through a window immediately after dusk that took him straight to the apartments above the bar where Arnie and Spiff resided.

Below, the bar bustled with activity, so he planned to be safe from any interruptions as Jay removed the small stepladder from the sidewalk, tossing it into the back of his truck. Since Mike had planned ahead, bringing rope up with him, he would be able to scale down quickly in case of emergency.

Not that the second floor was extremely high off the ground, but Mike didn't need to be hurting himself by leaping down on the concrete. His plan was going too well to mess it up with an accident now.

"Go," Mike said with a wave of his hand, indicating Jay should go sit in his pickup truck, which they had swapped for the Corvette upon returning to Carvers Grove.

He climbed inside the already broken window screen, finding instant access to the two doors above the bar. Below, music blared so loud he could barely hear himself think, but Mike came to the first door, giving it a few knocks.

If someone answered, he would pretend he was drunk and lost, in the hopes that it might work.

No one answered, and he tried the knob, but it was locked. A few shoulder thrusts later, and he was inside the shabby apartment, trying to find a light of some kind. He pawed around until his fingers found a desk lamp, and he illuminated the small apartment, much to his horror.

"Yuck," he commented, knowing he was inside Spiff's apartment.

Strewn candy wrappers, open boxes, a half-full trash bag in one corner, and mouse droppings were just the beginning of the horrific sights his eyes took in.

Deciding he had little time to waste, Mike quickly shuffled through the drawers of an old desk in one corner, trying to find anything that might identify Spiff, or tie him to the arson fires.

"What a fucking packrat," Mike commented to himself, finding all sorts of papers that meant nothing to him, but obviously held something important to Spiff.

Finally, after searching the man's desk drawers, he found a few old photos, and with them, several old ID cards, including one from junior high, and the man's driver's license, which Mike suspected was probably revoked. Perhaps Spiff just didn't drive, because Mike saw no evidence of a working vehicle outside of the bar.

He looked over the cards, recognizing Spiff from the photos. These were proof of Spiff's identity, and might help Greg more than they would aid in his own search.

"Julius Reginald Covington," Mike read the young man's real name aloud to himself. "With a name like that, I'd probably take up a nickname too."

He stuffed the cards into one pocket, satisfied there was nothing else to find inside the cramped apartment, and dashed out of the door, pulling it closed behind him. With the frame busted from Mike's entry, the door simply swung open again, but he didn't care at this point. Mike simply tied the rope to an old heating unit in the hallway, and descended to the sidewalk below.

"Did you find anything?" Jay asked quickly as the two clamored aboard the truck.

"I've got his real name," Mike announced. "Let's get out of here before the locals decide to put your truck on blocks and strip it."

Jay started the engine.

"I had a few looking at it, like they had just that in mind."

"Did you threaten to come back with your biker gang or something?"

"Nah. I just casually took out your gun and cleaned it for all of them to see."

Mike nodded.

"I see."

"What next?" Jay asked, as though getting excited about another challenge to find Kevin's killer.

Mike, however, had come to realize that even though one man was giving the orders, there were multiple parties responsible.

"Greg's on duty," Mike said. "Let's call him and give him an anonymous tip of sorts about the Dayton Hotel."

"What about that Gustin fella?" Jay inquired. "Everything runs through him, doesn't it?"

"You've got a point. Keeping an eye on him might help us learn when and where that fire is supposed to start."

"It's about eight o'clock. You want to swing by and see if we can't catch up with ol' Scott?"

Mike hadn't called Sandi all day. At this point, perhaps it was best he didn't, but he decided the one important thing left in his life was family, and she was going to be his wife in a matter of months. He didn't want to overwhelm her by telling her everything they had been doing the past few weeks, because he wasn't certain she'd understand.

He believed women looked at revenge and taking risks much differently than men, and considering the type of men Mike and his brothers were attempting to pin several crimes on, it was probably for the best if Sandi didn't know what he was doing.

"Run me home real quick," Mike said. "I need to let Sandi know I'm okay."

"What about Gustin?"

"See what you find, Jay, and give me a call."

"And Greg?"

"We'll give him a call when we have something more to go on."

Jay shrugged to himself.

"Whatever you say, little brother."

CHAPTER 35

On what was quite simply one of the most boring nights he had ever spent in the investigative offices of the Carvers Grove Police Department, Greg fought the entire afternoon and evening to keep his mind off the trio of conspirators, and what his twin brother might be doing.

After placing several calls to Sandi, he decided to give up. Hoping Mike knew what he was doing, Greg tried working on several mediocre cases, calling old witnesses here and there. Nothing new turned up, and he was about to see if he could use some comp time to take the remaining few hours off, when the phone rang beside him.

"Detectives," Greg answered vaguely as the investigators usually did.

"Is Greg Sheridan in, please?" a female voice inquired.

"This is he."

"Greg, it's Tasha."

She sounded distressed, as though someone might be listening to her, or watching.

"What's the matter?" he asked.

"I'm right outside your offices. Do you have a few minutes to talk?"

After business hours, the city hall offices were locked, and people had to use a designated phone outside for assistance.

"I'll be right there," Greg said, quickly hanging up the phone.

He snatched up his sport coat before heading for the front door.

There, he found Tasha clutching several files and folders, all secured by a rubber band. Her look was that of a desperate woman, or perhaps a woman whose life was just turned upside down.

"What's wrong?" he asked, seeing her ghostly pale face as she fought to calm herself in his presence.

"Can we go somewhere and talk?" she insisted.

"Sure," Greg said, leading her to the unmarked car he was assigned that evening.

A few minutes later, the two were seated in the car, settled on the edge of a nearby park where the most intrusive sound they heard was the occasional frog croaking from the stream. Greg chose to park in the picnic area, which sat beside the stream. Wildlife of all kinds inhabited the area, and some were docile enough to be fed by hand during the day.

"What did you come to tell me?" Greg asked, seeing that Tasha felt a bit more relaxed away from the center of the city.

"Here," she said, plopping the stack of files on his lap. "That is everything you'd ever want to know about the three men you were investigating, and their insurance claims."

"Good God," Greg said in awe. "You must have spent hours looking this stuff up."

"I just made the calls," Tasha said. "I had friends who looked up the information under a false pretense. In that business, it isn't that hard to find the information if you know the right people."

Greg stared at the files a moment, dumbfounded enough that he couldn't bear to open them with her present.

"You must have risked your job for this," he said, looking to her, unsure of how to thank her, or if he was supposed to.

"I quit my job today," she announced bleakly. "I…I'm leaving town tomorrow."

"But why?"

Tasha composed herself a bit more before explaining everything to him.

"I found one of Blaine's law books lying on his study table the other day, so I peeked at it, and discovered he was looking up laws about historical societies helping fund the buildings they contributed to, and I didn't think much of it at the time."

She swallowed hard before continuing.

"Later, I discovered he had written down a note to himself to check on the Dayton Hotel for his brother, and I, well, I finally put it together. Ronnie's friend Bryan Boyce owned the hotel, and I remembered reading about how the hotel would be a remarkable save for the Historic Society."

"But why are you leaving?" Greg insisted. "And why give me all of this now?"

"Because Blaine is part of their conspiracy, and helped in some way, to get your brother killed. I won't be a part of this when it goes to trial, and I won't have Blaine hunting me down forever if he gets away with it."

"But what made you decide to give me everything? I thought you were committed to your new life, and to Blaine Emerson."

"I was, but I realized living a lie will draw me further into his world, and I don't want any part of that."

"Why tonight? Why couldn't this wait, Tasha?"

"Because they sign that agreement with the Historic Society tomorrow, Greg," she said, as though he should have already known that.

"And?"

"And that means that building has to be destroyed before they sign those papers tomorrow, or legally, the insurance responsibility will be shared by Boyce and the Society."

Greg's face registered his shock.

"You're kidding."

"No, and that's why I had to tell you this tonight, and to make sure I get out of here before Blaine finds out what I've done."

Greg's concern turned to her for the moment. He could worry about the Dayton Hotel momentarily.

"Where will you go?"

"I've got some friends in Maryland," Tasha said easily. "I've got money, and it won't be any trouble at all getting a new job."

Greg felt his chest settle heavily as he breathed, unable to absorb all of this at once.

"Am I going to see you again?" he asked slowly, turning to her.

Tasha suddenly reached up, clasping him around the neck with both hands, pulling him into a long, deep kiss they both felt was overdue, though neither had admitted it to this point. Greg tensed when she reached upward, then fell into the pleasure of her aroma once more, moaning softly as their lips joined for the briefest of moments.

He wished it would go on forever, but his question was about to be answered.

"I hope so," Tasha said when she released him, stepping from the car.

"Tasha!" Greg called after her. "Wait!"

She didn't wait, and she crossed a footpath where he could not follow by car, leaving him alone with a pile of evidence and a broken heart.

Again.

Greg didn't have time to mourn Tasha's departure, because a building stood to fall into seven stories worth of rubble if he didn't stop it, and he would be damned if any other firefighters were killed because he didn't act.

Starting the car, Greg set the stack of evidence beside him before pulling out of the parking space, then the park, hoping to place himself inside the Dayton Hotel before anyone else did. He picked up his portable radio, deciding to inform his dispatchers he would be on a detail until his shift was over. Since he did little of significance in his division anyhow, no one would care.

A few minutes later, he parked the car in an alley a few blocks from the old hotel, assured no one would see it, or its city plate, where it sat. He placed the documents inside the trunk, locked every door, and made certain no one could easily see it from the road. The other end of the alley led to an old parking lot no one used, since it was sealed off from all sides.

He walked toward the old hotel in the darkness, seeing it loom overhead with windows occasionally broken out along the various levels. Barely a shadow of the great facility that attracted businessmen, foreign leaders, and sports figures during its heyday in the 1960's, the building looked as though it had been abandoned almost as long as it had existed.

In a manner of speaking, it had.

Used as a hotel for only a decade before it went under, the building later served as an extension of the local college, a training facility for the fire department, and as a museum, before officially being abandoned of all use a few years prior.

Still rented around Halloween for use as a haunted house by fraternities and high schools, the building held little other use to anyone in Carvers Grove.

Because of its status during the first decade of operation, and the people it attracted, the building was deemed historical. Two of the floors were constructed with literally tons of glass, which served to display art exhibits and give the building an unusual appeal. Another floor had imported tile on the floor, and original paintings on the walls by several famous contemporary artists, from the building's original construction era.

Through sheer existence alone, the building was a piece of art.

Greg started at it, and it seemed to stare back through its shattered windows, which looked eerily like eyes, challenging him to scale the mesh fence around the facility and come inside.

Taking a deep breath, certain his firearm was nestled at his waist, Greg planned to do just that.

※　　　　　※　　　　　※

While Greg waited for someone to show up at the hotel, Jay was busy observing Scott Gustin from a distance as the man loaded bundles of undisclosed items into his van rather hurriedly.

From a safe distance, Jay could monitor everything occurring within Gustin's property, and even had sense enough to bring his camcorder, so he could record everything Gustin did. Even if it never did any good, Jay decided he was going to be tailing Gustin anyway, so it made perfect sense to record the man, right up until he went to the hotel.

If that's where he was going.

Jay didn't trust Spiff any further than he could have tossed him into the lake earlier that day, but he wasn't taking any chances.

From his vantage point, there were several bushes concealing his presence, but also his view. Jay could see through the back yard where a giant in-ground pool let steam filter from the water surface on the cool August evening, and the garage where Gustin busily packed his van with several boxes before heading inside the check on something.

Jay picked up his phone, calling Mike at home.

Sandi answered, unhappy to hear it was Jay calling, but she put Mike on the phone nonetheless.

"What have you got?" Mike asked immediately.

"Gustin's loading up a bunch of shit into his van. Looks like the makings of an arson pie if you ask me."

"You think he's doing the job himself?"

"Well, considering you crippled his usual means of starting fires, yes."

"I can be right there."

"Not necessary," Jay replied quickly. "I've got the videotape rolling, and I can tail him anywhere he might go."

"Well, duh," Mike said sarcastically. "You know where he's going."

"Have you called Greg yet?"

"I tried, but he hasn't been in his office all night, and I can't remember his portable phone's number. If he caught Gustin in the act, that would probably get us what we've been wanting all along."

"Well, since Greg isn't around, I should probably let Gustin get in there and at least start the fire, right?"

"Why would you do that?"

"If I don't, we won't have *any* proof."

Silence on the other end.

"What are you thinking, Mike?"

"I'm thinking no amount of proof is going to help us, because of how we went about getting it."

Jay agreed, and both knew the legal system all too well from hearing Greg bitch about how many cases were dismissed on technicalities and botched evidence collection. No court would admit evidence attained by amateur detectives."

"If we can't use this for anything, why am I even following Gustin around?"

"Because *I* needed proof," Mike answered solemnly.

"And just what do you plan to do now?"

"What I should have done from the beginning, Jay. I'm going to make sure no one else's brother dies because of those fuckers. What is it they always say in those stories of revenge? An eye for an eye?"

Jay paused a few seconds, seeing Gustin hop into his van. He was getting ready to depart.

"You're scaring me a little, Mike. Please tell me you're not going to do anything drastic."

"By tomorrow morning, you'll know what I did, and why I did it. Good luck, Jay."

With that, Mike hung up the phone. Jay didn't like this new, dark Mike. He liked being hung up on even less, but he needed to see where Gustin was going.

"I already know where he's going," Jay said, berating himself aloud.

He took an alternative route that would get him to the old hotel that much quicker, and he found an old lot across from the hotel with a fleet of rental vans that were doing little more than collecting dust the past few months.

Parking his truck in the center of the vans, he shut it off, certain it blended in, and quickly turned on his camera as Gustin pulled into the lot, unlocked the front gate, and pulled his van inside, locking the gate behind him. He then pulled his van around the rear of the building, ensuring no one would see it from the road as he set about his business.

"Showtime," Jay said to himself, watching Gustin disappear from his view, then reappear around another corner, carrying a box into the hotel.

Jay forbade himself from entering the gates for two reasons.

One, he could possibly get placed as an arsonist, or an accomplice. Staying where he was, he would be perfectly safe, and no one would know any better.

Secondly, no one was inside the building but Gustin, and Jay wanted to make sure no firefighters risked their lives for that piece of shit.

He readied himself to lie if firefighters showed up, because he didn't want anyone risking his or her life for the old building under the pretense someone might be inside.

If the Dayton Hotel fell to the ground, no one would really care. After all, no one stayed there, it was an eyesore, and it only served to add to the growing list of damning evidence the brothers had against the conspiracy trio. That was, if they could use any evidence.

Besides, on larger scale fires like the hotel would be, the fire department called in almost every available firefighter to help. The list would include Wade, and Jay refused to see his son's life endangered on a lost cause, so he vowed to keep any of the firefighters from getting inside, no matter what excuse he needed to make.

Losing Kevin was bad enough, and Jay didn't want any other family going through what he and his brothers and sisters had. Taking care of his mother was more responsibility than Jay ever wanted, after so many years of her being the family's backbone.

It hurt him to see her so weak, so fragile, but someone needed to watch after her, and he was the oldest. By default, the responsibility fell on his shoulders, and for that reason he would make certain no one else lost any loved ones.

He sat back, watching Gustin carry several more boxes inside the old hotel, adding to the proof Jay no longer needed to satisfy his own curiosity.

CHAPTER 36

Inside the hotel, Gustin refused to stray from the first floor, knowing if it burned well enough, the entire hotel would crumble down after its weakened supports gave out.

Most of the first floor looked naked, since most of the decorative walls were removed, sold when the hotel underwent its last transformation. An overhead light swung gently in the breeze created by the hundreds of little gaps in the walls where air could flow.

Though the ceiling was intact, it looked dingy gray, rather than off-white, when Gustin's flashlight beam struck its textured surface. Every step, in fact, every movement, echoed throughout the mammoth building. Several times already, Gustin had felt a chill run down his spine, sensing he wasn't alone, as though the ghosts from the previous century were returning to impede his job at hand.

While the entrance lobby and check-in counter were primarily intact, little else around him looked very much like a hotel. Exposed drywall, wooden particle boards, and a few pieces of dusty furniture were all that remained in the main lobby where guests once read, ate, or waited for their families to arrive.

Gustin was too young to appreciate the hotel's past, because he saw it as little more than a financial gain. As he set down the flashlight, he looked at its decaying features, knowing the hidden beauty upstairs would be collateral damage in the wake of the overnight fire.

He could envision it as a modern day *Towering Inferno*, only without the people desperately scrambling to escape the flames stalking their every move. Gustin planned to be long gone by the time the flames actually embedded themselves in the walls and ate the tower from within.

After studying Spiff's technique, and talking with the man, Gustin had some idea of what he was doing.

He started by boarding up the two smashed windows on the lower floor so the flames would remain primarily inside, and not draw attention to themselves until it was too late. He needed the fire to grow large enough that firefighters would never dare try an interior attack. That sort of action might thwart his plan completely.

Most of the smashed windows were on higher floors, because teenagers enjoyed the thrill of trying to hit such a high target, and because the security fence blocked any straight throws at the two lowest floors.

Once both windows were blocked to the best of his ability, with the scrap wooden boards available, Gustin turned his attention to the boxes, unloading over a dozen rolls of paper towels before stringing them across the floor in every direction, then stuffing them up into the walls where cracks and crevices presented themselves.

With so many directions to travel, the fire would surely have a blast trying them all. Gustin didn't possess Spiff's talent, or love for fire, but he too believed it was a living creature of sorts, eating, breathing, and traveling.

He quickly dispersed several empty beer bottles in the corners, in the hopes pieces of them might survive the fire to implicate drunken teenagers in starting the blaze. Wearing latex gloves, Gustin knew fingerprints could be lifted on even the most charred of objects, so he took no chances. The bottles were from nearby trash cans, so other people stood to be falsely accused if their prints were lifted, but he didn't care.

After all, he was going to be taking a long vacation after this job was finished.

Placing a small board beneath the centralized web of paper towels, Gustin doused the center mass ever so slightly with some lighter fluid, knowing the fire itself, and any impending extinguishment efforts would wash away such a tiny piece of evidence.

He pulled one of the old chairs over to the pile, knowing the chair would catch fire, smolder, and if all else failed, slowly spread its wealth of radiant heat to the floor, and weaken the building from the ground up. Quickly stuffing some paper towel between the cushion and the base of the chair, Gustin ensured it too would contribute to the unimaginable destruction.

With so much rotted, dry wood, and plentiful oxygen from all of the drafty cracks in the ceilings and walls, the building would be doomed the moment a match touched the center pile of paper towel and wood.

Of this, Gustin felt certain.

Taking one last look around the main lobby, Gustin pulled a Zippo lighter from the right pocket of his slacks. He opened it with a ca-chink sound as the flame danced atop the metal frame, and he stared down at the pile of organized litter at his feet.

"Don't even think about it," he heard a voice say from behind him as Greg emerged around the old check-in desk where he had been hiding for almost an hour.

Gustin swallowed, unable to speak as a gun was pointed at his chest, the lighter still flickering in one hand.

His mind raced like a greyhound after a rabbit, but alternatives to surrender seemed limited.

"Set the lighter down, because you're coming with me," Greg ordered, reaching slowly for his handcuffs as he kept the firearm pointed at Gustin. "I know everything, so running won't do you any good."

Still Gustin said nothing, just standing there like a frozen popsicle, the lighter still flickering reflective light from his pale face. Greg began to worry just a bit as he approached the property manager, wondering what thoughts were going through the man's mind.

Surrender obviously wasn't one of his primary alternatives, and as the lighter dropped from his hand toward the board soiled with lighter fluid, Greg dove to catch it while Gustin dashed toward the back of the building.

Greg missed, landing hard on his right shoulder, injuring it as the gun flew from his hand, several feet away from him. Groaning to himself, Greg propped himself up with his good arm as several rows of flames raced one another across the paper towels, trying to see which could be the first to embed itself within the old walls of the hotel.

"Oh, shit," Greg muttered to himself as he stood, retrieving his gun from the floor after stepping across a row of flame.

He wanted to chase Gustin, but this situation would quickly get out of hand if the fire spread. Greg's primary concern, like Jay's, was to ensure no one died needlessly by entering the building. Feeling he had failed his father, Greg would make certain no one entered this building to save ghosts who weren't there.

Plucking his cellular phone from inside his sport coat, Greg dialed 911 to get the fire department on their way, but before he could hit the send button, Gustin sent an old wooden chair thrashing across the back of his head with a cracking sound as the chair splintered into a hundred pieces.

Greg landed face-first on the ground with a thud that echoed above the sound of the burning embers as Gustin stood there a moment to ensure the detective didn't move, even as the flames drew closer to him.

He started to reach for the fallen officer's firearm, but decided it might work out perfectly if people considered Greg Sheridan had sought revenge in a twisted way, setting fire to one of the few remaining historical landmarks in the city.

Originally, Gustin had wanted to run, but decided his operation, his cut of the money, and his life as he knew it, would be history. He was already facing a slew of charges, so murdering a detective and hoping everyone pinned the fire on the dead man seemed a logical way to go.

Seeing the cellular phone melt in the center of one of the rows of flames, Gustin felt satisfied his work was finished, as was the detective, and headed for the back door once again.

As he reached the door, Gustin realized the key ring he always kept hooked at his waist had fallen off at some point.

"Shit!" he exclaimed to no one but himself, turning around to find it before the heat of the flames became too much for him.

If he failed to escape the way he originally planned, Gustin would need to find another way out of there, or a wickedly good excuse as to why his van was beside a building engulfed in flames.

Desperately searching for his keys along the fire-laden floor, Gustin's eyes caught a glimpse of a shimmering object across the floor, and a closer look revealed they were his keys, but they were at the edge of a dancing firewall.

Kicking them out of the heat, Gustin walked over to them, kneeling down. He could see they were smoldering from the fire, so he dared not touch them. Instead, he grabbed a nearby rag to use in picking them up.

As he went to pick them up, Gustin felt something barrel into him from one side, realizing too late the detective was conscious once again, and tackling him from a low position.

Both men grunted as they struggled along the floor, the flames and heat growing more intense everywhere around them. Gustin's head hit a wall as Greg mounted his upper torso, laying into him with several fists repeatedly. He could have used his gun, but Greg doubted there was any way an arrest would stand, and he wanted just a little bit of retribution before he carted Gustin off to jail, or for questioning.

Before he knew it, his hands were wrapped around the property manager's throat, squeezing rather vigorously. He could hear Gustin gasp as oxygen failed to reach his lungs, and stopped himself before he went too far.

Realizing the flames were getting too dangerous for any human being to be near, he pulled out his cuffs, slapped one on Gustin's right wrist, then one on his own right wrist before trying to pull the man up to his feet. Instead, he received a quick blow to the head with one of the chair pieces from his earlier head shot as Gustin tried anything he could to escape at this point.

Radiant heat and the smell of consumed wood filled the room as the fire grew, trying to reach the grand ceilings of the lobby. Gustin saw this, and desperately patted the detective down for a key to the handcuffs while Greg lay on the ground, groggy from the two strikes to his head.

Gustin decided after a few seconds to skip the keys, and use the firearm to shoot the middle of the handcuffs, and possibly the meddlesome detective in the process. As he reached for the gun at Greg's waistline, the detective found enough presence of mind to strike Gustin squarely in the jaw, sending the arsonist back as far as the cuffs would allow.

"Give it up, Gustin," he ordered, feeling blood ooze from the back of his head.

Gustin started to reach for another striking object, but the sound of a cocked hammer from Greg's firearm froze him perfectly still. His eyes wandered to the sight of the gun pointed straight at his heart, forcing Gustin to realize his work, and the possibility of gaining so much money, were not worth dying for.

If he was lucky, he would find another route of escape before the detective could cart him off to jail, or to some interrogation room.

"Get up," Greg ordered.

Both men stood as chunks of ceiling tile and insulation began falling down around them, from the flames tickling the underside of the weakened structure. A deafening crash came to one side of them, and both realized the back exit was sealed off, because part of the back staircase had buckled under the stress of the heat, falling the only direction it could.

Straight down.

Greg's first thought was how they could possibly have conceived renovating a building that was obviously unsafe to begin with. The flames weren't even off the first floor yet, and the place was beginning to fall in around them.

He looked from the back exit to the two windows, both of which had drawn fire directly to them. For escape purposes, they were useless. Greg then turned his attention to the front entrance of the building, which he could not see in the darkness past the flames.

"Those front doors are boarded shut," Gustin said, a bit of panic setting into his eyes.

"They're just glass," Greg stated, knowing what the front of the hotel looked like after so many years of patrolling the area.

"There's two sets. The inside set has boards set in front of it, with all kinds of shit piled up against them to make sure no one gets in. Or out."

"Bullshit," Greg said, tugging Gustin along quickly through the few areas flames weren't touching, for a quick peek.

They reached the main lobby's entrance, which Greg had neglected earlier in his haste to hide himself, and he realized the first floor left them absolutely no way out. Box after box, along with pieces of furniture, were stacked in front of the door in such a manner that it would take close to fifteen minutes with both men working feverishly, to move every piece of heavy, dead weight away from the door.

By then, it would be too late.

Greg knew he could not release Gustin from his restraints, because the man couldn't be trusted.

"Upstairs," Greg thought aloud.

"What?" Gustin stammered in shock. "Are you nuts? That staircase on the other side just tumbled to the ground with *no* weight on it."

"You'd better come up with a better idea pretty quick, Gustin, or we're both going to be well-done steaks in a matter of minutes."

From his truck, Jay could hear the sirens of the fire department vehicles approaching in the distance. Flames were visibly reaching for the heavens from every open space they could find within the hotel's rotting walls.

Jay never expected the fire to spread so quickly, but he had underestimated how dry, and how ripe to burn, the hotel was. Strangely, he never saw Gustin leave the building, and the man's van was still parked on the backside, with debris occasionally falling around it.

Deciding it was time to make a speedy exit, Jay started his truck, deciding to use the back way out of the area. If Gustin burned up in the flames, it was his own fault, and Jay wouldn't give it a second thought when he read about it in the local section of the paper the next morning.

He maneuvered his truck around the parking lot, careful not to be spotted when he left the area, but when he passed a nearby alley, he caught a glimpse of a vehicle that looked strikingly familiar.

It could have been coincidence, but here sat a car less than two blocks away from the fire that looked like any number of those used by the police force.

In particular, the investigative division.

Thinking Mike might have reached Greg, and their brother might have come to the scene, Jay pulled into the alley for a closer look at the car.

"Shit," he muttered, finding the city license plate, and a radio unit inside.

He had little doubt it was Greg who had driven the car there, but where was he?

Jay panicked for a moment, pacing along one side of the car. Did he go look for Greg, or did his brother have everything under control? If he had everything under control, why wasn't he leaving a fiery building? Was he even in the building?

Positive he was about to be forced to do the one thing he vowed he would never do, Jay considered meeting the fire department at the gate to report someone might be inside.

He thought about Wade, and what if he was already called in, and what if they sent him up a ladder, and the building collapsed upon itself? Standing around to do nothing was the one thing he couldn't afford to do, so he fought his urges to follow through with his original intent, and began running toward the front gate where the fire trucks would likely stage while they waited for the scene commander to issue orders.

As he ran, he looked for any signs of Gustin or Greg exiting the building, but saw none. Jay wondered if he would be on time to save anyone, as his guts burned with the thought of seeing this entire plan end in disaster because of a lack of communication.

Taking one more look before crossing the last of the outskirts of the mesh fence toward the fire department, Jay caught a glimpse of something in a second story window, stopping him cold. Squinting, his eyes bounced like ping pong balls in search of another sign of life, and he finally spied Greg pulling Gustin along behind him, desperately looking out some of the windows on a side shielded from the fire department.

Whether Greg wanted the department to see him, or even save him, was beyond Jay's comprehension, but he dialed the emergency number on his phone to the city dispatchers nonetheless. He hoped to save everyone time and trouble by reporting Greg's whereabouts as a third party onlooker. If it saved the life of a victim or rescuer, Jay considered the risk worth taking.

As the phone rang once, he wondered again where Mike had gone.

CHAPTER 37

As Greg dared to climb the stairs, towing Gustin behind him, the smoke finally began to thicken from the fire below, and rose through the floor to make visibility, and breathing, that much worse for both men.

"This is crazy," Gustin insisted between heaving coughs.

"Shut up," Greg retorted, pulling his reluctant prisoner along.

Things weren't going quite as the detective might have hoped, but he didn't consider himself in imminent danger yet. He found himself above the weakest part of the building, with five more stories looming over him. A collapse meant certain death for both Greg and Gustin.

He needed to find a suitable window to jump from, even if it meant temporarily removing the cuffs to do so. If he waited too much longer, there would be no visibility whatsoever, and there was a definite possibility of getting lost inside the hotel.

Losing his way meant suffocating in the thick smoke, which usually led to a person's body shutting down.

Then death.

"You have no right to endanger me like this," Gustin complained.

"I'd let you go, but you've clocked me in the head twice already," Greg stated. "And where do you think you'd go anyway?"

"Back down where it's safe."

"Feel this floor?" Greg asked, turning to his prisoner, stepping heavily on the floor, to display how spongy it had become. "In a few minutes your fire is going to weaken this floor enough to send us both into a fire pit. We're either jumping out of here now, or we get to higher ground if we want to survive."

"We can't go to higher ground," Gustin said in total shock. "This whole place is going to collapse before long."

"Exactly."

Greg's year of struggling through the volunteer department had just paid for itself. Perhaps it would even save his life from such a grave situation.

He tugged Gustin toward a window, following the smoky streams toward open air, finding a sea of flashing white and red lights outside the hotel as the fire department began setting up a surround and drown operation, figuring no one was inside the hotel. Between the locked gates, and no witness accounts of victims, the department played it safe.

Battalion Chief Dan Walters surveyed the grounds with a critical eye, knowing full well he wasn't sending a single man near that building. The terrorist events in New York during 2001 were enough to keep him from sending loads of manpower in any kind of multiple story building, but Kevin Sheridan's death only added to that theory.

If a life was at stake, Walters would waste no time in sending someone inside, but he saw nothing to indicate any human presence, especially since he knew the front of the building was boarded up tighter than Fort Knox.

A large, gruff veteran with a thick head of peppered hair atop a face that looked chiseled from granite, his green eyes were usually in a shrewd squint, taking in everything his surroundings offered him.

He could sense this fire was moving too quickly, and looked far too dangerous to let any of his men go near it.

A call from dispatch a moment later changed his mind.

"Can you repeat that?" he asked the dispatcher, not sure he had heard correctly.

"We have a report of someone trapped on the second floor from a bystander," the dispatcher repeated a second time.

What bystander? Walters wondered, taking a quick look around. His captain, standing right beside him, seemed to be thinking the same thing.

"That first floor is toast," the captain thought aloud, apparently agreeing with Walters' usual take on sending men inside.

Walters agreed there was no salvaging the first floor, even as crews began putting water into the windows, blowing out the boards set there earlier by Gustin. Flames were finding their way out of new crevices as the walls began to deteriorate, and the battalion chief wondered just how much longer the first floor would support the weight bearing down on it.

"Get me four men in there," Walters ordered, wasting none of what little precious time he had. "Have them take a ladder and check the second floor. If they don't find anything, pull them out of there immediately."

His orders were clear, concise, and not at all unreasonable. The captain left to carry out his wishes, believing Walters was putting his men in the least amount of risk possible, considering the circumstances. Both knew the building was in peril, much like a floundering ship, but they had no idea when this ship might sink.

Meanwhile, as the firefighters set up rescue efforts they figured would be for nought, believing their officers would never send them into something that risked their lives beyond reason, Greg reached a window with Gustin close behind.

In his left hand, he still held his duty weapon, and stowed it away long enough to take up his keys. Undoing the cuffs on his hand, he looked to Gustin, who stayed some distance away from the window, afraid he might be identified.

"It's over, Gustin," Greg affirmed, barely hearing the ruckus from below as the firefighters sprang into action. "Come with me, testify against the men who put you up to this, and things might work out okay for you."

Gustin shook his head negatively. Either way, he would never lead a normal life again, but going with a cop in cooperation was not an option in his mind. He could hear the firefighters create a commotion below as they noticed Greg in the window, realizing their efforts would not be in vain.

"You don't know these men," Gustin said with a tone of defeat. "They won't let me live if you take me into custody."

"You'll be safe. Just cooperate, and everything will work out."

The building groaned beneath them from fire damage and the weakening of key support columns. Little time remained to get out of the building safely, and Greg knew he needed Gustin's testimony to make a case. Without it, everything relied on circumstantial evidence, and no jury would convict the conspiracy trio with the lawyers they could afford.

A ladder touched against the side of the building as the firefighters desperately tried to get to Greg, even though he had never really turned to ask for their assistance. His attention remained dedicated to Gustin, and even as the man began to backpedal, Greg refused to leave the sanctity of the window, knowing the old hotel was breathing its last, ready to die.

"Gustin, it's your only choice. Come with me, or you'll die in here."

Gustin paused, as though realizing how limited his choices were. He seemed to sense he was dead, one way or another. Prison would be no life for him, even if he did cooperate. He had no wife, no kids. He wanted to chance getting out for one last fling before he was captured, or killed by the conspiracy trio.

"Ronnie Emerson is the one you want," he heard himself say to the detective, knowing he would likely never get the chance to testify.

Soon, he would be dead, or on the run. He knew the trio well enough to figure they would spend money on having him murdered, rather than stand trial and possibly lose everything they had planned so long and hard to attain.

Even if his words proved nothing, perhaps he could redeem his soul for the wrong he had done, in case he didn't find a way out of the fire creeping up on him from behind.

Then, without warning, he darted off toward the back of the building, disappearing into the smoke almost instantly.

Without any thought to his actions, Greg started to pursue the arsonist, but a pair of strong arms clasped him from behind, pulling him back toward the ladder.

"Get out here, buddy," the firefighter who had him in a bearhug said, refusing to release his grip.

"Okay, okay," Greg said after a few seconds of thought, knowing Gustin was not worth risking his life for.

If Gustin did escape, it would be just a matter of time before he was apprehended. Besides, his van was parked out back, and there was no way he would escape with it. Rubble and fallen debris already made certain it wasn't getting past the hotel's mesh fence.

Greg voluntarily descended the ladder, and most everyone on the fire department recognized him as a Sheridan brother. Some eyed him suspiciously, as though he might be responsible for the fire, but most of them knew better.

After all, he was Mike and Kevin's brother.

Upon the battalion chief's orders, the firefighters pulled the ladder from the building and retreated. None of them had seen Gustin, and when the building collapsed several minutes later, Greg sensed the man probably never made it out alive.

"You okay?" Walters asked, putting a concerned hand on Greg's shoulder as he approached.

"I'm fine," Greg answered, looking at the combination of smoke, fire, and dust laid before him in a mammoth heap.

"You know what caused this, son?"

"Yeah, but I have a feeling all of my proof is buried under a ton of rubble."

"Rubble can be removed," the chief assured him with a bit of a smile.

"Yeah, but my key witness is probably crushed under it."

Walters turned serious.

"I see. Why didn't the boys bring him down with you?"

"Because he chose to make a run for it," Greg explained. "He was right there with me, but he decided to try running instead."

"That's crazy," the battalion chief stated.

"From our point of view, I guess so, but then again, he didn't have a whole lot to look forward to if he got out alive."

Walters began to understand, but it wasn't his place to discuss criminal matters with the detective, and he still had a scene to command.

"Not much of a scene," he commented to himself, turning to look at the pile of brick and wood before him, smoldering from the intense heat still trapped in its belly.

Such a shame, the battalion chief thought, that such a beautiful hotel ended in such a terrible way, especially with its redemption allegedly so close.

From the hoard of firefighters around him, Greg picked Wade out of the bunch, but the two merely exchanged glances and nodded. Wade had a pike pole in one hand, apparently grouped with a bunch of men who were assigned to dig through the outskirts of the burning pile to eliminate hot spots as they went.

Reminded that he needed to find Jay, and hopefully Mike, Greg excused himself from the battalion chief before heading toward his car.

"Can you give a statement later?" he heard Walters call as he walked away.

"To who?" Greg asked with a quick laugh, never turning around.

"Hell, I don't know," Walters yelled back. "Mason Gray, I suppose."

Again, Greg chuckled, knowing what little good that would do, as he continued walking. He thought about the conspiracy, and how none of it could be proven. All of his work, and in fact, Kevin's death, seemed like nothing more than a tragic incident about to be permanently swept under the rug.

Even the files Tasha gave him would do little more than plant a seed in the minds of the local people, *if* the information ever got out to the public.

As he approached the car, he spied a familiar truck driving down a parallel alley, knowing his older brother was watching out for him. He stared a moment, then waved Jay over, because he had questions he wanted answered.

Stopping suddenly, the truck sat a moment as the driver stared back. Each brother knew one another's purpose for being there, and basically what had just transpired, but Jay wasn't as ready to talk about it.

Not without Mike present.

Still, he pulled over to the alley, blocking in Greg's car for the second time that evening.

"You okay?" Jay asked without hesitation, his window rolled down.

"Never better," Greg gave a reply laced with sarcasm. "You and I need to have a talk, big brother, about what you and my twin have been out doing the past few days."

"Past week, actually," Jay said, turning his head away in an attempt to soften the truth of the matter.

"Well that's fucking great, Jay. I've been working my ass off trying to bust this open, and you two run around vigilante style, trying to ruin everything I've done. My star witness just got buried by a ton of rubble, and that could just as easily have been me. You two should have come forward with the truth long before tonight."

"Why?" Jay retorted. "So you could tell us to stop trying to find Kevin's killer because you alone were the only person capable of getting the job done?"

"That's not fair."

"What's not fair is not letting us help, Greg. We're family, goddamn it."

Greg let his brother's words soak in, realizing Jay was right. He was older, wiser, and most always right.

"Okay," he finally said. "Meet me at the all-night diner in half an hour. And bring Mike with you."

"I can't find him, Greg."

"What?"

"He said he had something to take care of, and not to wait up. I thought he was coming here to help you, but I guess that wasn't what he had in mind."

Greg sighed to himself.

"Fine. You and I are comparing notes, then. We'll catch up with Mike when we get the chance."

Jay nodded.

"Half an hour," he affirmed before driving away.

CHAPTER 38

Closer to three in the morning, the two brothers continued to compare notes. Jay recalled everything he could from memory, while helping Greg thumb through the notes Tasha presented him with earlier that evening.

While Jay sat with a cup of steaming coffee at the all-night diner's corner booth, his brother sat opposite with a stack of papers strewn across the table. Greg's eyelids were heavy, but a cup of hot chocolate and some cheesecake helped to keep him functioning.

"So we know almost everything, but we can't prove much of it," Jay commented.

"Gustin met with Spiff, Spiff set the fires, and the three bastards got rich off the insurance money."

"And Gustin was the link to everything, and now he's dead?"

"The firefighters confirmed it about an hour ago. When I called the coroner's office, they were still checking on the identity."

"How did they know who to check for?"

"I called the battalion chief and told him who it was, and he said they thought so, because they traced the plates on Gustin's van."

"So we're fucked," Jay concluded.

"Basically."

"What did you say about your evidence that doesn't work?"

Greg held up a few of the pages.

"Oh, it works, but it doesn't work in court without someone to testify. Maybe we can get that Spiff guy to speak against them."

"That wouldn't be a good idea," Jay said with an aloof stare in the opposite direction.

"You're right," Greg said, not noticing his brother's behavior, or having any knowledge of Spiff's last known condition. "He was only linked to Gustin, not the other three."

"Yeah, right," Jay said, quickly agreeing to avoid telling the truth about how Mike had beaten Spiff to a pulp.

"So how did you know Gustin was going to set that fire tonight?"

"I didn't for sure, but I didn't know how to find his arsonist, and I had a hunch they might meet up. Then I saw him loading his van. It didn't take an expert to figure out where he was going after I heard about the hotel scam."

Jay grinned slyly.

"And your ex-girlfriend told you all of this?"

"She did," Greg said, serious as could be.

Between them, they knew everything related to their unofficial investigation. The only piece of information Jay kept to himself was how Mike got Spiff to talk, though Greg suspected the arsonist didn't simply volunteer the information.

"From a legal standpoint, there's absolutely nothing we can do?" Jay asked one last time.

"Sure, I can hand this over to the prosecutor, but half of our information is obtained through illegal means, and the rest of it is useless without some kind of testimony. Maybe I could try sending it to the state police or the feds, but even then, there's no guarantee any of them will touch it."

"So you're saying the bad guys are going to win?"

"From a legal standpoint, yes."

Jay hung his head, looking at all of the papers, which proved worthless with Gustin's death.

"Ah, fuck," he muttered.

"What?" Greg asked, thinking Jay had come up with something to make their early morning even more miserable.

"I'm supposed to go on that bike rally this morning for Kevin and the other fallen firefighters."

"Skip it then."

"No way," Jay said. "I promised Mom I would go and bring some stuff to the memorial in Los Angeles. Besides, Wade is going with me."

"Sounds like you've got a tough choice to make."

"There's no choice, Greg. Just lots and lots of caffeine and pills to keep me awake for the trip."

"I figured the roar of hundreds of motorcycles would do that for you."

"That'll just serve to give me a fuckin' headache in this condition."

Greg paused a moment, finding a phone number stuck to the inside of the folder he had missed earlier. Grinning to himself, he realized Tasha had left her Maryland contact phone number for him, just in case he wanted to keep in touch.

"So, where is Mike?" Greg asked his big brother for the first time since they had met in the alley.

"I have no idea."

"You can quit covering for him now. It's over."

Jay sipped his coffee, giving his younger brother a serious look simultaneously.

"Seriously. I don't know."

For the first time, Greg realized his brother wasn't covering up for Mike, and that his twin was nowhere to be found.

Sandi hadn't seen him, he never showed up at the fire scene, and Jay had no clue where he might be.

"Damn it," Greg said, standing to use the payphone in the opposite corner of the cafe.

He snatched the phone from the receiver, put in some change, and quickly pounded out the number to the headquarters fire station. If Mike wasn't there, Greg had no clue where he might be.

Perhaps concern for Wade had drawn him to the station, because Greg knew he wasn't at home. Sandi confirmed that less than an hour ago, when he last called her.

"Headquarters," one of the firefighters answered at the station, since most of the men were still awake after getting some relief at the fire scene while construction crews took over.

Though they found Gustin's body early, at one edge of the building, tons of debris remained. Until they sifted through all of the debris, allowing Mason Gray to investigate in his usual manner, their job would not be finished.

"Hello," Greg said. "Is Mike Sheridan up there by any chance?"

"Uh, well, he was," the firefighter answered with some degree of thought. "He used the city directory for a minute, then left."

"City directory?" Greg asked more to himself than the man on the other end of the line.

"Said he needed the address to some guy with an unlisted number," the firefighter answered anyway. "Didn't say why, though."

"This is his brother Greg. Do you have any idea where he was heading?"

"No, but he left in a hurry after he tore out the page to the directory."

"Can you look and tell me what page?" Greg inquired.

"Sure, I guess."

Setting the phone down a moment, the man went to look while Greg tapped his foot nervously on the ground, fearing what the answer would be, and exactly what his brother had in mind.

Since Kevin's death, Mike was a changed man, showing signs of anger and depression Greg had never seen the likes of, except maybe in himself. They weren't so different after all, but Mike had more trouble containing his emotions, because of his bond with Kevin.

Greg looked to Jay, who was sipping coffee, looking over the early edition of the newspaper. While this was the end of the road for Jay so far as helping trace evidence, he would return to his normal, somewhat dull life of hanging antennas and watching over their mother.

Though Jay wouldn't admit it, he probably enjoyed the excitement of helping Mike track down clues about the men responsible for Kevin's death. Luckily, he was wise enough to never involve Wade, and his son would likely live out a full career in the fire department. Perhaps someday he would even follow in Kevin's footsteps and become an officer.

When the firefighter came back with the answer of which page was missing from the book by telling Greg the names appearing just before and after the missing page, the detective was not surprised, but horrified at the thought of what Mike might do if he couldn't reach him on time.

"Thanks," he said before hanging up the phone.

Leaving with little more than a wave to Jay, who looked stunned, Greg burst through the front door with a purpose. He needed to stop Mike from making a terrible mistake, and he hoped Gustin had told him right when he told him who the true ringleader of the conspiracy was, because there were two distinct possibilities.

"Shit," he muttered to himself as he stepped into his personal vehicle, which he had traded for the city car before meeting Jay. "Don't you do it, Mike."

His thoughts turned to a quick prayer as Greg raced from the parking lot, ready to trace his brother's footsteps in the hopes of saving a life.

CHAPTER 39

As a precaution, Greg decided to stop by the fire scene before checking where he believed Mike might have gone, just to make sure his brother had no intentions of seeking revenge on the arson investigator, who was still probing the scene.

Activity looked minimal as Greg stepped from his car. Few firefighters milled around the area, and those who did simply waited for orders. They provided free security for Mason Gray while he conducted his search for evidence, now that Gustin's body was removed.

Somehow Greg never expected Gustin to make it out alive. There had been no back stairwell, and if he jumped to the floor below, fire would have consumed him instantly. Jumping from the second story window to the hardened dirt below would have meant at least a few fractures, and no one reported seeing Gustin limp away from the scene.

Therefore, Greg had to believe the man was definitely dead. No one else could have been inside that building, and Greg's best lead was now nothing more than a mixture of charred tissue and bone.

Not wanting to waste any time, Greg gave the area a quick search, feeling certain Mike would not waste any time coming here. Deciding it was time to leave, Greg started toward his car, but the arson investigator spied him from a distance and started toward him.

"Nothing here to see," Gray said with a quick smile, as though he already had everything figured out.

Greg suspected it was easy to deduce a crime scene however he saw fit, when there was a reward waiting for him. He kept his emotions in check because they were the one thing that kept him from acting irrationally like his twin.

"What's your determination?" Greg decided to ask anyway.

"Well, with your eyewitness account, I guess I'd have to rule it arson," Gray said, in a manner indicating Greg's word wasn't worth believing.

Greg chuckled at the investigator's nerve.

"So you think I might fabricate some elaborate story, despite the evidence left inside?" Greg asked. "Hell, Mason, you're gonna find a lighter, you've already found a body, and I'm betting that van has some incriminating evidence inside those doors if you bother to take a look."

Greg had raised his voice enough to draw attention from the other firefighters standing around. He could see Gray getting a bit more nervous as he threw suggestions into the air. Perhaps the investigator had notions of sliding this case under the carpet as he had so many others, but Greg was determined not to let that happen.

Gray had pushed the detective's buttons by coaxing him into staying a few minutes more. Now Greg decided to push back.

"You trying to take over my investigation?" Gray inquired, as though threatened.

"No, because I know what your agenda is, and by God, I'm going to see that one way or another the truth comes out."

"What truth is that?" Gray asked, drawing dangerously close to the detective.

So close, in fact, that Greg could smell the onions from a Philly steak sandwich the arson investigator had downed several hours earlier on his breath. Like two male rams determined to defend their territory, the two leaned uncommonly close, ready to butt heads.

"The truth that you've been covering up fires for three men named Boyce, Shelton, and Emerson," Greg said just loud enough for Gray to hear, almost spitting the words he said with seething hatred.

"Prove it."

"I've already proven it," Greg admitted. "I know what you've been doing, and if the courts won't deal with you and your cronies, I'll find another way to make sure your bid for coroner goes down the drain."

"You don't have shit, Sheridan."

By now, most of the firefighters had returned to milling around the scene, realizing they weren't privy to the conversation as the two men bickered in voices just above whispers.

"It seems awful funny all of those fires were set in Washington Township's area, and that all of them were ruled accidental, or undetermined, when clearly there was evidence of foul play. Even the outside investigators said you missed stuff, or covered it up."

"You've got nothing."

"I've got insurance reports linking your three boys together in supposed accidental fires and explosions, one or two a year between them. Strangely, the fire reports at the station house make mention of the ownership of these buildings, but you usually leave that piece of information out of your reports."

"How the fuck could you know what-"

Gray's words trailed off as Greg gave a sly smirk. Knowing he had been under the magnifying glass longer than he cared to imagine, he simply shook his head. His face turned a few different shades of red, and he breathed in heaves.

"None of that will stand in a court of law, and you know it," Gray said. "Even if you do have some kind of alleged paper trail, it would all be circumstantial."

"I know it, and you know it, but I've got a few contacts in the media who might like to know it too," Greg threatened, just to push

Gray a bit further over the edge, weighed down by his own guilty conscience.

Gray responded, growing even more angry.

"You do that, and you might just wind up like your older brother," Gray said, nodding his head toward the burnt hull of the hotel to add the visual effect.

This time Greg was angered by the statement, and before he could think of restraining himself, his right fist hit Gray squarely in the jaw, flooring the man to a state of near unconsciousness. Every firefighter around looked in awe, and some smirked or laughed to themselves, seeing an arrogant prick like Gray get clocked.

"Fuck you and your precious career," Greg said, turning his back to walk toward his car.

No one but Gray would stoop so low as to say a bad word about Kevin, and the arson investigator had definitely toyed with the wrong man as morning drew near. Punching Gray felt good, even therapeutic, but Greg needed to find Mike and stop him before he did something they both might regret.

❦ ❦ ❦

Dawn's light broke over the horizon as Ronnie Emerson strapped a collar around his miniature poodle, ready to take her for a walk before his workday began.

Making sure the dog's collar was secure, Emerson wondered what his day would hold, and just how well things had gone overnight. Gustin always did things right, and Emerson had slept well, knowing the Dayton Hotel would be money in his pocket when he woke up.

He stood, punching in the code for his home security system before opening his back door. Stepping out, he saw his Mercedes in the driveway by itself, since no women had spent the night with him for a change.

Part of his money trouble could be attributed to his lavish lifestyle. Buying his new summer cottage, owning two luxury cars in addition to several collectable vehicles, and having a new love interest every week drained his bank account quicker than he could replenish it.

Emerson had grown accustomed to getting substantial chunks of cash.

And getting away with it.

Though his back yard was fenced in with nothing but wood, six feet in height, it was easy enough for someone to scale if they wanted to get inside. Getting past the home security system would prove more difficult, but Emerson had just shut that off, giving his uninvited intruder the necessary access and freedom to carry out his plan.

A hazy fog lingered in the early morning air, with a strange smell carrying over from a nearby pond. Emerson simply stood by, ignoring his dog's usual outdoor habits, feeling mixed emotions about his financial woes and the cure he had on the way.

After borrowing money from several major local players, who liked to be paid in full, with interest, and quickly, Emerson realized the error of his ways. Once he paid them off, he would slow down the arson fires to avoid detection. Although Gray was in their pocket, the state took no bribes, and knew nothing about giving favors.

While Emerson carefully dealt with the parties he owed money to, he paid attention to little else, including the family hellbent on getting one form of revenge or another. One man in particular was about to enact the only vengeance he knew upon the man he considered responsible for taking his brother's life.

Waiting until Emerson was ready to step inside his lavish house, Mike stepped from behind a nearby shrub, holding the barrel of his gun directly at the man's neck, not letting Emerson see him for a moment.

"Take whatever you want," Emerson said immediately, thinking the situation was a holdup, and he could bargain for his life.

Bargaining would not be so easy in this case.

"I'm not here for anything but you," Mike said in a low, gruff tone as the little poodle barked at his feet, starting to wrap its chain around both men. "Get inside and get that dog away from us before I shoot it, and you."

Emerson got free from the leash long enough to get inside and set the dog free, before turning to see Mike. Knowing Emerson was unarmed, Mike didn't keep the gun pointed at him, but he maintained a vigilant watch of the man's every movement.

Before stepping inside, Mike carefully stomped the mud and dirt from his tennis shoes on the concrete walkway outside.

"Who are you?" Emerson demanded. "What do you want?"

Accustomed to being in power, Emerson dared to make such demands now that the gun was away from his throat.

"Your brother's a lawyer," Mike commented. "Didn't he ever tell you arson was a crime?"

"Arson? What the hell are you talking about?"

"I'm talking about the arson for profit scheme you and your buddies have going. The same scheme, in fact, that killed my brother when you had Scott Gustin pay a man named Spiff to burn down the Brookshire Apartments."

Surprise registered in Emerson's eyes, but not long enough to keep him from denying it.

"I have no idea what you're talking about."

"Oh, don't you?" Mike asked, virtually emotionless.

Though barely in the light of daybreak behind him, Mike appeared fatigued, like he hadn't slept at all the past night, or perhaps several before that. Bloodshot eyes with deep blackened pools beneath them were proof enough, but his hair appeared more disheveled than usual, and he had a few days of stubble on his face from not bothering to shave.

"I can get you the help you need," Emerson said, trying to turn the tables. "Obviously you've made a terrible mistake, and I know some very good doctors-"

"Don't bother patronizing me," Mike said with irritation, cutting him off. "It's bad enough you had Gustin do your dirty work, but you even had Mason Gray helping you out. I put two and two together, and figured you were funding his sudden campaign bid. Wouldn't that be convenient having the arson investigator and coroner as a two for one deal?"

Emerson tried to laugh off the notion, but Mike pointed the gun at his head with a swift movement of his right arm.

"I want some admission or I pull this trigger, Emerson."

Weighing his options a moment, Emerson realized not saying a word was his best overall option, but if this brother of the fallen firefighter already knew the truth, he would definitely start shooting body parts if he figured Emerson was lying.

"What do you want me to say?" Emerson asked with a shrug. "I didn't set any fires, but I've had a few of my buildings destroyed the past few years. How do you know it isn't some kind of revenge thing?"

Mike smirked, lowering the gun once again.

"You know, I considered that at first, but when certain facts didn't add up, I started looking in other places, Emerson. It didn't take long to figure out who was setting the fires, and when I cornered Spiff, he didn't have any trouble saying who was behind it, or why."

"I don't even know who you're talking about."

"He knew you pretty well. He even fingered you as the man with the plan."

"How do you know he wasn't lying? Maybe trying to get back at me in some way?"

Mike thought back to the way he had left the arsonist in the middle of nowhere, and the condition Spiff was in. No one took that kind of beating and lied about it.

He still had no doubt Emerson was behind the fires, and ultimately responsible for Kevin's death.

"He had no reason to lie, because he was in the position you're in, Emerson."

Mike began to carefully circle around the man, pointing the gun once more.

"His life was threatened as well, and he made me carry out some pretty gruesome acts on his body before he talked, but after he realized I was serious, he confessed."

"Did you kill him?" Emerson asked, swallowing hard as he did, falling to a seated position on a nearby couch.

The way in which he asked led Mike to believe he wanted Spiff dead, so there would be one less loose end to tie up.

"He's alive, but don't expect to see him anytime soon."

"So what's it going to take to make you happy?" Emerson asked, thinking Mike could simply be bought for his troubles.

"You've got a brother, don't you?" Mike answered the question with a question.

"You know I do."

"Tell me how you would feel if I walked over to his house and set it on fire with him in it, leaving him no choice but to burn up and die?"

Emerson's look showed his concern and shock.

"Now you know how I feel, Emerson. Kevin went into that house to save two lives, and it could just as easily have been me who died. He saved the lives of two men who never should've been in there to begin with, because people like you pushed for that asshole Malovich to get a tax break in the industrial areas. You got your break in the amount of double the tax payment, and you got a half-ass fire department with inadequate training."

"Where are you going with this?" Emerson asked, feeling this spur of the moment terrorist was getting sidetracked.

"Those two firefighters never should have been in that building, because there never should have been a new fire department, and there never should've been a fire in those apartments your buddy

Shelton owned. But you, and your need to pay off your debts, pushed for that fire, and made the mistake of your life by selecting a building at the edge of city limits."

"You're making this up," Emerson charged. "You're bluffing. How the fuck could you know who I owe money to?"

"Spiff talked, and men like him know the word on the street, Emerson. You borrowed from people in his neighborhood, and nothing keeps quiet for long down there. It's bad enough you couldn't lay low after the fire that killed my brother, but you got greedy, and decided another building had to burn. It's a shame, too, because the Dayton Hotel was a great landmark. Even Spiff thought it was a neat place before I took a baseball bat across his shins."

Emerson saw his world crumbling around him, realizing Mike was not here just to sort things out with him by talking.

"What do you want?" he asked desperately. "Money? A memorial in your brother's name? Name it."

"There's only one thing I want," Mike said, turning just slightly to pluck an oversized pillow from the love seat behind him.

Emerson's eyes widened in fear as the firefighter slowly made his way across the room toward him.

"No, you can't-"

Emerson had no means by which to defend himself. He was not a thug getting money by throwing his weight around. He had other people to break bones and set fires for him.

Without another word, Mike approached the seated Emerson, stuffed the pillow down on the man's face, and pressed with all of his might, trying to suffocate the conspirator for the crimes he had committed, but Emerson refused to die easily, clawing upward at the pillow and Mike's forearms. His muffled cries and pleas passed through the material pressed heavily against his face.

Before the man could claw him, Mike launched a knee into Emerson's sternum, basically slowing his defenses to a stop. Despite agonizing pain, and the pressure put on his chest from the blow, Emerson refused to just let himself die of asphyxiation.

Unable to see his gruesome fate, Emerson continued to struggle as Mike simply pushed the gun into the pillow, using it as a makeshift silencer as he fired two shots toward where he figured Emerson's head would be. Though muffled, the sound of the firing gun was unmistakable. Barking and yipping occasionally to this point, the poodle squealed before running into another room.

Mike felt positive the shots were silent enough that the neighbors would not be disturbed.

Every ounce of fight suddenly left Emerson, and blood began to seep into several areas of the pillow as his body fell limp atop the couch. Mike removed the pillow from the man's head, seeing two bullet holes. One appeared distinctly in the man's cheek, and the other along the side of his scalp, where brain matter, skin tissue, and blood were apparent in the wound. The cheek simply appeared to fill itself in with flaps of skin and blood clots, which stilled themselves quickly in death.

Seeing bullet holes in bodies was nothing new to Mike, but he usually felt some sort of sympathy for the victims.

Not this time.

Careful never to make direct contact with Emerson, even when the man was clawing at him, Mike felt fairly reassured no major DNA evidence would be left behind, and for safety's sake, he tossed the pillow out back, into the pond, where it would soak up water. He hoped to wash away any fingerprints and other evidence it might hold.

Even if he wanted to backtrack all of his footsteps, he would never get them all, but he made efforts to do so in the yard. Walking one way, then stepping over the same footprint in the opposite direction ruined any chance of lifting the print for investigators. Beyond the yard, little remained but trees, and they would never be able to salvage a footprint in there.

Mike planned Emerson's execution the moment he learned the case would never succeed in court, even if it got there, and used what forensic knowledge Greg had bestowed upon him over the years to cover his tracks from the very beginning.

Never again would he be the chipper, easygoing firefighter at work, or at home, but Mike felt he could now begin anew. He could never replace Kevin, or any of his family, and when his father had told him to keep the family together, and Kevin died, he felt in some way he had failed.

This didn't make things right, but in Mike's eyes, it was a form of justice. An eye for an eye, his father always said when they misbehaved as kids. Mike didn't look at killing Emerson as just a form of justice, either. He hoped in doing so, the other partners would quit their activities, and perhaps other people on the streets thinking about arson for profit schemes would think twice.

Perhaps, just perhaps, someone else's brother wouldn't have to die.

He had never gotten the full confession he wanted from Emerson, but he knew the man was guilty, and his conscience wouldn't spend one second wondering if he had taken out his frustrations on the wrong man.

As he exited the back door for the last time, careful not to actually touch anything, Mike heard a car pull up in the distance. His first reaction was to run, but he might accidentally leave traceable footprints in the process. Instead, he simply ducked down along the interior side of the wooden privacy fence and peered through a hole in one of the slats.

"Shit," he muttered, seeing Greg's car pull to a stop with the main road some distance away.

Mike considered running, but Greg would likely be relentless and hunt him down, sensing Mike was the only reasonable suspect in the man's murder. Greg had no reason to be there, so he had to suspect Mike was on the warpath in the first place.

Making a quick decision not to disgrace Greg in any way, Mike decided to reveal himself and save them both a lot of trouble by surrendering. Unlocking the gate without actually using his fingertips, out of habit to avoid leaving fingerprints, Mike stepped out, holding the gun as his twin brother approached.

For a few seconds, they simply stared at one another, Greg on the concrete driveway, Mike on the outside of the gate. Knowing he was already too late to save Mike from some kind of trouble, he wanted to know the extent. All of Greg's thoughts of what this moment would be like if he was forced to confront it, washed away with the scene of his brother clutching a gun at his side, and Greg felt entirely uncertain of what to say.

"Did you?" he simply asked, figuring he already knew the answer.

Mike nodded slowly, saying nothing.

Greg looked skyward, but his look was not one of shock, or even dismay. He sighed heavily, rubbing the bald area of his head as he thought.

Positive he was about to be handcuffed and whisked to jail, Mike turned the gun over in the palm of his hand, walking toward Greg to surrender it.

"No," Greg simply said, his mind made up. "Get out of here."

"What?" Mike asked in surprise, thinking someone could be around, or maybe some hidden security camera had taped them, and Greg might unwittingly become a part of the evil he had just perpetrated.

"Go," Greg said again. "Take your clothes, shoes, and socks, and burn them all. Bury the ashes somewhere, and destroy that gun."

"How?"

"Take it to the smelting part of Jay's factory where they mold the antenna parts and toss it into a vat. Make sure you wash your hands real well too, so you get the powder residue off of them."

Mike still felt uneasy about his brother covering for him, much less getting involved, but Greg had reached the same conclusion about Emerson's group in a roundabout way. He knew a trial would never do anything more than give the group bad publicity.

"Make sure you didn't leave any trace evidence," Greg warned, "then get the fuck out of here."

Mike nodded, and carefully let himself back inside the gate as Greg walked to his car.

No one had seen him enter the driveway, much less approach the property, and no one would probably discover Emerson's body until that afternoon at the earliest. He would sit down with Mike to establish an alibi, and formulate a plan to keep his brother's name in the clear.

As he drove down the road toward his lonely apartment a few minutes later, he spied a band of motorcycles coming toward him. In a pattern at least a mile long, the group was riding from New York to Los Angeles to commemorate fallen firefighters across the United States.

Jay's group.

Traffic was moving so slowly with the morning rush crowd slowing to see the passing bikes, Greg decided to pull to the side of the road and step outside a moment. He watched the group pass, waving to some, wondering if Jay had joined in the ride, or decided to get some overdue sleep. With all of the events from the past few days, Greg wouldn't blame his older brother for sleeping an entire week if he wanted to.

Picking up firefighters and those wanting to celebrate fallen heroes as they went, the group would have a two-day bash in California. During those two days, they would raise money for the families of fallen firefighters, promote fire safety, and probably get drunk in the evenings. Greg felt they were doing the world some good by riding out there, and he somehow felt bonded with these men, because they shared the same philosophy on losing a brother firefighter.

Between the thunderous roar of the motors and the mild earthquake taking place under his feet, he felt like he was centered between tractor pulls in every direction.

Greg knew he was never cut out for the traditional family occupation, but he suspected Kevin and his father would be proud of how he handled himself against Gustin just hours before this sun-filled dawn.

As he stared into the reddish horizon, seeing the tip of the sun emerge, he felt a mist in one eye, thinking of Kevin, and everything he'd lost the past year.

Just like Mike.

He wasn't losing Mike as well, and he understood why his brother felt it was so necessary to use vigilante justice. His twin would soon be a father, and had a marriage to plan. Greg wouldn't ruin that, and further condemn his family to pain, if he could help it.

Looking into the face of a new day, Greg wondered what his life would be like from this moment on. Like his brother, his conscience would probably let him sleep at night, and maybe there was some good to come of Mike's actions.

Toward the tail end of the procession, Greg looked at the faces of the bikers, who seemed appreciative he'd taken the time to stop along the side of the road to wave and support them. He was about to step into his car when a pair of familiar faces emerged from the stream of bikers.

Greg cracked a smirk, waving as Jay and Wade passed on their Harley-Davidson motorcycles. Jay looked a bit fatigued, but he gave a playful two-finger salute as he passed, wearing his father's old volunteer department T-shirt. Wade wore his own department's shirt, so between them, they represented their fallen family members.

Both seemed content to spend time together on their bikes, with a group that would honor Kevin and hundreds of others at the end of their trail.

His heart warmed a bit to see father and son together, and it reminded him of the times he and Mike had gone fishing with their father on the few weekends John Sheridan seemed to have free from the fire station and his construction job. He couldn't relive the past forever, but Greg had his memories, and as fate would have it, he still had his own life to finish.

"Maybe things aren't so bad after all," he said to himself as he climbed inside his car, thinking he might give Tasha a call in Maryland to see if she wanted some company.

0-595-25445-4

Printed in the United States
19906LVS00004B/139